Contents

Part One -------------------- *1 - 129*

Part Two -------------------- *133 - 256*

Part Three ----------------- *261 - 402*

published on the
border of the death
spiral

dedicated to
the Shaman

The Asphodel

by Luke Delin

PART I

Hum Durgeon

1

When I got to university I spent the majority of my alone time below Ella Muntz writing a diary about me and the joyfully mad lot I never quite thought I'd meet. You never think you're gonna meet people like that. You always think you're gonna be stuck with the freaks. But in all honesty, I've got nothing against the freaks. The good friends I made turned out to be the freaks. The people I don't tend to like are the people like Ella Muntz.

And I don't want to go on about why I hate this and why I hate that. But I hated Ella Muntz. She was this knock-out stunner from Portishead who studied Business and she was assigned to be my housemate at BSU. When I met her on the first day she was great and all. I had a thing for her, actually. But when I hung out with her and her friends I realised how boring they were. I mean, I sometimes think that I'm boring. It's no big deal. But I was never as bored with myself (in all my life, and that's saying something) as I was with that sorry lot.

And I could have gotten past the fact they were a bit dull. I really could. But when I found out (irrevocably) how rude and entitled Ella Muntz was, I decided I would just be alone, because I couldn't stand her.

It all started on the third night. Some of the group were going to bed at nine. I mean, it was freshers and all, and they were going to bed at nine. I chuckled to myself at the thought of them cosying up in their beds after putting up motivational posters and listening to the terror through the wall.

Anyway, as you can probably tell, I don't like going to bed until it's two. And, well, it's probably got something to do with my insomnia. But I think even if I was healthy and all I wouldn't call it a night too early. On the first week, I went out nearly every night and didn't come back till three. I'm not saying that staying up later makes you a better person or anything. But I prefer the ones who'll risk their health happily rather than the ones who won't take any risk and will sulk about it.

On the third night I arrived, I was smoking a joint with a new acquaintance called Cody, who told me he had a katana collection but that his mum didn't let him bring it to university. I wondered if he was telling the truth. But in the end it didn't matter if it was true or not because the whole thing made me crease with laughter.

So it was me and Cody outside, and we were passing each other the joint while he told me all about the katanas, and that he used to open up pomegranates and grapefruits with them. He says: "And then I lick the blade." I start laughing like a real freak and then all of a sudden I hear this window open and it's Ella Muntz up above us on the top floor of the building and she just loses it.

"Dunley! The smoke is getting into my room! Please stop!"

Maybe if I was alone, I would have just chucked it and said sorry and been all horribly polite. But I wasn't alone, and Cody was looking over at me while Ella was screaming and it just made me laugh so much my stomach hurt. But really, that's not the bad part. The bad part was the morning after. It seemed as soon as Ella realised I like to smoke she went off me completely. Started being real rude to me out of nowhere (and everyone else who did it too) and it got to the point she thought I stole her ice cream and her booze. But I didn't. She just flipped from being my friend to looking down on me, figuratively and literally that night with old Katana Cody.

When I got into a more joyful and mad crowd, the hate just grew. She saw that I smoked weed sometimes, she thought I was a thief. And all of a sudden, she wasn't so stunning anymore. She didn't even realise she binged on alcohol all the time and that it was a drug like mine, arguably worse for you in the long run. She lost that beauty I saw in her the first few days. She was about as stunning now as current drug legislation. I mean, I'm nothing to look at. I've got a real half-pipe for a nose and bad teeth and I hate seeing myself in the mirror. I thought maybe it's just the mirrors this whole time. That I'm actually quite striking for a man, and the mirrors, all of them, are just wrong or something. In any case, superficial things like that don't bother me anymore. Like I said, Ella was a stunner, and I hated her guts.

It got to the point I couldn't be in the kitchen with her. So I just went to my room quite a lot. But it didn't take too long for me to find a new kitchen, and new friends, where no-one would get all sour even if you blew crack-smoke right in their damn nostrils. There were heroes, anti-heroes, beer-swilling zeros, musicians, poets, and they all accepted you. Everyone in that second kitchen always knew how to laugh. And when some real great conversations started occurring, I figured I had to write it all down. And when I tried to do that, I remembered that I had a terrible memory.

For months I was all holed up in my room avoiding the Muntz, writing. I figured to write a story about my new friends and what was going on, to make up for the fact I hadn't handed any work in or gone to any classes for four months. I had my reasons. I wasn't a slacker or anything. But I knew I was falling behind and so the diary became a mission, to write something great and hand that in. I tried to mesh the tale together with excerpts from a diary of psychosis (that I still carry around with me in a red-moleskin) but I could never fit the two together properly. I was worried that my plan to hand in a novel as my only piece of work was failing, because I couldn't write it. It was too hard. And anyway, things happened that not even me, a self-professed writer, would ever write down.

At the time I thought it was the greatest piece of shit ever conceived. Then when Erica Rye (a seething, great poet) read it, she told me it straight. I sent the bubbling story to her excitedly (she wanted something to read, she said) while she was in the bathtub soaking it up. But then I felt kinda sore because she told me it could have been better. And I sulked and shouted about it like a complete bastard. But she was the only one to tell me it straight. She would have done a much better job on the whole protagonist thing. I should have got her to write it for me. She was a great writer of prose. I, alas, ne suis pas.

It was trash what I wrote. And Erica's stern eyes saw it. It was self-absorbed nonsense. Still, I kept the illustrations I made under the spell of madness in that red moleskin S gave me.

I was feeling over the edge by December. Truly rattling my cage. And being so amazingly lazy as I was, when I arrived at BSU I forgot to refill my prescription of olanzapine. And because that first week was so extraordinary, I ran out of the pills and got distracted and decided to just come off the meds. They were used to suppress my psychotic episodes, which happened on a few occasions.

I was feeling lost. I never made the connection that not taking the pills was causing me this insomnia. But it was. I'd only learn about that much later (and also that withdrawal from those pills can cause you to go insane again). I'd been on the drug for two years since the episode which landed me in a psychiatric ward. I felt tired. Too tired to find them. Hadn't slept more than an hour every night since freshers ended (because withdrawal from olanzapine can cause insomnia) and that is why I had no energy for anything, even turning up to classes. I really wasn't a slacker. But everyone thought I was.

I just couldn't face going in feeling all sleep deprived and jittery and paranoid. I was partially deaf at the time and stupid and inept anyway. Deaf because I had these narrow ear canals which caused wax to form much more profusely than the regular Joe, and the reason why one girl had winced at the sight of me putting in my ear drops one afternoon. One canal was even narrower than the other (and this being the source, I now suspect, of my holy imbalance). Thus I had probably misinterpreted everything that really happened (and how I wish I did, because things got so horrible).

With my mush for mind and unusable ears, I was truly in the real animal soup. It was getting harder and harder to resolve. I was getting strange in the head. And so strange it was that on this Monday midmorning in January I had an even stranger idea. I was bored and I wanted to throw a party, but I thought, to let it be a surprise.

I was texting a few people as I couldn't hear anything clearly bar the heartbeat in my head, and I was feeling alone in my room. I sent a message to Beebee, who was currently in a philosophy lecture about Descartes and the mind-body dualism and his problem with the devil who controlled his reality. See, if I had turned up to that class, I would have left feeling psychopathic.

"How's it going B?"

"Descartes a fookn twat. O corse e exists. How paranoid was e?"

"I dunno. When I was a kid I was paranoid of god. Give the guy a break. He was torn weren't he? Torn. Get it?"

"Wot. Yh dualism. I kno. I'm tryna listen the guy speak about it nw. Leave the jokes to me. N stop msgin me."

With her northerly accent spilling over into even the texts, I left her to study. Or whatever the hell she was doing. I also left the jokes to her as she requested.

I didn't text Penguin or Kurt not because I didn't like them but because they were probably busy, unlike me. And well, I was tired as hell, so it felt like I actually was busy. But I wasn't.

Even though I didn't bother contacting them two, I could guess what they were up to. I imagined Kurt at this moment perhaps entangled in woman's clad as he was inclined to on occasion (and when I saw him all dressed up in a black dress and make-up for Halloween, I was shocked to find it wasn't some beautiful woman); in any case creating something as someone not content with mundanity would be forced to do, whether it was music or poems or unrelenting humour. He was mad and I loved it, That is, until he pissed on me.

I also mused on what Penguin was up to. Seeming unable to sit still I figured he would decide to climb down a strange way out of his quarters like a mad ape instead of walking down the stairs. Penguin couldn't sit still and that's probably why he was good at pulling girls. I was content with sitting for a long time and I wasn't good at pulling girls. There was no changing the either of us. And I guess you want to know why he was called Penguin and all. Well, the truth is, so do I. I don't know. I never thought to ask.

It was a dreary midmorning. Yet I had done the deed. I had fallen asleep. If only it was for an hour. I was proud of myself. But during that hour I had a horrible dream. I was trying to rescue the severed head of my father that was slipping away in a strong current of water. I swam over to it and tried to pick it up (the arms weak) and when I finally got hold of my father's head, I could almost hear it whispering my name. I woke up in shock, and my stomach was aching. Some deviant had stolen my bread the night before and I didn't have any other food. I didn't want to get up. I was falling in and out of consciousness, having that wretched feeling of having to pull yourself out of it, but the arms and head are weak, so you struggle for an aeon and keep falling in and out. It wanted to give me the kiss of death. Not today.

I jumped out the bed like a damn jack-in-the-box and put on some music. I looked for a cure to fix me up. In fact, the band The Cure was a good enough cure for me. What I like to do when I get up is play The Cure (something like *In Between Days*) and then spin around real fast in a circle. I wouldn't dream of doing it in public, though. I'd feel so old, like I could die. Anyway, it's a good trick to feel better from bad dreams, I find. You just spin around real fast in a circle. It was the drug of choice for not only six year old girls but twenty-one year old failures, too.

But as this twenty-one year old failure knew too well, every drug has some sort of side effect. I got dizzy from spinning and knocked over a lamp and felt all flustered again. It landed at my feet just below my window, the bulb shattered and glass all on the carpet. When I picked up the remains I looked through the window and I saw Tig down there in the courtyard with Moses, Jad and Molly.

Tig Dubois was a very small thing (I think I made a joke to her that she could be turned into a diamond), a French madwoman on the run, apparently. A beautiful girl who I no doubt would never catch or hook or whatever however the hell one wants to say it. I've got worn teeth from smoking for ten years. No-one wants that. I got a face for the radio. I'm broke, too.

Maybe old Tiggy (being a budding psychologist) had woken up realising a truth of subjectivity here in this plain, with its still as yet to be toppled monarchy; its casual spoutings of 'cunt'; the Sunday roasts left uneaten by the E-ravished offspring off the land; the working mass silent on the trains and loud in the pubs thereafter; Mrs. Brown's Boys, the Tory government and Jeremy Fucking Clarkson. I wondered did she regret leaving France to study psychology.

I gazed at the view outside. It was raining hard in my homeland. Whizzing it down in the homeland. Hard and wet in the homeland. It would have been the usual thing except there was thunder and lightning too, which was rarer.

If you ask me, England is both the best and worst country. And it's not got to do with the rain. If you want to know why I think that, well, there's eternal freedom for me here. But the only reason there is eternal freedom for me here is that someone else on the other side of the world is being chained to the basement wall. England fucked and pillaged the whole world and is still winning out because of it. There's freedom. But it's tainted, I reckon. Just look at all those damn treasures and artefacts the British Museum has. From all over the world. They just nicked it all. And yet it's meant to fill you with national pride? I am not proud to be free, and there's the problem. Yet I was still feeling bored and listless. I decided to check up on old Rye to see how her creative writing seminar was going. I was interested because I chose to study it. Rye was my go-between for those few times she did show up. A secret spy. She would feed me information that it was a total scam, that it didn't help her write and actually made it worse to write.

"How's the gang? Find ne other gd poets?"

"Jst gt out. Usual drivel. I red out a poem called Ur All Posers. Now no1 likes me."

"Send me it?"

I waited around while *Dreaming of You* by The Coral played through the bedroom air. I was curious to know what the girl came up with. She knew the beats, she could write better than me.

I decided to get up and walk to the kitchen to make a coffee (still naked, because I had woken up quite late and all). You had to drink coffee, and naked too, if it was raining in England. It was good luck or something.

Now, in the kitchen, where many empty bottles resided of all shapes, I was relieved to not find Ella (the beautiful witch) or anyone else there to see me in my leafless state. I was as pre-enlightenedly free as Adam and Eve before they had their damn coffee. The coffee that made them realise their shame.

I walked back to my room, set the drink down on the desk and began daydreaming.

You know, I like my coffee like I like my women. In a

mug.

I let the drink cool a little while I rocked my head to The Coral. I was dreaming of her in my lonely room. And when I finally picked up the mug and let the rim rest against my lips, my phone buzzed and I spilled the brew over my thighs and balls and I cried in pain. It wasn't good luck. It wasn't good luck at all.

> ... "*I'm a dozer*
> *A full blown cat*
> *Sleeping on the tin roof*
> *Of ur poetic crap*
> *U're all posers*
> *Ugly and fat*
> *I only meant literarily*
> *Not literally*
> *If u can't understand*
> *Then eat my fucking hat*
> *I am a dozing cat*
> *Cus u're all posing crap*
> *I read Keats*
> *U read Heat*
> *And u're all bardic slags*
> *U say ur hearts are weeping*
> *Like the rav'nous rain*
> *Well, bitches, my brain's steaming*
> *From all this fucking pain*
> *No, not pain like 'oh he hurt me'*
> *Fuck u and ur fifty shades*
> *I'm leaving this shit early.*"

Poor Erica was at the end of her thread, Dear Reader. Usually, she sent me wild ones about nature with sparse rhyming patterns. But today I guess she just got tired. It was still better than anything I ever wrote. I imagined her lips moving with cool determination, her eyes on them all with cat-like intensity, like a true poet who had something to say, and her little legs, storming out of a sinking unsalvageable ship. But, man. My balls hurt real bad.

"U're a genius Rye. Do I notice sum spite tho?" I didn't get a reply. I decided to check my emails on my phone to see if anything had arrived that was of interest. I had two new emails. The first had a tagline: WANT BIG PENIS? YOU BUY NOW! £££! And well, I don't know how they knew I wanted big penis. But I wasn't going to buy now. I couldn't even afford food. The second email was from Mrs. Gully, some head of education or other tripe like that. The tagline read: DEPOSIT RETRACTED DUE TO VIOLATION.

I clicked on the email, feeling confused.

"Dear Mr. Novak,

We have received information from security that Q kitchen has been damaged last night on 10th January 2016 and that you are responsible for the alleged party. For this reason we are retracting your £250 deposit in accordance with accommodation policy. The use of kitchens is NOT to throw parties and cause exit blocks or other such things (like broken glass) which could endanger the lives of other students. Your deposit will be taken in one to two working days.

Samantha Gully."

I was left even more confused. It wasn't true. I didn't throw a party. Sure, I was planning on throwing one.

But that hadn't happened yet. Then I recalled there was in fact a party in Q kitchen the night before. I had only turned up to eat a sandwich (because it was partly my kitchen, and where else was I meant to eat?) and there was already a party going on. That's probably where all the bottles came from. But the place wasn't damaged. There was no broken glass. Just loads of bottles on all the counters, some on the floor. I remembered that I left after I ate my sandwich because I didn't know anyone there. Someone had given security false information. Gee, and £250 was a lot of money and all, for something I didn't even do.

My eyes were hurting from looking down at my phone for so long, so I went for a walk in the storm (not naked, though, even though I would have liked to in order to ease my balls, but then again, they'd probably get struck by lightning). I put on whatever was around, to smoke a spliff and walk around in the rain and head over to the music department to see what whacked out things I might hear. And maybe hoping I would meet someone as unworthily wayward as me. Someone who might understand.

It felt strange being outside and looking in the windows of all the buildings, seeing so many bored despondent faces, youthful faces, faces of the new world, sneezing and snoozing and Snapchatting all over the place. I'm content with being apart from it all. They say it's education but I doubt it. It reminds me of that time the Shaman (a real benevolent soul from back home) corrected the lecturer when talking about Immanuel Kant. He said: "Sir, it's actually pronounced Kunt. It's the German. He was German, after all." And he was told to leave. Well if they don't want to hear the truth then why do they even have ears?

There was some sort of samba band thing going on in my own ears as I made it to the music block, though truth be told everyone, even students who didn't study music, made music with their lips and their brains. I heard everyone, in my mind, in the crazed and divided orchestra. If you took a dump you made music. If you breathed air you were Mozart.

By the time I got there the zoot had depleted and I was digging it so much I started dancing a bit. I went up to the window and started dancing more, like an uninvited freak, because I saw Jad Kinney beating a drum and I was trying to make him notice me. Usually I wouldn't be so audacious, as really I was very shy and too aware of myself. But there's something about being separated by glass, you feel invisible. Sort of. And plus I was bored and stoned and seeing Jad gave me some confidence. I knew he didn't want to be there. I could see it in his damn face.

He either wanted to be playing the piano, which was his eternal gift, or if not that then aiming to charm some girl, which was not his eternal gift. Probably his addiction, though. I had the same crutch, Dear Reader, but the difference between me and Jad Kinney was that he tried to get his fix. I guess I'm just a young cynic at heart (and echoing Maya Angelou, the real tragedy is I went straight from knowing nothing to believing nothing). I've never really quite believed in love. Romantic love I mean. I've been tricked about it, though. Same with old God. Show me some proof, then maybe I'll perk up.

It's not bitterness, I tell you. I *enjoy* not receiving Valentine's Day cards. I'm happy in my solitude. I'm optimistic about my impending death.

Anyway, to the point: there was something funny but also sad about that ebony face of Jad's when he was playing the drum. He looked like he was doing it right – playing it in time – but he also looked like he was not there at all, not in the music, which was strange because Jad Kinney was the music man to me.

He was looking at all the girls to see if he could charm them with his eyes or something. To see if he could beat their drum and all. I burst out in laughter like a madman in my parka with my hood up in the rain behind the window on this thunderous January noon and I genuinely felt happy to know my friends were stuck in classes. That's not mean. I want them to do well. Truth be told (and god I hate that expression, but I also hate wearing this skin and isn't that just easier to accept) they didn't all attend every class. But it was getting into the year and for some reason I hadn't caught on that my friends were actually right to be attending. At that moment I felt a prod on the back.

"Penguin? Oh, it's you. What the fuck was that dancing?" It was Erica. "You don't dance."

"Can't you see Jad in there? He looks bored as hell as if he's trying to chirpse the girls with his eyes. Playing the bongos!"

"How high are you? And where's my some?"

"I'm gone. Sleep deprivation certainly helps. Hey, I really liked your poem by the way, but the title was a bit ironic."

"You mean I'm the poser don't you? I'm watching you, mate." She stuck her foot out and tapped it on the wet concrete with some attitude, crossing her arms and leaning over my soul as if she were about to tear me a new one, verbally. But I got my reply in before she could:

"Well. Hipster."

"I'm not a fucking hipster."

"I meant angel-headed! Angel-headed!"

Erica was probably my favourite person in the group, and not just because she would get that I was referencing *Howl*, that poem I was trying to memorise and got to 'endless balls'. I was poking her back.

"Come on, if you wanna smoke let's go see if Beebee and Penguin are around."

"They're probably fucking." As it turned out, unbeknownst to us, they were about to.

"Beebee must have just got out of class, we have to find her before he does." We made our way in the rain. "Oh, by the way, do you know anything about a party in Q last night?"

"Yeah, it was shit."

"You were there?"

"Yeah. Apparently someone got their deposit taken away."

"Yeah. It was me!"

"That's peak, man."

"No, I mean. I didn't throw the party, but for some reason security thinks I did."

"Ahh. All I know is that Ella told security. Molly told me she was ratting the guy out. And it's you? Oh Dun, when will you catch a damn break?" She looked at me as if I was a dog with three legs. I nearly felt like one.

"Ella? Well, damn. Fucking figures. She's got it out for me for no reason."

We walked together to find Beebee and I decided to give her my parka as all she was wearing was a white-collared blouse.

"I thought you said you didn't give your coat to girls."

"You're not a girl, Erica."

"What am I then?"

"I don't know. But you know what I mean. Those girls in your class. They're girls. And you're not like them. I'm just using maths."

"Look, it's Bella! Bella, over here!"

"There's weather everywhere..."

"You're still deaf? I said Bella. B-E-L-L-A."

I realised what she meant, felt a twinge of excitement as if some angel was reported to have come down to Earth, then there she was, Bella Bowden. She looked over at me and gave me a cold glance, walking through the rain, accompanied by a thunderclap. Her eyes were so big, so sublime and deep, that when you talked to her, you got worried you might fall in.

I looked over at her. She's been doing it for a while, now. Giving me a cold look and all. I'm thinking she just comes to see Erica, not me. I just don't know what I did to make her all sour.

"Hey, guys. Man, I just had the weirdest seminar. Some guy tried to tell me my photographs were shit. You know what his were? Pictures of his fucking lunch!"

"Well, what was he eating? If it was a golden lobster then maybe he is good."

"Dunley's high," Erica says, as if excusing me.

"He was eating carrots! I took a photo of the lightning passing the field of sheep and he said it was pretentious. He's such a twat."

"There's nothing more pretentious than taking pictures of carrots, Bell. Don't stress. You're great. We all know you're great. I mean, you've got lightning in your lunchbox."

"Wow. That would be a good line for a poem!"

"I've got a patent on it, Dunley. Sorry."

"Well, could I use it in a story?"

"Fine... just make sure I'm the one who says it."

"I'm stressed. Could one of you write a story where we go for a spliff now? You know, I think we need to do it for Bowie. Like a commemoration."

"That's a good idea, Bell." The girls began to look forlorn. I was confused.

"Why so sad?"

"You didn't hear?"

"Hear what?"

"He died."

"Who did?"

"Bowie!"

"He did? When?"

"Yesterday."

"Oh god..." I looked down at the mud which had been softened by the rain and saw him underneath me. "I just got over Lou Reed's death!"

"Lou Reed was a womaniser, dude."

"Yeah, and Hitler painted."

"What?"

"I don't even know."

"You think Hitler's okay because he fucking painted?"

"That's not what I meant. I was just pointing out the... ah. Just ignore me. I'm all over the place today."

"We gotta put on some Ziggy," says Bella. "I need to hear his voice, guys."

"You're right. It's the right thing to do. Shall we just go and let Beebee's snatch get apprehended by the beast, then? They've got weed anyway for sure."

Penguin wasn't a beast. What I meant was he was a real man and I was just a little boy. But why say that?

"I'm up for it. We'll catch the lovers later."

The three of us began our route in the rain; Bella

warm, dry and prepared in her furry beige coat; Erica not prepared but still warm and dry; and me wet with melancholy. Bowie kicking the bucket certainly didn't help. I took one last look at the window of the music hall and for a second, I thought I saw his ghost. I wiped my eyes and then it was gone. And then I noticed Jad Kinney had vanished too. Everyone else was still there. I could hear the drums even in my weakened ears.

"What happened to Jad?"

"Probably fled to go try and fuck Molly, to be honest. She hasn't got classes today."

"God. Everyone's fucking everyone around here. Why haven't I got laid? What is it, guys? What's wrong with me?" They both look at me and then each other for what seemed a long time.

"Dunley, you haven't gone into a single class."

"Or a single arse." (Cue them two giggling to hell.)

"You don't even say arse, Bella. You say ass!"

"It had to rhyme."

"Dunley, man, you haven't gone in. You haven't met any of your classmates. You're not ugly or even a bad guy, they just don't know you."

"I don't think anyone knows me."

"Poor you. Why don't you just go for Khalifa? She likes you."

"Why is it that the one you don't want always likes you? I get it, it's sweet. And I'm weird as hell and she's normal and a great person who will probably do the best in the whole university. But it's not gonna happen. I'm not attracted to her."

"Can we *please* get some weed and stop talking about Dunley's unappreciated member?"

"Sure, guys. Sure. We'll go to my room and I'll roll a couple."

2

We started walking back from the musical window, the rain still pounding like Poseidon's drum.

I wanted to ask Rye for my parka back, but I just left it. I was gonna be drenched and I would enjoy it because she would be warm and dry. God, how pathetic I was.

We walked, with me on the left, closest to the buildings in order to keep as dry as possible (I wasn't completely pathetic) and the girls on my right seemingly excited to get out of their seminars (something I had never experienced) and off we went on our merry way to light one up for David Bowie. Bella started singing on the way as she often did when in a good mood, and I thought about why she was giving me such a cold look, and I thought about the golden lobster that never happened, and how perfect it was that such a beautiful creature wanted to see beautiful things and put them on a vision field.

We walked further and the girls were talking to each other. I tuned out because all I was thinking about was the rain coming down. The rain that was so ingrained in me that it was the most regular thing and yet every time I saw it, every time I heard it, every time I smelt it and felt it, it entranced me in a way that no girl or song or book or drug or even memory could do in its stead.

Before too long, we got to our halls. I said goodbye to my true wet soulmate (who I knew I would see again) and we went in and opened a few doors, easing their weight as if we were in one of those races with the little poles, carried on up a flight of stairs and arrived at the door of my bedroom. My new abode of boredom and loneliness. The girls followed me into the room, and immediately flared both of their noses in disgust.

"It's fucking rank in here."

"Can you spray something?"

I was starting to get why no girls, or in fact anyone, ever came to my room. The only person that did was my counsellor. Only sales people, drug dealers and counsellors try and contact me. I frustratingly grabbed my deodorant can and sprayed it round the room aggressively, though I was actually not that angry. It was rank.

"I'm sorry, your royal majesties. You're gold and I'm a piece of shit. I'm fucking ill! You've both probably had more sleep last night than I've had all term!"

"I didn't sleep!"

"Well then, Bell, you know the struggle. I just don't have time –"

"You never go in! You've had all the time."

"Okay, not time. I've had all the time yeah, but I've had no energy to clear up in here."

"At least there isn't flies and shit."

I pointed to the laptop on the table piled with unread books and sat on the bed next to the bedrest where the bud was.

"Don't worry...We'll be one song. Just pinch your noses. Song, guys?" The laptop was open, Youtube up, and it was connected to my speakers and ready to go. Some things I was prepared for. Things that mattered. But not things like life. I thought the girls both had good taste in music so I wasn't worried about that. I wasn't even worried that they would find some questionable material on my history. I was worried they would flee and leave me in my swamp. So I simply started to find the equipment. I did it quickly, trying to be impressive and trying to keep them around. Licking rizlas together, finding cardboard for roaches, grinding up the weed; I did it all quickly whereas if I had been alone I would have taken my sweet time. As I caught a scent from the weed, *Fools Gold* by The Stone Roses started playing, although to me it was muffled.

"I love this song, but can you turn it up? My ears, guys."

"It's well loud already. Just get new ears for fuck sake."

"Huh?"

"Nevermind."

"Huh?"

"Nevermind!"

"Oh yeah, that's a good album. But we don't have time to listen to that. Only one song."

"Fool with his gold..."

"Huh?"

Instead of saying something back, Bella just lost patience with me, quite rightly, and turned up the music, quite graciously. It was a good song. In my happy state I roll the two joints before the song finishes and I smile and raise them to the girls. Then they both laugh again. They were always goddamn laughing.

"Those joints look demented."

"Listen, I don't have big rizla. Beebee's not here with her magic hands, okay? I wish she was. That girl is the greatest roller who ever lived. But you're stuck with me, the nervous-handed stoner. They're not that bad, are they?" Looking at them as I held them up, and then each other, they burst into laughter again. Bella says:

"We'll take 'em. But we're not happy about it, Dunley."

It was like some strange thing in their minds that I rolled shit joints. I mean, I did. But I was always ready to share with them, and still the japery came, even when they were just slightly not perfect and they knew they would smoke just the same as a perfect one. I mean, I don't believe in Plato's perfect forms so didn't think there could be a perfect joint anyway. But Beebee got close. And she studied philosophy, so maybe she believed in Plato's perfect forms and maybe if you believed in Plato's perfect forms you would be able to obtain them, or at least get closer to them.

But I'm not too sure if she did believe in them. All this went through my head and I didn't speak it because philosophy, though highly interesting in the mind, when spouted out randomly to people, gets very tiring for you and them.

"Let's shmoke!"

"Hold on," says Erica, leaning over the laptop. "You've been watching David Firth cartoons?"

"You mean there's shit on there apart from porn?"

"It was a big mistake. That guy's fucked up. I watched a couple and now they're all over my recommendations. Locust Toybox is so much better than his bloody cartoons."

As we walked out of the room to smoke I knew that the girls would take a breath of fresh air through their sweet and golden mouths and would never return to my hell-hole of a room unless it smelled good. I dreamt of it smelling good and being tidy and there being a golden lobster on the table and fuck loads of flowers and the girls getting off with each other on my bed while I toked on a crystal bong.

It was fun to think of things that would never happen. Like any pleasant girl wanting to be with me or becoming a lawyer who dealt with cases involving drugs and the Vatican or getting signed or having a lot of money or saving someone or a way with words or a normal mind that didn't drift off into stupid shit. It drifted off so much I didn't even notice the journey my legs took from the room to outside and round the back of Hercocks, where there was some little brick lees where you could all sit and stare at the fields dotted with those mystically rooted trees and the sheep leaning in zen state on the slanted hills. I heard a 'baaaa'.

It was still raining and I had forgotten to bring a coat, but the lee covered us from the rain. Our bums slightly touched at the sides because we were next to each other and there wasn't much space and I just felt happy. I didn't feel horny. I just liked the feeling of the bums touching. They did too, I bet.

Then: *Oh! You Pretty Things* blaring out of one of their phones. "Wake up you sleepy head..."

I lit up my abominations, getting kicks from the song, and then handed one over to Bella who was next to me. She was in the middle because she bagsied it and ran there first like a little kid and thus got double cheek.

"Bella. Why do you like sitting in the middle? Is it for the double cheek effect?"

"Oh yeah! Nah, I just like being in the middle." Her eyes actually sparkled. There were reflections of raindrops as she looked up to a crack in the sky.

"...And a hand reaching down to me..."

"The double cheek effect. Lol."

"Who actually says lol in real life?" Ryc did not like that comment.

"People who are too cool for school," she says. "That's who."

The zoots were quickly depleting and we got higher and higher and were all enjoying the music so it seemed and life felt so good to me. I heard another 'baaaa' and sung back at it:

"You gotta make way for the homo superior..."

Like Bowie's mortal, physical life, I knew the smoke up couldn't last forever. The girls had classes to return to. I had one to go to as well, but I had decided I would never go in. I was utterly stupid. My plan to write a novel and hand that in as my only work was also stupid. I was a terrible writer. But at this point my insomnia and poor hearing made any extra effort seem like a mountain so big it was easier to avoid it. Avoid it all, just get lean with your mates and say farewell to a friend. You'll hear him again and ain't that the immaterial, and enjoy the thought that one day you could realise the dream of sitting in the middle and getting the double cheek effect and life would be alright.

"Look who's coming, Dunley," says Erica. "It's your Juliet." I choked on the smoke I was inhaling and started coughing so much I thought I was going to die.

The socially quaint yet vivid soul who was in my eyes misunderstood, had come round the corner, probably smelling the weed from her window and guessing we'd be out here. It was Khalifa.

"Hey, guys." She comes over slowly, but seems happy to see us. I wave. "Can I have a puff? I just got out of the worst cage-fight in psychological history ever."

"Sure, Khalif. What was the argument about?" I hand her the joint.

"It was that thing ... *puff* ... that thing where ... *puff* ... people say the mind rules the body ... *puff* ... and the other people that say the body rules the ... *puff* ... mind." She spoke very nonplussed, and while she did so she moistened the roach to breaking point. Another "puff" and another "baaa".

"And what side do you stand on?"

"I dunno."

"Wow, Khalifa," says Erica. "You're just like Morrissey. He didn't know either." Bella then let out what she had to: "She is like Morrissey!" Then: "She *is* Morrissey!"

In mere seconds a cage-fight in a classroom in Bath resorted into the fleer somehow unintendedly quoting *Still Ill*. How in mere milliseconds this short, sweet looking enigma from the countryside called Khalifa Rose had become the tall Mancunian poet who was pointlessly agnostic on tape and yet came up with a point. But I still felt annoyed at Erica and all because Khalifa didn't seem to know what we were talking about saying she was Morrissey and just bursting out laughing – and maybe she did – but such was the enigma of Khalifa Rose. She had curled locks and spectacles, was always being left out of things, or at least left out of the mess, so we made an effort to ingratiate her more into our lesser world after being, frankly, quite rude.

We would hide from her sometimes (never once my idea but I did follow once or twice I must admit) so we wouldn't have to deal with her, and the guilt got to me so bad that in fact one night when she went to give me a kiss, I didn't stop her. She had burst into my room and spoke a tome in three seconds and just snogged me. It was mad. She had wanted to. I do not know why.

I could imagine so easily being the outcast (not that she was one but she wasn't understood, the running away made that clear) as I was one for years and years and truth be told – there that goddamn expression goes again – felt I still was, and I guess I tried to imagine a girl letting me kiss her when I was a shy-as-hell boy and even now in my present state and knowing how happy it would make me, so that's why I didn't stop it. I wanted her to be happy. I definitely didn't want to be kissing her. But it wasn't so bad. It was nice, actually. It made it seem like it was important. Usually, necking with someone ain't important. Usually.

There was this joke about us in the group, because Beebee Gladstone (the devilish angel) wrote a fake love letter to me from 'her' and placed it under my door one day. Worse than the spit balls on the ceiling.

It was very like *'Dunley you are the man of my dreams and I would die for you.'* I then went to talk to Khalifa about the letter to let her down gently and all, and she seemed embarrassed and said she didn't write a letter and I thought she was just lying but she wasn't. There were mad things slipped in too which I should have clocked was Beebee up to no good. Things like: *'I need a strong man like you, Dun. I need a lumberjack. I need wood from the lumberjack. The wood of... love.'*

When I found out the truth, I thought about writing a hate letter explaining that 'I', Penguin, was done with her shit. But I never did. I wasn't good at actually being vengeful. Plus, you can't hate Beebee.

It made me a little depressed only because I always wished someone would want me and yet it was the only girl I figured wouldn't really work out. My mind was on the angel-headed hipster.

One day, she was about on a bench in the courtyard reading some new book by B E Ellis and asking me to come by later to check out her bookshelf. When she let me in I saw the shelf, which suffered some *Naked Lunch*; *Fear and Loathing in Las Vegas*; a copy of Vonnegut's *Cat's Cradle*; Salinger's *Catcher in the Rye*; a *Lord of the Flies* and seeing also Coleridge and Keats somewhere in the sheets and Dali's paintings coming out a big hardback. I think the shelf was bookended by *The Bell Jar* she had. I mean I wanted her as soon as I saw her, on the very first day, and before the bookshelf introduction regardless and when I did see her the first time I had a feeling she was special. (But as I said before, I've been tricked too many times in that regard.)

She was cool as hell, sweet to me, wild to us all and wise at nineteen. She was hilarious in those halls. Never spoke too much but when she did she had the most curious voice. Hoarse and yet something like dew. And she had that look like she'd been up for days which I really liked, but she must have been sleeping I reckon because that's where you get your beauty.

But even a lecturer who rated my notes I never wrote would have been okay. Even my soulmate the rain I wished would tell me it loved me. But in the end it didn't matter. We were all a sort of a strange gathering at one point. I remember the bee that came in unannounced that one night, too.

If you looked closely at it – you would see that it was fashioned in a delightfully amusing trick of the senses. We always thought a bear came in. For a week.

Probably longer than bees even live. I don't know. I'm not an entymologist.

The rain was included in the gathering as well as the bee in the bear onesie that always showed up unannounced (it's not that we were stiffs at all, we'd let near anyone come in that kitchen, but he just literally flew in all the time without warning or even knowing us that well, and flying in in the most peculiar way, and then he got sour but never left for ages) and I saw again that everyone was different and that's why it worked pretty damn well. I loved the fact that everyone was different. All a rarity.

Khalifa was shy and yet determined; I was intelligent and stupid; Bella was fun and curious with a bit of a dark beauty about her; while Rye was impassioned and mellow all at the same time. I think we all learnt something from one another, and misunderstood things about one another too, and that extended to the whole group, who weren't all around but who would be later, at the surprise party I was still wondering whether to execute. But I didn't want to invite Khalifa Rose, and the reason I didn't was not because I didn't want her around but because I was going to do something real stupid.

3

There is no introductory course to insanity, I reckon. It is like homelessness, or unrequited love. You do not plan for it to happen.

Some folks may restrain their madness. They are the people whose madness, or passion, is weak enough to be restrained in the first place. As Mel Brooks eruditely screamed: Either you got it or you ain't. I don't know if the bee had it or not. I suspect he wanted to be mad.

And we all looked sideways after he said "hey we're down."
And we all looked sideways.
"Look at me! I'm a bee!
In a brown delightful gown."

But I was no better than the bee. In fact, I was worse. I didn't wear a bear onesie all freshers week and turn up unannounced time and time again like the bee did, but I did plan on getting wine for the gang.

Getting some wine.

And lacing it with LSD.

I wasn't going to tell anyone until they all tried a little and then I would watch everyone trip, myself included. Khalifa wouldn't be able to handle it, I thought, and I wasn't sure if the others would either, and it was actually a very unfair thing to do but I thought it could end up being a right craic where nothing too bad would go wrong. I really did.

When I questioned whether something could go wrong well I just said to myself 'I've never had a bad trip and it's just paranoia getting worried about it'. Did I mention I wasn't sleeping and I was bored as hell? If only I was bored as heaven.

But I was going to trip with them, and we would all get drunk in the kitchen and when we got drunk in the kitchen we'd start to feel funny and then I would admit it, hope no-one got angry, and who knows, maybe something great would happen. Maybe it would be chaos. But I was bored, and I guess in a way I wanted to do something crazy. I didn't realise that I didn't need to go to such lengths. I was aware that bad trips were possible. Yet I was determined that everyone have a good one. I just wanted it to be a fun surprise because I thought no-one would do it with me had they the knowledge of it and they would just get drunk perhaps. But still I was playing with fire, and I still wasn't certain about it. But if you play with fire and you are certain then isn't that true insanity? Just asking.

I was telling myself 'it's just paranoia Dunley and nothing's gonna go wrong and it might be rude to lace it but how else are you gonna get everyone to do it?'

I thought I would get kicked out any day now and I

wanted to do something great before I got kicked out and had to go back to my parents. I'd only shown up for five minutes throughout these first four months. And the university wouldn't understand that I was partially deaf and severely ill from olanzapine withdrawal. Anyway that's what I told myself (common sense eradicated, you see).

And I couldn't execute the gold-dust of an idea my brother S told me upon driving me up to Bath, which was housing a sheep on the roof of Commons, so I settled for my original idea. They would either love me or hate me. I was willing to take that chance. I was willing to do it.

After I thought about it a lot, sitting there in the brick lee, a crack of thunder whipped me out of my thoughts. I was off in my own mind again and hadn't realised that Bella and Rye had left me alone with Khalifa. I guessed they were going back to their classes, or perhaps just getting away from me. A mere minute later I get a text from a random number saying: "Now's ur chance!"

Yet little did I know that it wasn't either of them two japers who sent that text – but a mysterious deity who had managed to find my number.

I was prepared for the worst, to calm down anyone that genuinely felt worried and soothe them and tell them it was going to be okay. The people who had done it before were going to be okay. I was sure of it. But Bella hadn't done it before and I guess quite a few of them hadn't and I did feel torn about doing it because of this. I hadn't either, really. I'd done 1P-LSD, some sort of knock off.

Yet I couldn't ruin the surprise effect by just saying I had acid and did anyone want some because chances were no-one would take any. Not on a Monday night. Not when there was bloody thunder.

No-one was as stupid as me, and no-one would have done something like this. That's why I thought I had to. I had to make an unforgettable university experience. I wanted to throw the best party in the world and have fun with all my friends and have them say they were so surprised but loving it. I really didn't want to freak anyone out.

But it really wasn't a nice thing to do in retrospect because acid was quite strong and it was a long time it would take effect. I was expecting them to be like – 'What the hell!'– but also expecting that soon after they would forgive me and we'd all have a right time. God. I wasn't thinking straight at all.

Not at all. Too much time on my hands, minutes and hours melting into my palms.

I turned to Khalifa, who seemed to have just been standing over me saying nothing all this time, only now finishing the wet spliff. I didn't hate the way she hung around and I perhaps would have liked to discuss with her the whole mind-body control thing, but I decided I would leave to go look for the stuff, and I thought about who and I reckoned Kurt Dashby would have some.

I suspected he had some at the time because first of all he was in a band and read Ginsberg and that was clue number one but not concrete evidence. Yet one night he came into some corridor we were all loitering in saying did anyone want 'tabs' and I didn't know what they were but I wanted to get one anyway, and Beebee practically stopped me because she was worried and all, that it wouldn't be a good idea since I did have psychosis some time ago (and Kurt suffered schizophrenia so the whole matter was very confusing). She was adamant about it and I see now that only meant she cared about me. But I sat there sulking for not getting to trip.

Kurt would be getting some back in the wine and it felt weird to think that, but he did like psyches. I had to pull the trade off convincingly. I needed to get enough for everyone but make it seem like it was for something else.

"Khalifa. I gotta go and, er, make some calls. It's quite important. Sorry to leave ya." I was a terrible writer and a terrible liar.

"Oh, it's okay. I've got this assignment to do anyway." She drifted off quite forlornly it seemed to me and I felt bad for leaving her so soon and all. But I knew she'd be alright. I had to go now before I admitted the plan to her, which I no doubt would have, and she no doubt would have spilled it to everyone only in goodness and that would have ruined it and I would definitely be a twat instead of only possibly being one.

I said goodbye and gave her a hug and went back to my room to go get my parka. I then realised Erica had it, but maybe she had left it in my room? No chance. Not the 'fucking rank' room.

When I made it to my room she had left a note on the door (I mean, I assumed it was her) stuck with bluetac:

abandon scent all ye who enter here

4

I went inside and saw that the parka was indeed still not there, so I grabbed my black jacket, an umbrella, my leather bag and a hundred and forty quid cash (student loans and good timing) hoping Kurt would take that for a little bottle if he had one and I'd have enough left for loads of bottles of wine – the clincher.

I pondered where to find him. He wouldn't reply to a text from me, there was more chance of the deity replying to a text, and I was too shy to call anybody but I guessed he would be at band practice, so I made my way out of halls to the music department where I'd been two hours earlier laughing at Jad Kinney play the bongos, to listen out for some killer song and follow it like a dog following the smell of meat.

I was getting nervous as I walked. I'd never thrown a party before. And I wasn't even sure anyone would come. But I reckoned if I got free wine for everyone there would be an incentive. Usually what happened was everyone congregated to a particular kitchen anyway and this was where the party was going to happen. It was going to be safe. It was going to be fun. It was going to be out o this world.

I made it quickly to the music department, this time from the other side, so I had walked up the more scenic route where grass and trees and a bouncing rabbit had calmed me down. There were some theatre folk proclaiming loudly their own delightful insanities out by the lake as I made my way, and their voices echoed through the campus. I never really got talking to them lot. They love to scream and I, well, I could stay silent for a decade if I had to.

I started to hear something like a band set-up playing.

Drums and cymbals being hit randomly, bass whopping in low hums and screechy guitar all going off. It was clear that they, whoever they were, were just getting started. I had to break in the front door and see for myself, something that was utterly rude when a band you didn't know was just setting up – and was probably rude anyway – but if it wasn't him and his band and some other band I could just pretend I was nuts and run out again. It would be easy actually, I wouldn't even have to pretend.

You couldn't just knock on the door of the band practice room. It was like tugging at the robe of 'God' or something. It wouldn't be noticed. You had to fire a nuclear bomb at His holy face.

As I got closer the three main sounds started to become more orderly. I would still come in but would probably have to wait until the song was finished. It sounded good, though.

I got to the door, the drums pounded in my chest. I opened the door and saw Penny Buslane standing by the mic with her guitar, brandishing an open mouth as if I had just come in at the moment she was about to sing the first word and all, and her eyes caught mine instantly and her mouth remained comedically open but she didn't start to sing. I startled her, I thought.

Penny was Kurt's girl. She had those similar tired looking eyes that Erica had and I never really spoke to her. It wasn't because I didn't want to. I just literally found it so hard to speak to people. The longer I waited not meeting someone properly, the harder it was to speak.

There were also a few other people I never really got friendly with unfortunately, because one night when I was off-my-face drunk some of them wanted me to let them into the building, and I was going to naturally but I was so drunk I couldn't open the door and they thought that I was just standing there, they could see my blur, being a nuisance and not letting them in. I tried for ages and then someone else let them in. They thought I was one of those people that would do that. I was too shy to tell them the truth.

Anyway, Penny played her guitar, Kurt played his guitar, the bassist played their bass and the drummer played their drums. The song went on but Penny Buslane didn't sing. They seemed surprised to see me but I'm glad they didn't stop the music. I simply made a friendly wave and hung by a cracked out wall as they played, but Kurt engaged with me verbally, shouting, as the song went on. It was very surreal.

"Yo, it's Dunley! What you think of that riff?" He turned his eyes from me and down to the ground and began rocking his head and his long brown hair followed, and I watched him and the three others in their awesome grungy harmony. I shout back, only since he started it:

"Yeah, man! Feeling it! I heard outside! And I had to come in to see if it was you guys! The infamous Hammyblink! Should I come back another time?"

"We're just practising, man! Is something up?"

"Kinda, dude! I was wondering if you got cid!" They still played the music. All of them. They were cool as hell.

"Yeah man! What you after?"

"A bottle! It's crr, well my friend's going to a festival and he wants to sell there! I don't mind giving you a hundred for a little one!"

"What festival?" And then I froze. I couldn't think of a damn festival in that moment. I had been to a few. I knew about many. But I couldn't think of one and didn't want to get into a longer conversation which would end up in further lies. I was quick to make one up:

"Flippy...Whippy." I kept on going. "It's really, er, low-key! Almost to the point no-one's even heard of it."

"Oh yeah? Where is it?"

"Kent."

"What do they play?"

"Psytrance."

"I've got one for you man, don't worry!" He slings his dark green jaguar behind his back in a movement that seems so swift and elegant, and turns to the corner of the room by his guitar case and bends down for a few seconds. The other three began a conversation but I wasn't aware of it since I was so excited about the acid. Kurt then bends his body back up and walks over to me, showing me something that looks like ear drops.

"You got the hundred on you?"

"I do."

"Sound, man." I then got out my wallet, the wallet that gave off some impression I had wealth, when really I was quite poor and the system just strange. But I did wonder if perhaps I were the thing that was strange and the system were the thing that was poor.

I took out five twenties, counted them in front of his relaxed countenance, but before I did anything else I made important small talk: "Yo, you about the kitchen tonight? I'm getting wine for everyone and we're just gonna chill like usual. Jad's got some new speakers, you in? You can bring the band, too. Everyone's welcome!"

"I'll see, man. Possibly. I need a bit of a wind-down after this mind-fuck of a new track we've been working on."

"Alright, man," and just then I slap the scores into his

hand. He then in turn throws the bottle up in the air so it lands safely into mine, and gives me a wink. It did seem kind of like a weird performance, but the fact was he was just a very at-ease guy and he wasn't trying to be cool or anything, it just happened that way. I was real jealous of that. I never winked at people.

It was no big deal to him. He could probably get bottles and bottles of the stuff from all the people he knew just by charming them. But a goof like me had to pay up. It was fine. I didn't mind. I look at the bottle.

"Cheers, man. My mate will be very grateful."

"No problem, dude." He swings the jaguar back to its rightful destination and gives a nod to the drummer whose name escapes me and they all start playing again. It was my cue to leave, and as I went for the door I heard Penny scream her first lyric. It was the lyric of something like accepted anguish. I can't tell you what she said here for legal reasons. But it was real. A real manic voice.

I kicked open the door and walked out, popping up the umbrella for the rain that was still there – didn't I tell ya? – though seeming to have more portentous tone to it now; shoving the bottle into my leather bag and bopping my head to the song, which got better but more muffled as I walked away, back through the scenic route but not the way I came. The way to where the shop would be.

The way to where I would fool all my goddamn friends.

5

The day was getting on, and most of the gang had

finished their classes, but there was probably revision to be done and gladly, as I wasn't ready yet. But I couldn't be certain that my friends were revising now. They weren't really the revising type. They were all quite intelligent. They didn't really need to.

I couldn't be spotted with the wine until it was laced and I was texting some of them about the free wine already and to come by the kitchen later tonight before they made other plans. I was enjoying thinking what sublimity might hit me. What I would see. Whatever it was, I was ready to see it.

Jad Kinney the all-living Brummie said he'd be there, but only to use the piano and bring his speakers in return; Molly Jones the caustic dancer (also a Brummie) who had been my neighbour of gold and whom I dined with during the Christmas holiday for a near questionable feast when we ransacked the kitchen after everyone else had left, said she might; Beebee Gladstone, the utter delight of a northerner who was really quite beautiful and mad and easy to warm to, even though she had a mouth (chrysostomos, it was), lived in the block of that kitchen we all usually went to and with little doubt would be there, so I didn't speak to her, nor Jamie Penguin her blonde lover, because he was sure to want to be with Beebee; then there was Nossie Godman, the dark-skinned 'gentleman' who literally was a godly man, at least he went on about it all the time, said he might but only if he could bring this peng chick (his words) who he was having deep meaningful conversations with, which I reluctantly said okay to; then Bella and Erica said they would be there 'probably, dunno' and if they ever decided they'd bring Tig with them, the cute French girl who was a psychology student like Khalifa Rose.

I remember Tig one night desperately handing out questionnaires to us which reminded me of all the bullshit questionnaires I had to answer during counselling, but I was happy to help her I guess. She also handed out codeine to some of us at one point which she had about her person from some injury and I tried it for the first time and it was well nice. Better than a questionnaire if you ask me. But questionnaires don't make your eyes itch the next day. Then again maybe they do.

I said in the texts not to invite Khalifa, pretending I just didn't want to see her but hiding the fact that I cared about her too much to drag her into this. It was my only morsel of good sense. They all agreed we could take a night off from her. It was just strange, as we had given her such a rough time (how rotten I feel about it now). She never clocked on or anything and just stayed with us, letting herself be teased and joked with just to not suffer being alone. Well, I perhaps would have done the same.

I cared about the others too but thought they'd be alright. And I didn't care if I appeared rude or spiteful for not inviting her. I was doing what had to be done. But I was beginning to have doubts now. Did it even need to be done... Was it fair... Was it okay? I was starting to think that it wasn't. And yet I had already made it to the shop. I had already got the acid. I had already probably lost it. And I was already in the queue holding the five bottles of wine: three white, two red. And suddenly I saw Jad Kinney again, loitering around the front of the shop with a couple other guys. He comes up to me – this is in public and all – and shouts:

"Yo, Dun! What was it like when yoh went mad? Paint me oh picture."

Now, I don't hold self pity or embarrassment for what happened to me, and I didn't mind telling him (he was curious about it and asked me what it was like a lot) but he really wasn't doing me a service shouting out that shit at the shop.

"Well, Kinney. Imagine not sleeping a whole night yeah? Now multiply that by thirty five, chuck in some Messianic delusions and fear," (still in the queue) "fear... and confusion of the most maniacal kind, a thousand different beings which all possess you... the fear you will never know what it's like to be safe from your own thoughts. It's a maze. It's a fucking maze, Jad."

"That's deep as shit man. You should write this down. Would be sick."

"I tried. It doesn't work."

While the shop staff girl looks at me and I see I'm holding up the queue I realise what the shit I'd just been saying. And off Jad Kinney goes, laughing his joyous yelps at my strange existence.

But perhaps there was concern hidden underneath those questions he so fervently asked me. Perhaps he wanted to help me. But in all honesty I thought Jad was just interested and not really concerned for me. And maybe if I had told him my plan, he would have talked me out of it. I needed myself to talk me out of it. I needed to clap my own hand. And after all this, I was still seriously considering it. God might not play dice with the Universe, but poor old Dunley would shoot dice all night for the price of a priceless mind. What a damn tragedy.

By now the plan had got me so excited and twitchy that I felt I couldn't back down. And I really wanted everyone to have a wild time and maybe being surprised would make it better. Maybe I was overthinking it. Getting paranoid and all. But was it just paranoia? Maybe I wasn't overthinking it. Maybe it wasn't a good idea. And then it just struck me, I didn't need to do it. I could still buy the wine, sure, but it would be clean. Just get drunk like you've done a hundred times before.

I resolved that it was a stupid idea. Yes, most likely nothing would have gone wrong. But I was defeated by internal thoughts. How it wasn't actually a good idea or a right craic or anything. It was just plain rude.

I paid for the bottles. Yes. Just good old drunk. Nothing could go wrong with booze.

On the way out of the shop, I had my umbrella ready but I noticed for once the rain had stopped. The thunder and lightning had stopped.

It seemed like a good omen, and to my surprise, it seemed the majority of people would be at the party (which would still be happening but now acid-less). And though it was only getting on for four now, it was already on the way to getting dark and I needed to try and rest for a good few hours. I had been running on empty since seeing Kurt.

I had to be rested for later on and I also knew I had to have at least three hours in bed in order to achieve something as pitiful as a dozen minutes sleep. I could not be sidetracked at this point. But I did get sidetracked. My phone started buzzing.

"Hello?"

"Hello, Dunley. This is Samantha Gully. I need to see you in my office. Could you come to Stable?"

"Umm, yeah. Sure. What time?"

"Now."

"I'll be there in five minutes."

I walked across the square towards the building housing old benevolent Gully. That was a joke. She wasn't benevolent at all. I wonder what I did to upset the poor wretch. Probably just the party I never threw. Well, I could tell her the truth. Maybe she'd believe me.

When I walk to the front door, it opens on its own. I introduce myself and am told to take a seat and wait for Mrs. Gully. I end up waiting twenty four minutes. She then shows up and invites me in to tell me that there will be 'repercussions' for not turning up to class.

"But I'm telling you. I'm ill. I can't sleep."

"Does that excuse the fact you haven't handed in any work at all?"

"I can't hear very well, and I haven't slept, well, at all. I promise I'll catch up."

"I'm sorry Dunley. But first there were the drug violations. You remember you were taking drugs in our accommodation?"

"Yes. I remember."

"Well, we can't tolerate that. And the party last night?"

"It wasn't me." Then she let out a big old sigh. God, I really hated her guts.

"You have to take responsibility for your actions. And the fact you haven't shown up or done any work tells me that you aren't fit for university, Dunley."

"But, I've. I've got a novel I'm writing. I'm writing it right now. As we speak. It's in the process of being done, I promise."

"I'm sorry Dunley but we only accept the adhered to assignments. In any case, we can't keep you here, Dunley. You have to go."

After that I had cried right in front of her face, stormed out and felt myself being pummelled into the ground by life itself.

She didn't even care. Didn't care that I was ill. Didn't care that I didn't throw the party. Didn't care that I could have done all the work and caught up in two weeks. But no. Well, to hell with it.

I started walking home, seething with anger. What right did they have to kick me out? Like hell I was going to turn up to her next meeting. What, just to be told how incapable I am? To be told how misguided and astray I was? That I had to be gone, disappear, never to be thunk of again. I decided to hell with it. The plan was back on. I was going to trip with my friends while I still had the chance. I was going to 'take drugs in the accommodation' and there was not a damn thing they could do about it. Not anymore.

I had to get home and try and get that sweet twelve minutes of sleep and after that put all the drops in the wine bottles without anyone being around. If I could do that, and arrive at the kitchen for eight with it all sorted and no bad luck then I could relax and the plan would be set to go. So I walked with at least some sort of hope, rolling a cigarette and lighting it up and the sun, though low in the sky, had fleetingly revealed itself before its coming getaway, as if waving from the crowd, as if it needed to be noticed just once, and pretty soon I did get home. When I made it to the front door, Ella Muntz had come out.

"Dunley, what did I tell you about smoking weed?"

"What the hell, Ella? I haven't even been here."

"Well someone's smoking weed. I can smell it and it's turning my stomach."

"Why don't you just dip your face in vodka or something?"

"Are you sure it's not you?"

"No, you're right, Ella. It was me. Every single scent of

weed is coming from me. In all the hundreds of students here that smoke weed, it was me. It's all me."

"Don't be funny."

"Why shouldn't I? You got my deposit taken away, Ella. I didn't throw a party in the damn kitchen! Why did you tell security that I did? I only went inside to eat dinner and there was already a party going on. I left after I ate my food. You cost me two hundred and fifty goddamn pounds."

"Well, you were just going to spend it on drugs, weren't you?"

And with that, I realised there was no point in talking to her. Some people like to be entitled, well, let them. They'll dig their own grave.

As she stormed off to her Business seminar I took one last drag from my cigarette, threw the fag-end onto my shoe and kicked it up to the air. Sweet air never ratted you out. Sweet air never lied. Sweet air never accused you of stealing its ice cream and beer when you didn't steal its ice cream and beer. Sweet air. Cold and wild with westerly freshness, still charmed despite the smoke by that enduring scent of rain that still lingered in my nose. I went inside. And going up the stairs I see Penguin moving a goddamn mattress. My wine bottles clink together in the bag.

"Dude, are you moving?"

"I wish. Just taking Kurt's mattress. Do you have any superglue, by the way?"

"Why?"

"Need to spread it all over one side of this," he says, slapping it. "It's gonna look lit on the ceiling."

"Sorry man, I haven't got any superglue."

"Ah it's cool. I'll just raid." As he walks down, holding the mattress with a single tat-clad arm, I walk up and notice Rye and Bella sitting down on the floor outside my room. I hadn't left it on the lock but I'm guessing the horror scent drove them to the hallway. But why were they waiting for me? Erica was still wearing my parka. The note was still on the door.

"So, he's back."

"What you guys up to?"

"What're you up to?"

"I'm not up to anything. Penguin's the one fucking glueing beds to the walls." They get up from the floor.

"Listen. We were hanging out and thinking. You know you said you were, well, unfulfilled and all that, well – go on Bella – you tell him."

"What? What guys? You found me someone?"

"Sure did."

"So?"

"The truth is Dun, we both think you're not that ugly. But like, you're just a mate. And, well, we felt bad that you hadn't been with anyone, and we tried to find someone, but no-one was up for it. So –"

"So we were talking and someone had tequila in their room....We're willing to sort you out, so to speak. No strings attached. But it's our little secret, yeah?"

They both seemed really drunk and were giving me the eyes and leaning against the walls and biting their lips like they were getting frisky or something, and I seemed like I was having an aneurysm. Some utter out-of-this-world dream. Except it was a nightmare.

I would have liked to think I would have done it, had I not been almost to the point of collapsing in exhaustion. I found them both beautiful. They were so damn beautiful, Dear Reader. Bella was from Swindon and looked like a gothic daisy punk with dark hair and those big sublime eyes I was on about, and Rye was from

Cheltenham and small with lighter hair, and she looked good in anything. I remember seeing her wear black trousers one day and she wasn't going to work or anything I don't think and I wanted to rip them off her they looked so good. I wasn't really the ripping type. But I sure as hell wanted to be. It sounded like something people did at university, a real mad thing with no strings attached (apparently) but I needed to sleep. And I needed to be alone when the time came to adding the drops to the bottles. I was literally frozen to the ground. I didn't know what to say.

"Aw, he's nervous. Isn't this what you wanted?" They were definitely drunk. They were stumbling all over the place.

I guess I could have asked them to come back later after my nap. But that felt rude and moreover the more I thought about it the more I felt on the edge. I was scared, scared that it would ruin something, and I was sober now and paranoid for so many reasons. I looked at them.

"Nah, you guys are trollied. You're kidding, right? This is a joke?" They didn't say anything but Erica took off my parka and left it on the floor. She was only wearing a red bra and knickers. I couldn't believe it. Bella didn't remove any clothes but looked excited and that was turning me on, too. I didn't get it. I thought she didn't like me. I had a feeling they were messing with me. It was something they might do so they could laugh later on and tell everyone too, and if I said okay they would scream 'Ha!' and revert back to their regular old selves and I would be a fool. But I couldn't help but stare at them.

Even though my body was crying out to just do it, it was also crying out to fall to the floor, and I decided that saying no was the only thing to do because I wouldn't be fooled and I could get my nap and still spike the wine and it probably wasn't true anyway.

"You two are my mates. You're making me uncomfortable."

"Then why have you got a hard-on?" I look down like an idiot.

"I'm... hiring a prostitute. Like right now. That's why. You two gotta go. Now. She's on her way. She doesn't like to be disappointed. She gets angry."

"Calm down," Erica says. "It was a joke. Of course we wouldn't do that! But you believed us. That's funny as fuck." I began to blush and my hard-on went right down and I felt like a little boy. A little goddamn boy. They laughed and stopped their drunkenness.

"But we'll still hang out. Come on, it was just a joke. Let's have a spliff and laugh about it together. Not at you. With you."

"I'm serious. I hired a prostitute. Look, it was all very funny guys. And we will hang out later. I'll ask Beebee to roll a Plato spliff with my bud and we'll all get zonked to fuck. But right now you gotta go 'cause I gotta get ready for, umm, Ramona."

"Ramona?"

"Erm. Okay, Dun. No judgement. I mean, it's a bit weird and creepy to pay for that shit. I mean I know we just got our loans come in but if you're that hard u-"

"I'm not hard up! I'm doing it for a bet I lost. Just," I pick up the parka on the floor and hand it to Erica. "Just please leave me alone for a while. Don't even wait around outside to see her arrive. Promise me."

"Jesus. Fine. Come on, Erica. We'll get your clothes from my room." They walk down the stairs. "Don't drink all the wine with her! And don't bail on us tonight!"

"I won't bail on you. I'll meet you at the kitchen later." They finally went on their way and were out of sight but I could still hear them laughing. I was really angry. Though in all honesty it was still a strange rush and all to have them flirting like that. But they fucked with my head. I was nervous as it was. At least Kurt didn't show up naked with a trilby on his cock (which he did when he knocked on my door one day. Only legends foretold of the men and women with hat-wear down there).

When I got into my room, I walked back out with a pencil and turned to face the note on the door. Underneath Erica's pithy observation, I drew a bed with a stickman inside and ZZzzzz's above, so people would know to leave me the hell alone for a while.

I went in and closed the door, put down the shopping and laid onto the table the five bottles in the bag and eased the bag down the necks until I was ready to open them up. I still had to decide how many drops for each bottle. Not too much. Not too little. Goldilocks shit, Dear Reader. I had never bought a bottle of acid before and didn't know how precarious it would be, so I loaded up *The Jean Genie* for some dutch courage from the ghost of David Bowie and twisted the tops off them all in my hellholeyardcasaswampnewabode. Then I got out the little bottle. I decided as there were at least ten people coming that I would put twenty drops in all the bottles – four drops in each. I had no idea what one drop was compared to two or anything like that. Had no idea how pure liquid acid compared to little 1P tabs. But it didn't seem too bad, really. I figured the more reckless people who would drink more would get more trippy, and the people who only wanted to sip the wine wouldn't feel much. That felt fair. It felt like it was going to be okay. Then my mother called.

I had aired her for a week and I wanted the gods to look down on me and my friends with kindness during the festivities, so I turn down the stereo and pick up the phone.

"Hey, Mum."

"Hi, son. How's it going, dear? How's your day been?"

"Oh, pretty uneventful. I read some stuff. Hung out with my friends a bit. Are you alright? Is everything at home okay? How's Dad?"

"Oh, he's okay. Still recovering from the accident. But he's pulling through. We both miss you, son. Is everything okay? Have you been eating alright?" I look down at my hungry belly and all the crisps and chocolate still not eaten and imagine the golden lobster again.

"Yeah. I'm eating fine. Everything's fine. But I'm really tired. I might go to bed real soon."

"This early?"

"I'm not sleeping so good at the moment. I need a nap."

"Okay, well just make sure you're not out tonight when you wake up. Don't be pressured into doing anything. You've been really good so far." (I hadn't.) "You don't want anything to mess this up, yeah?"

"Okay."

"We love you. Lana's here by the way. Do you want me to put her on for you?"

"Mum, I'm sorry but I'm really tired. I don't have time." There I was again saying I had no time when I had all the time. "I'll call you tomorrow, okay? I love you too."

"Oh, okay son. Well, just remember to eat well and get all your work done. And don't forget to wash your –"

"Mum..."

"Alright, alright. I'm going now. Give me a call tomorrow."
"Will do. G'night Mum."
"Night, son. Have a lovely sleep. Bye!"
"Bye."
"Bye!"

After that ordeal I felt both angry at her and ashamed of myself. I had lied to her and said I had in fact been attending my classes. The lie just kept getting longer. And it irritated me, her constant bye's. She always had to say bye more than once. But that just meant she loved me twice, I guess.

Yet it soured me to be reminded of my mother at this point. At the point where I was feeling really unsure about it all now and how I still had the chance to maybe stop this whole thing and ram the breaks and go back to bed and get up early for the Creative Writing seminar the next morning – but I shook it off, and switched the music to Nirvana's *Incesticide* and played the album from the beginning.

I breathed out a big sigh, got the little bottle out again (I had hidden it from my mother as if she could have seen it) and started putting the drops in. I took my time with it as the music blared. I was being very careful, still rocking my head. Then, I put the lids back on all the bottles and shook them all good so the acid was spread evenly. I was pretty sure that would do it. My stupid plan was done.

After *Sliver* finished and *Stain* began I leapt into the bed without turning down the music or taking off my clothes, and writhed about banging my head on the pillow, and banging – I might add – not in the despair one might feel after a devil has eaten your heart but in

digging the music as one might feel after you yourself
have eaten the devil's.

"An' he never sleeps 'cause he's got bad luck..."

I divided my time between moshing and lying there still,
seeming to be neither asleep nor awake. I tuned in and
out of the world as *Incesticide* played over and over
again, perhaps four or five times it was playing, with
eyelids shaking as if they couldn't decide to open or
close. I was in and out of the music, in and out of
movement, in and out of the bed and in and out of my
mind as I heard *Molly's Lips* and she said she'd take me
anywhere as long as I stayed clean.

"Kiss, kiss, Molly's lips..." and I drifted into a vision and
saw my friend Molly Jones and there was a trickle of
blood coming out of her mouth and I winced and fell
down into a massive field where a little sheep was laid in
front of me with sweet mad eyes and it says to me:
"Don't do this, Dunley. It's a baaaaa-d idea. Baaaaaaaa-d."

6

I woke up encased in the ageing evening and felt
strangely rested. My laptop had died sometime during
the revery. And after a weird day – after a weird life – it
was about to get weirder. But I was sort of relaxed. I
took the bad dream with a pinch of salt and decided it
was good that I finally got some sleep, and that it was
just nerves and not some premonition and that hearing
the sheep 'baaa' had only made me chuckle as I
remembered it upon awakening. And then I too
remembered about the whole prostitute thing and
hoped no-one would bring it up. The sad thing is they

believed me. But I guess it was good otherwise them two wouldn't have left.

I was ready to mess with their heads like they messed with mine. Except I was going to make them feel messed in the positive sense of the word and yes I really believed at that time, Dear Reader, that there was too an apex of mess as well as the zenith and that you could really justify anything as long as you had the right intention.

I looked at the clock on my phone. It was 8:26. I ate some chocolate and changed my shirt and put on some deodorant; began my short route to the gang who were probably there, and brought all the bottles and food with me too. I took a few, more than a few to be accurate, sips from one bottle of red to add to the authenticity. I was feeling on top of the world. When really I wasn't in the world at all.

When I arrive at the kitchen door, Penguin's outside hanging from the ceiling.

He didn't get stuck from the superglue. He was climbing up and down the stairs and got to some woodwork right near the ceiling. I really thought he was brave and all for doing that kind of shit. I admired it. He sees me and says 'hey' and jumps down and opens the door for me. There were a few familiar faces there. I'd guessed Jad Kinney was there before I saw him because I heard some classical music which was probably him. But even over that loud piano I could hear Beebee Gladstone talking to the others. She was getting them all curiously riled up in this conversation about what 'brewing' and 'treads' meant or something.

"What you onnabout?" etc. Erica looks at me and shouts: "How was it?"

"...It was alright. But after I got a call from Gully. I'm getting kicked out."

"Seriously? Man, that's shit."

"I know."

"You do kind of deserve it, though."

"Oh well. I brought a shit load of wine. What's everyone saying tonight?"

"Dunno. I've been making poem/s all day. I just got here." Yep. She said it like that.

I blurt a collective 'yo' to everyone and then notice Molly doing the splits. That song about the lips was still going through my head, and she was dancing around the room with her beautiful movements, lighting up the low-lit kitchen and making it lively. I couldn't see Kurt or the band; Nossie and the mysterious chick; nor could I see Tig but Tig was in fact there, she was just so damn tiny I didn't notice her on the sofa. Then her head popped up. Beebee was next to her, she was there skinning up something vicious. Something dreamt up by that Greek guy I was on about. The perfectly formed joint.

She was talking a lot too, and it wasn't annoying. The group were loud and we all talked so it wasn't always her, but she did tend to override at points. But she wasn't one of those who talked a lot and got tiring to hear. I never had a bad thing to say about her. She climbed inside a freezer and stayed there once so I'm inclined to trust everything that comes out her mouth. Her teal dyed hair clad in glorious icicles. And no, there was no damage. Only joy seeing Beebee in the freezer.

If I ever talked a lot, it was definitely annoying. So I tried to keep quiet. But it was good for the group to hear the Lancashire melody of Beebee's spoken thoughts.

Even her 'what you onnabout?'s were eloquent. And when she and Kurt were talking, the conversation was often funny as hell. Their dialogues were so funny they often got into a scrap. But Kurt Dashby wasn't here. I look at everyone and they all look tired from a long day.

"How's everyone's day been? Bella, did you manage to get over the carrots stuck up your arse?"

"The what?"

"You know, that guy."

"Oh, yeah. Some guy took pictures of carrots for his portfolio the fuck."

"What a bastard," says Molly, still dancing around.

"It was ridiculous," she continues. "I'd sure like to stab him in the eyes with his fucking weird ass lunch."

"Haha, someone getting brave."

"Molly!" I say. "I haven't seen you all day. Is the spider still in your room? I'm real sorry I couldn't catch it."

"Don't remind me, Dun. But nah, it's cool. I think I stepped on it when I was doing my practice."

Then Tig chimes:

"Who's your practice? Jad?" And the guys start laughing a bit and it was real noticeable because Jad'd heard his name and stopped playing the piano, turning around quickly with that erratic quality he seemed to be bestowed with.

"Peak, she's only training for the best, innit."

"Not quite."

Meanwhile, Rye leaps up from the sofa with a bottle of Hooch in her hand, so high I see those red knickers again. I wondered if she had said anything. She got up to fill the empty noise in the kitchen no doubt, now that Jad had been distracted from the piano, and went over to him to figure out his new speakers. I liked to imagine that Erica had thousands of songs in her head, like some manic mix-tape in which the number of tracks outlived her ability to contain them all. She once hacked my Spotify and I found a playlist of 1992 songs. Not songs from 1992. One thousand nine hundred and ninety two songs. It broke my phone.

"Ah," says Penguin. "This one!" And this 'one' which was unknown to me had got me bopping my head and then out of nowhere the kitchen door opens and Nossie Godman appears, indeed with a chick as hyped.

She had dark skin (not as dark as his) and long wavy black hair and big eyes and generous makeup which accentuated her looks and she was undoubtedly attractive and yet to me seemed quite a thing apart from true beauty, like roses in a vase and not roses coming up out of the concrete. Nossie seemed content and was holding three bottles of half empty spirits and looked wrecked as usual.

"Yo, it's the P block crew! Wagwan ma bitches! This is Ramona, guys."

"Ramona!" screams Bella and Erica simultaneously. Then they look over at me.

"Fucksake. That's not her."

"What you mean that's not her?"

"Tig, Dunley hired a prostitute called Ramona earlier," says Bella. "But it's obviously a different girl. Right, Dunley?" Jad did his trademark dying laugh.

"You hired oh prozzy?" he says, his face looking like it was gonna blow up or something, and Penguin was laughing too. I was embarrassed but there was something about Penguin's laugh. Penguin was a fucking penguin. From Norwich.

"Yes, Jad. I hired a prozzy..."

I wondered there, how could something not even true be so embarrassing? I don't like saying prozzy. Or sex worker. To me they are people. People, who bone and get boned and run with scissors for money. It's well dangerous to run with scissors. But I imagine some lesbians find it quite the activity. Will never know.

Once though, I had a dream when I was fifteen where in the dream I woke up and I was a girl. It was a full blown lucid dream. While rudeboys at school were saying I was like a girl because I couldn't get a girl, their brains imploded from their own stupid paradox.

'I'm not like a girl I was one and I'm a fucking man now and I'll smell flora if I want to. I had a fucking vagina in a dream you twats.'

But I never said that to them at fifteen. Never said that to anyone actually. But it was only that one dream and I never had it again.

And embarrassing, this whole lie about 'Ramona', because I made it up and that was perhaps even worse than actually hiring her. But I decided to let it go, and laugh at myself. People thought I was pathetic anyway, probably. And I was going to spike them all with acid and that would show them.

I started by opening one of the bottles of red wine and taking a big glug. Nossie and Ramona (the fucking twat) were both hammered and so I reckoned they probably wouldn't want any wine. They were all over each other, and Nossie was talking about all this deep shit to her in the back of the room like always and I went over to Jad and Erica and pointed it out, bringing a bottle of wine with me in my hand.

"Nossie's giving her the DMC."

"Nossie goes in. I mean he actually got a girl though, so..."

"Can I have some wine, Dunley?"

"Sure, Erica. Red? To match your-"
"Nah, white. Bring me a white one."
"If you let me choose the next song."
"Sorry, Penguin's got the next one."
"Fine. Where's Kurt?"
"Don't give a fuck."
"Ooh, harsh, Molly!"
"Yoh mohm's harsh, Tig."
"Fuck you, Jad." Then Nossie comes over.
"Oi, did you know Chid's outside? He's pinging off his nut on mandy."
"Really, Noss? He's never done mandy before."
"Like, he's saying he's seeing pink unicorns."
"What?"
"He's lying. Off mandy?"
"That's fucking jokes."
"Can I put on a song?"
"Play Smiths!"
"Fok the focken Smeths!"
"Excuse me? What was that Bee?"
"Literally man he's chatting shit. I've done shrooms and I've not seen pink unicorns."
"Drugs oh subjective. Depends on the person."
"Yeah. Like some people realise The Smiths' greatness, others don't."
"The Cure are way better."
"Why can't we just enjoy both of them?"
"Smiths are overrated."
"Every band's overrated if you keep talking about them for fucksake."
"Za whaney cont." And though I liked the music of the Smiths, I couldn't help but laugh.

And so it goes (in the vein of Vonnegut) that the evening

went on pretty much like this. Everyone was funny I found. Ripping on each other and everyone seemed alright about it, and we were slowly getting stoned and drunk and real good music was being played on the speakers. But I was stuck thinking about Chid quite pensively for a while, looking out the window hoping to see him – Chid – the big beautiful bear who had come by the kitchen every now and then and was always laughing at something, he never stopped. Even when he tried to dye his hair blonde and it went full blown ginger he laughed. And now apparently he was seeing things from his first time on ecstasy. But I wanted to believe it. I wanted it to be true. I imagined Chid, riding a pink unicorn into the mystical night.

7

When Kurt and Penny happened to arrive a while later it seemed I was beginning to f e e l s o m e t h i n g . This wasn't the s a m e as 1P-LSD.

I look around and notice no-one was saying anything about it. I realised I had been drinking the m o s t , and everyone else – apart from Nossie and the unfortunately named girl who were drunk on clean stuff – had only sipped at the wine. My stupid plan was not quite working.

"Guys, please. Drink up."
"Bot we're getten stohned."
"You can drink and get stoned, no?"
"Wuhl yeah, bot I wanna get real stohned first."
"I'll drink and get stoned."
"Good on ya, Penguin. See guys, that's a real man."
He took a massive glug.

"Urgh, we get it, Dunley. You wanna screw Penguin."

"Nor. Ee's mahn." Then Penguin jumps on her, seeming to be so happy. He was lucky. And while I saw them fighting and loving all at the same time, I noticed Penguin had drunk quite a lot. I had a feeling he would feel the come up before the others. He was definitely lively. But he always was.

Soon, I noticed that my head was buzzing and I was starting to find it hard not to say anything. I was freaking out slightly, unsure as to how many drops I had actually put in now. I was really coming up.

"Guys, I just wanna say. I love you all. Like, like, like I'm gonna write a story about you guys."

"Ooh, really?"

"Are ya gonna portray yaself with moscular arms anna throbben beg welleh? Remember, realism is key."

"It's gonna be wicked." I lean over to Beebee to give her a hug I'm so ecstatic and she in turn lets me have a toke on the piece of art. I mean, I looked at it and it actually looked like a piece of art. In a painting. But I was gone now.

"And you're gonna be the protagonist?"

"Yeah. Cool, huh?"

"Dunley," says Erica. "I think we should change the protagonist. To me."

And in that moment Dunley realised that I was right all along.

Then, in a moment of weirdness, Kurt says:

"Guys, we have something to declare."

"Go on ya crease merchant."

"Me and Penny took some drops before we rocked up here. If we start licking your faces you'll know why." He seemed so joyful that his sweet pudgy face could not contain his excitement. He was tugging on his leather braces and shining his smile at us.

"Oi Kurt, you seeing pick unicorns?"

"Jad, mate. I am a pink unicorn."

"You're tripping?" I say to him. (It's me now. I think.)

"Yeah. It's actually the most we've ever had before. We're coming up now. Just enough to handle."

Right then I see Kurt holding a bottle of red. It was near empty. It had been shared out, but people had only sipped on that red. I was so waved I was mixing white with the red thinking it was rose´ now. I began to look worried and feel sick.

"Kurt, maybe you shouldn't have any more wine, man. Penny, have you had any wine?"

"No," she says. "But thanks. I would love some."

"You always share your drinks with me, man. Didn't you invite us all here t-"

"Kurt, I really think you should stop drinking that wine!"

"Look who's concerned all of a sudden. Chill out."

It seemed I couldn't stop him or Penny, unless I told everyone now. Well, it seemed like a good idea to. I had guessed any minute now Penguin was feeling it and the others would be feeling something. I noticed I couldn't see him. I wasn't worried about him, though. But I wouldn't want the guys to start tripping and then think I was never gonna say anything. So, with a big breath – feeling all freaked out – while Kurt and the others are looking at me, I brace myself.

"I laced the wine."

"You what?"

"I laced it with acid drops. All of the bottles."

"Are you serious, Dunley?" says Erica in a mean, raspy

voice. "Is that why I feel like I'm coming up on cid? I thought I was going mad."

"Me too," says Molly. "I just thought this was real good wine!" At that moment Molly ceases her dancing and looks frozen. She then, out of nowhere, runs out of the kitchen. I felt like everything was going wrong. I wasn't even paying attention to who was drinking how much.

"Dunley," says Kurt. "What have you done, man? Didn't I say I couldn't have more? I've drunk so much of this bottle. How much did you put in it?" He stares at the bottle in his hand and his eyes protrude out like a cartoon, and that is no poetic exaggeration or hyperbole but what I saw with my own eyes.

"There were like three or four drops in each bottle. I don't even remember anymore. I'm sorry, man. But listen, you're gonna be fine. You can handle it. Just power through. And girls, I'm sorry. I thought you'd be feeling good. It really wasn't meant as a mean thing! I wanted to surprise you, and I was gonna tell you all, it's just I started tripping hard and well –"

"Yoh mean O'm gonna trip?" says Jad with curiosity. "Like, nah. What?"

"Exactly. What? What is the word," says Bella. "I'm not drinking any more. I didn't want to trip! Fucksake, Dunley!"

"Well, I actually did," says Erica. "Still. Dick-move, man."

"Good one you bloddy idiot. Ah mean, I'll be able tuh andle it. Bella? Ow you feelin?"

"Just a little tingly, I actually feel okay I think."

"I feel strange," says Tig. "But, like, it's kinda nice."

"Yeah!" I scream (weirdly). " Everyone's just freaking out 'cause they're surprised and coming up. Trust me, just chill out. I drank loads didn't I? And I'm okay."

I didn't feel okay, Dear Reader.

"I'm gonna reach epic levels. You're a cheeky cunt, Dunley. I'd be more angry but fuck I'm flying."

"Look man, I'm genuinely sorry. I didn't know you'd be on it, I didn't know you'd do the most you'd done before you got here. But you're gonna be fine. Penny, you're gonna be fine. I'm gonna be fine. We're all gonna be fine!"

"Where's Penguin and Molly gone?" After Bella had asked the question, everyone noticed it too. We had forgot Molly just ran out of the room. And to my knowledge, no-one even saw Penguin go. I decided the night wasn't going to plan, but right now it wasn't clear that I had definitely fucked up. I was trying to stay positive.

"She's probably gone to run around and dance outside. Acid makes you kinda weird."

"You're weird. Who spikes their mates?"

"I thought it would be... was a good... idea..."

"Well it's not. I guess we're gonna have to buckle up and enjoy it though, it's not fun to be angry on cid, guys. Plus I really wanna check on Molly. I'll go down there, bring her up, then we can all try and chill even though Dunley's been a dick. We can't let him stop us having a good time."

After Erica's reasonable words, everyone seemed to calm down. She started walking to the door. The rest carried on, but no-one was talking to me.

I looked out of the diamond shaped window of the kitchen, feeling the acid was not helping my mood, and it was then that I saw Molly. She was dancing outside.

"Guys. Molly *is* dancing outside. She's well into it." Erica stops just before the door and turns around.

"You sure?" asks Jad quite seriously.

"Come look." Then, everyone gets up from where they were and looks out the window together. The rain had returned, but it was dripping quite beautifully to me now, and we all stood there watching Molly. She danced like an angel from hell. Split leaps and pirouettes, tendus, jete´s and arabesques.

"She's great."
"She ehhs."
"And the view looks amazing to be fair."
"The raindrops. The raindrops!"
"They're changing colour."
"D'fuck. I am too."

It seemed no-one was freaking out, not even Kurt or his girl Penny, nor Bella who I was perhaps worried about the most. But it was fair to say we were all blitzed. I looked around and noticed Nossie and Ramona hadn't even been aware of what was going on. They were at the back of the room on the floor snogging and Nossie had his left hand all over her legs and was still holding a bottle of spirit with the other in an image that was so absurd and yet so fitting. Was God giving him a hand, so to speak? Did he pray for this very scenario, and was gifted, why I, an outcast of faith, a heretic, am made to only be lonely? I had to hire an imaginary prostitute to get laid.

We continued to watch Molly. She made some mad leaps and positions, before getting off her legs and deciding to lie down on the grass. She looked up to the night sky. Rain was spraying down onto her pale white face and dark brown hair. She was laughing in utter joy. Looking up through the raindrops and seeing stars behind them. Then I looked up too. Something up there was shining amid the rainfall, glimmering. Specks of golden galaxy entwined in purple black.

"The stars, guys..."

"Foohk."

"Let's go outside."

"Ah mean, ah do wanna. But ah wanna look fuh Penguin first. He jost focken vanished."

"Oh wanna hear the music," says Jad. "O'm staying."

"How can the stars be out if it's raining?"

"Huh, good question Tig."

"We're seeing shit."

"I guess our eyes are just funky. I mean, the stars are always there, they never leave."

8

The night drew on, and everything looked like a painting. A moving painting, where the artist had remained unknown to me, and who was etching my thoughts and dabbing stars into my eyes. Nossie and Ramona had left, seeming to think we were all a bit weird and laughing a lot, but they were bound to leave the floor anyway to fuck and would have left even if the world wasn't a painting. I looked at the wine bottles and all had nearly gone except one white which was about nearly half full. It shined as if giving off a holy glow. Jad had returned to his position of pianist, and even the notes he was playing were starting to glow. The sound had vision, and it was heartbreaking and very intense and I got lost in such deep thought listening to him play. He didn't seem to be impaired. He seemed to be even better. The crescendos thundered (much like the thunder outside) and the high notes plucked the highest emotions out of me (like hovering fairies). It gave me a sense of such depth that I began to sink into the music, literally I was finding myself trapped in his song. I almost wanted to ask him to stop, but I couldn't do it. I cried and everything was glowing and finally I reached up out of the keys and saw everyone again after what seemed a whole hour.

I noticed Kurt and Penny were gone. Beebee was too. Penguin still hadn't shown up. I hoped that he was alright. But by all accounts if anyone was going to be alright it was going to be Penguin. He probably found Beebee and they just went to bed or something.

Yet I was still very aware that I wanted to make sure everyone was okay. Still in the world, still trying to remember what I'd done. But I couldn't really remember. It was all getting further away from my mind the more I searched for it. Eventually, after watching the room getting longer and expanding out of itself while the walls went on melting, while my head buzzed eternally; everything was a holy combination of visions and vibrations. It felt like sitting in a boat in your bedroom with friends who appeared to each other deranged and yet joyous. Eventually *eventu*ally, the music of the piano released me from its intensity, and I just let go.

Kinney continued to play, yet it was taking a background effect now and no longer confusing me. Erica and Bella started laughing, but it wasn't annoying me this time because it wasn't at me. I don't know what it was at. A mad hoarse yelp came from Erica's mouth:

"I think I'm O'ing, guys..." and no-one really seemed to care if she was serious or not amid all the laughter. It was laughter of a bizarre hilarity, as if the gods were Us and there was no pain in anything & you had to laugh &

for nothing in particular except for itself. The girls had me going.

"What's funny? I mean, it's funny as hell. But what is it?"

"Don't even ask," says Bella, as she chuckles and looks at Tig and she chuckles and looks at Erica and she chuckles and looks at Jad and he doesn't chuckle but his piano does.

"Kinney, man, that song is so good. You're astounding me."

"Safe," he says, without looking up or stopping. It seemed he couldn't stop playing the piano. He was getting so into it he seemed to be one with it, one with the piano. Erstwhile, I myself was one with the wine. I had drunk over a whole bottle.

Erica, Bella and Tig were all on the long red sofa lounging around like cats, and they were laughing and goofing around so much that I knew I had pulled off the greatest thing. The stars were shining. The rain was shining. They were shining. The only thing missing was Molly Jones. If everyone else just left to get laid, well to hell with them. Molly would keep the party going.

I got up from a chair and felt I had moved up about forty feet, and went over to the window and I couldn't see her anymore. I stepped closer, bending my body and pushing my head to the glass to see where she had gone off to. And then I saw her. And she was flying. No. It's not what you think.

She was flying and there was a bus there and then I heard a scream that was even more anguished than Penny's which I heard earlier. But it didn't seem accepted.

I shook so much in fright that the others noticed and

stopped laughing and Erica says:
 "What's up, Dun? Is Ramona with another client?"
 "You're so silly for hiring one."
 "It's well funny."
 "Guys, now isn't the time! Molly got hit by that bus! Fuck! Fuck! Didn't you hear her? She was dancing and then flew up and the bus was there an–"
 "Shit off. Don't!"
 "I'm serious! We have to go down there!" Then, the three of them looked at the diamond window from the sofa, wondering why I still hadn't left it and looked sick. Then they looked sick. Jad was still playing the piano, unaware.
 "Molly!" Bella shouts. "She's not moving! Dunley was right, the bus driver's getting out and he's next to her. Jad! Jad! Stop playing, Molly's hurt!"
 And then the music stopped. It stopped instantly, like a knife being pulled out of a heart so big that its beating had stopped and everything was so silent and yet so loud with fear and time was stretched and Jad turned around, looked quickly at the scene outside, and didn't say anything but ran out of the room, nearly faster than Molly had earlier. He looked so serious as if he was unable to do anything else. We all decided without agreement to follow him. We all had to be there and there was no time for us to do anything else either. They would yell at me later. They would eat me later. We just had to go down there.
 When we get outside, the rain falls hard on us. It felt so weirdly wet to me, as if I had never been rained on before. Nothing like this I had ever felt before. She had stopped screaming but we could see the carnage. Her legs were smashed and looked ravaged to pieces and melting into the concrete. The blood was so bright and

yet so dark.

Molly's legs. Her dancing legs. Broken and lifeless and weeping into the concrete. She looked so scared. There was bone visible through her black tights.

I was ready to break my own legs. I wanted to ask the bus driver to run me over right then and there. But I went over to Molly, following the girls and Jad who had gathered round her. They were stroking her and whispering into her ear: "Molly...Molly...It's okay, babe. Look. Look at me, yeah? We love you and you're going to be okay."

"I..." she says very slowly, in a wheezy voice. "I was flying, guys. I was dancing and then I felt this thing and I was flying. And my legs... I can't feel them." Kinney was over talking to the driver. I assumed he was enquiring about an ambulance. Being a real man, while I was a wreck wanting to smash my own god damn legs that had dragged me all the way through my horrible, ill- conceived idea. But still I say nothing and just stand there.

"Dunley," says Bella. "Look what's happened. Look what you've done! You fucked with her head you idiot!"

"It's okay," Molly says, as if things are fine. "But my head, it really hurts. And my legs... they won't move." I saw again the trickle of blood coming out of her mouth.

"Well I'm fucking mad! If he didn't do this weird ass thing and betray our trust you'd be okay Molly. You should be mad at him!" Then Jad comes over.

"So there's an ambulance already on the way. Dunley, you should just go mate. Oh don't think you're wanted here by anyone."

Tig was still stroking her hair. Bella looked starstruck and there were tears in her eyes. I was sure now that giving her the acid was the wrong thing to do. She already hated me anyway. There was no need to hurt her more.

She was bent down with her hand on Molly's leg asking if she could feel anything, halting off what seemed strange thoughts, and looking stressed and tired with it now being midnight and eternally dark. Erica gives me the coldest look before returning her attention to the poor girl on the floor.

"I can't. I mean, I'm in a lot of pain... but my legs won't move."

"Molly, I'm so fucking sorry. I'm sorry everyone. I want to help but I don't think I can. I'm just gonna go."

"Good!" she says, finally seeming to acknowledge me. "You've fucked up my life. How am I supposed to still do dance, like –" she looks down – "like this? If I could move I'd cut off your hands, Dunley! Fuck!"

It was then that I took a final look at the blood-dappled painting and cursed in that instant not myself for making it but the painter who had remained unknown. I resolved in some way that there were people looking after her, and I walked away.

I then hear Jad say as the ambulance was heard whirring in the distance:

"O'm gonna go with her, guys. You can come if you want."

"We'll come!" And then some steps are heard, and Kurt appears with Penny behind him. They both run over.

"What's happened? What's? Molly?..." He begins to shed a tear. "No. I'm tripping so fucking much. Is this really..." and he trails off and notices me walking away. "Dunley, I'm actually gonna kill you!"

I turn around and he's leering at me, that tear still wetting his red cheek. I could see it even among the rainfall. I had wanted to get away from him, but I wasn't going to make it worse by running. He walked over to me and when he was eye-to-eye with me he threw a punch, and I felt his fist hit my jaw so sharply that I fell to the ground and he clambered over me and was shaking me as if he were trying to get a demon out of me. He smacked my face with his forehead, and again, and again, and I could see blood pouring out of his forehead and it was then that I tried to get him off me.

"Kurt, stop..." But I didn't have the strength. He kept on doing it. And then more blood, and I could see the pain inside of him. It wasn't the pain in his forehead, or mine. It was something deeper. And in my mind I had a vision of when I first met Kurt Dashby.

It was the first day I arrived at the university, and I was alone and had given up on meeting anyone, so returning to my room sulking I picked up my guitar and began playing *Pay The Lady* and singing all the loneliness out of me, as perhaps that song was intended for all along, and when I finish I hear something, someone shouting through the window:

"Nice song, man! You have a beautiful voice!" And that coming from a voice I had heard earlier that day talking fervently with everyone on the courtyard and causing riots of laughter and holy pauses and well just conversations flying all over and feeling that I wasn't alone and that it was a strange song to even appreciate, and so I knew I wanted to meet him, but afraid as he seemed to be so popular and I not, yet still lighting up my day which before had seemed so tainted with my own failure to light my own or anyone else's as he had mine in just that short comment alone, and then later that evening him coming to my door so unexpectedly and inviting me out with his friends and me accepting and not being alone that night and perhaps meaning I wouldn't be alone for the whole three years as I was certain would be the case, because it had happened at school and college too, and then there with him in this neat little place in the city with friends around to feel less dread and happy even and all because of him and I was fond of him and fonder still when I heard he suffered schizophrenia and how a brutal thing it is, and even an affinity I felt for him within that; within the joke he made that I was Ginsberg and him Kerouac; playing Dylan and Libertines in the kitchen and him listening and eyes glistening and then finding out he wrote poetry. See that was the great thing about that open mic night at the Student Union all those moons ago, when the moon itself was large and purple to more than one eye, the night of the urination.... It's why I couldn't punch him after he did it.

    We came back from the Student Union after the readings and I went for a whiz in some bush and he comes over and just pisses on me... down my arm dripping piss drunk too and angry wanted to punch him but...I couldn't do it. I looked at him and shook my right arm like a wet dog would. He was half laughing and half apologising. But I just couldn't hate him. I couldn't do it. I was sure of it. Sure of his performance that night anyway. There was something undeniable about his voice and what he said but it was the way he did it too. Mad moans came from his mouth so effortlessly – the pint of Guinness in his left hand notwithstanding whereas me that night I remember a sub par stolid poem about the ward orated quiet and nervously. But his so full of boundless energy and not just the reading but him, his very presence was a poem and what a soul he was and how I loved him and realising now that I had destroyed it all and he was knocking us both near to concussion.

I would have let him do it to me but I couldn't let him do it to himself, so with my strongest will I pushed him off me so he couldn't bash his own head in, and I got up and he was lying on the ground his hair a soaked mess and blood and mud in it too and I knew I had to get out of there as there really was nothing I could do anymore. But I noticed that the bus driver was looking over. And it was in an instant that the ambulance was seen and the sirens were at their loudest now. The sound of whirring and the colours of the lights made everything seem far too real and yet far too unreal. Things were so bad. I was beginning to hear an evil voice in my head, laughing. I was going insane again and I knew that I had done the wrong thing and everything was fucked and I couldn't even help.

'It's Satan laughing in my ears.'

I could still hear the voices of the girls to Molly, and Kurt wailing on the floor in some mad trip I could not even comprehend, and now with Jad getting him up and calming him down but Kurt still yelling at me. I hung around still from a distance; I didn't know if I should leave. Then the bus driver comes up to us.

"She came out so suddenly," he says. "I couldn't even break. There's an ambulance which is going to take her to the hospital. Anyone who wants to come can. But let's clear things up first. Why did this girl jump out? And why were you two fighting?"

"Because look what he's done to Molly!" screams Kurt. "To Bella! To everyone!" And then he began to really lose it. He looked like he was trying to shake off his own body. He looked like he was in a horrible trip. He fell to his knees and punched the concrete and threw himself onto the concrete and writhed about and grabbed his own head and he truly looked like how I looked when I was in the psyche ward and I was throwing myself against the walls to hurt myself because I could not take the insanity. And I didn't want to admit what I had done, because I thought they might get in trouble. I was so confused. The driver's face was morphing into different animals.

"I... She. She didn't jump out. I pushed her into the bus. She's a bitch and she deserves it." Satan laughed in my ear with the grimmest sound I've ever heard.

"This is very serious, young man. Why were you fighting? Why is he so angry?"

"He hates me. He hates me for doing it. They all do. Well I don't care!" I didn't know what else to say. Kurt probably did hate me. They all probably did and I knew they were in their right to. But I couldn't say what I really did. It was too bad to admit.

And then, as I looked down at Molly, and over at Kurt, I came to the conclusion that this painter I had imagined was not real and that I was the only one who had allowed this to happen. They weren't going to be in trouble, I realised.

"Hold on. He hates me... But not because I pushed her. I'd never push Molly. But it is my fault. I laced some booze with acid, sir, and I gave it to my friends. They had no idea. I swear." He looks at me with a very serious face, though it was changing: panda – bear – horse – pig. I was utterly gripped by the worst feeling I have ever felt in my life. Complete shame and fear. And the laughing in my ears which was disgusting and wouldn't go away.

"Is that so?" He looked around for an answer from someone else.

"It's true!" says Tig. "He didn't tell us! Luckily we didn't have too much. But Kurt, he, he, he was spiked the most."

"Listen, everyone. This girl is going in the ambulance right now. Her friends can come. But this boy who had too much is going to the psyche ward for now. He's too erratic. And you –" he stares at me with a stare that made everything around me fizz and shake, as if reality itself was breaking apart – "are in a lot of trouble."

9

It was then that I decided to run before I was arrested, which was definitely going to happen. The others would be in the same position regardless. I wasn't going to prison.

I then remembered about Beebee and wondered if she knew. I ran and ran the fastest I ever ran back to the kitchen to avoid the bus driver and to find out where they were. When I got there, I was already out of breath and the evil laughter still hadn't left, seeming to follow me wherever I went. I closed my ears with my palms but still I heard it. I started to see apparitions come out of the walls. And through it all I heard something.

I ran again and followed it, my ears were unblocked now. I climb out the window and onto the roof, and Beebee's standing there, looking down over the edge.

"Beebee, what are you doing up here?"

"It's Penguin. Ah found im."

"Oh. Good."

"E was hanging off the roof. Jost messing around."

"Is he alright?"

She says nothing. After a long pause I repeated it: "Is he alright, Beebee?"

"E was olding onto the gotter. Ah thought e'd be fine. Then e looked at me. Ee said not tuh worry. E said e loved meh. And e fell." I looked at her. "Why…"

She couldn't finish. She wanted to blame me for it. But she was too concerned with him. I decided to look for myself.

When I walked, I noticed the rain on the roof tiles was hitting hard and it, which had been around all day and which brought back my memory of the day, the sweet day, when everything seemed good and I hadn't yet done this; when the worst that had happened were mere embarrassments and missed work; was the hardest hitting it had ever been and it almost felt like hail it was so bad. When I reached the edge and was next to her, I saw him. For the first time in his life, Penguin was still.

10

I try to give her a hug but she pushes me away.

"Fock off! This is all ya fault! Ya didn't even tell im! Ya didn't say shit! Just fock off, Dunleh! Just fock off forever you otter cont! Jamie!"

I was so scared to tell her about what else had happened, and didn't want to make her more upset, but everything was fucked now.

I had more than likely killed her boyfriend; I had sent Kurt mad; I had ruined the life of a girl who was innocent and all her friends were fucked up by it. The only thing I could think of that wasn't fucked was that Khalifa wasn't there to be hurt by me.

But still, it was, because she would no doubt be traumatised by it all when she found out, like how Tig and Bella were now, and I would return to having no-one give a shit about pitiful Dunley Novak. Nothing was right and everything was completely destroyed.

"...I'm so sorry, Bee. But I need to tell you." My whole body was shaking. The rain and the darkness had warped my vision so much that everything was a blur. "Molly got hit by a bus. Her legs are broken. And Kurt's being taken to a psyche ward. They've all gone to the hospital." She didn't look at me. She still sobbed, but I knew she heard me.

"This is the worst naht in the world." She then stopped looking over the ledge and turned to me.

"It's like ya evil... Why did ya fucking do this? Penguin's not done acid before and you foken spike his drinks? He had a whole bottle worth!"

I was afraid, she looked crazy in the eyes. She ran up to me, beating me in the chest and making it go one hundred mph. After a while she stopped and just grabbed me. I knew she didn't want to give me a hug, but she was lost and I was the only thing to hold on to in that moment. She held onto me and cried into my chest, telling me I was a cunt and why and why and why and smacking my back with her fist and I was so sad that I cried and the tears fell on her hair.

I decided to grab her arms, took them off me, and turned around and ran back, stumbling on a wet tile, and jumped back in through the window to the kitchen, now silent and without the people who should have all been there.

I had to stop this. I had done enough and there was nothing more I could do. Thunder clapped in the empty kitchen. There were ghosts still coming out of the walls, wailing. I went into a drawer and found a machete, and as I pick it up, the animal-headed bus driver, now bestowed with a snake's head, is standing in the doorway looking at me again. In one moment that seemed to last so long, with the strongest force I could muster, I slice my throat open and fall to the ground. The horrible laughter, and everything, had finally gone.

11

I opened my eyes, and noticed that a squirrel was leaning over me and looking at me straight in the face. It was eight foot tall.

I remembered, I was tripping on acid and this must have been the peak. I didn't remember anything else. It seemed my brain wasn't working right.

"Look who's up."

It then picked up an acorn which was as big as my head. It started munching. It munched on the acorn for so long, still looking at me.

It was strangely entrancing to see its big black eyes and bushy red face with the nose and little mouth, proportionally little I mean. I was there thinking what rare chance to see such clarity and pause in a squirrel – a red squirrel at that – and that they always run away, but this one was over me and still and staring intently as if it wanted to be around me. I wondered if the acorn was the starter, and I was the main course. But I decided not to run. It didn't seem dangerous.

"Are you a snollygoster, boy?"
"What?"
"A snollygoster. Don't you know what that means?"
"No."

"A snollygoster is one with intelligence but no morals."

"No one even says that. And by the by, I don't have either."

"Well they used to. The last boy I had knew what it meant. But I guess that was nearly two hundred years ago."

"What do you mean last boy you had?"

"It's not what you think. I was only helping him." He continued to eat. No, he didn't seem dangerous at all.

"Can you cut that munching out? It's getting a little tiring."

"As tiring as the laughter?" It lowered the nut as it said it. I started to remember that there was some bad laughter going on in my head some time ago.

"Well, no. That was horrible." But why was it horrible? What made me hear that?

"You were hearing that laughter because of what you did to your friends, Dunley."

"My, friends? I don't have any friends, only Shaman." I looked at the squirrel's face. It was beautiful and calm. Tilting its head at me.

"Are you sure? What about – what's her name? Molly?" The name rang a bell in my brain. I then remembered she was my friend, she liked to dance. And then I saw the blood that was so bright and yet so dark.

"Molly... I... I remember now. She ran out of the room. And then... and then..."

"She ran out of the room because you worried her with your drugs. You 'fucked with her head' as Bella said."

"Bella... wait. How do you know my friend's names? How d'you know mine?"

"Because I saw everything. I saw what you were doing

today. Tonight. I saw what you have been doing your whole life. It was me who sent the text, Dunley. I was trying to warn you. It is my job to watch over one human with all my patience. But I could not stop it from happening. I have told the others." It picked up the acorn again and munched on it, its ears sticking up.

"The others?"

"The other squirrels, Dunley. We have friends here, too. A squirrel may have all the acorns in the land, but eventually, it will go nuts without a friend."

"Is that a joke about the acorn?"

"Is it funny?"

"Well, you said it so deadpan. Like it wasn't a joke. So yeah, I guess it was kind of funny. But to be honest, that joke is a bit old hat. And I'm not in a mood to laugh."

"I've been trying to work on a comedy set. You really don't like it?"

"I said I did..."

"I'm only trying it out because I've been watching you. You've been doing it much of your life. Except when they got you on the meds, that changed you. Before then, you used to want to make people laugh, even when you thought you weren't funny. You became a recluse, but really it started when you were eleven years old. It took you a long time to get over it. You never quite did."

"Huh, I mean, that's all true I guess. But listen, squirrel. I'm not here for a therapy session. What's happened to my friends?"

"Call me Navi. We're all squirrels, here. Do I call you human? Hey human! How's it going, human?"

"Okay, point taken. Navi." I couldn't believe what the hell was going on. "What happened to my friends? Did any of it actually happen?"

"It happened. It happened. And you're not tripping

anymore. There are no trips here."

"Well, no. It might not be a trip. But it could be the psychosis coming back?"

"Psychosis? No, Dunley. You've just got the hum durgeon."

"The what?"

"Hum durgeon. It means imaginary illness. I guess nobody uses that word now either."

"What's your point?"

"You don't have psychosis, Dunley. You've never had it."

"Right."

"I'm telling you."

"A giant squirrel telling me I'm not mad! God, what am I supposed to think? So it's not a trip? It's not psychosis? It's all true?"

"Yes."

"You, you must think I'm a bastard... I didn't mean for it to get so bad."

"Yes, my friends will need convincing. But they haven't been watching over you your whole life. I have. Do you remember when you were two years old? It was your first memory. You were on holiday with your family. When you realised your father had gone away on a boat on a stormy night, you got so ill you thought you were dying. You were thinking of your father on the boat, lost and alone. That's what drove you ill. It drove you mad."

"You're right. That was my first memory. I love him."

"And when you were nearly four? You were bored, and you found some matches and decided to light them up and you saw the curtains in the living room and went to go light the curtains. When your mother grabbed you, she said 'you can't do that, you'd hurt us.' She said you'd all burn with hot fire and when you finally realised what you had nearly done – you cried for two weeks straight. It's proof you are not perfect, Dunley. Far from it, really. But you loved your family and you imagined them burning and it made you feel like you were burning. You couldn't stop imagining it. Your mother said it was fine the next day, yet you cried and cried and cried for weeks... I was watching even then."

I was starting to think maybe he did know about me. "Do you... know what I did to Bella, then?"

"Yes, Dunley."

"Why is she so distant with me? I mean, before all this... What happened? What did I do?"

"About a month ago you took seven ecstasy pills and drank a big bottle of whiskey and started punching her on the arm. Then you groped her leg. She told you to stop. You didn't. You took an irresponsible amount of drugs, Dunley. Then you blacked out. That's why you don't remember."

There was a silence that lasted for an aeon.

"Why do you bother with me, then?"

"If you had been sober, you wouldn't have done that."

"I was sober when I gave them all acid, Navi!"

"Sleep deprived, Dunley." He looked at me with those big beads, his fur rustling as he stared at me. "You haven't been sleeping well for months. It's making you-"

"See things? Like you?"

"It's making you lose your sense. You have to trust me."

"Fine, okay. Whatever. I trust you. Where are these friends of yours? And mine? And where are we? And what's gonna happen? And how com-"

"Dunley. Too many questions. We can answer them, but you must have patience. Here, eat some of this acorn. You need nourishment." He handed me the acorn.

"Well, thanks." I didn't know how to eat it. It was really heavy. I bit on it and it was hard and brittle. I managed to get a little in my mouth and I chewed it and it didn't taste good. I dropped it onto the floor.

"Hah, that was another joke. Just trying to lighten the mood. You don't need food here. We're in the Asphodel."

"What's that?"

"It's the land we Watchers come from. It's a kind of limbo."

"Limbo? What the hell? Isn't that just another joke?"

"We do not joke about our home. The Asphodel is where we are." And picking up the acorn from the floor, he puts it below his pit like a football, and moves his free arm across the vista. "You came here because things are unresolved."

"Well, yeah. They are unresolved. I love my friends. Kurt... Molly... Rye... everyone!"

"Then may I ask, what made you not invite that girl, the girl that likes you?"

"I didn't want her to be scared. But the others, I don't know. I thought they could handle it. They all seemed strong. But Khalifa, she is the strongest in so many ways. But I couldn't do that to her. I shouldn't have done it at all. I know that now. And now I'm here. Well, I guess it's better than Hell."

"It can become a hell. Look," he says, grabbing the acorn with both paws and hurling it into the air. It flew far away and I was expecting some crash to resound in the distance.

"I don't get it."

I looked out and saw the surroundings and it was like

being on top of a mountain.

"That nut will never stop. It will never land. And the time. The time will too."

"The time will never land?"

"It may end up that way. It must be decided at the Great Nut Courthouse. That's where we gotta go."

"Oh, come on! That's got to be a joke! That sounds like something I would write in a stupid story."

"It's true, Dunley. There will be a hearing up there. So we better start moving."

12

Back on Earth, the bus driver started running up to the body of the boy who had just slit his throat. The machete twanged against the floor.

He went over to the body and bent down and looked at the blood rushing out. It was already too late. He was in shock, but he didn't startle. He didn't cry. He didn't go mad. And he didn't have a snake head.

"This is unbelievable. What drove him to this?"

Meanwhile, Beebee had appeared, her hair and makeup mangled from hard rain, and saw the bus driver and the boy who was on the kitchen floor.

"Sir, ma boyfriend. I think e's dead." The man looked up at her. In a way, he was not surprised.

"So is this one."

There was no time to be idealistic, or hide the truth. The bus driver had never witnessed so much carnage. Yet he was determined to stay on track, and do the right thing. Whatever that was.

"Dunleh, he's dead too?"

"I'm sorry if he was your friend." She said nothing.

She was not sobbing any longer. She seemed to have no emotion at all. Beebee, the girl with the loudest soul and spirit, had become as silent as the boy who was still bleeding from his neck. She watched him close the eyelids. "I'm sorry about your boyfriend. What happened to him?" She stood there, silent. Then:

"E fell off the roof. E's owtsahd. Not moving... Dunleh, he gave im LSD and didn't tell im. I'm on it too, bot I didn't know either."

"It's okay." He gives her a reassuring look, then gets out a walky talky and sends a message: "HQ, we need assistance. A boy fell off the roof. No, well we don't know. He might be. Okay. Okay." He put the phone down. "Do you want some tea? You look cold." He then got up and walked over to the kettle and began to prepare some tea. "What's your name?"

"Beebeh."

"Your other friends have all gone to the hospital to be with your friend Molly. And Kurt, he was taken to the psyche ward. You shouldn't be scared, it's just temporary. They're going to help him. And they're going to help her." He handed her a cup of tea and then reached for a blanket on the sofa and draped it around her. "You are a very brave girl. Keep strong. I know this must be hard."

"I jost don't get it. Why would e do somthing like this?"

"I don't know. It doesn't make much sense to me, either. To be honest, this is the most crazy night I have ever experienced. I just drive buses. I am used to thinking you students are just, like, well I just drive you." He looked at the boy. "This night has opened my eyes."

13

I had drifted off after my encounter with the giant squirrel called Navi. When I had awoken, he had disappeared.

  I decided to get up, and I looked around at the view which was so sublime and endless it frightened me. Yet it was beautiful. There were three suns straight above. Red, orange, yellow. I then looked down over the mountain in awe, it was indeed true that I was on a mountain. The clouds were gathering below me. I tried to see if I could spot anything, perhaps my friends, but I didn't see anything except the blue air and white clouds. And then, looking down over the edge, I gazed something. What seemed a strange and unidentifiable bird, some bird of paradise flying up just below me. But there were no other birds up here. I assumed it was too high. I watched it as it flew up to my head, flapping and expanding some electric blue wings, with a four foot long beak. It lowered itself down to me and began singing:

  "I am Homa. What brings you to these heights?"
  "Who?"
  "Homa. And you are?"
  "Dunley..."
  "Dunley, I sense you are in trouble."
  "You sensed right. Do you know Navi? He was here when I got here."
  "Navi, Yes. I believe I have heard of him. It is said among the Gods of the Heights that he is a very good squirrel. And he is your Watcher, then?"
  "That's what he said."
  "What happened? Were you killed?"
  "I killed myself."

"But boy, why would you do such a thing?"

"I gave my friends this stupid drug and I'm on it too, and well things got real bad. I wish it would just end and I can be sober again. You know, I'm starting to think maybe none of this is real. Is it just you, Penguin? Are you goofing me? Have you turned into a bird? And I bet Erica and Beebee are over there too, aren't they? Guys! Can you hear me?" It looked at me gravely.

"I am only Homa. You seem to be confused as to why you are here. Let me explain. We are in the Heights. It is a place where the purity of existence is maintained. You were sent here so your Soul would not evaporate."

"But, who are you?"

"I am Homa."

"Yeah, you already said that."

"I am the only bird up here. It is far too high up for the rest. But I am not normal. I am Homa. I fly forever."

"You, fly, forever? Right...Good one Penguin. I know it's you. Now stop messing around."

"It's true. I have flown and will fly for eternity. It is my fate. Here, here's something to help you on your journey."

It spread out its wings and a blue feather fell to the ground.

"A feather?"

"Stroke it against your forehead. It will heal you."

"Heal me, eh? With a pigeon's feather? Don't make me laugh. You need to fucking help me, I'm seeing shit."

"No need to be rude."

I still wondered if it wasn't someone messing with me. If I was really just tripping still and someone just got a pigeon from somewhere to freak me out. "I must leave you now," it says. "Don't lose the feather. And good luck on your journey."

In a flash, the song and shadow of Homa had left, falling into the mist and leaving me there on the mountain peak.

I took stock of my senses, remembering again the body I had left on Earth. I went to feel my throat. There was no opening. I was still breathing and, though this being had blessed me with its unlikely appearance, I thought about Penguin who was not breathing. I didn't cry, but I felt so bad. I wondered still if any of it had actually happened. If it was all a dream or still within some mad trip. I wanted it to be so. I'd thought much more confusing things. But I also knew that I couldn't give up now or doubt myself. If it was true or not, I had to accept it.

After I put the blue feather into my trouser pocket, I looked up to the sky again. I saw a small red speck. It came closer and closer and I thought that it might be Navi, but I wasn't sure if it was perhaps another one of his kind. It flew down to me. It was using its tail as some sort of propeller. It was him alright.

"Sorry I had to leave you. I had to consult with my friends before I took you there. What do you think of the view?"

"It's unbelievable. But I have to tell you something."

"What?"

"I saw Huma. Or was it Homa? Anyway I saw this giant bird up here while you were gone, and it talked to me in birdsong and I understood it. It gave me this feather, look." I got the feather out and showed it to Navi.

"Dunley. That's absurd. There is no way any bird could withstand these heights."

"But it's true."

"I assure you. You're just imagining things. Don't worry. I will guide you through." He snuffled his nose.

"So, you didn't try and jump off the mountain, then?"

"No, I didn't. It wouldn't work anyway, right?"

"I'm glad. You would have fallen into Molocth."

"Molocth?"

"It's an underworld. As above, so below. Up here is what you humans call Heaven. Down there is, well. It's not worth thinking about."

"Bloody hell, Navi. You could have told me earlier. What if I did jump?"

"I had to make sure you were ready. Now, Dunley. I think you're ready. I think it's time. Time to head north and find the Great Nut Courthouse. We'll be flying above Molocth, so you must always be holding onto me. You will be safe with me. I promise you, Dunley. But know this, too. You will encounter squirrels that do not know your life story. Still, they have heard what you have done today. They know. They're ready to lock you up, torture you and leave your friends to suffer. But I know you. You weren't in your right mind. You must be like your father. Your father who was all alone on that boat in the storm. He never gave up even when it seemed like he was lost. He came back to you. You must be like him. Are you ready?"

"I'm... I'm ready."

"Okay, come on. Get on my back. I'll take you to the courthouse."

I knew it sounded crazy, but I was so glad that Navi had come. I was glad that I had a chance to maybe resolve what had happened. It sounded crazy and all, but I found a friend – a friend which really I didn't deserve – in him. He was not aggressive, he was not spiteful. He was wise and he was funny and he was serious and he was beautiful and he was now underneath me, jumping off the mountain with his hind legs and becoming airborne. His tail vibrated joyously. I held onto his fur and I was not scared. I looked around. It seemed we weren't getting anywhere but it felt so fast.

"Can I ask something?"

"Of course."

"Is Penguin in the Asphodel too?"

"I know you're concerned for your friend."

"Is he here or not?"

"Look, I think it's time to have some quiet. Don't dwell on all the things you do not now know. There is no need to worry." In the silence that followed I didn't feel up to all this. After a long while he began to speak again: "It's okay though, you have it, you have that curiosity. Otherwise you wouldn't have done what you did. These things which have gone wrong, were borne from it. But all the good things you have done were borne from it too. Without it, you would still be alone in your parent's house. You'd be alone in your bedroom and would have done no ill or no good. Having a hand-shandy. Right?"

I saw that he was right. For once, I was not going to fold. I wasn't going to hide. For the first time, I laughed at Navi's joke.

"You know me too well." I held onto his magical red fur and put my head down and let him take me to where I needed to be. "You know me too well."

14

I had fallen asleep yet again.

It seemed my friend, possibly the only friend I had at this moment, had such comfortable fur that even I, a self professed insomniac, couldn't help but drift off when touching it. I did not fall into a somnolent rest, though. I had been dreaming about my time in the mental hospital I was taken to after an overdose of AMT and falling into psychosis. Navi said I never had it. But maybe Navi was just part of the psychosis.

I saw again the myriad insanities. The plain monastic rooms full of nothing but lonely mind-ravaged patients. Nurses banging on doors with medication on their lips. Other's minds being seared into my own. The evil doctor creating deformed apes and shoving them in cupboards, and Rory, who playing so sweetly her blue guitar out in the courtyard found herself trapped in a manic fear in which she screamed so loud the crows all took flight.

Not to mention the body-swaps, the continual deaths and rebirths, the unending doors which led to a maze of rooms I could not escape from, and a final memory of me trying to bite my own face off, bleeding all over myself after being restrained on a bed, thinking I was at the end of *1984* where the doctors would show me the thing that I most feared. I woke up just as the door opened.

"You've been having a bad dream, Dunley." I rubbed my eyes in fright, remembering that Molocth (whatever it was) was right below us. I grabbed onto him tight.

"Don't take it personally. I always have bad dreams when I'm stressed." I looked out at the eternal distance.

"This must be hard for you to deal with."

"Hard for me to deal with? All those people down there... wherever they are... they must be finding it hard! I deserve all the nightmares I get. Don't you get that?"

"Look. If you care about them, then there must be a reason for it. You must have seen something in them.

But I'm not here to talk about them. They all have their own Watchers."

"Just, please, stop saying all this shit about how this is bad for me! You didn't see them down there like I did! You didn't see Erica's face. She looked at me like I was... the devil."

"Is that the one, the one you thought about when you were alone at night?"

"God, why don't you leave me alone! I found it nice at first, that you were watching over me. But you've seen all my patheticness!"

"Do you love her?"

"Not that it's any of your business....I do." I stared at him.

"Love will get you through this. Not hate."

"I had to fall for her. Now I've lost it with her for good. It just hurt so much, seeing her look at me like that. Seeing them. Because I did this evil thing. I am the devil... And you're treating me like I'm not!"

"Do you want to be evil?"

"No. I don't want to be. But that doesn't mean I'm not. You should have thrown me off, thrown me down there." I took one hand off his fur and pointed to the infinite drop. "Because, because, you fucking twat of a squirrel can't see that!" I started punching his back in a madness I could not contain. "Does that hurt, you... Throw me down there! Throw me off and end it all now!"

I started wailing, trapped in a confusion. I could not tell if I was evil or not anymore. I was being pulled by either side and saw the faces of all the people I had left.

"I am not going to do that. You have to calm down. Listen to me. You did not want this to happen. That is what separates you from true evil. It was idiotic, but that is not evil. It was crazy, but that is not evil either. Madness is not evil. If one is insane that does not mean they are a bad person. You found that out at the ward yourself. This is breaking your heart, Dunley. You are breaking your own heart."

I stopped punching his back. But I was still crying into his fur. It was too much. I did not know what was going to happen at the courthouse. I did not know if I could help them. I did not know if I would ever see them or Shaman or my family ever again. And having left my mother on the phone like that when all she wanted was to know I was okay. I cried again into his fur and it became so wet it glistened and I realised I had been punching him. I had been punching the only one who believed in me. My anger had gone, but my heart felt weak.

"I... I just don't think I can do this."

He said nothing, but carried on his flight. I put my head back down on the wet fur and breathed hard and tried not to fall asleep again. I knew if I did, I would enter an even more despairing nightmare. I had to stay awake.

"How long is the journey going to take?"

"Well, we've been flying for about three days now. So nearly there."

"Three days? I haven't seen a sunset. And there's three bloody suns."

"Because you were asleep."

"So it's been three days on Earth too?"

"It's been about nine hours on Earth."

"Oh. Well, aren't you tired and all after all that flying? I mean, I am and I've been asleep for most of it."

"I need to take you there. It's the only place where you can stop all these things that are hurting you. I know you said you didn't want me to be concerned for you – because you don't deserve it – but I'm being honest now. I want you to be happy, Dunley. You have no idea what it's like to watch over a boy his whole life, and see someone who is so fraught with sadness. There are so many things I have seen watching you that made me feel you are special. Never a dull moment."

"I'm not special. I'm a loser. I'm a fool... I get too emotional about everything. I couldn't just back out of doing it, could I? I had to let my emotions override my reason."

"And now you've got your reason, no? Look, can you see that building?" He raised his right arm and extended it to what looked like a little castle out in the distance. A castle resting on top of a giant acorn, floating in the white void of this strange and yet peaceful world.

15

When we got nearer, Navi had slowed down and his tail had become like a wind-catcher. We floated down and I saw that from its foundation, the castle's framework tailed off into what looked like scorpion tales that pointed up to the boundless sky, and the three suns still glimmering their trifecta of light. The castle was a deep black, with windows that pierced through my eyes like those of a cat's. A lurid yellow. After the horrible dream, after everything I had witnessed back on Earth, it was a haunting that I could finally handle.

We got to ground and I sat there for a minute on his back, looking at it. I tried to think about what he had said to me. Why I had gotten angry at him. Why I had to stay strong and see this through. He crouched so I could jump off.

"Okay. You see the castle door?"

"Yeah."

"That's the entrance to the courthouse. I will knock on the door for you, but then I must leave you."

"What? You're not coming in with me?"

"It is not allowed." In that moment, I felt even weaker. "Don't worry, Dunley," he says. "I'll still be with you. I'm still right here." He raised his arm and put his paw on my head.

"I'm... I'm sorry I got angry at you. You didn't deserve that."

"Think nothing of it. Come on."

We walked to the door together, and he raised his arm and knocked three times on the wood. I almost wanted to tell him I loved him in that moment. I wanted to ask him more questions. I wanted to stay with him. But I realised that there was something beyond that door that was more important.

I looked at his beautiful bushy face one last time, peering into those deep black eyes, his cute sniffing nose and the ears still sticking up and pointing around, and as I turned away, the door creaked open and I walked inside.

16

When I entered, I could not see a thing.

I mused anxiously on whether it was really happening. And if I tried to tell someone, well, no-one would believe me anyway, right? I heard the door creak again behind me. It had closed of its own volition. I stood there, not in shock, but in deep thought.

I was wondering how on earth I could do this, when

for every interview I had ever attended, every presentation at school and every tense situation I had ever been dealt with, I'd always given in to my absolute anxiety and had always fucked it up. But this was not something I could fuck up, I realised. I couldn't enjoy being a fuck up any longer.

I took a few steps in the darkness. The walls on either side became visible. They were lit up by fire lanterns on either side, with shadows underneath them, and I could see that the passageway was very narrow and seemed to go on forever.

I carried on walking, the lanterns lighting up as I moved through. There were portraits of royal squirrels on the walls. I mean, I assumed, because of the jewelled crowns.

I must have walked for a long time. My feet were starting to really ache and I was feeling paranoid. But I thought about my new friend, who had flown me here for such a long time. What a thing he was. What a thing to tell the others. That they all have their own Watchers. I wondered if they too would come to the Asphodel if they ever died. But I guessed most people weren't real wretches like me.

Yet Navi took a chance on me. I carried on through the pain.

A couple of times throughout the journey, I had turned around to see what was there – maybe anticipating I would see something grotesque or insane – but there was nothing there except the dwindling fires on each side and the shadowplay underneath them. My eyes were tricking me again. Knowing how easily I got lost I had to try hard not to end up walking the wrong way.

Eventually, I could see in the distance that there was

another door. It was curved at the top and looked bigger than the door from which I had entered. Probably to fit all the Watchers. I felt small. I could see myself getting closer though. It wasn't going on forever. I neared it, and began to hear a strange muffle of sounds. After a while, I had reached the end and was standing by the big wooden door. At that moment all of the lanterns went out.

Shrouded in darkness, I raised an unknowing fist to knock on the door, but it had opened before I had the chance. Looking through the opening, I couldn't see anything clearly but I could hear what the sounds coming from behind the door were. Munching. What seemed two hundred mouths munching in a mad collective.

When the door had fully opened, I saw a thin red carpet flowing down the middle of the hall, many glorious crystal chandeliers on the ceiling, and when I looked on either side of the place saw benches fifty feet high that housed the squirrels Navi had told me would be there.

They were all red but varied in their colour. Some were brighter than others, some seemed to be more well groomed than others, but all had the same black eyes. I wondered if they were all Watchers.

Noticing one in particular, it in turn caught my eye, lowered its nut and pointed at me.

"Look! It's here!" The munching stopped abruptly. There were a few moments of silence and then I began to hear jeering. Through it all I picked out a few random phrases:

"Ooh. What a pretty little boy!"

"Well, it showed up! Didn't expect that!"

"Time to face the firing squad, little boy!" I did not

feel anxious at this moment, though I admit that it was strange and all to see. I put on a fake, confident smile and kept on walking down the
carpet. There was a mixed barrage of both munching and jeering while only a few had sat silently, seeming to be entranced by my appearance.

"So this is the drugged up loser Oswell was talking about!" Then I felt a horrible shock to my head and my vision went blurry. I fell to the ground.

"Hahaha!"

"Good shot, Rocko!" I picked myself up from the ground and felt blood coming out
of my head. I was dizzy and in a lot of pain and yet I continued to show a straight face. Then other squirrels started throwing their acorns.

"Take that you monster!"

"Make it feel like it made them feel!"

"Nah, I'm keeping mine, Deb. Still hungry."

I was being pummelled. Some were hitting my chest. Some hitting my shins. Some missing me completely. After it all, I was still standing and no-one else had managed to hit my head again. But I was ready to topple.

I looked down at the floor around me. There was a huge pile of nuts that had gathered. Above the top of that pile, I noticed a squirrel that was even bigger than all the others I had seen. It was behind a pulpit, looking grotesquely fat and holding a gavel. It was using the gavel to smash acorns against the sound block, cracking them open and with the other paw stuffing crushed nuts into its gigantic mouth. But as it was doing this, its black eyes never left mine. I don't know if you've ever had the misfortune to have someone leer at you while they eat food, Dear Reader, but it's not very nice. And this wasn't just a guy. It was a giant goddamn squirrel.

"Order in the court! Order!" The jury of squirrels had lowered their din, deciding to whisper before finally halting their voices completely. I looked at the judge.

"Dunley Novak, you have been taken to the Great Nut Courthouse for a situation down on Earth which has been flagged up by your Watcher. He has told us what has happened."

"Evil!"

"Completely evil!"

"Silence in the court! You were taken to the Asphodel after killing yourself in what can only be described as the coward's way out."

"Coward!"

"Scum!"

"Silence! We let it slide your whole life. The drugs. The lies. But this is too far. You have been charged with the most grievous of crimes. Spiking your mates with LSD."

"Spiking its mates!"

"With LSD!"

"LSD!"

"Silence! How do you plead?"

"It's true. I did it." What broke out was a wave of moans and jeers which had seemed to be more in sync than at any other moment.

"And tell me, little boy, why would you do that?"

"Yeah, you fucked up cunt!"

"Because it's evil! It wanted them to suffer!"

"That's not true. I–"

"Oh, he knows the truth!"

"Coward speaks the truth!"

"Evil speaks the truth!"

"Scum speaks th–"

"Well are you going to let me speak? Are you going to listen to my side of the story? Or have the acorns numbed your god damn squirrel heads?" I checked my pocket for the blue feather. I had a feeling I would be needing it. Another juryman had decided to throw another acorn, but it flew past my head.

"Do you think you can speak to us like this? You pitiful boy. We will let you speak. But one more insult to us and you're going to get –" his eyes grew bigger and his jaws became wider – "what you deserve."

"It deserves all hell!"

"Hell!"

"Hell!"

"Silence! Let it speak." I cleared my throat.

"Well, your honour. It's true that I gave my friends acid without telling them about it. It's true that it all went horribly. A boy is most likely dead because of me. But I must tell you, I did not want anything bad to happen. I realise it was completely stupid and without foresight. But I love my friends. I wanted them to be happy. And I didn't kill myself because I'm a coward. I mean, I am a coward. But I did it because I couldn't handle what I had done to them."

"It just didn't want to get arrested!"

"I would rather be in jail than be up here. I'm not saying I'm a good person, your honour. I'm not saying I'm intelligent or that I even deserve anyone's forgiveness. But it hurt me so much, it still hurts, to know they're still down there on Earth, having to deal with what I did. You've got to fix this for me." It didn't sound too convincing but I didn't know what else to say. I was very much nervous now.

"You say you love your friends. Can you prove such a thing?"

"No, it can't! It's lying!"
"Liar!"
"Murderer!"
"Lying murderer!"
"Well, I... I don't know how to prove it. I just do."
"The mask is slipping!"
"Slipping off its murderer face!"
"Evil lying acid-head face!"

I was afraid of the thing that I 'deserved', but my blood was boiling. I stared out at the crowd. There was nothing in those eyes which resembled Navi's.

"You want me to prove it? If I could go to Earth right now... I've got poems. Written about them. A story about them. I did those things, worthless though they may be, because I cared about them and I thought they were all decent and interesting and I don't even care if they all hated me from the start! They took me in, they accepted me... Kurt... Erica...Bella... Beebee... I loved them, your honour. And I loved it when Jad played his piano, there was nothing but goodness in that. I told him all the time how I felt. And Tig, well I didn't know her very well but I still cared about her. And Bella... She was so full of life... Even though things were hard for her, and I was so cruel to her. And Molly, she always made me laugh, and she was so talented too. And Beebee... It was like a knife in my heart how I left her like that. I never wanted ill for any of them. And I don't need to prove any of it because I know it's true."

"Oh, it doesn't need to prove it!"
"Save the tears!"
"Arrogant murderer!"
"Acid-head murderer!"

I looked out at them all, rage filling my veins. I wished

that Navi was there. I wished there was someone like him there. I wished it wasn't true. I never felt so alone in my life.

It was at this moment that I knew whatever I said I would get torn down. I didn't care anymore. I had the blue feather from Homa. I was ready to use it.

"Shut up. Shut your god damn faces! All of you! You don't know me... You don't know them! And it's all bullshit, what comes out your mouths. Navi understood me, he didn't tear me down at every god damn moment! You're all petty! I came here because I thought you would listen. But you already seem to have made up your minds. I'm not here for any other reason than to stop what's happened on Earth. So give me what I deserve, because you god damn squirrels don't even deserve to be talking to me! Shove your precious nuts up your fucking arseholes." I stared at the judge. "You too, you fat fuck."

And then an avalanche of acorns. The feather flew out of my grip. I was turned to pulp before I could even move.

"Take it away!"

"Yeah, take it away judge!"

"Boy, you didn't listen. You have disrespected me far too much." He looked insane and it began to frighten me. Foam was frothing out his clenched jaws. I could fit in those jaws.

"Guards. Take it to the anteroom."

"Yes, judge!"

"The anteroom!"

"The anteroooom!"

They all seemed to be cheering now. Justice had been done in the Great Nut Courthouse, Dear Reader. I felt my arms being pulled from my side and I was dragged along the floor and they began pelting acorns down at me again, the cheering getting louder. I couldn't reach for the feather now. One medicine ball of an acorn had me right in the crotch, but before I could cry out, another smashed into my forehead and I blacked out.

17

I had been in the room for so long that all my bruises and cuts from the pelting had healed. My body had seemed to regain its basic vitality and yet my mind was falling away. There was nothing in the room. It was all white and there were four walls, a ceiling and a floor but nothing inside except me. There was no door to get out.

I did not know how long it had been, and I was unable to fall asleep at all during this time, but I knew it must have been a very long time because my bruises and cuts were gone and I noticed long bristles when I touched my chin.

I quickly began talking to myself when I realised I couldn't handle the silence.

"This room is hell," etc. "Will they ever let me out? Is this it? Is this what Navi meant when he said the time would never land? Navi." I began to cry. "Navi, can you hear me? What do I do, Navi? I failed, didn't I? I got angry again when I should have stayed quiet. Did you see me in the courthouse, Navi? Can you see me now? Please, give me a sign that you can…" I choked on the last words in a sadness I could not halt and lowered my head.

After a while, I sulkily raised my head and looked around wearily, maybe hoping he would give me a sign and all. But nothing appeared. I only saw the white walls. They mocked me.

I had lied down on the floor in the fetal position, closing my eyes, trying hard to fall asleep. I thought that even if I went into another nightmare, it would still be better than being in this room. But I could not fall asleep.

Maybe it's because I am already asleep? I thought. Maybe it's not real? Maybe it's just the LSD? I was absurdly tired, and wondered if it was some horrible case of insomnia due to all the trauma my mind had experienced, or just a trick of the anteroom, that it would never let me sleep, and I would have to sit here, awake, forever, with nothing and no-one except myself. But I still had hope that maybe Navi was looking over me, watching me as was his one duty. I just didn't know.

There were moments when I would reach a meditative state by focusing on my breathing and I must have entered that state for hours and hours at points, becoming separated from my own self and forgetting I was in the room. But it would not stay that way. Something would jolt me out of it. A creeping thought of a certain person would pierce through, or a movement of my leg which had to stretch due to an ache, would drag me back in. After I was back I would be calmer, but I would not be happy. And soon that calmness would dissipate and be replaced by questions that no-one could answer. It became so maddening that I began not only talking to myself but screaming at the walls

This must have gone on for days and days. Perhaps even weeks. I had been thinking about all my memories. I started from the moment I was on holiday in Croatia when my father had left me to ride his boat in the vicious storm, and I pieced back my life from that moment until I was nearly four years and almost burnt the curtains down; to jumping on cushioned chairs at five with a girl I've never seen for twenty years; all the way to primary school when the recurring nightmare I used to be tortured with had begun; football and Pokémon with Dan; Mike getting hit by lightning; the gigs with Shaman and O'Finnley; Day 1 in Rose Ward; Day 2 in Rose Ward (a maniacal feeling place); 1st love; 2nd love; how many memories? O yes the night I slept on a red sofa in South Kensington which was situated outside for some strange reason, and bought stale bread for sixty pence and laid there for hours in Winter England Night eating stale bread on a red alfresco sofa because I missed my train (arriving in London only in an attempt to meet Jazz Deane, a first rate poet, do a reading, but couldn't find the place, and got lost and couldn't get home for hours). Or the more recent time I got lost in the city of Bath after a night of continual sweat from too much ecstasy, walking back in monsoon rain and thunder from town to the campus getting lost again and paranoid I would be stabbed or raped watching endless ambulances driving past thinking there's my stop and ending up nowhere near home but stranded in a huge forest at five in the morning on a Friday night my phone dead and lost alone in this strange forest and meeting that Lithuanian there thinking this is it my number's up only a madman would be alone in a forest at dawn (!) but him lost as well and simply trying to find his way like me! Ended up sleeping in the forest for four days he told me. Worried I'd have to pick berries with him and make spears but finally getting out of there and landing home at eleven gobbling up my medication and sleeping for two whole days. I helped him get to Bristol, he helped me get to Bath. We escaped the forest. And we saved each other's lives that break of dawn. That was the most mad thing about it.

To memories of playing collision on Shaman's trampoline and him handing me potions and entering new worlds. Memory of meeting him. It was perhaps the greatest day of my life. It was a school day, 2007 2008 something like that. It was Music. We had this teacher called Mr. Bloomsby who was thirty and going bald and he told me I was playing a 'wrong sequence' of chords. I made up progressions on the guitar that he, a certified music teacher, said were wrong. But could that be true? I didn't care what the hell Bloomsby thought of my chords. And anyway that's not the point. The point is it was a lesson where nothing was going on (the holiest type) so we just watched a film. *School of Rock* was on and I could see this boy infront of me really rocking out to the TV and I was getting excited like maybe I could finally go up to someone and talk to them. I was sitting there while this Asian with dark skin and a lock of black hair is jamming along, and so I suspected he wasn't a phony or a brute. So with this new confidence while *My Brain is Hanging Upside Down* plays throughout the classroom, I poke him on the shoulder and he turns around and I say to him: "I can play this song." And then, he got excited like I wasn't expecting.

"No way! That's awesome. You've got to teach me how to play, man. I've got a guitar at mine. Maybe you could come over after school and show me some chords or something? I've heard you're very good on that old guitar. Yessssss. Come round."

We've been best friends ever since that day. Hell, nobody ever wanted a damn thing from me. Really.

Then Shaman (a name I would later bestow upon him like an unordained freak, and well it just caught on) wanted a damn. He wanted a damn from me. Nobody ever wanted a damn from me. Platonically, I love him perhaps too much.

Memories. Good and bad alike. I imagined it all to pass the unholy time. To the day we went to McDonalds and Rye leans over having eaten all my chips and says to me:
 "Bet you that guy is a serial killer." And after Beebee rolls everyone a cigarette and we stumble to Boots and on the high street Rye gets sucked into someone's 'forcefield'. And then we're all in Boots me looking for ear drops to fix my ears and Penguin picking up a tube of lipstick and saying: "Look, guys. It's Jad-coloured!" And everyone laughing including Jad. But Jad unable to control himself, ungraciously digging his key into Erica's neck that day while waiting for the bus, and passing her a two's on a cigarette only as the bus we were all waiting for came. And I heard again, loudly, the copper pennies Beebee and Penguin threw down at her and which rang bells around the cobbled ground that day we all went to town. I couldn't help but laugh.
 Memories. Dreams. Nightmares. And O yes the nightmare I could not explain, the nightmare that felt like I was trapped in a moment where time was infinitely leaping and yet seemed to be on the point of collapsing altogether at any moment; struggling to escape in time and there's so much panic trapped in such a small space that I would eventually wake up, utterly deranged, every night until I was fifteen, past the worst moments of my waking life as I started to not be a little child anymore and became an older boy, a boy who hated himself and wished he was someone else, wishing it upon stars,

because he had no talent in anything and couldn't speak and no girl wanted to hold his hand. And the panic of staying like that forever...

I found myself falling.

Where was Shaman in all this? Even he, the soul who had in a certain way saved my life, the only person outside of family who ever believed in me and who in fact believed in me to mystical levels, was gone from the room like everything else.

I still remember the days leading up to the first acute psychotic break. It was with him. We had agreed perhaps a month before to go see The Libertines play a show in Hyde Park. It was early July, and after I had overdosed on a deadly drug but I was not yet psychotic or in fact had any idea that I would become psychotic not a week later on my brother's birthday 16th July 2014. Before that, just terrible physical pain, sleep deprivation. Deathly dehydration. I almost said no to the gig, because I was so ill. But he dragged me out and convinced me like he usually did that I was not going to miss our favourite act because I felt ill.

We drank cans of Special Brew he had acquired as we chugged along on the underground, and I remember him casually going up to a woman waiting at the platform to remark that the umbrella she was holding was 'beautiful'. Oh and potentialities, he was going on about potentialities to me on the tube getting real into the subject while us drinking and yammering delightfully out in the eye of everyone chugging along this steam train mind, and me, without sleep but a band to see, a night to remember. And just a few days later. I lost it.

I wondered why as a boy I saw beasts and evil creatures encased in my bedroom wall when I went to sleep at night, these horrid things which were not there in the daytime, and turning over to the open room and still afraid, feeling they would attack me from behind, and deciding to lay half off the bed in order to be further away from them. I wondered why I saw strange colours and patterns when I strained my eyes looking at the grey sofa in the old living room, or when I just stared into space long enough for these strange images to appear. I wondered why so many things had scared me, my brother's CD case of Radiohead's *The Bends* with the strange fuzzy head was a notable example of unexplainable horror, when at that time I had never taken any drugs.

I then began to think if any of it happened. Not just the encounter with the squirrels, not just the terrible night when my friends had suffered under my hands but my whole life – everything that I had ever experienced I began to think had never even happened. Illusion. And the only thing that was true, was the room I was now trapped in. I couldn't take it anymore.

I got up and went over to the wall on the left, slapping it with my hands.

"Let me out! Let me out! I can't take it anymore!" I began punching the wall with my fists. "You sadists! You sadistic bastards! Let me out! Let me out!" I let out all my rage, all my sorrow, all my confusion and regret into a madness of anger that did not even show one dent on the white wall. But I had to let it out. It felt like letting out both an angel and a demon.

It was not long before I grew tired, and had stopped pummelling the wall and just held onto it, just wanting to feel something.

"I'll do anything. I'll do anything you want. Just let me out. Please. Please..." I slumped down, knowing no-one could hear me. I had no strength to ask any more questions. No strength for it or for any more movement. Yet I crawled, back to the centre of the room. I was lifeless now. No hope, nor fear. Nothing.

18

When I heard the wall I had been slapping and punching and holding onto begin to crack, I didn't even move. Another illusion, I thought. A fitting metaphor for how my mind was falling to shit.

But I heard it get more pronounced, and then I began to think 'so damn what if it's illusion.' It wasn't so bad to hear something that wasn't my own voice.

I turned my head, and beheld cracks in the wall forming, and the wall began to shake and in one glorious moment the wall was shattered completely and there was a squirrel with a black mask holding onto a long spear standing in the open space.

"Get up. We're leaving."

I got up, and walked over to the ruins of the wall. When I got close to him, he grabbed my arm and nearly broke it, and began dragging me out. I did not even feel like being angry with him. His presence, which should have been startling, was not so.

"How was it in there?" I didn't reply.

"That's a nice beard you got. It almost makes you look like a man." Still I say nothing.

"Cat got your tongue? And stop dragging your feet on the floor. I'm not carrying you." I did not pick myself up, but neither did I let him take all of my weight. "You and your Watcher..." he began, seeming to be enjoying a thought in his mind. "It's quite funny really, how you ended up with such a pathetic one as him. You suit each other well." He laughed again with a strange malice. "He's an embarrassment to the Asphodel."

I finally felt like I had stopped being a lifeless robot. The guard had put my friend back into my mind. But though it had angered me, I decided to let the anger pass. I took a deep breath. There was no point giving into his remarks. But I still had to say something.

"If you can't see what's special about him, then I feel sorry for you. I really do." He grunted and carried on pulling me through the dark passageway.

"Just keep on walking, little boy."

*

I had left my eyes closed during the walk. I was not concerned about where I was. I did not ask the guard where we were going. I did not thank him for releasing me. I did not yell at him for his cruelness. I simply let him take me wherever it was I was being taken to.

I kept my eyes closed and it was then that I saw Erica staring back at me.

It was not the look she gave me which tore me apart after we ran out to see Molly. It was the moment I fell for her, sitting on my bed with her, after we had written a short poem for each other, which being her idea and so spontaneously too I could not say no to. I saw her eyes. They lit up mine in the dark passageway and in my darkened mind – her words on the notepad I felt had once again disentangled me.

And how good this poem was and how I didn't need to lie about it and in fact feeling inferior as it was not achingly romantic as mine was to her and yet it was still enchanting (I treasured it above anything despite losing it) and really that is what I wanted to read and what I wanted to write to her in turn – but distracted by this love creeping into me at that moment, I was giddy like a little boy poet, and as you all should know, the best poetry comes not when thou giddy but near death. Yet I was free in that moment. I opened my eyes and my heart was there again. It was warming me and I did not hold onto it in desperation, but neither did I try and block it out.

She had given me that perfect memory, and yes, Dear Reader, I did say earlier that I found it hard to believe in the perfect forms but if there was one proof of evidence that Plato was right then it was that moment. She had given me something which made me feel I was not that dull, ugly and worthless thing I had always thought I was. So I smiled for my old-friend, whispering 'thank you' as the guard dragged me along the darkened passage and we arrived at a door and he pushed me in, and there I was, once again in the courtroom where the long red carpet cut through the benches that housed the jangling jury.

I was not disgusted by them, or held anger for them. I simply saw them and my heart was still warm and I was not going to let anger or fear take hold of me.

"Order in the court. The defendant has returned."

"It's even uglier with the beard!"

"How was the room, murderer?"

"Yeah, how was it?" I noticed there were pockets of curiosity, many mouths spouting 'yeah!' as if they wanted an answer from me.

"Well, I'm here. And I'm ready to continue."

"It couldn't take it!"

"No way could it take it. A coward could never take it!"

"I'm ready to continue the trial, your honour." At that

moment, the jury had stayed inordinately quiet. They looked down at me and I could feel that they were staring, but I did not need to put on a fake smile of confidence this time. I was ready for whatever they were going to say.

"Dunley Novak, for your obstreperous behaviour thr–"

"What's ostreperous mean?"

"It means he's a cunt, Zara!"

"Order! For your sickening behaviour three weeks ago in this very hall, you were taken to the anteroom for punishment. But you are here now, and we will continue. Have you calmed down?"

"I have calmed down, your honour."

"The first order of business," he says, still munching on shards of acorn. "Knowing it has been three weeks since your disgusting actions, you may be concerned for your friends and are perhaps wondering what has become of them."

"Yeah, right!"

"It doesn't care about them!"

"Silence! Jurymen! Let it not be said that I disagree with you, but please, I must hear its reply. This session will drag on far longer than it needs to otherwise."

"I am concerned for them, your honour."

"Then we are going to show you the reality of what you have left behind. Guards. Show him." They took his order at once, and walked over from the sides of the pulpit where they had been waiting at the judge's helm and began heading towards me. Their steps echoed through the hall. They then stopped at equidistance from me and the judge, and turned to a hidden door on the left and vanished into a side room.

Not long after, I heard a deep sound emanating from the room, and then my eye caught a sharp glint which pained my vision. But I could see what it was. A huge and sparkling crystal acorn, as tall as the guards, had been rolled into view. It glimmered a luminous cry of mystery within itself and the guards appeared alongside it, rolling it into the middle of the hall and easing its movement until it halted twenty feet in front of me.

"Walk forward." I began walking towards it. It strained my eyes. The light reflecting off the crystal seemed holy.

"Will this send me to my friends?"

"Yes, but only briefly. You're coming back."

I figured that it was my only possible connection to the world I had once lived in, where once I was indeed sane and that normality which before had seemed a dull thing to shake off now not, now realising it to be a holy thing too which I had abandoned; this the world of streets & fields & lamp-posts & institutions of all shapes, the mysteries of conversation & the will of its speakers & the will of all human nature & gift of the original nature around like an aura & yet within too; trapped in the manuscripts the polaroids the canvas the engravings film-reels shrieks songs stories & voices of the mind which carved the stone rose from the stone & drew the dawn from the den of thought & the joy of it all & the dread of it all these moments when history was seen piled with the coincidences & tragedies bound by beating hearts & misted in the rainfall of every man woman & child alive in the blues of the beaten down bus-stop where not knowing was part of the race & damned if one ran the same old path & damned if one never loved oneself nor ever left the room for fear of a glance that would meet your own & drag you out of the isolation but isolation still a thing! Still felt! Whether loss of a lover or a sour hangover these things still felt.

Still. In this place I had left and what sublime connection & connections of everything there & really there & unseen & godly stuck to the sky with head in the roof tiles of humdrum heaven whereof the stars & Homa & Shaman too were dreamt unseen as these connections are unseen but nonetheless there with brutal melody pounding in the chest.

I longed for my sanity as I neared the crystal. I longed to be home.

As I got closer I could hear it humming. And now from the angle it had concealed fully the judge from my view. It was beautiful to look upon. Like a prism it was shining the entire spectrum back at me, undulating colours in all directions and now being so close to it I could feel an icy chill.

"Now," the judge says. "Place your hands on it."

"But, wha–"

"Do it!"

I placed two weary hands on the crystal. The coldness pulsated through my hands and up into my body and into my eyes and my eyes began to harden. I then appeared in a white field. There was a tundra of whiteness all around. I couldn't see anything. But I could hear someone talking.

"It's going to be okay."

"How is it?"

"You're still alive. That's what counts."

"Yeah. Alive. Without... I look hideous, Jad."

"You don't. They had to do it, Molly. They were too infected." It was then that I began to see them through the mist.

Molly was lying in a bed and Jad was perched next to her on a chair and I could see that she was bandaged up to the knees and there was nothing beyond those knees.

The true horror of seeing that – the consequence of what I had done to her – now painted before me in this hospital bay. And she was still beautiful and she was still Molly Jones and there was no question about that, but I could tell she probably thought she was not those things anymore, and it was nearly unbearable to witness. I closed my hardened eyes, leaving her there not alone but with Jad, who I suspected would care for her and say the right things and tell her she was beautiful and still the light that was Molly Jones. I just wasn't sure.

I fell back into the tundra and kept on walking. I had found the familiar voice of Jad without seeking it out; I knew what I had to hear and see I would find, so I walked around without a bearing and without a plan and sure enough soon I began to hear a far-off scream... And it growing louder and louder and sadder and sadder in my ears. But I could not stop moving and I knew I had to hear it and soon I had found where it was coming from. The wail was so clear through the silent mist.

"What is that?"

"It's just a little injection. It's going to calm him down."

"But what is it?"

"Haloperidol." And then I saw him. He was being restrained by someone and another was injecting a syringe into his arm and he was shaking hard and his eyes were manic, resisting and screaming while Penny stood over the bed watching him with a hollowness in her eyes.

Pretty soon after the doctor had injected the medicine Kurt had lowered his screams until they were reduced to mere sighs, and he stopped shaking and was still on the bed and his eyes were not manic any longer but hollow too like Penny's. And I knew from personal experience that this was no cure but something which would only cease the madness for a short while. I looked down on them as a ghost in the ward and feeling I could no longer watch anymore, I closed my eyes and drifted off up into the ceiling and fell out back into the tundra to see the all-enveloping whiteness which had surrounded me.

"It's only gotten worse... And all I can do is watch it."

*

I was feeling very weak and afraid of what else I had yet to see. I stood there still for a while, not knowing where to go. All I knew is that I had to try my hardest to fix it. And I didn't know how. But I had to be patient and see it through. I took a random direction and began walking again but I did not find anything as quickly as I had the other times. I walked and walked hoping to hear something, all I heard was silence. Yet I walked and I walked and it must have been an hour I was walking. And I didn't hear a sound. But I began to see something in the distance.

A blur at first – I edged towards it and the blur then dissipating and I saw from overhead a teal dot resting in a pale green field and I recognised that coloured dot and I knew that it was the hair of Beebee Gladstone.

I moved towards the ground and the colours became rich and vivid. I could see the graves all around the cemetery and the flowers too amongst them, and when I had approached the ground I heard her crying again as she was on the roof.

It seemed so long ago now – nearly a month had passed by in the Asphodel – but I remembered what Navi had said about the time dilation and that it was perhaps only a few days past here where Beebee stood alone in front of the tombstone that read her lover's name.

JAMIE CURTIS (1994-2016)

Flora surrounded the grave. Dozens of carnations. I didn't want to look over to see her face as I knew what had happened – proof now, this cemetery scene – and there was no need. His death was on my hands. I had to stop this.

But it felt like prying and unfair to catch her alone there, so I turned around towards the entrance of the cemetery and saw a girl in the distance walking over. As she got closer I could see that it was Erica.

"Beebee," she says. "You've been here an awful while."

"I know. I jost can't leave yet." They stood together in the January chill.

"It was nice to see so many people come."

"Yeah..."

She then turned to face Rye and when their eyes met, they both looked into each other's deeply and sadly and with love and pain they embraced in a hug of what seemed deep significance. I realised I should leave them. Yet I wanted one last time to see Erica and see her beauty as she really was the most beautiful thing I had ever seen and I knew that most likely I would never get the chance to see her again, but I did not hang around for that. I closed my eyes and felt myself floating again and all light dimmed and the world was washed away and left below me as I fell up again harshly into the snowstorm encased within the crystal.

I laid there on the icy ground as I struggled to get up.

And then, while taking rest, the ground beneath me began to crack, and I fell down into the depths of the ice and was free-falling. During this I had heard a voice. A voice I knew deeply. The first voice I had ever heard singing songs into my ears, which now seemed crackly as if it was contained within a machine. My mother on the phone.

"I... I don't believe it. No. He was the sweetest boy. Yes... He's had trouble with drugs before. No. Nothing like this..." She was trying hard to breathe and I knew there was despair stuck in her throat. I did not hear the other person talking – only her.

"Yes... I'm okay. Thank you for calling... Yes. Please tell Jamie's family we give them our deepest condolences. Yes... Yes... Okay... Thank you. Goodbye."

I was trapped in not only the plummet but now the sound – clear now – of my mother's crying, which was always and will always be the saddest sound I have ever heard and unjust as she a diamond and what horrible guilt I felt in that moment. I wanted to see her face but it was not there and all that was there was her crying and I couldn't take it. I fell and fell and she cried and cried and I remembered that somewhere in the courthouse my hands had been resting on the crystal which had shown me these things. I tried to see them there and began to feel their phantoms and they were cold and frozen and numbed, but feeling this torture of my mother weeping and only because of me I took all my pain and focused it into the numbed phantom hands, until they shook and cracked, and then, feeling them giving way, they were finally released and I was back in the courthouse having fallen back onto the floor in a loud thud that drew attention from everyone.

"Did you have a nice time seeing your friends?" says a

juryman up in the balcony. I was crushed by it all too much to answer. I had not the slightest idea of how horrible it would be.

I laid there on the carpet, looking around and seeing their black beady eyes all on me and still how they all seemed to be judging me with them. I looked away and noticed there were shards from the crystal scattered all around me.

"Get up."

The crystal was still blocking the judge but I knew it was his voice – it was a hideous thing. I then looked back down at the shards around me and saw one right by my left hand. I rested my fingers over it and furtively placed it into my pocket.

"Get up!"

I picked my body up and stood there as the guards were rolling back the crystal acorn into the side room in which it had come from, and I saw again the judge and saw again that he was still eating from a pile of crushed nuts with murderous eyes.

"I don't want to be here all day. So let's make this quick."

"Okay."

"Would you like to go back to Earth, Dunley?"

"Of course I would."

"Would you like to go back to Earth, knowing that all that has happened has still happened?"

"What do you mean?"

"It's very simple. You go back. Or you stay here. If you want to go – we will let you. I'm sure your mother would like to see you. Alive again. But nothing else there will have changed. The only way we can change what has happened, is if you stay here, in the anteroom. It's your choice."

It wasn't simple. I had never been good at decisions. Even very trivial things I found it hard to decide. And now, having been horridly awake and all for nearly a whole month and not since that ugly dream while resting upon Navi's back, possibly the hardest decision to make was presented before me and I could not shirk it.

I even wondered – in my resistance to decide – that perhaps maybe I could shirk it. Run away. But it didn't make sense and I knew there was no way to get out of it.

"But why, why are you giving me the choice?"

"The room will drive you mad. But to return to Earth would make you guilt-ridden. There's no way out. You would never be able to forget it if you leave here. And, having to decide this yourself, will be punishment enough I think."

I thought about my friends, how if I returned Kurt would perhaps still be in the mental ward and Molly's legs would still be amputated and Penguin would still be dead. And the only way to stop it – to stay in the room which had maddened me more than the psychosis in Spector Park. And I remembered Navi saying how the time may go on forever and no doubt that is what the judge meant when he said I would have to 'stay'.

But maybe I could do it for them. Maybe this was my chance to do the right thing. I thought about my mother. I thought about Shaman. These souls who would never see me again. The world my mother had brought me into, the world where Shaman had saved me, this world, which would also never see me again, or I it.

But I could. I could see them again. I could see the world again. And I could make new friends. I could try and forget about everything I had done and maybe at first it would be hell but over time maybe it would be okay and then maybe it wouldn't, but at least I would have that excitement of not knowing what would happen.

19

It was a regular day at university, a Friday afternoon in February, and while the gang were out living la vida loca, I was inside, not living but still loca.

Erstwhile, two staff from the university had come to my room to track me down and ask me why I hadn't bothered to come to the follow up meeting with Mrs. Gully. I heard them knock on the door. Nknnknnk.

"Accommodation!" Then nknknknnk.

"Dunley? Are you in?"

"Hello?" Still I was silent.

"We're coming in." And then the door opens and the two staff, two women of about thirty years of age with curious faces, and now with nostrils flared as Bella and Erica's had been upon entering all that time ago, had peered inside and saw that the bed was not empty.

"He's here," one of them whispers to the other.

"Mr. Novak. Please wake up. We need to speak with you." But I did not reply to them.

"He's being stubborn. Just pull down the blanket. Then he has no excuse."

"What if he's naked?"

"Just pull the top half down." And so the taller woman had leant over the bed and pulled the blanket down and both their faces lit up in madness.

"Becky, do you. Do you see that?"

"Yeah. I see it."

"He's. He's not."
"No. He's not."
"It's. It's a lobster?"
"It's a lobster. A giant gold lobster." The woman who had lifted half the cover off then lifted the whole cover off and there it was. A golden lobster on top of Dunley Novak's bed. No sign of the man himself.

They looked in wonder as the gold sparkled. Its pincers were as big as them. Becky then leant over and knocked it with her fist. She heard a sharp twang.

"But what, what does it mean?"
"It means he's giving us the finger, that's what it means. He doesn't want us to find him and he's left it here to give us the bloody finger. He's probably some god-awful art student thinking he's funny or something."

"I mean, I know he hasn't shown up all year. But, this is really well made, Trish. It's so intricate. It looks like real gold."

"I doubt it's real gold. He's a student. But it is impressive. He's got to be around somewhere. Come on, let's go. We'll find the sod."

They left the room and walked down the stairs and out of the building and as they paced through the bitter cold, they passed two girls who had been sitting on a bench talking in the middle of the courtyard.

"Do you even like him, Tig?"
"He's such a weird teacher. I mean, I know he's a psychology professor but man, he needs some psychotherapy himself. Why's he always leering at me?"

"I'm so sick of hearing about mental illness as well. It's making me feel mental."

"You are mental, Khalifa."

"Haha. Well, I guess genius is mistaken for madness quite a lot these days."

"Oh, did you manage to get that assignment done by the way?"

"Actually I haven't yet."

"Really? Not like you... It's due tomorrow."

"To be honest. I've just. I've just been lazy. Well. It's not really that. I'm just wondering where the hell Dun's gone, you know? He hasn't replied to my messages and no-one else has seen him in weeks."

"He's a lost cause. He probably got kicked out for not showing up. You really need to stop thinking about him, Khalif. I don't want to hurt your feelings, but, it's not worth it. He's a junkie. You need to forget about him. Look for someone else. You deserve someone better than him." At that moment a little blue thrush had landed on the bench before flying off again not a second later.

"Maybe. Maybe you're right. Thanks, Tig. I'm not upset or anything. But I do wonder where he is."

*

The two women from the accommodation team were walking up the path that led from Hercocks towards the rest of the university.

"Should we have taken it with us?"

"Oh, I'm sorry. Did *you* want to carry that bloody thing?" And the little blue thrush heard them overhead. It flew through the chilled air and left the arguing twosome.

It was so high up that it was above even the highest buildings, where through the windows one could occasionally see students leaning joints out and blowing their misdemeanour mist into the frozen sky. And the little blue thrush noticed one window in particular and decided to land there – there was music playing inside.

It hopped up to the ledge and looked inside and noticed a pair of hands, one holding a spliff betwixt two fingers, trickling digits and ash onto the keys.

With a warble of excitement it flew into the room – passing a cloud of smoke – and rested on Jad Kinney's shoulders. And warble warble as Kinney plucked his matching trill of a nocturne dreamt by Chopin and together, they warbled wonder and pain – pain being from the sound and wonder of the sound, in their mysterious duet, accepting that sadness and awe through its release onto the clavier and from within the beak of the little blue thrush that had found its way inside. And seeing a little shadow printed onto the white keys, Jad turned his head slightly with his hands still dancing through the climax of the nocturne, and he saw the bird swaying its head and warbling along and they caught each other's eyes as Jad overturned the climax with a glittering collapsing mash of the highest keys before the final ease of the notes, and when the piano had ceased, the bird jumped off his shoulder and stepped onto the clavier and looked up at him, flapping its waxy blue wings. A blue feather fell onto the piano.

Jad looked and, taking a final drag of the joint, blew it out of the window, and it was then that the little blue thrush leapt up into the exhale (thinking this smoke was perhaps the source of his talent) and flew into it warbling still and now as high as him, though even higher as it flew out into the heights of the frozen sky with the nocturne ringing through its stoned little head and falling out joyfully from its little grey beak – wondering where next.

It glided through the afternoon, perhaps too whacked out now and so deciding to find the fresh air which was placed in the huge fields that surrounded the university. And thinking too *warble warble there's got to be a stream somewhere to clear me throat*

It flew down with its little belly flipping from the pressure, hoping to get some much needed fresh air and perhaps some water from the stream. Gliding over the tops of trees – enjoying its exploration – and soon found a little cascade by an edge of woodland. It rested on a bark and looked at itself in the water's reflection.

Warble warble someone got out the wrong side of the nest this morning huh

After it had drank some water its throat seemed to clear up and it gave a loud impassioned trill in celebration, and wondered how all those students could have that smoke day-in day-out as it had seen them do ever since it upped-sticks to its new nest, located in an unassuming tree not far from Hercocks.

It decided not to hang around the woodland in case some beast was lurking there, and jumped up with its little feet and bound through the air to find an open field. It flew far and happily and seemed to be over the real nest-lock feeling when it found a big open field where some sheep had congregated, gliding down to have a little look at the odd creatures. And as it landed, it saw a girl with a camera taking photos of the sheep.

"Black and white? Or colour..." The little blue thrush had seen her taking a photo of one sheep up close and thought to itself *warble warble I'm much more beautiful than that damn sheep*

It puffed out its wings hoping to catch her eye but the girl was too absorbed by the sheep. After waiting a while, it decided to intervene, flying over to the sheep in question and landing on its head, and it was then that Bella Bowden noticed it.

"Aww! Little blue-bird! Don't move! I'm gonna use the fisheye on this one..." And the sheep was baaa-ing seemingly bewildered and the little blue thrush was trying to suck in its belly. She aimed the camera at the pair and wandered over gently to get the closest shot and snap! the sheep lost it and hoofed around making the little blue thrush dizzy. It flew away and left the girl with a photo that she assumed would get her a 1st for her degree.

The light from the camera had made its vision blurred and the blubbering sheep had made it far too dizzy, yet it continued to fly as it noticed still slightly being affected by Kinney's smoke had made it quite a psychedelic experience for the little blue thrush. But soon, it grew tired and decided to land on another window ledge. It looked up. It was dreaming of Homa, its ancestor in the Heights. While it regained its strength it peered into the window and saw another girl. But it didn't fly in as the window was shut. It was Molly Jones doing a pirouette.

She had been spinning there for so long that the bird's dizziness had returned.

Warble warble that girl is such a good dancer but curse her for making me this way and in a fit of anger it bounded off again.

It flew far in irritation. When it had come overhead the university grounds it noticed some students and felt to do a shit on one of them and give into the anger. But it realised there was no way to justify it. Then it started hearing more music, music completely different from that of Kinney and his friend Chopin.

Warble warble this is some good music and it followed the sound and flew into an open door and there lay Hammyblink.

Kurt and Penny and the others all playing their new track (which had been a real mind-fuck to get together) but which now was fully formed and no longer embryonic but mad and alive as were the people who had made it. And the little blue thrush moshed around the room, weaving in and out of the band-members and their instruments and through their arms and over the fret boards and under the drum supports and well everywhere just digging the music, which was so different to that of the ebony pianist's, yet still with pain and wonder – only pain and wonder augmented in a new way. The little bird found it hauntingly good but due to its little ears could not handle much. It flew up out of the door and left the band to ruin their own.

"D'ya see that thrush? He was feeling it!"

"How'd you know it's not a she?"

"Maybe it's like you, Kurt," the drummer says. "Like, he's a he but he likes to dress up as a she."

"Well then," Kurt replies. "They're destined for glory."

The afternoon was now getting into the evening, and the light had drifted away long before as it being February. The blue thrush decided to head back to its nest to find its partner and lay down in a peaceful rest.

Warble warble uni is so tiring but I wouldn't change it for the world

In the darkness it found the unassuming tree and saw it getting closer and closer and thus closer to that rest it so needed, but then it caught something in one of the windows and it being a curious one decided to check it out. Another joint hanging out of the window. Another joint with the cherry at the end lighting up the surroundings. No big deal. But this one, it noticed, was nearly two feet long.

I've never seen one of them so big

It flew up to the ledge and saw the girl who was responsible. It was Beebee.

"Bring it over here."

"Old on, Jamie. Aww, there's a lettle throsh... outsahd the winduh."

"Oh really. Does it have a joint for me?"

"One more poff." She stared at the bird for so long, she didn't realise she had smoked most of the spliff.

The thrush continued to watch Beebee as Beebee continued to watch the thrush. Neither of them had any idea of her boyfriend's resurrection. Then Beebee looked down and saw the joint was smoked near to the bone. She turned around. "Jost com over ear, Ah'll give ya blowback."

He got up from the bed and leant over to the window with her and she put the end of the joint into her mouth and he cupped his mouth against hers and inhaled.

Warble warble aww they're kissing well I'll just leave them lovebirds and go see my own I guess and off it went towards the unassuming tree, landing gracefully in the nest where its partner was there, sleeping. And through the window it caught the eye of Erica Rye.

There that little thrush is again

She picked up a notebook that was rested against the ledge and turning around, seeing her lover asleep on the bed, crept in gently so as not to wake him. When she had buried herself under the sheets, she rummaged around for a pen that she had dropped there some time ago and, feeling it there, she drew it out and put pen to paper and started writing:

> *Wild-eyed wanderer*
> *Where did you go?*
> *You used to be around*
> *But now you don't show*
> *So how does it feel*
> *To be alone?*
> *What's it like to lock madness in solitude*
> *And have it be your home?*
> *You said you were shy*
> *With nowhere to hide*
> *And you leave like this*
> *Without a goodbye*
> *Did you end up lost*
> *No direction home?*
> *What's it like to lock madness in solitude*
> *And have it be your own?*
> *What demon provoked?*
> *Did madness grab you by the throat?*
> *You should know I would soothe those sighs*
> *Those tired eyes*
> *Make it known that you deserve the universe*
> *The stars, the genealogy*
> *Not so much melancholy*
> *I think of it here in my bed*
> *With a head full of spent angels*
> *Are you alive or dead?*

And it was then, Dear Reader, that Dunley lowered the crystal shard from his eye, put it back into his pocket, looked at the surrounding four white walls, closed his haggard eyes of time, and finally went to sleep.

PART II

Weird Halloween

20

The world is in my eyeballs. I didn't want this.

I wanted to be a writer. Here come the jeers. Don't blame me. There's not much else I can do. And I can't even do that right. Because as in life, in writing there is Heaven and there is Hell, just as art displays to us illusions of both, and a third place is created, and we get trapped in ink. The scene of all those half-finished stories of mine was always Hell and not Heaven. But why does Hell seem the lesser of two evils? I can't write about happiness. I just can't bring myself to do it. You gotta write what you know about. Or draw what you see about. So anyway, I don't know about happiness any more. I know about madness, though. Or to phrase it better, madness knows about me. All too much. Hi madness, I say to it. Dear old enemy, I sing to it weeping. I never really thought for a second it would be me who got carted. 'Life, eh?' is what they say. They don't say 'Death, eh?' though, do they? No, they never tell you the side effects. Or maybe it's because you forget what they tell you. But surely isn't that the follow up conversation? It goes Life, Death, then maybe Life again, who knows. And then maybe Death again. They keep on going on about it. These voices that whisper from the window, the window that's not even open, hear these voices going on, three or four at the same interval, all clambering over each other so it becomes a swamp of whispers:

"Life...Death...." and then a shot of panic runs up my arms and my head floats away. The red light in the top corner of the room blinks. It's sending me a message. It's from Simon. Simon says that the world is just energy. Simon says there are people working for the government who are posing as patients. Simon says I'm going crazy. "No Simon," I say to him. "You're going crazy."

There was a study done showing that voices and visions

conjured from 'irreality' emit the same waves and frequencies in the brain that real voices and visions do. Anyway that's what Old Bull said out in the courtyard the other day. Irreality is his favourite goddamn word. He says we're receiving real signals to our brains when we hear those things that we are told are not there. Either that or nothing at all is real. But I like to think that real and unreal are both real rather than a world where nothing is real. In a way, both the true reality, and the strange imaginings, are the exact same thing when perceived by consciousness. So I guess all those times I thought I was a great writer I perhaps was. Yeah, and perhaps I was a good looking woman with a knack of literally anything. Perhaps I was moral and conscientious and all that unbelievable stuff. Perhaps I was sane. I'm not unaware (and neither is Old Bully) about the consequences of this study. The future possibility of emitting signals into your brain to replicate love, and would it really be any different from real love? I mean hey we've got neurological proof it's all the same damn thing, right? That would be terrible would it not? And might it not have happened already? Love in a memory stick. Closing down sale. All stock must go. All soul must go Monday. The apocalypse future of everyone boning robots and popping government tested drugs while all the while no-one could figure out how to save the ecosystem and handle totalitarians with untold wealth and the use of new technology. They say it's paranoia. I'm just daydreaming. I miss you. And it's really not the thing to do to point this out and all, but what's good about going crazy, about being carted - you have something to talk about. It's given me a reason to stick around. I gotta stick around. Because I need to figure out what it all means. I need to figure out what's real and what isn't, before it's too late. Eighteen years I have seen the world but it is only the last year I have seen what the world is not. I have seen gruesome things but even that doesn't compare to the feeling. More maniacal than anything I have ever previously conceived of or experienced. Not being able to know what your own name is, well that is merely a timid manifestation compared to the others. Yet mental function doesn't stop altogether, rather it mutates. There is no way to describe the feeling. Some writers may have tried, and most definitely they did a better job than I ever could. But I know the feeling now. Mix paranoia into dream and you're halfway there. Do I dare ask you to listen to it, as I have? Hear disembodied voices? See ghosts coming out the wall? Believe you are someone else? Believe you are dead? Believe you are born?

No sense of time. No sleep. No respite from fear of thoughts. I can feel my mind, actually decaying. And there's pictures in the skull. You don't understand because I don't. Everything is a conspiracy, my love. For example I saw eyes closed other night dozens of unexplainable orbs of lights which I interpreted as angels. But I realised I was not one of them. I was looking up at them in Hell. Every eureka is a goddamn brain zap. There is pain in the brain. Feels like it's eating itself sometimes. The only thing I can cling on to in some sort of hope, is that it can't get any worse. Right? Should I test fate? My perfect timing? Some force has decided to choose me, to ingratiate me into this world which I don't understand. Why me, though? Why not someone else? And do I really wish it upon even my worst enemy? I've struggled to get these words down (it has taken an hour, I think) but it has been a pretty low part of the episode where I can handle holding a pen and getting it down. But I still feel paranoid and don't trust anyone today. And it's going to come back. The loss of sense. At that point, these words will become meaningless again, merely unknown symbols. The haunting will follow. It goes with the confusion. From this the emaciation and insomnia will occur, which heightens the confusion and therefore the haunting. All this will surely go and then come back like clockwork. As a stopped clock is right twice a day, so I too will have two seconds in the day where I understand just what the hell's going on. But given time, that will be forgotten again. And that's what I am. A stopped clock. A stopped clock that's gone up the wall.

I'm getting this down because who knows when I'll forget how to hold a pen and how long it will be. I think I can even predict when the next episode will come. It's written on my forms. I can see it now: "Maya Maney: Not Fit for Consumption."

Insanity isn't just a word in a library. It's said all the time you forget its original meaning. It's been diluted to hell. And everyone takes their sanity for granted except us. God, if only everybody knew what malicious horror it really is...Worse than Death. Moloch of Mind. Mind sacrificed to Moloch. Destroyer of all Sense and Order and yet worse than Chaos. Moloch of Misery. Moloch of Mind!

Usually most everyday I hear people whispering when no-one else is around. I don't know what to believe. Are they really there or not? Are they trapped in my head? Will they come out through the ears? It's been a common talking point in the ward, the fact there's no common talking point. Can I tell you something that is quite apart from sensible? I have a tail. I have an invisible tail that I feel sometimes when I get up or sit down. It's really strange, and at first I was afraid of it but it's actually one of the few nice things that occurs. And it feels so real and I tried to grab it the other day but it wasn't there. But I feel it. It's there. It's both there and not there. Maybe it's the not sleeping that's doing it. It's been twenty four days so far. I can't close my eyes. Because when I do, I see a face staring back at me right up in my skull. I wish you were here. It was really nice when you came last time, but that was so long ago. I'm not allowed a phone as you know.

These letters are just my way of letting out the demons.
Hoping to see a letter from you. Hoping that you wanna visit
me like you used to, put in the same room next to me, mad and
carted too and we could be neighbours and then it wouldn't
seem so bad.
M Xxxxx

21

It all really began when I ran out of the Halloween party. I didn't know where I was going. But something deep and unsettling was happening within me. I ran for hours. Then when I was too tired to run, I walked. And as quick as anything it became light again and I realised I had been out all night. I slumped down for about an hour in this alleyway in town, and was roused by some passer-by. He handed me a coin.

"I'm not homeless, mister."

"Then why are you sitting out here? So early? Shouldn't you be in bed?" I ignored him, closing my eyes to see snakes. All around me. I leapt from the ground and started to scream. The passer-by ran away.

I sat there for a while, afraid my brain was turning into something new and grotesque. It didn't feel right. I had a strong feeling I was dead. That I was in Hell. I tried walking again. I didn't want to sit down any more because whenever I was still I'd see these strange images in front of me. And so I'd get up and shake myself like a wet dog and carry on walking, because it felt safer to do that. I still had no destination. But I needed to keep moving. The day went by as I walked through town, circling the high street as many times as I could stand. I walked past people and heard their thoughts. They were all thinking about me. I couldn't take it.

I ran again, out of town to a nearby field where there would be hardly anyone. When I got to the grass I fell down in exhaustion. It started to rain. And even the rain had thoughts just like the people did. But I couldn't understand.

Eventually, after two days of no sleep and wandering around the town for reasons unknown and yet definite, I fell at the door of my sister's place. I wasn't intending to go there, but I ended up there somehow. I knocked manically. When she opened the door, she was struck by how run down I looked.

"Maya. What's happened to you? Why are you all ragged?"

"I'm Emily Davidson."

"What happened to you?"

"I don't know. I don't know, Beate. I feel like I'm dead. I feel like I'm in Hell. Have I died and gone to Hell?"

I was taken to a hospital. Just a regular hospital. My sister rang them. She didn't know what else to do. I thought I was God. I looked yellow like a lemon. See, I really want to tell you about what happened to me, and I really want you to understand, but it's hard, because none of it made any sense. And it's been a long time, too. The longer I wait to tell you all this, the more I'm forgetting it. So I have to say it now. Maybe it will help someone. Maybe it won't. I don't really care. I've just got to get it out. It's a demon inside me.

I've been afraid to tell people I meet that I was in Spector Park a while ago. You don't know how people are going to react. Even now, almost a decade later, the memory of it is still somehow tormenting me. In front of my vision, this mad jigsaw puzzle with all the pieces rammed in the wrong way. A story written the wrong way. So I'm untangling this lump of memories to try and make some sense of it, because after all, no-one gets far without sense. Imagine if, like me, you lost your sense. You may have already. But if not, you've possibly never even imagined such a thing. Perhaps you have been so accustomed to your brain acting normally that the thought of going insane hasn't even struck you. Perhaps you think it's like lightning. Unlikely to strike. But it happens. I know it does. It cracks in the sky of the mind. If you ask me, I'd rather be hit by a big old bolt of lightning than go topsy turvy again. Over the years still it haunts me. Because it wasn't just the insanity. It was Somnus too. It was everything. I remember having that first sensation of losing my mind. It's like your brain splits and everything seeps out... Your thoughts linger through the air like wind. A cloud of paranoia encircles you wherever you go. You can't escape it. Not with sleep anyway.

Leo was my rock through it all, until the rock stopped showing up. I would write him letters, every fortnight, but eventually he stopped replying. And then there was no word from him. Everybody has a poison heart.

I was pessimistic about finding love. But I was still on the lookout. To try and forget about him once and for all. There were many people at Spector Park Mental Hospital. But everyone was ugly. Beautifully ugly. The thirty year olds looked like forty year olds, the twenty year olds looked like thirty year olds. Everyone had sad sunken eyes, staring desperately into the abyss. It was all the meds they stuffed you with.

I wanted to meet someone. But at the same time I was content with being alone, because my alone time was and still is very important to me.

One day, a while after Wickman stopped visiting, I saw a new arrival coming in. He wasn't a struggler. By that I mean he didn't resist, didn't complain. He just walked in coolly. But there was something about him that made me think he was sad and sunk-eyed like everyone else.

He stayed in room seventeen (next to mine) and he was always silent and eating on his own at lunch. He wasn't ugly like all of us. But maybe that was just because he was new.

At the time I was too busy entrapped in a mental game of horror and psychedelic monstrosity beyond any Hunter Thompson novel. And beyond which can even be explained in words.

I was too scared to talk to anybody when I showed up. I wanted to die, and I'd die happy, I thought, because I could then have peace. But I couldn't figure out a way to do it. This depressed me even more. Didn't talk to nobody, not even Old Bull. But when this new guy arrived, I wanted to talk to him. He never smiled. I liked that in a strange way, as if the smiles were saved for when they really mattered. He had eyes like there were vampires inside them and skin so pale he might as well have been one. I thought about sending him a letter, because I was too nervous to confront him. He was very tall with deep pits under his eyes and a look like 'hell it's all going to shit but what you gonna do?' except without smiling. It was strange. He carried many books around as well, held nervously in twitching hands. They were always twitching. Like mine did. When I noticed him, looked closely and all, I saw feeling not so much in his appearance but his absence, the way he drifted without an end, a lone ranger in the same damn jungle, absent in it, called in sick, and apart from reading, which he did often, there was absence in his eyes, the eyes that were so deep when I first saw them, which was odd in of itself because he never used them - if you get what I mean - well reading yes he used them perhaps to the point of insanity, but never wanting to take the glance and make eye contact with me or anyone else. And noticing how often I'd stare at him, secretly, clandestinely, from across the lunch room, and so much so that when sleeping at night (in fact not sleeping) I would see and imagine his face with eyes closed and so much I did this that I remembered his outline and all the details of his face. Sometimes it replaced the creeping face. I was trying to catch his eyes in the lurid light of the lunchroom, in the activity room, in the communal area, and always falling short. Noticing the continual books he had - his eyes jumping along with the text with willing animation as he walked like a ghost across the ward with a copy of Plath, and well one time he was reading *One Flew Over The Cuckoo's Nest* and actually thought the book had flown away up the corridor and so began to chase it, not knowing it was in his hand. I was watching him wherever he went, seeing the page turns, the low cough made at intervals, the scratching of the nose, seeing the curves in his eyebrows. I was really getting obsessed. But he was a madman. I didn't know in fact the truth of anything about what he was, who he was. But knowing who Wickman was never helped me. Still, there were times when I felt like he really could be the one, Leo. He was so sweet in the beginning. But it all turned to nothing.

Anxiously, I got up from my bed and picked up a stack of letters that I kept bound with a purple elastic band. I picked one up and read one of them. Just thinking about him made me angry. I crumpled the letter and put it in my mouth and chewed it all to hell until it was nothing. It was time to focus on other things. Like how I was finally allowed outside. I remember wanting to go outside for months and they wouldn't let me. It was because I was considered a 'bad' case. I bit on occasion. Sometimes I was taken to Confinement for that. Patients who were taken to Confinement were considered too rowdy to coexist with other patients. You were taken to an en-suite room which was locked from the outside. The regular rooms were not locked, so you could wander around, though usually there was someone waiting by your door to drag you back. Confinement for acute inpatients was apparently to curb violence. But I wasn't evil or anything, it was the illness confusing me. I didn't want to bite anybody. It was someone else taking my place. A cheap get-out you might say. But utterly true.

The only time they let me out was for going to the courtyard to smoke a cigarette, which I didn't do often. I could see glimpses from windows, seeing the outside world as if it were an ultra high definition painting on a glowing canvas, thinking 'if I go out there I'll finally be free and smell the flowers and hell maybe try and leg it, I mean they're operating on us aren't they? They got us under control here, so to hell with them too!'

When I got outside for the first time my legs ached, the late May light shot my eyes. The nurse who was watching me waved to another nurse. I looked around, thinking what would happen if I just ran away. But I quickly became distracted. Weirdly and gloriously distracted. I could see in full 360 vision. I was feeling confounded and queer like my head would just float away or something, and the light so bright it made my eyes weep from the door walking out to the outside steps and seeing fantastic displays of trees, each phantasmal fern signalling a note in the orchestra of nature all around me. Round the back of my head I could see them all. It was so bizarre, and I walked as slow as a sloth in-taking all this mad amount of vision and it bending from the intensity, the gravity of it. I curved round the entrance in a perfect circle with my watcher, the vision weighing down my eyes with light like thunderbolts and causing everything to bend round the back of my head into 360 (perhaps 320, more than usual in any case), though calm head from air hitting the face and freedom in a sense. I walked as slow as I could to savour the moment and the Sun and its angels shone down on me if only for a moment, because alas I was made to go back inside after, and feeling it phoney and not genuine freedom at all.

I returned to normal 180 and was ushered back in from that vision of trees, and in a faraway jukebox in my mind they called my name. I neared the desk as I slinked past the queue, sweaty from the Sun, and saw a man rubbing the wall with his hands. In one of the rooms nearby a woman yelling, something about murder. There was an eerie sense of panic in the ward. So nothing unusual. The man touching the wall lets out a groan and says: "The Masters do a fine job of dragging me out from bed. Drugs! Get yah drugs, here!"

I walked into the dispensary room and saw a huge stock of meds on one side, bending like the outside view bended, so much that I could read the fine print on all the bottles. To the other side was a sink with a dripping faucet, which dripped in the most delightful way, and not at all like you'd think it would be in Chinese water torture. There were two doctors inside sitting down reading notes, giving each other a perfunctory nod, mumbling to each other about various things I couldn't fathom. Lots of things ending in zam. The female doctor looked Chinese. Well, maybe Chinese water torture after all. I looked down at the cup she gave me, not knowing what was going on. I then looked up at her. She smiled. "You take these, yes?"

I put them in my mouth like a helpful guinea pig. But I wasn't going to swallow. When you're in a real cosmic confusion you might not understand why they're giving you pills. You might make up your own explanations. And in fact I did, as she leaned closer to check I had swallowed them. I spat them out in her face. They would have ricocheted off her face but for the fact that saliva had congealed on to the pills. I was glad, because I thought I had resisted a horrible disease by spitting them out. See, it seemed true (as many other things past and future would seem true under derangement of the senses) that the pills contained AIDS. Why? To poison me. Simple as that. This wasn't mere paranoia, or a hunch, it was complete belief. The final evolution of paranoia. And what the hell makes the brain do that? Or is it the brain even? Is it something else? This whole AIDS conspiracy may have happened because I saw a newspaper somewhere earlier that had the words 'doctor' and 'aid' on the front page headline. With hindsight, I was half starting to understand it. You see what you imagine, and fear heightens it. They weren't full of AIDS. No, now they made your hands disappear.

Daily struggle to tell the nurses this, with import, with anger (and by now you really must know I am telling the truth, and leaving no stone unturned). There was a certain level of understanding because I went through phases, waves, coming in and out of chaos, like how the sea washes up on the shore and falls back in. My mind gets clearer and I debunk all the crazy things that have 'happened', telling the doctors that 'I really am better now honest and would you please let me go I don't belong here,' only to be hit by a new episode and a hundred more delusions. And these delusions all link together in one vast and frightening web. The malfunctioning mind finds myriad ways to connect everything, usually in sinister ways it's connected. But everything connected. The newspaper headline. Me being there to see it. The medication. Even the journalist who wrote the piece. It was all connected. Later, connections would be made so fiercely I would become literally entangled within them, and my brain and its receptors would remould into a new structure, something which would change me forever. Anyway, those words on the newspaper left in the communal room were enough, enough for me to really believe these doctors were trying to poison me. I remember I began crying and tried to run out but either got restrained by the male doctor or just bumped into the wall and fell down. Everything was sideways, I remember that much. The woman put her hand on my shoulder and whispered: "It's okay, yes? Don't spit them out this time."

I took the yellow and pink bastards and left, and saw again the man rubbing the wall and another woman who was levitating.

At first I pretended to take the pills. But eventually, I just gave it up. They crushed my will. I succumbed. Three four times a day I succumbed. I would have to deal with whatever they wanted to do with me, and my soul be condemned if I didn't take their pills. While I didn't know it at the time, Somnus also had psychosis. The new arrival. He was given pills just like me and spat them out just like me. I named him Somnus unbeknownst to him himself as it was just a little joke and all, for me and me alone. It was because I heard him scream in bed one night, he was in the room next to me: "The dream! The dream!" And it happened again another night a few days later, again saying 'the dream!' (this being the only thing I'd ever heard him say) and sounding possessed in the voice, and well Somnus is the Roman god of sleep, and it was on my mind that day I decided to name him, again clandestinely, because I was reading it in a poem in a book left in the activity room, where strange pieces of art by the patients were hung up.

It goes:

The God called Somnus
Is the God of Dreams
A shriek in the night for all the Visions seen
He can drag you by the hand
To another planet's land
The song that's sung in sleep
Is but Somnus and the band

And though I thought I was reading it in some poetry book, I realised it was my own notebook. I had just written it down and had already forgotten that I had done so.

I 'knew' about Somnus, or Hypnos as it's sometimes called, because I was interested in Greek Mythology. I imagined deeply this God who had a thousand sons, called the 'Somnia', who appeared in people's dreams during times of great importance. Apparently, they travel the dream world, entering and hiding in people's dreams. Sending messages. At the time I made a connection in my mind between the Somnia and what I was going through, and that perhaps within this mythology the truth had been hiding all along. That dreams, and therefore hallucinations, are the work of sentient forces.

And so, for a goof, I named the new arrival Somnus (in lieu of knowing his real name or in fact anything about him other than his appearance, mannerisms, outline of the face) after hearing as I said 'the dream!' from the wall of his room and I remembered the poem and that was that. But it was mystery. What was the 'dream'? What was the need to wail in the middle of the night? Well, of that I understood. But was he 24 - 7, did he ever sleep? Did he dream, without sleeping?

22

The morning after the first release into the open outdoors – 'schizo alfresco' as I'd written in my diary, next to the poem about the dream god – I was told I had a meeting with Dr. Malik. Dr. Malik was a psychiatrist. He was going to tear me to shreds. Tear me to shreds and force me to self-immolate to top it off. He had a strange grin. A grin so sour it made me want to end it all there.

"Hello, Ms. Maney," he says as he leads me into his room. "Nice to meet you." When we sit down my tail wags. "Have you been hearing any voices today?"

"No."

After a long pause, which seemed to last twenty minutes, he says:

"Are you, quite sure?"

"Well, no. I'm not really."

"...Not really what, dear?"

"Well, you just said 'are you quite sure?'"

"I'm sorry. I didn't say anything. Do you know how long you've been here, Ms. Maney?"

"No idea. A thousand years?" I was getting sick of him calling me Ms. Maney. Maney was my father's surname. And I hated him. The dead bastard.

"You came six months ago from Wexham General Hospital. You were running around at five in the morning and scaring the patients. Do you remember?"

"No." (I did.)

"You were a real handful for them. Now that you're here, your... progress... well, let's just say things could be worse."

"How on Earth could they be worse?"

"But let's not focus on all that," he says, grinning weirdly. "It's nearly June now. How have you been getting on d'you think?"

"I want to be out of here. That's how I've been getting on."

"When you get better, then we can do that, Ms. Maney. But you're not quite there yet. So, have you heard anything? You need to tell me what's going on with you. I can't help if you won't open up."

And falling prey to that strange sour grin he had, he had me opened up alright. There were yellow horns beginning to crown on his head, coming up out his skull. I tried to ignore it.

"Well, I have heard people talking when there wasn't anyone there. In my room just me and all. As if, it's like some narrator in my head. But I thought it might be that theory where someone says something in say Glasgow and the words travel through the wind and carry it all the way to London. You know, like they're real voices but they've just been from somewhere else. Sometime else." He gave me a look of uncomprehending concern. And the horns, well they disappeared. But then they came back. Like a television tuning in and out of static. "And you've got horns."

"Are you, quite sure?"

"Ahhah! You said it that time! Don't tell me you didn't! And no. I'm not sure a goddamn bit! Why are we here?"

"We're help to help you, Ms. Maney."

"But why am I here?"

"To be helped." His horns grew sharp at the end and I could see his shadow on the wall moving independently from him.

"Well, if you could help me then?"

"Of course."

"Could you not call me Ms. Maney?"

After the meeting, which lasted around twenty three minutes, the chair now definitely reeked of my sweat and no doubt caused an impervious groove to form. It's what happens when people have meetings with me for twenty eight minutes, I get horrible ass-sweat and I sit there in the chair full of anxiety sweating everywhere and nonplussed about it all at the same time if you could imagine such a thing. It didn't matter what the psychiatrist had to say. Nothing made any sense anyway and I still hadn't had confirmation if what was happening was reality or whether it was just in my mind. Was it the Somnia, infecting my dreams? Was I even in Spector Park? Perhaps they sent me to Broadmoor instead, and I was wearing a straight jacket in a marshmallow room imagining everything. Could it really have got that bad? There was no way to know. You give up knowing things when you come across psychosis. If I talked to someone, they might simply have not existed but in my mind as a hallucination. To this day I am still unsure if the people I met were even real, but at the time I was certain they were.

And why did they insist on asking me endless questions about what I understood and what I knew to be true? What my name was. How old I was. The street I lived in growing up. What was the point. And well Old Bull (the old man I met out on the courtyard smoking, as I used to do myself quite a lot when I first arrived at the ward) might not have even been real either. He looked the spitting image of William Burroughs to me and so I named him Old Bull, and I wondered with mystical import if he was real, really real, because he looked so much like the real William Burroughs who was dead and I couldn't believe it, and was surprised to hear him come up to me and say in an English accent that his name was Thom. I had a feeling it really was Burroughs, that he was just lying to me. And because I knew William Burroughs had died long ago, it struck me that he might not be real. And that's when the paranoia grew to untold levels. How, for that matter, to tell if any of them were real. Was Som real? Was Dr. Malik? Was I? Was the man who always seemed to be disappearing at whim real either? The one who looked like Allen Ginsberg (again to a t) wearing a long white robe and appearing inside windows? (Yes, not outside of the window, inside it. Inside the glass. That's how he kept getting away.)

Surely if I took the position that the yellow horned Dr. Malik wasn't real, wasn't there, then surely wouldn't I have to take the position that they all weren't there? Or just some? And how to tell them apart? They look the same, the voices hit the brain the same. And that day of the meeting being a wild hot noon, I wracked my brain, mulling it to shit, ruminating on the mind I watched fall away in front of my eyes. Sad, mad and sunken.

23

The night was even worse. No sleep again. Heard voices from the window again, the window that's closed. I looked yet again at the iron bars covering the window from the outside, and wondered if I could melt them.

"*Life...Death...*" That was the voices seeping through. Maybe they just weren't double-glazed windows. Maybe it was a Scottish man talking the day before. Through the wind and all.

The tail wagged uncontrollably throughout the night. I felt something was going to finally destroy me beyond repair. I just wasn't sure what. They got in some nurse to calm me down. And she, a tall Zimbabwean called AJ, sat next to me and held my hand but she didn't have a head. She had a red balloon.

As she talked I could hear it squeaking. Her face was drooped over the balloon. She made no comment about it. Couldn't be bothered to tell me where the head went. Maybe I was next?

It floated from a string coming out the top of her smock. Then out of nowhere she grabs my arm and gives me a Chinese burn. I recoiled and looked at my arm. Right where the Chinese burn was, a ? appeared.

"Breathe, Maya. Breathe with me." And I held her hand and did what she told me. And pop went her head. The loud bang filled my ears and I turned around and there was no head or balloon or anything on her body. Just empty space. But I could still hear her talking to me.

The morning after, having slept not one minute, I walked over to the 'kitchen' that was built into the communal area, where you could make yourself tea or coffee (they gave most of us that luxury) and well that place always brought to my mind this fella called Bruno who I met in the kitchen when I first arrived in December. He was sorta the rule breaker to the self-serving of hot drinks gimmick. I remember he wore a black tracksuit and a big silver chain around his neck. He was black, he was young, his head was all shaved. He had this mad shake thing going on with his whole body, and walking over to make myself a cup of tea (didn't need coffee, was already charged from horror despite being sleep deprived) and seeing the mugs not made of china but some sort of plastic, pink plastic, no sharp things anyway and well this guy was talking to himself, but what was stranger was that it was going three times the speed of a normal dialect. He was physically charged and you could see and hear it. Spilling coffee grains all over the floor while he yammered on, pouring boiling water over five mugs spread out all over the counter in one fell swoop like a skilled waiter would except not skilled at all – water covering the counter and coffee grains too, a whole mess and this guy was jumping up and down the walls spewing mad collages of nonsense and paranoia, I mean he looked like he was going a different time than the rest of us. He saw me and his chain sparkled in the light. "Yo, I'm Bruno. You new here?"
   "Maya. Yeah."

"Can I give ya some advice, Maya?" He picks up the mug and it's shaking like there was a damn earthquake or something coming and the ripples in the coffee proof of the matter.

"Sure..."

"Keep quiet in your room."

"What? Why?"

"There's bugs in the walls. In the skirting. They've got us on lock-down. Just keep quiet."

"Who's got us on what lock-down?" His hand was shaking so much the mug was getting hotter. Guess it's a good trick and all, for the winter months.

"I'm not supposed to say," he says, putting ten spoons of sugar in the spilt cup. "But I'm gonna dash out of here. Go ask Thom. That guy's got some sense." And off he ran holding three mugs in his lap.

I never saw Bruno again. Maybe his paranoia had driven him to find a way out. He filled me with a new horror going on about the bugs in the skirting. But it was good sense for him to recommend seeing Thom or 'Old Bull' to study the theory more. He was perhaps the smartest and most sympathetic of the old lot who smoked outside and hung out in the courtyard with all the other manics, like a beer garden you'd imagine but obviously no booze anywhere and hell no-one needed it because the meds made you fuzzy all day. Still, they managed to sneak in booze. Old Bull was an intelligent cookie. In any case, a radical cookie. I remember when some concerned patient was worried his cigarettes would kill him, he replied: "Smoking saved Bertrand Russell's life. Why wouldn't it save mine?" He'd be there doing his duty in the courtyard talking of which conspiracies in the ward were real and which weren't, that unsurprisingly lead to a savage debate which no-one could say a final word on. But he was eloquent about it. When I asked him whether they really did have bugs in the skirting, he said: "Don't know if it's true or not. But why risk it? Might as well be quiet. Think of Winston Smith."

"But why are they doing it?"

"I didn't say they were, Maya. But if they are, the hypothetical sons of bitches, it's just another form of control now ain't it, just like how they keep us here. They'd have us buried alive if they could. In fact. Some days they do."

I was still unsure if it was true. It could have been a joke, a dark joke. But that didn't stop me being as silent as I could in my room. I even hesitated coughing, for fear that devils were listening to the recordings.

Though I had friends here, like Old Bull and Rudie, I wasn't interacting that much with anyone. I just watched it all happen. The nightmares spilling out of your head and all. Half the people I didn't know, but I saw them everyday and recognised them all. They appeared in many of the delusions. Waking nightmare is best way to describe it.

Perhaps, I thought to myself, as I were a detective on a case, there were people at Spector Park who were actually fine and didn't need to be carted. But then again who did need to be, if in fact man needed to be carted at all? Maybe Somnus was fine. Maybe he was doubted. Maybe Old Bull was doubted. Maybe I was doubted. Hell, and which is worse, unlawfully trapped and doubted by everyone? Or simply crazy? And perhaps there were people here who were actually fine but they just lingered around because it was shelter and food. But really, who'd think to up-sticks here?

And so the mystery of this, alongside all the other mysteries, beamed a hidden light that was just beyond my sight.

24

Sometimes I ate cigarettes. I don't know why. When smoking them, I had cut down to one cigarette a week. But sometimes I ate it. One time, I swallowed one and then heard tiny voices inside my belly. Everyone was yelling as in a disaster, but they were so small you couldn't see them. But they were there. In the cigarette. Old Bull was the one who gave them to me, as there was no way of getting them from the mystical 'outside'. He gave me a lighter too, which I wasn't supposed to have I don't think. You were supposed to put your cigarette in the machine on the wall out in the courtyard where it lit it for you, but Bull didn't. Anyway, I hadn't got any more addicted than one cigarette a week. But sometimes two or three because I ate them. And well, it was for some unknown reason. The first time, my stomach turned nasty and I felt to vomit. I was trying to figure out what made me eat it and I wasn't understanding. I curled up in a ball in my empty room on the hard floor and rocked back and forth holding my belly hearing screams from the little people trapped there and wishing for at least one thing to make sense in this place. I realise only now it was because I didn't want to burn them. I wandered around the corridors holding my stomach hearing the tiny screams, and there were hundreds of ghosts all hovering around the ward. Perhaps a thousand. And they were all crying.

I wondered to myself how lucky I was to be crazy in

this decade, and not sixty years ago. There was no electroconvulsive therapy, or mallets. But the drugs they gave you. The mind-numbingness. Well that was just as bad. And yet, numbness couldn't numb my visions. It only numbed me. My time in Spector Park was the strangest experience of my life. Yet I was only one.

What outsiders may think is that there's blood and shit on the walls but it wasn't like that in the place I went to. People are just loopy. And with that loopiness anyone can imagine anything. Even the blood and shit. I remember one time *Trainspotting* was playing in my head like VR for some reason, and I fell into the worst toilet in Scotland.

But insofar as reality was concerned it was clean and everyone was wearing their own clothes (though that made it strange somehow) and no straight-jackets in sight (still that wasn't proof there weren't some being worn) and well quiet yes but only in certain wards. The ward I was taken to first (after the insane month spent in the general hospital) was significantly more rowdy and dangerous and loud than the one I was taken to after that. I remember I was paranoid of everyone. Nevermind the ghosts. And there were terrifying shadows on the walls and Godzilla was climbing out of the communal TV screen every night. And I remember grimly those horrible times my thoughts were on loudspeaker all over the ward.

People ran around all the time as if they were each escaping from a demon under their beds. Like a bomb had gone off at Heathrow or something and everyone was running around, just like the little people in the cigarette, not intending to go anywhere but just running from their own foreheads. God, how afraid I was in that first ward. And early on in the illness too, which made it harder to have any foresight or smarts about it. It was hell in Thorn Ward because all the degenerates were stuffed there and there alone, and why that place was so gruesome. Perhaps degenerates is a strong word. Megalomaniacs, then.

   Dewdrop Ward was where I was taken to after, and where I stayed until the end. It was nicknamed 'Dumbdrop Ward' among Old Bull because he said everyone here had a floating head. No anger. The anger was drugged out of you. The place meanwhile was made to look like it was some sort of benign bubble. It was ungodly clean and clinical, there were uncomfortably comfortable bright blue chairs everywhere, violet walls, pink cutlery for the tea. Even the pills looked like some hopeful kid had imagined them. Meanwhile Thorn Ward had white walls and daily graffiti. In any case, it certainly didn't hold up that Dewdrop was an evil place on the surface. Most were charmed by it, a few resisted it for fear of something deeper and darker underneath that calming surface. I remember Old Bull said to me he saw the devil in those bright blue chairs.

*

It was one cold January evening when Bull invited me to play rummy with him and his friends. I was hesitant at first, I didn't know how to play, but he said he'd teach me, and I left more confused on the matter than when I started. But it was a nice gesture and all. And no blame on his part when I started eating (like the cigarettes) a pack of cards that he gave me.

   I had got into the idea that if I wrote words on the cards and ate them, that the word would manifest, like a wish. I wrote 'escape' and 'love' and 'reason' on some cards hoping for all three. But nothing happened and I only felt sick, and sore too that I'd eaten Old Bull's gift.

"Off with the fairies. The sad and rheumy eyed lot. Dumbdrop Ward." He had a point. Everyone walked around all spacey. Whereas in Thorn Ward everyone ran up and down the walls.

"They've taken the lot but they won't take me," he says. "All's what happens to me is I see visions in my brain" – points his finger against his temple – "with eyes closed, of horrible things. It's not my fault. But I get angry or panicked and they grab the butterfly nets thinking I'm after them. Me! After them!"

I began to realise after becoming acquainted with Old Bull that there was more going on that I first thought. I was trying to figure out what it meant when the balloon-headed nurse gave me a Chinese burn and a question mark appeared on my arm; what it meant when my sister Beate visited and I thought the hospital had killed the real Beate and replaced her with a clone; what it meant when the floor turned into water and I had to swim through the hospital (I remember just before that wet hallucination I had been trapped inside a painting for many months); what it meant when I saw that door people disappeared into and never came back from; what it meant when those strange alien spirits arrived to meet me in the night; what any of it meant. I didn't exactly see it all with my eyes. Yet I know that I encountered it. There's just too much to explain. You should see my old diaries. I believed in at least ten different grandiose delusions every single day. I hadn't slept properly for almost a year. My thoughts were spilling out into the world again. The sons of Hypnos felt near. Daydreaming things that didn't make sense.

And that's what it felt like, like being in a dream. And never, never being able to wake up.

These hallucinations, deaths, delusions, nightmares, rebirths, visions and sicknesses congregated in my mind as one fantastic conspiracy, and I wanted to know what was going on but things were so complicated. I sought answers from the psychosis. But though it showed me things, it was incapable of explaining to me what it meant. It could have been thirteen years. It could have been an hour. No way to tell. No way to differentiate between imagination and reality any more. Had to at least try.

But the tail wagged and defied all reason. The night of a thousand ghosts defied all reason.

There was also this need to find patterns in things. The way people walked, the direction their eyes made, the movement of their hands. It was all a secret code so people could communicate without saying anything. Paranoia strengthened this need to find the patterns. My brain saw everyone tilting their heads or scratching their hands or looking left as a secret code to be unlocked. What was everyone really saying when they blinked or scratched their nose? They were plotting against me.

Paranoia is everywhere, basically. But you can also become different beings. I still remember the time I became a mouse. I reincarnated into twenty different forms. Basically every time I died, I came back as a slightly stronger slightly smarter mouse. Each death from the mad doctor I got wiser and wiser, thus being able to get smart about it all and escape him, not knowing that it was just a hallucination. Before I escaped, he whispered to me strangely that he was going to 'enjoy killing this one'. He picked me up by the tail and looked at me with his huge face. He had a big machete and was slicing off the other mice's tails. I heard faint high-pitched screams and saw blood spattered everywhere and the huge sound of the machetes falling down onto the floor where I had, now at the third reincarnation, escaped to the floor, but he quickly found me and sliced off my head. Then I returned to the incubator – which was just my bed – where the next rebirth would leave me wiser, through to the fifth reincarnation, then sixth, seventh, all the way to about twenty rebirths. And then becoming so enlightened and familiar with the room that I could get off my back, move off the table, get to the floor and escape. When I finally got out of there, I had already transformed back into myself and the day went on as usual. No need to tell anyone. No-one believes you anyway. And I know it sounds like nonsense but I'm telling you I heard those machetes, I heard screams. I felt the mouse body. The machete's unnatural selection carving the perfect creature. One who could get away. I wrote in my diary that day:

I have to be careful what I think. A thought could kill a woman.

Most of the time I was not myself. I was other people, other things. And I don't mean to be all dramatic and phoney because I really do hate that crap, but I was always near something worse than death.

Being wheeled around the general hospital in one instance I remember now... I believed people were about to operate on my brain. This was early on in the sickness. I remember that ugly hospital gown and how I looked anaemic when I looked in the mirror. I was taken on a stretcher which felt and looked like angels carrying me, then I got in this thing. I was aware everyone was watching me from afar. They put my head into this strange machine. My mind ran, trying to figure out what it was. Or that strange night when I had just been born, as a baby, from myself. It was the night after I threw a mug at Beate's head because I thought she was an imposter (and luckily I missed). She wasn't really an imposter, and the machine was just an MRI. But I didn't know that. I thought here's the fabled lobotomy. Conducted by strange white ghosts looking on over me. And as if it could get any less plausible to you (doesn't mean it didn't happen, and it's the truth even if it didn't happen) I realised I could freeze time all the way back then, and I did whatever it was that I did and then time stopped. Everyone stopped moving. But me. Silence, dust particles frozen in the air. I'm not saying it really happened but like a vivid dream, I felt it just the same. I stood up from the stretcher and walked about with everything still and silent. The nurses were like ivory statues and the whole place was just still as anything... and then unfreezing it (again without knowing how) and the wail of noise coming back, the nurses melting back to animation while finding myself thinking I was about to be raped by some policemen that had all sat down in one room talking to each other and laughing (and by now you must really know that a butterfly could set me off on paranoid waves).

But to add a bit of joy to this whole thing, (I must remind myself to do that) throughout the thousand horrible states, there were a couple states that were glorious. Like the tail. There was nothing sinister in the tail. Or when I became the form of a single sensation, that too was nothing sinister, it was something akin to being a simple cell of the body. No eyes, no head. No mind. No sense of who I was. But a peaceful hallucination. Just a feeling of tension and relaxation. Contracting, being a sensation. I lost my ego and sight you see, and so I was not afraid. Then after a while the world came back and I gave birth to myself and all hell had returned.

While I'm remembering – I can't leave this out – I recall those numinous creatures that mad Christmas night of tears and visions (creatures who'd I later name the Alphazites); the three-eyed aliens who spoke like whale-call and healed my aching head by pressing long claw-like fingers upon it, knowing that they were kind after I was left unharmed and even feeling much more sane and together after they left. Noticing them crawling out of the empty space in silence for the first time. It was in Bay 13 in the general hospital. I was wearing the ugly gown and saw the strangely fluttering blue curtain set around me, whereupon they appeared. They always arrived to meet me in silence. Their whale-call was not exactly sound but something I could definitely sense. And the same with seeing them. Not exactly vision but something I could see. Tall and thin bodies, big craniums, three terrifying eyes.

25

I had forgotten what sleep was. I envied everyone who rested soundly in their beds. Well, I guess that just meant I had more time to figure out what was going on. But I couldn't stand the insomnia. I mean, who can stand eternity? And, as if a miracle had been bestowed upon me, I found a way to finally conk out.

It all happened when I started panicking in my bed one night. I was screaming and wringing my hands underneath the sheets and sweat was pouring out the top of my head. I was stuck in a bad trip feeling, a kind of trapped, seemingly unending feeling. I screamed so loud they took me to an Observation room where they could watch me go nuts. There was a table with a bowl of cereal placed on it and they asked me to sit down and eat. But I was afraid they were trying to poison me again, so I chucked it on the floor. I heard them talking from the viewing room as if my hearing was heightened.

"She's showing signs of intense paranoia, panic disorder, severe anxiety, severe confusion, hallucinations. Apparently she is hearing whispers in her room, and seeing many things. Orbs of light she says. Aliens. Ghosts. And a face staring at her when she closes her eyes."

"We might need to raise her dose on risperidone, olanzapine and haloperidol. Tell me more about her physical diagnosis."

"Her temperature is extremely high. Blood pressure's up. Heart rate is sporadic. She's underfed and won't take food. She's very pale as you can see. Eyes are twitching a lot. She's sweating. A lot. The bed is soaked some nights. And no sleep."

"Again? How many days has it been now?"

"Well, according to these notes she had a good rest about five weeks ago, since then I'd estimate half an hour a week, not enough at all. She currently believes the doctors around the ward are really a group of self aware robots that are going to kill her, but I'd imagine soon she'll be over that and onto something new."

"How to pre-empt this is key. We don't want her to be a problem."

"Sometimes she crawls on the floor. I don't know why but it's very strange, for instance one morning she crawled around on the floor and screamed 'I'm drowning'. When a doctor came to get her up she bit him on the arm. It's not quite aggression, I think it's more a desperation."

"Has she gone AWOL since then?"

"No. She seems too afraid."

"Any progress? Anything positive?"

"Drawing seems to calm her down, though that being said even that seems to be a problem. She handed reception a piece of paper yesterday, and she had drawn a spiral on it and she said - 'Can you take this away? I'm falling into it.' So. We'll see how she's doing tomorrow, you never know with these things. Just have to hope she gets better. She's only eighteen. It's very sad."

"It is. I feel awful with one night of bad sleep. I can't imagine what it's like." Then, they abruptly stopped talking and I heard the door go. They came in and led me into another room. I didn't know what room it was. I saw in front of me a dancing ballerina. As she spun, the room also did. I turned around and saw the doctors had gone. The door had gone, too. I turned again and felt dizzy and looked at the dancing ballerina and her eyes turned red. "Missing sleep, are we? Or are we asleep right now?"

"Who are you?"

"I am you."

"No. I'm me. At least for now I am. How do you know about the sleep?"

"Because I live in you, Maya."

"What?"

"C'mon. Dance with me." Her red eyes were getting strange to look at now. But I decided to ignore it, like I ignored everything else. I took her waiting hand and spun around with her as the room spun around too and there was no mortal way to know of north or south or up or down or left or right any more. After an endless time, the ballerina stops me and says:

"I have something that will help you sleep."

"Well, that would be ideal, bu-"

"It's a ring."

"A ring?"

"Yes. But before I can give it to you, first you must do something. You must encounter Icelos."

"I feel like I've heard of that before. Wanna catch me up?"

"Icelos can change into animals of all kinds, strange images and demonic shapes. It could be any beast you encounter."

"Such as you?"

"No. I am Morpheus."

"Wait, I feel like I've heard that before too. Was it something I read? Can I ask, Morpheus. Why the ballerina get up?"

"I get bored morphing into the same old humans. Sometimes you have to change it up. Don't you feel like that sometimes?"

"Okay. But why the red eyes?"

"Why white eyes?"

"You got me. So what do I gotta do, Morpheus?"

"There are precious rings inside the belly of Icelos. With diamonds, sapphires, rubies. But one in particular, a simple bronze one, beholds the wearer of the ring the ability to fall asleep immediately with no exceptions. It comes from his father. Well, our father. He is the god of Dreams."

"Mad. So, this beast is your brother?"

"Yes. Though, with my human existence I perhaps am the beast."

"What do you want me to do?"

"I want you to gut Icelos, and find the ring. That is my gift to you, Maya."

"Gift? You want me to kill your brother? That's your gift?"

"No. No. It will not actually be him. Only a figment of your subconscious. But it will seem as though it were real. No exceptions."

"So could it kill me and then I'd be dead?"

"It will only feel that way." I took the hand of Morpheus, and she spun me around till our legs were hovering off the ground. It was like entering hyperspace or something, 'cause the next thing I see is the planet Jupiter right in front of me as if I were floating in space. It was so clear. I looked down and noticed I was on an icy ground. Everything was ice. I figured it must have been one of the moons of Jupiter. That's where I was. What had that damn ballerina done to me? And then it didn't get better. In the distance, a howl shot out. I looked over in horror. It was a polar bear, except it had giant white claws. Like scorpion claws but pure white, white as the polar bear and white as the icy ground. It used its claws to glide over the ice, leaning on them. I looked in amazement. Then it saw me, shot out a long black tongue and started howling again. I turned my back to it, saw nothing but ice below me and space beyond me, and Jupiter looking on.

"What do I do? I haven't got anything." And then, like a gift from God itself, as my arms were outstretched looking for an answer, a large icicle fell into my hand. It was very sharp on one end. I put it into my stronger hand and ran toward the beast, while it roared and slid

to me on its claws. We were approaching one another. I
then got a big hit of fear. It was so insane, this creature.
And there were precious rings inside its belly. What did
it mean?

We were so close to each other now that time
stretched and slowed down. It struck out its right claw
and grabbed me. I felt my torso being sliced open. It
held me up and looked at me with its polar bear eyes, its
jaws open ready to eat me. I readied the twelve inch
icicle in my right hand, felt the cold emanating from it
and so real it felt it scared me, and stabbed it in the eye,
far so that it would enter its brain. I realised I was only
meant to gut it, but it had been done now. It struggled
for a while and then it fell motionless on the ground. I
was free. I took the icicle from its head and stabbed
along its belly, and guts came pouring out. Lights shone
in the muck. Sure enough the rings were there. My first
reaction was to take everything, but I realised it was all
mostly worthless to me in my current situation. I was
trapped in Spector Park, right? Maybe Spector Park was
on Europa. God knows how Morpheus sent me here.
And was there a return ticket?

I picked up the bronze ring and wiped some guts off it
using my skirt, and looked at it, twirling it between my
thumb and forefinger. It had something that looked like
Sanskrit etched on it. And then the hyperspace feeling
again, and the ballerina was in front of me again. It
seemed as if she was shrinking. I rubbed my eyes and
then even smaller she appeared. Smaller and smaller
until only the size of a beetle, and beyond, into nothing.

I turned around and left the room and went through
to the next room and found myself walking through
door after door. It felt like seventy two doors. The world
was spinning again. As if we were all in some giant

bubble floating through space, going through door after endless door, as if I was still dancing with Morpheus. I fell into doors, down them, up them. I ran up the walls.

Eventually I got to my room after being escorted back because I went into a staff-only area without even being aware that I was there. When they left me I put the ring on. And after months upon months, I fell asleep long enough for it to be considered a full night's sleep. Yet it was a peculiar sleep. My finger began to tingle and vibrate after I put the ring on. Then I noticed being pulled into a somnolence, feeling dizzy again like I would finally nod off and then not only my fingers vibrating but now my arms and legs too, my hands vibrating my toes vibrating my eyelashes vibrating my vagina vibrating vibrating vibrating.Vibrating so much I couldn't help but orgasm. It wasn't erotic. It was holy. My whole body was releasing itself, everything was vibrating. Loud so I could actually hear the buzzing. It ended with my head doing it, too. And then I couldn't move anything. I floated out of my body and rose out of the room beyond the ceiling, and there were comets falling into my eyes and twelve heavenly hours later, I woke up back in bed. You may have no idea how it feels to finally sleep after being unable to for weeks (unless you have a baby, you poor thing), but it's complete heavenly. It's funny. They say it's the enemy. If anyone's gonna be an enemy it's insomnia. I remember one time during that wretched time awake, it was noticed by one nurse remarking: "It's the longest I've ever seen anyone awake." And at the time thinking I made the goddamn Guinness World Record or something (though now I know of people who have gone without sleep for far longer, it's insane). But by all accounts it wasn't helping the craziness. What else to call it. Evil of the mind.

Moloch of mind. The ring stopped that. I didn't even question it. It seemed far fetched but I had the ring and I fell asleep just like Morpheus said. Still, I decided to test it more, to see if it would make me sleep every time. So the next night I put it on and bang I fell asleep uninterrupted for ten whole hours. And no encounters with the Somnia. Apparently I only see them when I'm awake. Shouldn't it be the other way round? Shouldn't dreams... is it dreams? Or reality? And how strange it was, when usually there was no sleep for weeks on end. And how blissful it was to escape the living nightmare and enter a dreamless sleep. Whoever said it's the enemy is but a hopeful fool.

Though I managed to catch up on some rest, I still felt anxious and depressed. And I was still bummed out even after finding the sleeping ring in Icelos's belly. Nothing else that exciting was happening in the ward (though paranoia was making me question everything). So in order to distract myself from the fear and also the bleakness, and too cowardly to try for the tenth attempted suicide, I did some pencil sketches in my room to make the time pass a little less weirdly. I had a technique I favoured above all. Sporadic hand movements on the paper and see what happens. I would draw faces like this, sketched with brutal force, moving the hand in flicks and spasms with every stroke of the pencil. I didn't know how to draw like a normal person. I just sat there in my room trying to draw a self-portrait. But I couldn't do it. I hadn't seen my face for months because there were no mirrors in the ward. The last time I had a look at my old lousy face was back in March when Beate came to visit and I used her pocket mirror. I remember thinking that I looked dead, as if I was someone else, and as if this person in front of me was from a distant future. Yet now, I had completely forgotten what I looked like. I knew my hair was dark brown, I could see it falling down my shoulders. And I could see that my skin was caramel and there were goosebumps taking a permanent vacation on my limbs. But I couldn't remember what colour my eyes were. I wanted to draw Somnus. I knew his eyes. They were green. I thought maybe I could draw one of him and give it to him. Sort of like a greeting gift. You won't even need to talk to him, you'd just have to slip it under his door. It's right next door, right? Do it. Do something girl, for once in your life.

So I did what my gulliver said. I trusted it for once. I got out another pencil and drew something resembling him, his pale skin, those hauntingly green eyes, the small tuft of blonde hair, the big ears. After I did it, I felt my gut tighten. It wasn't a cigarette or anything like that. It was emotion.

I opened the door of my room, walked out and turned to his room, looked through the little window, saw he was not there, walked in and placed the picture under his bed. At the bottom of the drawing, I had written:

From an impenetrably secret admirer

Thinking – 'well he's never told me his, why should I mine?' I was nosey to find out more about him, but all that was there was a few books. I wondered where he was, then noticed a small wooden box on the table. I picked it up and saw that it was locked. I put it back down on the table, and left his room for mine.

Now in hindsight, after thirty six minutes strewn across my bed in panic, I regretted doing it. I started talking to myself.

"What if he doesn't like it?" I wrung my hands. "What if I get better and then can't see him again? Yeah, like that's gonna happen."

An hour later, I realised I couldn't find the ring the ballerina had given me. The sleeping ring. I couldn't find it anywhere. I left and wandered about, hoping to see the ring somewhere on the floor, while peeking through the thin square windows that were on all the patient's bedroom doors (and consequently privacy was destroyed) but nothing appeared. I then decided to go into a random room to see what I could find.

If I was going to lose something this precious, then I was also going to gain something precious. I looked in the window of door number three. No-one there. I crept in. Some trainers on the bed, writing on the wall. I began looking on the table and there was a bible with a piece of paper taped to it saying: 'by Marlon Hughes'. Without thinking I took a pencil from my skirt pocket and used the rubber end to remove Marlon's name and replace it with my own name, all in the shared delusion that whoever 'wrote' the Bible, was 'God'. Yeah. I know.

I looked among all the little trinkets and I couldn't see the ring, which didn't surprise me. It had to be somewhere I was earlier. I didn't want to hang around so I walked out of the room, looking left and right in case I was caught. The release of sleep was something akin to an opiate. At one point I actually believed sleep was heroin, because I'd gone without sleep for so long. I needed it. I needed to feel myself vibrating like that again. And I needed the ring in order to achieve it, and to avoid the horrible vision I'd see when I hadn't slept for three plus days, which is the ominous face staring back at me when I close my eyes. It's so invasive and cruel that I can't keep my eyes closed. Yet that's what you have to do in order to fall asleep. There's no out.

Try and ignore it but it's right there in front of your damn vision, closer than any real face could be. And the closer you get to falling asleep, the more vivid it appears. Like a devil inside your head. So you can understand perhaps why I could never sleep. And why finding the sleeping ring was so imperative. Imperative, I heard in my head. Heard in your head. Life, Death, heard in your head. You could try the lost and found.

   I kept on hearing it. Like a spectre of rhythm. It just went on & on. Heard in your head. Life, Death, heard in your head. All the way through me walking to the lost and found and asking but no luck, hadn't seen any ring nowhere they said. Life, Death, heard in your head, and the voice so confusing I no longer knew if it was just what I had said. Life, Death, heard in your head. As if my existence wasn't perhaps being described, by some writer of my soul. You really need to find that ring.

   It got to the point I just let it say its thing and be done with it. Over time, it became more than just a whisper, it helped me orientate myself as it were, flowing with it, letting it be me. Be you, dead in the head.

   And why would this particular voice come about? Don't question things that are helpful, I guess. Maybe the voice came to warn me not to do what I wanted to do since I got here, which was leave here. Leave forever. Number ten. But no belts, no rope, no knives, no things to jump off. The writer of my soul chose this, I reckon. My fate. I guess, unlike me, it didn't want me to die. I settled for holding my breath. But it didn't work.

26

I was truly in the gutter when I happened to make a

close encounter of Somnus. Not the Roman god. The one I was obsessed with.

It was in the lunch room. I was looking at the food, recalling how I left the portrait of him in his room. I turned pale. Well, there's no way he could know it was me, I thought. As I hovered over the food I noticed his arm spreading out just behind my left shoulder to take the same sandwich (yes, being this voyeuristic of him I knew the shape of his arm and the clad surrounding it). I felt guilty and then put the sandwich back so that maybe he could have it instead, but he just walked away to where the hot food was. I felt sour. It wasn't a good first impression. Taking his goddamn lunch. I sat down on a round wooden table in the corner of the cafeteria and sulkily ate. I heard some laughing twang in my ears. No visions today. Well, the walls were changing colours, but that wasn't anything to be suspicious about.

My tail wagged as I bit into the food. Just an ordinary day. I wondered where June the White Witch was.

She was hardly in the lunch room, and if she was she was sly about it. She was usually washing her hands with boiling hot water to get rid of 'the demons', or performing exorcisms to many an unwanted spectator. She went by June, but everyone else called her June the White Witch due to her wrinkled pale skin and white-blonde hair. Not everyone got on with her. But she had been there the longest out of anyone, over thirty years. She made qualms with the others due to her always insisting there were devils inside them and that they needed to let her do her thing on them, her exorcism. She would jam her palm onto some unwitting bystander's forehead and shriek: "Demon be gone!"

She never did it to me though. But then again, she was hardly around. When I met her, she told me to wash my hands in boiling hot water and said that boiling hot water is holy water and that it will get rid of the demons. I was slightly freaked out. She had light blue eyes and a very wrinkled face, with long majestic white-blonde locks, and well, her hands seemed fine despite the constant hot water. I can still hear the tap rushing now.

"Just soak it in some hot water, love, really hot, and it gets rid of the sin." And I replied: "What sin?"

"The sin of sin."

"Well, I don't really believe in sin. I believe I was a mouse. But I don't believe in sin."

"Don't let the Lord hear you, petal. He'll be giving me an earful all day." She wasn't joking. She admitted she could hear God talking to her. All the time. She had this prophetic seriousness about her, but with the polarity of being very silly and bubbly too. She was a strange one, and well thirty years in the funny farm no doubt she'd be this way. She said I could call her 'mammy' and that if I never needed anything she would be there. But she didn't get on with some of Old Bull's friends, who made these scandalous rumours about her which circulated round the ward, and rumours which I didn't know were true or not. It was doubtful. But not impossible. Rumours grew that she flung boiling water over a man's face and raped him. Rumours grew that she had killed her own daughter in a cauldron of boiling hot water. Rumours grew that she was a witch. But June would never do something like that. At least that's what I thought. She cried when she recanted the tale to me, pulling out some pictures of her daughter and showing them to me.

"She didn't make it very far. Look at her."

"How old is she there?"

"Oh, ten. She went missing soon after this picture was

taken. And I never found her. My sweet Jane..." Her face turned forlorn.

"She's very pretty, June. She looks like you."

"Thank you darling. I think so, too."

While I sat there daydreaming about June the White Witch and wondering if she did actually burn her daughter Jane in a cauldron, I noticed that Somnus was making his way out of the lunch-room. I figured I would go up to him and apologize and all for being so rude and taking his food. Not rude for being greedy per se, but rude for making an awkward situation out of it. I got up and started walking towards him, and then something very weird presented itself. My right palm had grown a mouth.

I stared at it while I continued to walk. It was pouting at me. Just like the mouth in *The Blood of a Poet*, that old 30's surrealist film Wickman had shown me. In the movie an artist draws a face, then the mouth flows up from the canvas and appears on his hand. My very own smirked, mesmerising me as I slumped through the lunch-room. And then I fell down. I fell into him.

"Oh my god. Sorry..."

I picked myself up, then bent down and picked up his notebook that had fallen. On the open page I saw manic handwriting. "Here's your book. I'm real sorry."

For a moment, he looked panicked in the eyes. Then he took the book from my once mouthless hand and made a little smile to me, but didn't say anything. The panicked look came back. Then he ran. He just got the hell out of there.

I looked at the lips on my hand. It was trying to talk to me. But all I heard was a mystical muffle. Then I kissed my hand in a kind of possessed madness, hoping it would be satiated. I looked as mad as anyone else. And as quick as Som had legged it, the mouth had disappeared. I was alone again.

27

In the ward, there was this patient called Rudie Walker who saw the Illuminati. She'd be talking to you one second perfectly fine and cogent, then just lapse into madness and cry out about how they use 'mind control' on us.

I found out where Rudie was most of the time by following the sound of a saxophone. As well as seeing the eye everywhere, Rudie played saxophone and was usually performing in front of everyone, right out in the open. Sometimes she would scream spasming on the courtyard ground. But it didn't make anyone too sour because she was exceptional on the saxophone. I followed the sounds until I was outside in the courtyard. She was jamming with Old Bull who was sucking on a harmonica.

"Hey guys."

"Hey Maya."

"Listen, Rudie. I don't wanna interrupt you. But could I talk to you for a bit?"

"Sure." We walked over to a vacant corner and leaned against the ramp railing. "What's up?"

"Do you know anything about opening people up?"

"Well, I have thought about it to be honest. But I wouldn't want a murder on my hands."

"No. That's not what I meant! I mean, getting people to open up and all. There's this guy who's really shy and I want to know how to get him to talk."

"Why do you think I would know?"

"You got me to open up. When I got here I didn't know anyone. It's like Somnus is now."

"Somnus? That's his name?"

"Umm. Yeah. That's his name."

"Who the fuck would name their kid Somnus?"

"Well, I don't think they did. I think someone else gave him the name. Anyway, he's really shy. What can I do? You know, apart from learn the saxophone."

"Is he that one who's always reading? Blonde hair, quite tall?"

"Yeah!"

"He's a quiet one. He comes to Gardening Club though. That's how I know him. He does the gardening group on Tuesdays. Just sign up and then you'll get to talk to him. Bingo bango."

"I knew I could trust you, Rudie. Thanks. I'm gonna sign up right now!"

"Glad I could be of service."

When I walked off to sign up to Gardening Club, Rudie and Old Bull were really getting into the music. It seemed on the whole that music helped people with mental disorders. Music is powerful, I reckon. It's the reason musicians continued to play on-board the sinking Titanic. They knew they were dead, yet they carried on playing. They needed the music like a junkie needs a hit. I remember being so afraid and confused one early time in the illness, that when Beate arrived to meet me from America she had brought an iPod which had all this classical music and stuff from the Amelie soundtrack on it, and I put it on and closed my eyes, and this frightening music came on. Not scary, but haunting. I felt I had lost my body and was swimming in an ocean, yet I was higher up. I could see the hospital building below me, and see everyone, every single person, walking from room to room. I immediately forgot about all the bullshit and yet I felt it all too much. But it made sense. For once, something made sense. I cried so much throughout that song. It felt like a haunting salvation. I saw myself and everyone else in a magnificent togetherness. A holy harmony. I saw the light in all these souls I was around but hadn't realised till now. I saw the sadness too in everyone. And we were all in the same boat. Sinking, as the music carried on.

As I entered the building, the saxophone and harmonica had suddenly stopped and been replaced with feet slapping on the floor and murmurs and telephones ringing through the clinical air. I looked over to the wall that was covered in a big frame where all these flyers were put up. There was a woman sitting against the wall looking up to the ceiling frantically. I figured it was on there. I got closer, and scanned the flyers.

Do you have depression? You're not alone. Feeling suicidal? Talk to someone. Recovery: We want to help you.

Yes I was depressed. Yes I was suicidal. I didn't need to be reminded every five goddamn minutes. I then found the sign up sheet in question.

Enjoy GARDENING?
Then come to our Tuesday group 1 pm - 2:30 pm to learn about growing plants, meet new friends, and have fun! Let your potential bloom!

I looked at the names on the sign-in sheet. His had to be

there. I looked through them.

Spencer Dustman, Rudie Walker, Venus Miles, Phil Blake, Elena Maccabee, June Jangle, Ivan Limpsky, Dunley Novak, Beth Reed, Mo Monk, Elijah Azir.

I guessed one of those names was his. But I wasn't sure which one. It was a Monday, which meant that the class would start the next day. I prayed to no god in particular that I wouldn't get struck by a bad episode. I was starting to feel jittery, good jittery, the butterflies of the stomach and all. I was excited for the first time in months.

Weeks went by. Som hadn't shown up, which I didn't expect. But I met a few new people, and thus was closer to cracking the code of what his name was. It wasn't Phil Blake because I met Phil Blake, he was this slightly too banterous guy with a terribly crooked nose. And it wasn't Dunley Novak either, because I met him too. I felt bad for poor Dunley. He seemed to be totally confused. He was telling me all about his troubles while we watered some dahlias. The flowers were talking to me too and it was hard to keep track. I looked at them and saw every atom comprising them. Atoms shone fuzzy light. Dunley and the flowers mumbled on. A bee came to assess the situation. I realised I was a giant compared.
"I've been in this anteroom for years. They locked me in here." I didn't feel like mentioning to him we were out in the garden and not in an anteroom, but he seemed really confused. He was going on about these giant squirrels and a place called the 'Asphodel'. He was saying how he was destined to be in the room for all

eternity, because of something bad he did in a past life or something. I felt really sore for him. He had the fear. I could tell.

"Don't worry Dunley. I'm sure you'll be okay."
"Yeah?"

While it was nice meeting Dunley, that 'yeah?' was never truly answered. I was enjoying the Gardening Club but I felt sour that Somnus hadn't shown up once. I wondered if he knew I was coming and just left. I was getting paranoid thoughts. I mean, more than usual. How he actually despised me and couldn't wait to get away. It was like a damn tumour in my head. I needed to lop it off. I needed to talk to him.

I asked Dunley the next week if he knew about Somnus. I didn't mention I called him Somnus, because really I was embarrassed by the whole thing. I just mentioned the 'quiet boy'.

"I actually spoke to him, because the girls asked me to find out why he's not showing up to gardening. I think he's going through a tough one at the moment."

"Oh. I see. Well if you ever see him around again can you tell him the girl at sixteen is looking for him?"

"Yeah, no problem. You like him don't you?" I hesitated.

"Yeah, I guess I do."

"I hope you get to tell him. He looks like he needs it. Man, I can relate. If I had a girl I would be a lot happier. But I'm stuck in this room..."

Even though Somnus never turned up, I still went to the gardening thing every week, because I found that being allowed outside in the garden just felt so nice with it being June and lovely hot and still the cool air because of the garden and all. I made friends with the flowers, and Dunley, Venus and Beth. We would mess around and shoot each other with the water hose, and no-one got angry at us because we were special and all. Rudie came to a few but then stopped going. She had severe psychotic bouts that were becoming untreatable. She would be talking to you seemingly happy as a daisy, and then wringing her hands and screaming and falling to the floor and yelling of the 'eye' and the 'trap'. Yet I too did just the same thing, only I didn't remember it.

Then there was Venus Miles, this African beauty who always wore the most amazing clothes and had a real funny personality, but it was only one of multiple personalities she had. When you talked to her you got confused quick. But she smiled, which was rare. And Beth Reed was this quiet poet with chronic schizo-affective disorder who looked like a vampire. She orated poems in her room, practising for the final reveal when she'd crack her version of *Howl* and how she too saw the best minds of her generation 'destroyed by madness'. We talked me and Beth about that strange time in Literature when Ginsberg was stoned declaring tranquillity and Kerouac drinking his brain an ongoing freight train headed off rail but somehow somewhere linguistically infinite. Meanwhile Venus didn't seem to know what we were talking about, and I don't think even I did. But I was having some fun (as promised in the sign-up sheet) and it was nice to do something other than tear my own hair out. But later on I felt kinda bad that Som was going through a tough time. I decided to draw some more portraits of him. I spent days doing only this. Eventually I ended up with a whole folder of them, and decided to sneak a peek at him through the window on his door one day to get a better angle for a new drawing. But when I saw him, he was levitating.

I opened the door, walked into the room and saw the bed was turned up so the bedposts were against the floor and the ceiling. He was dangling off it. I reacted quickly, running up to him and holding him up high by the legs and torso so the noose would stay loose. But I couldn't free him from it. And I couldn't let go of him. The door had closed automatically. I screamed as loud as I could, waving my head frantically to the little window on the door. He looked unconscious. I couldn't hold on much longer. I wasn't strong. But I was keeping him from breaking his neck. Finally, someone had heard me shouting and came rushing in. Then more people came in. It was like an avalanche of people. I released him into their hands. Two guys were holding him up while another untied the rope from the upended bedpost. I decided to leg it out of there but some woman was goddamn praising me for what I did.

"You saved his life." But I didn't want the attention. I really didn't.

"Well, I'm glad he's okay."

"Hey..." he says, now on the floor where a couple people were crouched next to him. "You tried to stop me?"

"I couldn't let you do that to yourself. I'm sorry, though." He looked embarrassed. "You really scared me, you know?"

"Yeah. It was a stupid mistake." He felt for his throat, and a tear was falling from his eye. Two guys started pushing the bed back to its right spot. I didn't know what I had done. Should I have saved him? I thought. Did he want to be saved? But all I asked him was: "How'd you get the rope anyhow?"

"Oh, it was in the garden shed."

"Doesn't that have a lock on it?"

"I found the key."

"Where?"

"In a dream." I looked at him, he was still breathing heavily.

"I mean, you must have been in a bad way. But look at it this way, it might be better that you survived. Maybe it's fate."

"Yeah? Do you believe in fate?"

"I kinda do. I believe my life is being written actually. I think it's like some writer of the soul or something. But I guess that's just silly."

"I can understand that." He looked at me and I almost lost it seeing his eyes staring back at mine. It filled me with a secret joy. For months, finally getting our goddamn eyes to synchronize.

"Guys," I say to the others. "I think he's okay with me now. I'll look after him. You guys go, it's fine."

"Is that okay with you Spencer?"

"Yeah, that's fine."

28

And then I was alone with him.

"So you're Spencer Dustman?"

"How'd you know it's Dustman?"

"I saw your name on the sign-up sheet."

"Oh, right. Well. It's funny really. I just use a fake name."

"Oh. So what is your name?"

"You don't want to know."

"Try me."

"Well, the truth is, my brother used to call me something. But I forgot what it was since he died. I just use Spencer Dustman most of the time and no-one seems to question it."

"Oh, your brother passed? I'm so sorry."

"It's okay."

"But really, no-one else gave you a name? Not even your parents?"

"They never gave me a name. I was just 'boy'. Now they're dead. They were in the 7/7 bombing. Well, good riddance. They don't need a name either." He looked defeated. His hands twitched.

"I know how you feel. My parents are dead too."

"Really?"

"Yeah."

"How did it happen?"

"Mum had cancer. Dad had a heart attack. With Mum it was awful. Dad didn't help a goddamn bit just sat there drinking. And he used to hit me. He used to touch me."

"That's terrible. I'm so sorry..." he scrambled for my name.

"Maya."

"What a lovely name. Maya."

"How did you get here anyway? Like, why are you here?"

"I don't know. I think it's because I was a butterfly from another planet four thousand years ago. But I'm not 100% yet. How about you? Why are you here?"

"I don't know any more. All I know is that everything is different now." I felt myself frowning and so I tried to lighten the mood. "You know, when I saw 'Spencer Dustman' on the sign-in sheet I thought hell what a name! Why do you call yourself that anyhow?"

"Because I'm nothing but dust," he says. It was the strangest thing I'd ever heard.

"Gee, Spencer. I'm sure you're more than dust. You know, it's funny. I actually call you So-" I had to stop mid-sentence. He was clutching onto the ring. "Where did you find that ring?"

"Oh, it was in my room. Cool, huh?"

I didn't want to tell him I'd been in his room, but I really wanted the ring. I didn't know what to say. "I just found it on the floor."

"It's very nice, Spencer." I then noticed that the drawing I made of him was also on the floor, under the bed. It was covered in dust. It meant that either he saw the drawing and chucked it, or he actually hadn't found it yet.

"It's more than nice. It helps you sleep. It really does. No kidding." I looked at him, feigning surprise and doubt. "Hey, I'll let you borrow it for a bit if you want," he says. "You can see for yourself. May I?" He picked up my hand very gently, raised the ring and slowly hooped it onto my finger. "It looks good on you," he says. "But really, it'll send you to sleep. So you better get out of here and into your bed before you topple."

"I'll just keep it off for a while. So were you wearing it when you were, well, you know. I don't want to go on about it or anything."

"Yeah. I was keeping it on so I'd fall asleep just at the moment I left. Just at the moment the rope would tighten."

"Wow. That's heavy. Sorry I asked."

"It's okay. But, man. I was just thinking how strange it is that I'm even alive. I thought today was gonna be it. I really thought today was gonna be it. It's given me, it's given me some hope, you know? Like I can actually talk to people and it won't be all hell."

"See, you're coming out your shell already. Not that

you're a turtle or anything." I grinned like an idiot. Then forgetting that the ring was still on my finger, I conked out right on his goddamn floor.

29

The morning after Som's attempted suicide, I had a very long sleep. When I woke up it was twelve. I had missed the morning medication. (That is, unless they injected me with something while I was asleep.) I took the ring off my finger and placed it on the side table. Today was an important day. I was meant to have a check-up to see if I was getting any better. Dr Malik was waiting for me in his office.

"Hello, Maya. How have you been?"

"Oh. Okay. Nothing special. Bit depressed. Tired." Furtively, I was hiding the fact that I truly was happy, because Malik would have snuffed it out that I was only happy because I was falling for another patient and all. See, I didn't want old Malik to know about any of that because romance between patients was not really allowed in the ward for various reasons, such as that it heightens emotions and can cause vendettas and jealousy and all that terrible stuff. So I kept my calm. "Yep, nothing special. Just another day in the ward, Dr."

"Are you seeing things?"

"Not today."

"Heard anything?"

"No, sir."

I then started thinking if he thought I was all good and fixed and all, that he might let me go and let me be free. The problem was, I would have nowhere to go.

"Actually, yeah I have been seeing stuff today. There's

gargoyles in my cigarettes. And... ummm... I'm hearing the ghost of Anne Frank."

"Okay. What about the horns? Are they back?"

"No." But then they started to be.

"Are you scared?"

"I'm scared enough that you should keep an eye on me, not so scared that you should be worrying." My tail wagged against the seat.

"Just remember nothing is your fault, Maya. Things might scare you or confuse you, but you must remember we're here to help you. And you aren't alone."

"You know, Dr. Malik. I'm starting to think maybe you're right."

After the meeting, I felt better for once. Usually those meetings weren't what you'd call healthy or anything. But I was finally happy, and it was rubbing off. It's strange how you can be so sad and in the dumps for so long, you forget that happiness and being content even exists. It's a trip. Once you feel it, well, it's like meeting a long lost friend. I wasn't going to let anything drag me back down.

When it got to lunchtime, I bumped into Old Bull in the cafeteria. He said he wanted me to join him later for a game of rummy with his pals.

"Go, on. I can show you again if you forgot how."

"Sure, Bully. Can I bring a friend?"

"The more the merrier!" He left, cackling. I wondered to myself in that moment if I would ever get real old like him. I wandered over to the lunch cart and grabbed a sandwich and a bottle of drink. I then decided to take another sandwich. I don't know why. I guess I wanted to embrace everything. The rummy, the ward, my youth, the two plus sandwiches. Hell, anything. My good mood had seemed to turn what was once fearful hallucinations into spangling light and kindness. For now. I sat down on an empty table. But I didn't feel alone. The room echoed a beating heart. My beating heart. And everyone's beating heart. And then it started pumping like there was no end.

"Hey, Maya."

"Oh, hey Spencer. How you doing today?"

"I'm pretty good thanks. How are you?"

"Can't complain."

"Did you sleep well then?"

"Yeah. I did. You know, that ring really did send me to sleep! You were right."

"You can keep it if you want." I didn't bother mentioning that I found it first.

"Really? That's very sweet of you, Spencer. But, won't you find it hard to sleep?"

"Maybe we can take turns with it?"

"That sounds fair. You can have it tonight. Oh, I was gonna ask you. My friend Bully asked me to play rummy with him and his friends tonight. Do you want to come along? They're real old. But it could be alright."

"I don't know how to play."

"Neither do I. Still, it might be fun, though. What do you think?"

"If you're going, I'd be a fool to miss it."

"Oh, Som."

"Huh?"

"I mean, Spencer. Spencer."

"No, what you said before."

"I. I. Okay. Here's it straight. Before I met you I saw you around quite a lot, and I ended up giving you a name. I know. It's stupid."

"You know, I kind of like it. Som..." He looked at me

and smiled, then tucked into his pasta bake. I was already on my second sandwich. I was hungry for once.

"Hey, guess what. I took two sandwiches."

"Woah," he says. "Looks like we got a real criminal in our midst."

"Well, sometimes you gotta break the rules, you know?"

"Aren't you afraid I'll rat you out?"

"Not really. Because if you told someone, you'd already be dead."

After that horrible awkward day when he ran off after I bumped into him, I couldn't believe how easily we were conversing. It was as mad as the mouth on my palm.

"You know," he says. "It feels nice to talk. I haven't talked in years."

"Years?"

"Years." I leant over to him and in a fit of mad inspiration, like the gods were looking down on us and destiny had been cast, I delicately touched his cheek with my index finger. I was trembling.

"You can talk to me all day, Som."

We were so close to each other now, I wanted to kiss him, I was preparing to kiss him, I could feel his breath on my face and it made me lousy with lust. He hadn't moved his head back. We sat there, face to face, and then he lowered his head and kissed my neck, just once, softly, sweetly. He moved back and looked me in the eyes. Then I just leapt at him. It was the most intense kiss I'd ever had in all my twenty seven years. A kiss fit for nineteen. Or was I eighteen? Couldn't remember. My birthday was long forgotten amid everything else.

By the time we stopped, everyone else had left and we were all alone in the cafeteria.

"You know. That was great and all, Som. But someone might have seen us. We should be more careful. They don't take too kindly to romance between patients here."

"Gee, I'm sorry. It's just, it's just. Do you know how beautiful you are?"

"God, no. I'm a wreck. Still, that's sweet of you."

"And kind too. I mean, I nearly died. And you saved me. I didn't even want to be saved." He held my hand. Strangely, they weren't twitching this time.

"What were you thinking anyway? What made it get to that?"

"Being alone. It's been hell here."

"I can understand that. I'd be pretty much alone if it wasn't for my sister. But she's in America right now."

"Yeah? What does she do?"

"Oh, she's the founder of this newspaper there. The Peak Times. It's like an alternative look on the news. She's really great. She's uncovering this cocaine scandal in the White House at the moment. She's making a success of it. If I didn't have her I don't know what I'd do. Here, do you want to see a picture I have of her?"

"Sure." I got out my little purse where I kept no money but had old pictures of my family tucked in there, along with a key Beate gave me for her new home in Seattle. I got out a photo of Beate.

"That's her on the right."

"She looks a lot like you. Where is that, anyway?"

"She was hiking up this mountain. Hozomeen mountain. It's in Washington."

"Wait," he says, sounding confused. "I know that mountain! I've been there!"

"You have?"

"Yeah, well, it was in a dream. Still, that's the place!

It's where I found this." Then he reached into his pocket and produced something I didn't know what. It looked like a wooden block with spoons attached to it.

"What is it?"

"It's an African musical instrument. It's called an mbira. See, you pluck the metal things here and it makes this wonderful sound." He plucked the spoons. They produced a sound something like steel pan drums, except much higher. He was right. It was a wonderful sound.

"Wow. That's awesome. Can I have a look?" He passed it to me. I plucked one of the spoons. It gave a little trill. "But, wait. How did you get this from a dream? You mean it was like a dream, or something? You're being poetic?"

"No. I found it there. And then when I woke up, it was in my hand. I bet I could find other things, too."

"Really? That sounds kinda funny, Som. Are you sure someone didn't give it to you?"

"Well, the way I found out about it in the first place. There's a nurse here I met who showed me a video of an mbira being played on her tablet. She sat with me all night because I was afraid and she showed me it. The music made me feel something I'd never felt before. So I knew about the mbira and what it looked like and how it sounded, and it just so happened I had a dream a few nights later when I finally slept, where the mbira started playing and I followed it up a hill to a mountain and found it. I woke up. It was in my right hand, just like in the dream. And I thought to myself it's probably a dream right now and how the hell could you tell otherwise?"

"I'm holding it right now. Either it's true, or you're lying to me. You're not lying to me, are you Som?"

"I'm not, Maya."

"It just sounds a bit funny. But I guess my tail sounds kinda funny, too."

"Tail?"

"Yeah. I have a tail. It's invisible. That's why you haven't noticed it."

"Does it wag?"

"Often."

"That sounds kind of cool, actually. I'd like a tail. Consider yourself lucky!"

30

Later that night me and old Spencer Dustman were in the cafeteria again, except now it was dark and the food counters had all been closed down. We were sitting at a table with Old Bull and his friends Joe and Murray playing a game of rummy. Joe was short and plump with a grey comb-over who had a habit of being very loud and assertive and twitching a lot, while Murray was tall and thin with a grey comb-over who seemed very timid and unable to speak his thoughts. Old Bull had them going on about the reason we were all here.

"I'm just saying Joe, you're right that it's to keep us away from society. But you're wrong that it's all for the best. Say they let us all out now, said 'hey fellas it's time to turn in this whole enterprise, go home,' well we wouldn't destroy the world with our filth. What filth? That they have as well as us. We're all the same. Everyone's insane, it's just we were stupid enough to get caught."

Meanwhile old tall Murray was looking very anxious for some unknown reason, and started making a house of cards with his part of the deck.

"No we're not. We're not the god-damn same. They would never embrace us, Thom. They see us as mutants, they're afraid, and consequently that turns into hatred. We'd never get along if they let us all out. And it's not our filth. It's theirs. They'd find another way to lock us all up, keep us away from the oasis. It would turn into a real war, them and us. So it is for the best. Not that I like it here, I hate it. But it's for the best of the whole society. We're martyrs for the sane world. Well, let it be. And if they let us out (like that would even happen!), that fear of us would turn into hatred, that hatred would turn into war. I'm telling you. Better that we're hidden. Better that they don't see us. Because if they did, they'd want to eradicate us. And well I know who I'd be fighting for. It would be honest warfare." He slammed his cards down as he said it.

"It seems you want this war, Joe."

"On the contrary. I say it's better they keep us all here. So the norms don't infect us!"

"I'm not convinced," replies Old Bully. "We'd get along fine. But we seem to agree on the main point. That it's not treatment. It's confinement. They're keeping us away from the rest of society, so that society seems on the whole not insane, but orderly. Like a magician's illusion. They want order in their society. So they take us away from society, shove all us 'disorders' away and throw away the key. Imagine all the great minds we have here, and they are told they need to be isolated from the world. There's no treatment here. It's just for show. We're rabbits in top hats. We don't need to be here."

"Gotta be somewhere," spurts Murray out of the blue.

"True say Murray! Gotta be somewhere!"

I was listening intently. They seemed to still be playing the game during their heated conversation but I couldn't keep up. I was trying to figure out who 'they' exactly were. Murray was still lost in his house of cards. I looked at my hand. I had a Jack of Diamonds, an Ace of Diamonds, a Jack of Clubs, a 2 of Hearts, a 5 of Clubs and an Ace of Spades. I reckoned I had a pretty good hand, although in truth I really didn't know. Old Bull was the dealer, and I looked up at his old wrinkled hands when he dealt out the cards to us and saw a ring on one of his fingers and wondered if it wasn't another enchanted ring. Implausible, but then again everything that happened was implausible.

"Maya. Your hand."

"Ummm. I'm sorry. I just don't get this game. Plus, my Jacks are staring at me and I don't like it."

"You're not supposed to tell your hand. Ah, shall we just give it a rest then? I think we're hurting Maya's head."

"No, I'm fine. Well, to be honest, your argument's got me all nervous. They're not here to make us better?" They started cackling. I felt embarrassed and lowered my head. "It's been a long game isall."

Old Bull seemed sympathetic in his side-glance look to me, while Joe was still cackling like a madman. Then he got out a bottle of vodka from under the table. "Perhaps you know the drinking game?"

"Where did you get that?"

"You don't have to, me and my boys are gonna drink some anyway." I grabbed the bottle and took as small a sip as I could. I hated vodka. But I liked hanging around with those guys. They were all old and subsequently weren't insufferable like young people. They talked politics and big madhouse ideas intelligently. I passed

Somnus the bottle. He took a real big swig.

"That's ma boy," cackles Old Bull. There was this unwritten rule amongst guys that drinking somehow made you more of a man or something. But to be honest, I was a bit put off by Somnus drinking such big swigs.

"Take it easy, Spencer." Then he whispers to me from behind his cards: "I don't even like it! I just want to fit in!" and then I burst. The rummy game had all but disintegrated and after a while everyone was drunk and Murray was still making his house of cards, but the funny thing was, it didn't topple once. And he had drunk loads of vodka. It just kept getting bigger.

"Wow, Murray," I say. "You're good at that, aren't ya?"

"I used to hold the World Record, you know." Alas, it got to the point he ended up using all fifty two cards. It was still standing strong. It was as if doing this calmed and centred him. "Anyone got any more cards? I ran out."

"Maya," says Old Bull. "I gave you a pack didn't I?"

"Sorry Bull. I ate those."

"You ate them?"

"Most of them. It's a long story."

"You might as well eat a long story," says Joe. "Get the nutrients."

"I've got some paper," says Som. "We could cut them into card shapes with those kid scissors they have." Then he got out a little notebook, and I saw some of the pages as he flicked through them that were completely covered in inky jottings. He handed a plain sheet to Murray who looked at him very strangely.

"Do you write, Spencer?" I ask him.

"Well, sometimes."

"What do you write about?"

"Well, usually it's dark stuff. Not happy endings."

"Happy endings aren't all they're cracked up to be I guess. They just don't seem realistic to me. Nothing ever ended happy isall I'm saying."

"I've been trying to work on a happy ending. I think I figured it out. Would you like to hear the premise?"

"I'd like to read it, Spence!"

"It's not done yet. It's just a short story. Just notes."

"Okay. Tell me about it then."

"You ever seen those elephants that can paint?"

"Oh sure. It's cool, right?"

"I guess you don't know they're tortured into doing it."

"Gee, Spencer. I thought it was going to be a happy story!"

"It will be!"

"Okay, go on." (And by this time we had both forgot company.)

"Basically, they shove spikes into their ears and keep them in crates and abuse them, until they break down and paint like they're told, you know, it's just for tourism money. It's horrible. Anyway, the story is about an elephant in Africa that is forced to paint. And she goes through hell from her abusive human master. The spikes in the ears, the confinement. But one day, during a live show, she paints the words 'Leonora Go' on the canvas, breaks free from the shackles on her ankles and kills her master by stampeding him. Then the crowd of people run away. When she escapes, she goes into the wild. She finds a forest. And brings a paint brush in her trunk. She paints her old friends on trees, being free and alone in the forest, a certain happy ending but not completely, because of past and present mixing, and umm, but yeah, that's pretty much it."

"It's a good idea, Spencer. I like the Leonora touch too. As in Carrington?"

"Yeah."

"I love her."

"Her paintings are amazing aren't they? And wasn't she Mexican like you?"

"Well, she moved to Mexico. She was English born. I am Mexican born and moved to England. Man, I wish I could paint like her."

"Me too. I'm awful. I can't even draw stickmen very well. I try and stick to writing nowadays. I'm just stuck on the prose. I wish someone else would write it for me."

"It would make a good kids film. Kids love elephants. And painting. Heck, it'd make a good painting!"

"Would you like to come back to my room and you can help me write it?"

"Sure. Hey, guys. We're gonna go. But thanks for a fun night." We both get up.

"Anytime. Have fun you two." Then the old fellas start cackling again. As we begin to leave them, I knock the table by accident and the cards finally fall. Murray looks up, mumbles 'curse you Father', then laughs. As we walk across the corridor I say to Somnus: "They probably think we're going to bed or something."

He looked nervous after I said it. Then he decided to just run off, leaving me there in the corridor.

31

The next morning I had woken from a dream. I saw the elephant that Somnus was going on about. Leonora. She got carted. She was trapped in a white room with a straightjacket across her huge trunk. All her little paint brushes were snapped in two, lying on the floor around her, crying red. Then she started to wail in that way elephants do before a charge, but it was muffled from the straightjacket. And then I woke up and the sound morphed into the voice of one of the nurses on med call.

Naturally, I got to thinking all this medication wasn't even fixing me. Because, well, it didn't seem like it was being fixed. I had been in the ward eight going on nine months and I didn't hardly feel any better for taking these 2,880 pills. I was counting. My eyes were always puffy and red and today was no different. There was a terrible leg-ache too. From being in the bed all day and all night. And they didn't like you walking around so much. And if you ran they immediately called for help and seized you like you were a zit that needed popping, and tranquillised if need be.

It was foolish to think I'd been getting better. Somnus had reminded me what it was like to be normal again, and I was a damn fool for thinking it would finally save me from the torments. In reality, the torments have never left me, they've clung on. God, how my legs ached. I just wanted to run around to get them to stop aching but I knew better than to do that. Sometimes the pain got so bad I wanted to cut off my legs and be done with them. There was even a time I remember I was convinced I was being turned into a cyborg. My legs felt like giant rectangular boulders built into the ground, so heavy I was unable to lift them. I was tied to a chair. And so then believing it was part of some mechanical surgery to turn me into a cyborg. On days like that, when I was forgetting where I was and who I was, the Somnia showed themselves in mad visions before me. The tail wagged portentously throughout it all, as if something real bad was going to happen, and I believed it 100% because the tail never lied.

Suddenly there was a loud knocking on my door. The tail felt electrified. But still I lay there, not making a sound. There was a storm coming outside. Outside the door, I mean. I didn't want to leave the room. There was a mystical fear gripping me. It squashed me to pulp. No, not a storm. An earthquake? Or was it just the knocking? I didn't have the strength to decide. I just chucked the blanket off my body, wiped my puffy eyes and pulled myself off the bed. My legs were shaking like they might break if I walked. The knocking got so loud I was convinced it was an earthquake, and the real reason my legs were shaking. And then I realised that if I could go out there, maybe the quake would kill me and I wouldn't have to have all this fear and aching of the body. But I walked out and everything looked normal. All the violet walls were there, in the right place, too. No earthquake. But a single crack in the floor. Yet as I stared at it, it grew bigger. Bigger and bigger. I lost my balance as the floor opened and I fell into a dark pit and was free-falling and there were evil glowing faces big as Big Ben and claws scratching at my brain and I was falling so fast but not getting anywhere and this went on for an hour in total darkness.

Finally, I strained to see the bottom of the pit. There was a man down there. A man down there with four arms reaching out ready to grab me. I screamed so loud my voice-box practically broke in two and I couldn't make any sounds now except a little hoarse moan. I fell into the man's arms and he rocked me like I was a baby and I saw that it was the face of my father. A long red serpent tongue then flew dementedly out of his mouth. I was crying. I tried to shout but I couldn't make any sounds. He whispered maniacally: "Just say stop....and I'll stop."

Still I couldn't make any sounds. I cried like a little girl lost in a supermarket with no voice to shout out to mummy and all there was was this demon with my father's face with four enveloping arms clutching me and stretching me out as if I was tied up on a bed by my wrists and ankles. He carried on. I felt like this was no dream. Was it Icelos, this beast? And if it was Icelos, was it a dream or reality? With a force I obtained from sheer fear and adrenaline, I tore my right arm free from his grip. Then he punched me in the jaw with one of his free hands and grabbed me again. I was coughing up blood, it felt real. I wasn't ready to die, even if it only felt that way. I grabbed his tongue and curled it round his head until it started choking him. I didn't let go for nothing. It was hot and slimy in my hand. His head then started to swell and turn puce. His eyeballs began to pop out his head and suddenly I was released from his grip. I watched as he shrivelled up (just as the ballerina did) like a date, as small as my hand, and then there was a blinding light above me and I started to hear that scream that I myself had made when I first fell into his arms and it was still going on and as if it wasn't me who was screaming but someone else. The blinding light then began to dim and a female figure was looking over me while I continued to scream, so loud she had to shut her eyes to avoid the spit. Eventually, I ran out of breath and lay there still, on the bed, panting. She put her palm on my forehead and it was burning so much I was afraid it was that evil thing with the four arms getting into my head again. But I didn't scream this time. I just wept, like that girl lost in the supermarket. The supermarket of sanity.

"Ya gave me quite a scare," says the nurse.

"He gave me a scare."

"Who, darling?"

"I. I don't know. My. But I hate him. I hate him!"

"Dayo's got ya. Noting's gonna stop me protecting ya, darling. Now, come with Dayo to tha dispensary. Ya need ya medicine." When she picked me up, I calmed down. Her bosom was so big it was like sleeping on five pillows. I remembered my father was dead. The creature I saw must have been Icelos in a hideous form. Meanwhile, the nurse was humming some tune, something that felt like it had come from the other side of the world. Mystical, ancient. Like that little musical instrument Som showed me.

"Now, Dayo's going to make ya a cup of tea. After ya go and get ya medication. By God, ya went a bit off the rails, girl!" She was laughing at all my madness right before me. "Ya see how ya need ya medication? Ya see?"

I didn't reply. I just pulled myself away from the five pillow bosom and drunkenly wandered to the dispensary, where there was no queue, because I had arrived late for the morning dose. Once again I saw the Chinese doctor. Once again she gave me the pills. I got the fear all over again. I didn't know what the pills were and no-one told me anything. When I ran out I was immediately restrained, and they held me down, and when, failing to get the pills into my mouth, suddenly injected me with a syringe. It felt like I was falling quickly into a deep sedation. All my fears had evaporated. I melted into the air.

And woke up to the sound of.

For once everything was quiet. There were no discernable voices, strange thoughts yes, and strange feeling yes, such as the tail that always wagged and then disappeared until the next time it would come, always in perpetual surprise. But now silence had overtaken me and overwhelmed me. And in that giant pool of no-sound a voice began echoing throughout my eardrums. It faded away and there was silence again.

It was precarious to have to depend on these voices in the brain. Who was I, exactly? Was it this girl Maya or was it someone else? And who was the voice of the soul? Who was it who tormented me?

Sometimes I felt like everybody. Then I felt like nobody. All Aboard the Risperidone Rollercoaster. Funny. Now that I think of rollercoasters, it reminds me of that crazy ambulance ride after my sister called 999. She started to become ill-at-ease at my presence that day and worried I'd gone truly mad. This was when she still lived in England. It was the morning I arrived at her door after I ran out of the Halloween party and left Wickman behind. I started to really freak out, but I tried to hide it. I remember she gave me a copy of *The Bell Jar* and I was reading it in the garden and I got so scared the characters were coming to life that I threw the book across the garden and hung there in fright. I remember thinking that I had died and gone to Hell. I remember thinking the binmen were Nazis coming after me. I remember seeing angels. I was looking up at them in Hell. I was finding out that Hell wasn't fire and brimstone. Everything looked the same, except something had changed. This was Hell. Everything looked the same. Except now the devil was inside me.

They came and took me away. In the back of the ambulance, I laid down on a stretcher and saw a tattoo on a man's arm of a tiger. It started moving around. I thought it was going to attack me. Then the car took off and the ride felt just like a rollercoaster. It felt so real.

Like it was going to crash in hyperspace. Like that old ride at Thorpe Park called X No Way Out. Did I ever tell you about that time I nearly died on X No Way Out? Well, I was just sitting in the seat ready to be checked and all. But when I tried to put the harness down to secure me with the seat-belt, it didn't go in properly and click. When the assistant came over, he didn't see that it wasn't secured. He was in a rush to check everybody he didn't check me properly. He then started the ride, and I started telling my sis: "Beate! It's not fastened! It's not fastened!" But she just laughed.

I held on hard. Then it felt like it was going upside down in a giant loop and I thought I was going to die and fall out right there on X No Way Out. Its gimmick was that it pretends to break down halfway, right at the top of some hoop. I vowed never to ride a rollercoaster again.

"C'mon. It was kinda funny. Do we want the pictures?"

And that ride at Thorpe Park felt just the same as the ambulance did, the one that was on the hyper-way to true insanity in future hospital corridors racked with malevolent fear. Though it was daytime everything was dark. The ambulance lifted off the ground to avoid hitting any cars going one hundred mph through the streets of Maidenhead. People flew past, their faces hung in slow motion as we drove into the day-night of Absolute Irreality to remove my freedom from under my grip.

The thing about all this, all these things, is that you're never schooled, clued in. No-one is there to explain to you why you have a tail, why you hear voices, why you turn into mice. You want it to be a simple beginning, middle and end and in that order. With reason at the helm. But it's not like that. It's more real than anything, in a way. As Harmony Korine said on Letterman in 1997: "Every movie there needs to be a beginning, middle and end. Just not in that order." Which explains why I died before I lived. Most of the people around here were older than me, and they had died so many times it was hard to keep count. We all just kept dying every morning, then ate our breakfast. On a big hamster wheel going backwards in time, our dreams slipping out from the future. The fact of the matter was there weren't any clocks anywhere. But I reckon if we saw them, they'd be going the wrong way.

One rainy day I was telling Somnus how I went into the toilet and there was a sign above the cistern that said : PRESS HERE FOR DEATH. And I pressed it. But I realised I was already dead. And that's what I said to old Somnus that rainy afternoon.

"I think I'm already dead. It's the only way to explain everything."

"Guess so."

"But maybe it's okay, you know. Maybe this isn't the only death. Maybe I'll be born again and that will restore everything."

"Maybe we'll see each other again?"

"You know, my old friend used to say that. She said when we met, we had already met before in another life. And that when we die, we'll meet each other again as different people."

"Huh. I hope I'm not crazy in my next life." In a moment of nervousness, I ask him:

"Do you think we'll ever get out of here?" He turned quite solemn in the face and looked down at the floor for a while.

"They'll never let us out."

"Really?"

"Well, they'll never let me out. I think I got this forever. You could get better though. I think you will. And anyway, Doctor Russell says they'll let anyone out who's showing sane behaviour for an extended period of time."

"So let's do that. But god knows what he perceives as sane."

"Do you think you are sane?" He looked away from me.

"I hope I am. I don't want our encounter to have been an illusion, Som."

"Me either."

"So why did you run off the other night?"

"I had to get to my room. My room protects me. They can get me if I'm not in there."

"Who can get you?"

"Oh, it's nothing."

"Okay... So, you really think you'll never leave here? And you really think I could get better? But even if I did get better, I would still be here, because I want to see you."

"I want to see you, too." Then he looked off to one side. "We could find a way out, maybe."

"Escape?"

"Phantas told me that there is a gemstone somewhere in the dream world that can give you powers. I've been trying to find it for months. He says it came off an ancient amethyst geode centuries ago, which had hieroglyphs engraved on it."

"Really? This again? You're really convinced, aren't you? And who's Phantas?"

"He's in my dreams. He inhabits inanimate objects."
"What's your point?"
"The gem. With it, we can leave undetected."
"And where would we go?"
"That I haven't thought of yet."
"I don't want to bum you out, Som. But this whole dream thing doesn't make much sense."
"Please. You have to believe me."
"Believe?"
"Look. I'll prove it to you. I'll find a rose in my dream. I'll give it to you in the morning." He took my hand and kissed it.

When it got late we decided to sleep together in his bed so that when we woke up I would 'see the rose'. It felt more natural to be in the same room, given we were neighbours. He made me search his room for hours to prove there was no rose he was hiding beforehand. We lay down on his bed, and I guess it would have been the usual thing to maybe have sex with him, but we were both so tired we just lay there. It was against the rules to share beds. I sat there awake all night next to him. At one point I decided to take the ring off him and put it on my finger, and then I dozed in the early hours.

When I awakened it was late. I turned over in the bed and felt something. It was a thorn in my arm. So there was a rose there, just like he said there would be. Still, that didn't mean anything. I took the ring off and put it in my pocket. Som was gone. I leant over and saw that wooden box on the table again. It was moving around, as if possessed. I went over to the table and handled the mysterious box. I wanted to know what was in there. In case there was a finger, or a voodoo doll with my face on it. But I remembered from before that it was locked. One the side was etched: DREAMS.

Was he trying to give me hope with the rose? That one day he would finally find the magic gemstone in one of his goddamn dreams and use it to break out? It seemed like something in a fairy tale. *'There was a knight called Somnus. And Somnus had a dream box....'* Something too good to be true.

I then began to wonder if he was even real. Had I conjured him up? Were they dreams? It perhaps would have all made sense if that was the case. And days went by and I never saw him, which made me think I was right. Where could he have gone? Where did I go? Weeks went by as I continued to wonder what was real and what wasn't, and never figuring it out. And then one day he knocked on my door. He started telling me that he had been trapped in a dream for two weeks, and that's why he wasn't around. I was getting angry because I didn't believe him.

"Tell me the truth."

"But it is the truth. They froze me. I believed everything that happened to you. Why can't you do the same?"

"God! Just stop it, okay!" He walked out of the threshold, not saying anything.

As the day went on, I felt sour for yelling at him. I went to his room and knocked on the door like he had mine earlier. There was no response. I opened the door and saw him. He was holding the red rose. He was cutting his left wrist with a thorn, longways (the death way). Blood was seeping out over the bed. I went over to him and his face was spasming, his forearms doused in blood. Then his head finally stopped moving. His eyes were still like space. And then I woke up again.

I rushed to his room again. I was afraid of seeing it all

again. But I could see from the door window that the rose was in a vase on his table. He was reading a book, and when he saw me, he took the rose and put it in the book like a bookmark, making the book wet, though he didn't seem to notice that. His eyes lit up when he saw me.

"Hey. What were you reading?"

"It's my diary. I was just checking it to see who I was. I forgot again."

"Listen. I'm sorry for yelling at you before. You didn't deserve that."

"Oh, it's fine. I know it's hard to believe."

"If you really do believe it, then I guess I do, too. We're a team. We can't turn on each other."

"I'd hate to think I'm confusing you. It's confusing enough just being here. But having someone around, it really helps." He leant over and kissed me. I was kind of getting worried for him, and it was making me angry. Through the little door window a figure was peering through. There was a knock on the door. Neither of us said anything. Then the door opened and a man walked in.

"Maya. Can you come with me?"

I hesitantly walked out with the doctor through the corridor. The ghosts were still there, hanging two feet off the ground and looking dark oily blue in colour. They were still all sad-looking. We got to a door and the doctor led me in. Man, how many doors I've had to encounter.

"Listen," he says as we sit down. "I know you don't want to hear this. But you can't be kissing other patients."

"I wasn't. I was giving him mouth to mouth resuscitation."

"You do know about Spencer's past, don't you?"

"No. What past?"

"Look, I understand. You're young. So I'm going to let it slide."

"That's great and all, but what were you saying about th-"

"But if I see you doing it again, you're going to have to go into Confinement for a while. We can't let this happen. We can't let people see it and start doing it themselves. We have to maintain order, you see."

"Got it, doc. Can I go now?" I didn't even wait to hear his reply. I just walked out. But not before cheekily blowing a kiss to him. The whole situation just made me laugh. He probably just didn't want anyone to kiss anybody because his doctor ass was never kissed once. He'd probably maintained a eunuch-like order his whole life. The scoundrel.

I left the meeting feeling no different, except I wondered what he meant by Som's 'past'. Anyway, I wasn't going to stop it with Somnus just because it was the rules. I wondered what on earth they could do to me. What exactly could they do? Cut off my lips? Put his cock in a blender? I was already in a bad way, I was at my limit. The voices weren't just at the window now, they were everywhere. In the blank shadow. Inside the drawers. In the mind. So what could they do to me now that would ever rise in comparison? I was already dead.

32

I started going to Art Club in August. The room was extremely warm and the fumes off the paint were strong in my nose, and I must have died twice every time I showed up. One day some woman was getting up and going over to a tube of paint like it was the most important decision. Then she opened the lid and leaned back and squeezed the red tube into her mouth until all of it was gone. She tried to swallow, but threw up red bile on the table instead.

I wondered and still do now, if she chose red because she too thought a devil was inside her. It was unclear whether she wanted to kill herself. Sometimes the illness makes you think stuff that is not food is food, and then other times you do it to hurt yourself. I was always in the art room at least once a day ever since I found out about it, and I never once thought of that. A bit like Van Gogh and his ingestions of yellow paint. Was he, like that woman eating the tube, trying to hurt himself, or was it the illness making him think it was soup? Or sunshine? I believe it's very easy for things like that to seem true. It happens. I'd heard from Bully that when he was a young man, he had a girlfriend who drilled into her own temple to get the voices out. What I would have done is simply ask the voices to leave me be. But sometimes in a desperate state you do anything to fix it. I wondered as I sat there in the activity room if the voices really did leave as the drill went in. And where did the person go, and if they were in some new plane of existence, like a sort of Heaven, would the voices still be there? And then what drill could be used then? "Hang on," I whispered to myself. "Paranoia."

I secluded myself in my drawings and quickly forgot about it. Usually I was doing a portrait of someone. If they had a face then I would draw it. Some other people were drawing like me, but most of them just coloured in those already drawn images with felt tips, usually soothing things like birds and fruit. By mid August I had two portraits of Dr. Malik (one adorned with horns), three new ones of Spencer Dustman, one of Dayo the nurse, two of June the White Witch, two of the Alphazites (adorned in cloaks as they sometimes were), one of Venus Miles, one of Dunley Novak, three of Beate, three of moi (which probably looked nothing like me), one of Old Bully and one of Gill Madison, who up to now I haven't spoken of but he was a real character I remember distinctly his happy and drooping face and that '95 Liverpool shirt he wore; his intelligent ramblings about where he was when The White Album came out in November 1968 (his father's balls) and that he was the real Elvis Presley. I made a joke to Old Bull that Gill was a 'mad guru', and then everyone started calling him Guru instead of Gill because of my comment. He knew the exact date of things that had happened years ago and made connections between them through strange 'recollections'. He talked very fast in an accent that I could not pin down. But I enjoyed when he came up to meet me, stumbling a bit, and being real nice and all and offering me a can of Coke, calling the nurse he was smitten with 'Kate Middleton'. Oh, he'd say stuff like that all the time. When I first met him he said "Kate Middleton just made me tea, she did," and I thought he was just confused like how he thought he was Elvis Presley. He gave everyone different names. He called me Angie Baby. It's from the song of the same name. He'd sing it to me all the time.

"It's so nice to be insane, no-one asks you to explain." But maybe he was just making a joke. It was hard to tell. And he always repeated himself at the end of a sentence. So he'd talk like this: "You know I knew David Bowie, I did," or "I'm the real Elvis, I am." He was about forty I'd say, though I never asked him. An old kid with a weird mind that was insane intelligent when it came to certain things, but usually just playful.

I was particularly proud of the portrait I did of Gill. I made him look like a real guru with rags and all. It was near professional. I was getting better at drawing. Yet that became a curse. Sometimes when one of the drawings was done, it would start talking to me. I wanted to rip them up at those times because it frightened me. But really, I was more afraid of the voices still being there after I tore them up, like how the balloon headed nurse still spoke. They felt almost human-like. I didn't want to kill them. I just kept them, under my bed, adorned with stitched up mouths.

August carried on in the Activity Room. Art Club was strange again this particular day. Some guy was bashing his head against the table. I had a portrait I was working on of my mother. I never really knew her, she died when I was two. I didn't know what she looked like, and had seen no pictures of her, except one which was stained and old and barely viewable. She looked happy, though. It looked like a happy figure. Quite tall, like how Beate's tall. I myself am short and wonder what went wrong in the genes. See, I wish I knew my mother and I wish she didn't die but I gave up on wishing a long time ago. I remember when I used to wish, I wished that my father would die so my mother could come back. At least Beate was still here. Beate was a functional human being. She was beautiful and exuberant and confident and kind. In essence she had everything I didn't. She had it together, whereas me, well I don't really need to say at this point, do I? I'll say it anyway. Not Fit for Consumption.

I continued to draw my mother's face of mystery. As if I could bring her back to life, so long as I could just get it looking right. But I strained my eyes to see what couldn't be seen. My hand in use was doing its usual thing. Moving independently from me as if it were possessed, and making everything sporadic just like it had before. But I couldn't control it. It stabbed the paper into shreds. Everyone looked up.

33

"Would you rather be deaf or blind?"
"Gee Som, that's a deep question."
"Well?"
"I'd have to say deaf."
"You'd rather be deaf? Why that one?"
"I hate the voices. Plus I want to see your face as much as I can, now don't I you big idiot?"
"So you wouldn't miss my voice?"
"Yeah...Where is that accent from anyway? You never told me."
"I don't even know."
"You must know!"
"It's just another thing I forgot. What does it sound like to you?"
"Well. English. But there's something off about it. Anyway, what about you? What would you pick?"
"I would rather be blind. I hate the voices, too. But still, it's better than seeing all these people talking at you and you don't know what they're saying. Most people can't do sign language. And imagine if you went to a gig or something. Would be very strange."
"But you wouldn't be able to see anything if you chose that one."
"That's just the surface."

"True. It's a blessing we have both, I guess."

"It's not really a blessing to me." He looked downcast as he said it. "Sometimes I wish I didn't have either. My sight and hearing have been jacked up to the max. It's like those dolphins that are kept in concrete tanks. Their sonar bounces back at them and never goes away. It drives them mad. I feel just like that. It's too much. My brain can't take it, Maya. It would be nice, to just, disappear from it all."

"Som... Remember what you said to me. You said you were happy now. Like you could talk to someone and it wouldn't be all hell? Remember?"

"I am talking to someone. You. It's just. Sometimes the days are just too hard. My brain is starting to really hurt. It really hurts. It feels like it's gonna burst." He grabbed his head and cried right there on my bed. I didn't know what to do. I patted him on the back. Then, I started to hear a voice that wasn't either of us. I panicked, and looked around my room. It was underneath us. I took in a deep breath and titled off the bed with my head and it was dead loud now. It was one of the drawings, coming to life.

"Erase me. I do not belong here."

"God, not you too."

"I do not belong here."

"Yeah, well I don't belong here either. Get used to it." But it kept on saying 'I do not belong' over and over and it was driving me nuts. It was only a doodle. So I folded it up into an aeroplane and threw it across the room, hitting Som in the face by accident. I wanted to laugh but he looked sad still.

"Look, I know how you feel. I've tried to end it nine times."

"Nine?"

"Five pill overdoses, one hanging, two alcohol poisonings, and one wrist slitting."

"But you seem so together."

"Nope. My scarf fell off the tree branch. You'd be surprised how many people have tried to end it. People you wouldn't suspect. But you should be glad you're still alive. I'm glad you're still alive."

"You know. You're the only reason I want to stay." I didn't know what to say. I just smiled awkwardly.

"There's something I gotta ask you now it's in my mind. Doctor Hurst said something about your 'past'? Is there something you didn't tell me?"

"Past? Yes. There's something I haven't told you. I wasn't sure how to."

"What?"

"Do you remember I said my brother had died, and that's how I forgot my name, because he wasn't around to call me it?"

"Yeah... So you do remember it, then? What is it?"

"No. I mean. It was me."

"Me what?"

"Who killed him."

34

I hung there for an aeon.

"What?"

"I know I should have told you earlier. But I was afraid."

"Why? Why did you kill him?"

"It's not what you think. I'd never want to hurt my brother. But I thought it was a clone."

"Okay. And your parents? Did you kill them too? Was

that 7/7 thing just a lie?"

"No. Not them."

"So how did you do it?" He stared at me darkly.

"I strangled him while he was asleep."

I began to feel sick at the way he said it so calmly. But I too believed my sister was an evil clone, and threw a mug at her head trying to kill her. If it had hit her temple she would probably be dead, too. So did it really mean I could have been evil and wicked for throwing that mug and killing her? Did it mean Somnus strangling his brother was likewise? I had been so blinded by my obsession with him and then infatuation with him that I took him for a saint. His own brother. Would he do it to me, if he thought I was something else? And what exactly was I anyway?

Soon it became September. I was planting some flowers in the garden with Dunley. The garden was cold and bright. I was wearing my Pixies hoodie under a long baggy denim jacket and still I felt cold. While talking to Dunley I found out he overdosed on AMT and said he spent two months in Spector Park, which was long before I turned up. And he said he got better, and they released him, and he went to university to study Philosophy and Creative Writing, but something bad happened the second term of first year and (though he didn't know it himself) was taken once again to Spector Park, and had been there for two years and counting, enough time for me to show up and find out about his strange belief with the 'giant squirrels'. And while I gathered some soil, he recanted to me more about the drug.

"It really fucked me up. Actually," he says, now

seeming to be rather coherent and confident in his words. "My old friend Shaman is all love smack crazy for this Russian girl. Katrina Barkova. And I never knew her at the time, but anyway she took too much AMT too and fell into a coma. And the weirdest thing was. She died in the hospital and then came back to life. AMT is a monster. I thought doctors were injecting me with it. I saw it written on the syringes. I'm still not sure if they were really doing it."

Erstwhile, Venus was pouring a watering can on Beth the vampire's head. Som hadn't bothered to show up. I was kind of glad. He was probably going to tell me he got trapped inside a dream again. But he had to be there in the ward, didn't he? In his room? How could he have escaped without being in a dream? There was no way to escape. I'd tried a couple times. But maybe he was telling the truth. Was I going crazy thinking he might actually be right, and that under certain conditions one could identify an object in a dream and teleport it to the waking world? And maybe you had to be mad to do it? My mind was swept to derangement at this point, a deep schizophrenic state, in which any theory I heard or imagined both became the reality. So I believed him. I believed he was real. Looking back now, all these years later, I still wonder if it was ever real. But the love, and the pain, felt realer than anything.

I left the garden and went to his room to check he hadn't escaped into his dream. I walked up to the door and looked through the window. There was no-one there. I checked everywhere. The courtyard. The cafeteria. The activity room. The lounge. I even looked through all the windows on all the patient's doors. I saw people, but they weren't him.

Though I really did care for him and felt a real

connection with him, still distilled in my mind was the feeling I felt when he said it. It was like a vicious beating heart, beating, pounding in my chest. But it wasn't my chest. It was his. Lodged in mine. I imagined him doing it, as if it were me. Looking into his younger brother's eyes and actually killing him right there with his own hands. It frightened me beyond anything, and I almost didn't believe it. How was he capable of doing this? Him? The quiet reader? It was the way he said it so calmly too, when usually he was nervous around me. I mean, as soon as I mentioned sex he vanished. Maybe this was eating him up inside. Maybe that's why he was so sad. I tried to decide whether I still wanted to see him. Part of me wanted to, and then there was another part of me that just wanted to get away from him. I didn't know what to do. Forgiving him was one thing, I still had to figure out how to deal with the fact he might, if, driven too much by delusions, try and hurt me. How could I be with him, and feel safe, knowing he might strangle me, too? How could I be with him, knowing full well myself how 'clones' and 'imposters' can infect someone's head? And isn't it the people you love most who you end up hurting the most? And was he intending to hide the fact he did it? Even from himself? Too many questions, girl.

Nothing could prepare me for Som's revelation. It was the thorn in the red rose he left me that morning he mysteriously vanished. Yet little did I know at the time, things were about to get a whole lot worse.

35

While feeling paranoid and tired, I had the luxury of

being interviewed by some American called Sal Goodman. He was a journalist and he wanted to talk to me.

He led me into a small room with a table in the middle. There was a lightbulb dangling above our heads. The guy wore ray bans and a reddy orange Hawaiian shirt. I couldn't pin down the accent. I wondered if he lived in Seattle like Beate. He kept on asking me to close my eyes and say how many fingers he had up. I was confused but I did as he said. When I got them right, five times in a row, he looked up at the lightbulb dangling above us, and asked me to leave the room and stick my fingers in my ears. When he let me back in, he asked me how many times he flicked the light-switch while I was out. I told him. Then he asked me to guess numbers he was thinking of, colours, what words he had secretly written on cards. He was testing me for something. But I didn't know what. They weren't run of the mill journalist queries. Then he says: "Have you ever seen aliens, Maya?"

"Aliens? Maybe."

"Can you contact them?"

"No, they only contact me."

"Can you summon them?"

"Why are you asking me all this?"

"It's for an article on schizophrenia."

"And why all those questions before? Sounds like a strange article you're writing."

"Well madness is strange."

"Is there anything else?"

"Explain to me more about these aliens."

"What do you want to know? I encountered them one night. Ever since then they come by whenever I need them. They help me." He scribbled on his pad.

"What do they do?"

"Sometimes they give me a third eye. It's strange, I know."

"Nothing's strange here, Maya. Go on, what is the eye for?"

"I see my past and future in one. It makes me realise, umm, something. It's hard to express in words, mister."

"Very interesting. The magazine is gonna love all this, Maya."

"Great."

"Okay. Look. I've run this bit as far as I can take it. I'll level with you. I'm not a journalist. I work for the Secret Intelligence."

"Yeah right."

"It's true."

"That Hawaiian shirt begs to differ."

"I had to go undercover. Even the ward doesn't know. I'm just a visitor. A visiting journalist looking for a story on psychosis. See my badge? Look. I just need one thing. For you to bring these beings to me, so I can proceed to Stage Two."

"What's Stage Two?"

"That's none of your concern."

"Well, I'm sorry to break it to you and your 'journalistic endeavours', mister, but it's not possible to just bring these things to you. They're not in our dimension."

"But they came to see you? So they were in our dimension?"

"Gee, I don't know. I'm as clueless as you, okay?"

"Find out how to bring them to me. I'll be back to check up on you."

"Why don't you just find some other poor freak?"

"I have. But no-one else got every question right in the

quiz. There was an old man called Thom Hyper who was nearly at your level. But nothing like this. There's something special seeping from your illness. Let me harness it. I'll make you a lot of money."

"I don't want your god-damn money. I had the chance to have diamonds and rubies. Money is useless to me."

"Fine. Then I'll get you out of here. I'd bet you want that?"

"It's still a no. I don't trust you. What's the Secret Intelligence got to do with psychosis anyway? You still haven't told me what's going on."

"This is strictly confidential. But now you're in the mess just like me, so. I'll tell you." He adjusted his shades and cleared his throat. "The service has assigned me to talk to mental patients like you, for the reason that the psychotic state may reveal the future. I know it sounds kind of funky, but the new administration has got a lot of far out ideas, and well they got the money to back it up. The service wants access to the psychotic state. And to find the beings which are undetectable by any other means. That's why I'm here. You seem to have extreme extrasensory perception. And you have seen them, you say. You are clearly our best shot of reaching them."

"If I'm your best shot, the Secret Intelligence really is scraping the barrel."

"Just hear me out." He took off his sunglasses and paused for a moment. "If you help me, I'll get you out of here. I can take you wherever you want to go."

"It's a no. Goodbye, Sal."

When I left the room, a man was running across the corridor, screaming.

"My baby! My baby! Someone ate my baby!" No-one

seemed to pay attention. People were sitting in the lounge drinking tea, reading newspapers and magazines and looking at old photos and remarking of the cool weather and the ghosts of children running around the place. I sat down on a big blue chair there next to Gill, who was drinking a can of Coke. He was always drinking Coke. But they never had any vending machines in the ward.

"Say, Gill. Where do you get those Cokes from?"

"Oh, they give 'em to me, they do, Angie. I also got a TV and DVD player. Usually they don't let you because the wires can be used to hang yourself, but it's all wireless now, it is. The future don't look too good for suicide, it don't."

"But how come they give you all this stuff? I don't have anything."

"On account I've been really good, I have. I've been here twenty three years and never rustled a feather. I have *Fantastic Planet* and *The King of Comedy*, I do. Oh and *Jason and the Argonauts*. Funny thing about the real Jason. The one in the film ain't the real Jason. There's this guy who comes in to see his little brother every day, he does, sits next to him, he does, calms him down, gives him food. Every day. He's the real Jason, you know? The really real one. I don't think the boy even realises he's here every day visiting him."

"Which boy?"

"I think his name's Dudley."

"You must mean Dunley. Yeah, he's really out of it. Wherever he goes, he thinks he's always in the same room. With no door. He doesn't see doors."

"But did you see him earlier? Jason gave him a guitar from home, and he just started playing it. He made everybody look up, he did. No-one knew what the hell was going on, but I could see his soul coming out of his fingers, I could."

"Damn, I must have missed it. I had some interview with this guy." I didn't mention any more about it. "So you've got *Fantastic Planet* on DVD? I love that film. I only watched the French version, though. And I don't understand the language so it became even weirder. Anyway, that's so cool you get a TV. I guess like you said, they treat you nice when you've been here a while and don't cause a fuss."

"Well, Bulldog causes fusses all over and they let him have porn mags for Christ's sake."

"Bulldog?"

"The one who looks like a bulldog."

"Oh, him. Well, that's a bit sad isn't it? I don't have anything in my room except a diary, some sheets of paper and a pencil. And they were all brought by Beate on her first visit. So, they give him porno in exchange for not killing anyone with his bare teeth? If I want to see a naked guy, well I just draw it."

"Well, I've seen you and Dicaprio together quite a bit, I have. Are you two..?"

"His name is Spencer, Gill. And no. Well. Yeah. I know it's not allowed. Please don't tell anyone."

"I won't, Angie. I've got a crush on this Kate myself, I have. So I know what you're feeling, I do. Just be inconspicuous. Invisible."

"You know, he said this thing to me. How there's a gem that can make you invisible."

"Ooh. Wouldn't that be lovely! I could walk around naked with that, I could!"

"But he really believes it. What should I say to him?"

"Sometimes that's all we got, our beliefs. And when you try and destroy someone's belief, they feel like a piece of them is missing. I mean, with me it's different. I know I'm the real Elvis Presley, but do I really care if the others don't believe? I am what I am, I am."

*

It was a few days before I was taken to Confinement. For biting one of the doctors on the leg. I maintained he had created me, and turned me into a deformed creature. So I bit him.

I was avoiding Som at all costs. I still didn't know how I felt about the whole thing. I confided in Dunley Novak.

His room was number six, and I went there and saw his acoustic guitar lying against the wall through his window. I went in and said hello and all. He looked as if he was lost. He still believed he was in this 'anteroom'. I didn't bother telling him it wasn't true, after what Gill said to me about people's beliefs and all. That crushing them is like crushing the people themselves. I just tried to distract him from it. We got into a conversation about sleep, naturally. You tend to talk about things when they're not happening to you.

"It keeps people up far longer than their mind can bear."

"What does?"

"Psychosis. Schizophrenia. Madness. Losing the plot, the thread, the conversation. Whatever you wanna call it, Dunley."

"I wanna call it something vicious. God, if only I had Soogy's way of thinking."

"Who's Soogy?"

"Oh, well he was this homeless guy I met once when I was at university. Used to be a deliverer in some hopped up VW Camper, but things got bad and he had to sell it. I just saw him on the pavement outside Sainsbury's one day, I was walking back from getting food there, and I look over and see this homeless guy sitting down and smiling. Smiling. So I go over and give him a 50p or something and we end up chatting for two hours while my oven pizzas thawed in the Sun. He keeps on giving me cigarettes even though I told him I had a full pouch of tobacco, but he insists, telling me they're good for me. He was really cool. Anyway, the reason I'm saying all this, well he asked me about myself and I told him I was mad for a while and couldn't sleep for thirty days straight, thinking he'd find that impressive. Then he puts his cigarette out on the floor and says to me: "Thirty days? So ya ken, then?" and I say: "What?" and he says: "Ya see things. Ya realise things. It's the strongest drug known to man." He stayed up on purpose, telling me he got mad enlightened when he did it. He treated it so positively. I was baffled by his serenity. I mean, I always thought it was hell, staying awake that long. But he seemed to enjoy it."

"Well, me and Soogy are very different people. Enlightened? Not me. No chance."

"He was a bit peculiar. But then, all the best people are."

After a while, the conversation became darker, and it was mostly my fault. I was distracted and couldn't help telling him my bad lot. I told him about Somnus and how he had killed his brother. How I felt I loved him. How I didn't know what to do. He listened attentively while I rambled on. In the end, he didn't know what to advise, other than a shrug of the shoulders. But I wasn't expecting him to fix it. It might not have even been able to be fixed. We talked for a while longer, him seeming to be more coherent than usual, and there was no talk of the 'giant squirrels'. I asked him if there was any girl or boy in his life he had fallen for.

"Yeah. You know, falling is the perfect word for it. You can break your neck falling. I'm done with falling."

I realised I was making things depressing, so I asked him about university and what it was like, since I had never been to one. But unfortunately it was just as depressing. He said he didn't turn up once for classes, had no money, wasn't eating, was nearly always alone, was sad with everything in his life, and felt he was a failure. He said he got so depressed, that he, just like me and Somnus, and even Old Bully, had tried to kill himself. And of course thousands of others all over the Earth, including the legend of Seymour (whose joyful way and tragic story shall be left for another day.)

"Saved up two months worth of meds and downed them with whiskey and valium. An old lady or somebody found my body on the floor of some park at dawn. When I woke up, I couldn't believe I was alive. My heart was in hyper arrhythmia. I should have been dead. An angel was looking over me that morning."

"You believe that?"

"Yeah."

"In angels?"

"Well, yeah. Everyone's an angel. It's like that poem. The bum is as holy as the seraphim."

When they finally put me in Confinement, I imagined if everyone really were an angel like Dunley said. Then I imagined if everyone were really a devil, too. Was a human not just the combination of angel and devil? Was that not what I was? Was I even human any more? I was locked in a room with nothing but the voices and an occasional meal. And then, something began to really torment me. I was starting to believe there was a bomb in my stomach. I could hear it ticking. When the idea quickly came to absolute belief, I banged my fists against the Confinement room door frantically, hoping someone would hear me. It was two hours later when they finally let me out. I ran out like a snowstorm.

"There's a bomb! Inside me! I need to leave! Let me go! Or everyone's dead! Please! Listen to me!" I ran for the exit. And you know what that gets you? Tackled to the ground while some people lie on top of you, and the medication is on its way to debunk the delusion. When they sat down on me I thought they were going to abuse me, because they were laughing to each other and it made me paranoid. And it really wasn't just a ploy to escape the place. I truly believed I had to save the lives of everyone around me by getting out of there, because the bomb was set to go off. I was yelling that they 'can't do this' and that they had to 'believe me'. I had closure of my death. But not everyone else's. Not the other angels. I had to leave. But in the end the bomb never went off. And I have still never forgotten how much I truly believed it.

Strangely, the night, now back in my room, was very hot. There were windows open, but they were the type of windows that didn't open all the way, so it got very humid. Voices seeped through the iron bars. The tail wagged incessantly.

I stopped going to see Somnus and sleeping in his bed. It was his turn to have the sleeping ring one night a while back, and I just let him keep it for weeks because I felt like torturing myself. And I felt like being alone, and my psychosis was on full speed, disorientating me with pure fear and confusion. I saw Jean Cocteau and Salvador Dali climbing up my walls on either side like spiders. Later, in the corners of my eyes, I saw flames in the otherwise blank night thinking there was a fire. And then he knocked on my door.

"I know it's late. But I need to tell you something. I was supposed to tell you earlier. But I was, well, I couldn't do it at the time. I'm sorry. But. Maybe you should sit down."

"I'm already sitting down, Som."

"You know The Peak Times you told me about?"

"Yeah?"

"It got bombed."

"What? Bombed? Are you crazy?"

"Well, when you told me that your sister worked for them, I wrote to them asking for a copy, you know so I could read it. Today I got this letter, which said they couldn't send me a copy because that building where the paper had it's HQ was Columbus Building, which got bombed. Everything's on hiatus there."

"Let me see that letter." I grabbed it from his hand, started reading. "When did this happen?"

"Two days ago."

"And what about Beate? Was she there? Tell me she wasn't in the building, Som."

"I'm not sure."

"And you're telling me this now?"

"I'm sorry. I know it's late. I'll go. I just thought I had to tell you."

"How can I even believe you! You're going crazy just the same as me, Som. How can I believe this? I can't. I love her, Som. I remember this time I went hiking with her when I was fourteen, she fed me grapes as we climbed Hozomeen, you know, that mountain you went to in your dream, that picture I showed you? And she told me all about university while we hiked and what it was like to get drunk and get with guys and all that stuff, but she was so smart too. She came to visit me so many times in the ward. And from America. It's just. She can't be dead. It can't be true."

The night after Som told me about the newspaper bombing, I had a horrible waking nightmare. All I could see was her body in pieces. But surely someone would have contacted the hospital looking for me, if she was in fact dead? Or maybe they thought the news would just drive me over the edge. But I was already over the edge.

A week went by and Sal Goodman turned up again. This time he was wearing a black suit. His brown crew-cut belied his crazy gestures and the manic yankie voice he had.

"You again. Why the change?"

"I need to change outfits everyday. I'm undercover."

"Why did you come to this country?" I ask him quite randomly.

"You know, I like it here. Everything's small. Which makes me feel huge."

"Great. Listen, Mr. Goodman. I need to know if something's true. What do you know about the bombing of The Peak Times?"

"Oh, yes. The Peak Times. Terrible. Just terrible. Why do you ask?"

"My sister works there. Well, she's the founder."

"Your sister is the founder? Your sister is Beate Castro? But your last name is Maney!"

"She took my mother's name. Didn't figure that one out?"

"Oh my. Listen. This isn't easy to say. They took your sister."

"Wait, what?"

"I'm sorry, Maya."

"So she's not dead? She wasn't in the bombing?"

"No. But some far right militia apparently hired by cronies of Trump initiated the bombing. They're keeping your sister as a hostage. If only I knew at the time your relation. I apologise. See, the Trump campaign is shifting the blame on ISIS for the bombing and kidnap in order to protect itself, since the information about your sister has been leaked to every news outlet in America. So Trump is blaming ISIS. But it's an inside job."

"How do you know?"

"I went to his conference in Washington, bugged him with a new device my scientist friend Buckwell just recently invented. Basically, it involves nano technology. It's invisible to the naked eye. Anyway, so I posed as a journalist for the New Yorker at this conference and bugged him with this new device and got the device back two days later, since I knew his whereabouts at that time due to the bug that was on him, so I got it back without him even knowing he was wearing it. The info it sent back. Well, it's all there clear as day."

"So, Beate has really been kidnapped? By a far right militia?"

"I hate to say it. But it's true. How strange that I would run into you, her sister. It's ironic as you Brits say, right?"

"Yes, what I care about is the irony, Sal." He looked at me strangely as if deep in thought and continued the (unbelievable) story.

"We don't know exactly who these people are, but we

can assume they're dangerous."

"Well it does actually make sense now I think about it, since she is such a vocal liberal and condemns Trump herself in almost every issue. But why the whole building? Why'd they blow it all up? There were nineteen stories."

"Do you think Trump's cronies really care about collateral damage?"

"Mr. Goodman. Please, help me find my sister. I know you have the skills. You bugged the goddamn President." He looked at me with a stern expression, and sighed.

"Hate to say it, but she may already be dead. But I'll help you find her. If she's alive, I mean. But first, you have to do something for me."

"What?"

"Find the aliens. I want to see them."

"Listen, I don't think it's even possible."

"Either you do it, or your sister is as good as dead."

Following Goodman's second visit, I spent the whole night thinking about what he said. I tried to figure out how I could get the aliens to meet him. They only appeared to me, so how could he see them? And what was it that he wanted from them, anyway? Their powers of healing, perhaps. The way they healed my head with their long spindly fingers. Or perhaps their extraordinary ability to calculate faster than a quantum computer. Or even their ability to perceive time as a single moment. All past, present and future in a single moment. Beyond time. They could tell him the future. Maybe that's what he wanted.

When I thought about it, it started to make sense. The Alphazites were very powerful creatures. He could harness a lot from them, if only they could be harnessed. First they had to appear again. Then I could talk to them and see if they would agree to meet with Sal. I didn't want to do it. But I had to. Because it was my only chance to find Beate.

*

I was feeling down on a cold evening. I took my lighter out and looked at it in my hand. Hm. What if you set the duvet on fire and wrapped it around yourself? Would that work?

I went out to the courtyard to have a smoke. Rudie was playing her saxophone. No-one gave her coins because no-one had any coins. The music was haunting in the dim light.

My mind was completely destroyed. It began to hurt like how Som said his hurt. I ran into the ramp banister and tried to hurt myself more. Break a bone. What did it matter? Again, I wanted to torture myself. But the saxophone stopped, and Rudie came up to me, looking distressed at my distress.

"Maya. Are you okay?"

"I just want to get out of here."

"Me too. We should both escape."

"I've been hearing that a lot."

"You know, if we did, I could play sax on the high streets. I could make actual coins. But it's not about the coins, really, when it all comes down to it, it's the music. Pure and simple. If I don't play or hear music, the demons come. Demons are mute. Angels are megaphones! Haha!"

It was beautifully queer that she said that, because

Som's hypothetical deaf or blind question had me realising that music, and hearing, were superior to merely seeing. I realised he was right. To be in a world without music, would be a horror of its own. I prayed to some unknown deity that I would never lose my hearing. Even if they were voices from the damned. My very own sonar bouncing back at me.

October came and left. But before it left for another year, there was one last day. October 31st. It was a terrible time to be in the ward, because everyone was paranoid of ghosts and spirits, and Halloween was the one day of the year where even sane people became concerned. But here, well, some were possessed, and some were trying to possess.

I ate alone in the cafeteria. Dunley saw me and came over to the table and sat down. Well, can't avoid people your whole life.

"Hey, Maya."

"Hey Dunley."

"You okay?"

"Yeah. No."

"So, which one?"

"Dunley, my sister's been kidnapped." He hung there in silence.

"What? How? Why?"

"I'm not sure yet. God," I say, as if I was only talking to myself. "If that damn gem was only real, I could escape without being seen and go find her. If it was real. God, but what's real now? And all the while the voices whispering to 'come' and 'see this' and there's nothing to be seen but pure horror. Pure horror, Dunley."

"I know how you feel. Well, I don't exactly hear things much these days, but I have been seeing some strange stuff."

"Have you seen, aliens?"

"Yeah. How did you know?"

"What did they look like?"

"Well, all I remember is they had three eyes. And I have this three-eyed smiley tat on my wrist to sort of symbolise the time I saw them." He showed me his forearm. "Though actually, now that I think about it, I think I got the tat long before I met them things." He looked quizzical.

"You know, Dunley. I saw that too. So maybe the Alphazites are real after all?"

"Alphazites?"

"It's a name I came up for them. They don't call themselves it or anything."

"Oh, right." He smiled with intrigue. "I wonder if anyone else has seen these things? They're unreal aren't they?"

"Well, Rudie hasn't, neither has Beth or Venus. Bully didn't either, but he did say he was sent to the future once where humans had all been extinct and a new species emerged. But it's hard to trust what people say here. It's hard to trust yourself. I mean, there's this American guy who's telling me he works for MI6. And Som tells me there's a gem that can give you powers. He says it can make you invisible and all. That it heals you, and makes you live for hundreds of years. He said it can even turn you sane again. But I'm starting to think he's the one who isn't being sane."

"Hey, if aliens are true, and giant squirrels are true, then an enchanted gem ain't too far out in the woods, right?"

"But even if I did make it with him and escape, we would have everywhere and nowhere to go. I don't know if I'd want to see him. He killed his own brother,

Dunley. It wasn't evil, I don't think. But it happened. I'm just afraid that he'll do it to me, too. I still love him. I just can't handle it. I can't even handle myself, you know? How another?"

"Are you afraid when you're with him?"

"No. But that was before I knew. I've avoided him for weeks. He keeps coming to see me and I tell him to go away, that I'm seeing devils and I want to be alone. I'm really bad at this sort of thing. It doesn't help that my thoughts are spilling out of my head."

When it was night, I kept on thinking about it. I couldn't help myself. I wondered if I was capable of doing something like that. Were we the same? Could any minute any one of us turn into an Icelos of our own? A beast? A murderer? And while I sat torturing myself with these thoughts that lonely night, I heard him on the other side of the wall screaming again. After he didn't stop, I decided to walk in, and saw he was shaking. He didn't look right. He was talking to himself, and he was spasming.

"There... There..." Then moments after a voice was heard in my head as loud as a quake:

> *"Halloween on Hozomeen*
> *Mountain monster*
> *Wails a dream."*

I jogged Somnus with my hand until his eyes lit up.

"Why did you wake me? I nearly had it!"

"Som, this is crazy. There's no gem. There's no gem okay? I wish there was. And I don't want to crush your belief. But there's not. You have psychosis, Som. You got carted just like I got carted."

"Yeah, but sometimes people get carted even when they're fine. I'm fine, Maya. I understand now."

"You don't understand, though. It's not real."

"Maybe you're not real."

"Doubting my existence. Nice job. I could do the same to you, you know."

"Why don't you tell me if this is real?" He held my hand. "Is it real, Maya? Is it real?"

"But I don't know. Just because it feels real doesn't mean it's real. I just don't know." I gripped his hand tight. If he was real or not, I knew I loved him. Everything else evaporated. It was just me and him, holding hands, not letting go. But then he said something that just broke me.

"I'm being transferred to another ward."

We stopped fighting and fell to his bed in shared exhaustion, until it was dawn and the ghosts of Halloween were sent back from wherever they came from, and out the thinly opened window a lone red hawk kite was dangling its spanned wings across the lint grey November skyline, as if its freedom was literally bounding through the air, never to be touched by these insane human hands.

We were together all night. I kept on thinking about him getting moved somewhere else. It emptied me. But he breathed on my nose and I didn't care. I felt strangely safe with him. He kept the ghosts away. But I still hadn't forgotten what he did. It never left me. I just learned to bury it, like everything else.

When I left his room that morning and returned to my own, I happened to see the Alphazites again.

Such evil looking things they were, yet evil they were not. They had these claw-like fingers that looked like they could decapitate a lion, and eyes that stared into your soul three god-damn times. But evil they were not. If they were, I would have been dead already.

They crept in like clouds and began talking to me, but it wasn't sound. There was only a mysterious little humming and vibration but I knew what they were saying somehow. It was like telepathy or something.

"Maya. I sense there is something you would like to tell me and my cohorts."

"Yeah, there is. This guy who works for the Secret Intelligence Service wants you to meet him. But it sounds like a bad deal. They're going to use you for something."

"They cannot do such things to creatures like us. We know the future. We live our fate the way we always have, always do, always will. And may I ask, why did you accept such a request from him?"

"He can find out where my sister is. She's been kidnapped."

"I'm sorry it's come to this."

"So what happens to her? And to me? And can I stop Som getting transferred to another ward? Does that pan out?"

"We know all these things, yet as we have told you numerous times, it is not a good idea to tell you. You see, humans aren't capable of handling eternal present. Rather, you can, but only temporarily. You will forget eternal present even before the eye goes." Then one of them raised its ghostly thin arm and extended a finger to my head, its long sharp nail grazing my skull. I felt a pulsating motion in my brain and the third eye emerged from my forehead, and suddenly I understood everything and everything made sense and I knew what would happen as well as what did. But very swiftly it seemed my brain couldn't handle it, and I forgot it all as quickly as I had discovered it.

"Is that what you call living in the past, present and future at the same time? Eternal present?"

"A lovely wording as you humans say, isn't it?"

"Can you tell me where Beate is? I know you said I shouldn't be told. But I'm desperate. I love my sister. I'd dread to think what they're doing to her." They made a peculiar sound in unison. I understood it as their display of sympathy.

"She's still in Seattle."

"Where in Seattle?"

"I can't tell you any more. I've told you too much already. But I do want to help. We want to help. You humans are a troubled stream from a pure source."

"Can I just ask one more thing?" Their three eyes all blinked.

"We're listening."

"Do me and Somnus ever, you know, get married and have kids?"

"As we have said, it is not conducive to know too much about your future, Maya. We can handle it. But we are different to you. You see, we have three eyes which symbolise three things. Past. Present. Future. You humans have only two. Past and present. But with a third, you become one moment in time, which slips beyond your simple three dimensional world. And oh yes. Speaking of that, your eye should disappear soon. Do not blink too much. Goodbye, Maya. And good luck."

They disappeared through the wall. My new eye was again seeping back into my brain. The thing was, it felt strangely normal when the eye was there. Like it really belonged there after all. Like it fit. Like it always had. I touched my head and knew something strange and incomprehensible and frighteningly beautiful was behind it. I went back to Som's room to tell him all about it.

36

When Leo got to the station, instead of buying a ticket, he jumped over the turnstiles and ran towards platform four, somehow lucky enough that the train to Reading, which would get him on the way to Spector Park, was right there waiting to leave. The guards saw him jump up at the turnstiles but couldn't catch up to him he ran so fast, and in an instant he fell in through the closing door as if he were Indiana Jones or something, leaving the guards no choice but to watch the train disappear into the horizon.

When he was inside the train, he sighed and slumped down in a window seat. There was an old nun across from him, constantly sneezing. Greenery flew past. To pass the time, he tried to get some rest, as he had only slept half an hour and felt real gruesome. It was Thursday, but it felt like a Sunday. A Comedown Sunday. He smelt of booze too, and people on the train looked at him as if they were not looking, but they were, they saw his ripped red chequered shirt and black jacket with dust all over it and cuts all over his face, sweating madly, looking deranged. The nun sneezed again. Greenery flew past. He was still thinking about the previous night. It was hard to remember it all, but it was there. The giant bee nearly stinging him to death. Jimi Hendrix coming to life from a poster. The voices from the books. It was so incredibly weird, even for

Halloween. He was glad the drugs effect had worn off.

Soon the train was pulling in to Reading Station. The grey concrete of the platforms encompassed and swam past. The train halted and he got off. He didn't manage to get any more sleep. As he stepped from the platform edge, hordes of people clambered up the escalators while few took the steps. He preferred to go up the steps because there was more space, and he didn't like being all bunched up with other people. He didn't like sleeping with other people. He liked being alone. He found song in the sound of the train, and always enjoyed taking trains, going places. But now wasn't a holiday.

He reached the top of the grey staircase, and the sky above wasn't seen but was grey as well. His eyes were grey too. His skin was grey. But his mind and soul and heart had colour. It had a reason to go on.

As he got out the front entrance, he walked two and a half miles west, using his phone's GPS to see the quickest way there. It took him three quarters of an hour. When he arrived, he was met with the big blue & white sign saying 'Spector Park Mental Hospital'.

The car park was full. That wasn't a good sign, he thought to himself. As he stared at the sign, he remembered when he first visited Maney and saw that sign for the first time. He remembered he was worried about going in, expecting to be yelled at and freaked out, but it really wasn't that bad. Then again, he wasn't the one with the mental illness. He felt pity for everyone there. He understood no-one and no-one understood him. It was that very first time, when he walked in for the first time and was taken to her room for the first time, that he understood just how bad she had gotten. He was told that she was an 'acute inpatient', basically the worst of the lot. Her eyes were crimson, her hair was being ripped out by her own mad, shaking hands. She looked grey then, like how he and the sky looked now. And he remembered bitterly how one nurse had ignored her when she was screaming that a devil was inside her.

He steeled himself and went inside. The place was busy. Nurses with dark blue collared smocks were filing past, and he looked around to find the reception desk, whereupon the lady behind the counter asked him his business.

"I'm here to visit someone."
"Have you booked an appointment?"
"No. But it's really important."
"Okay. And who are you seeing?"
"Maya Maney."
"And your relation to her?" He stared blankly at her.
"I'm her boyfriend."
"And your name?"
"Leo Wickman."
"Okay. We'll ask her if she wants to be seen."
"Oh, she will. There's no need. If you could just show me to her room. She knows I'm coming."
"Well, please. Wait for me to ring someone and just check she's okay to be seen. You know, just making sure things are all clear. Protocol."
"Look, I don't have time for this." A light flicked in his head and he remembered the number of her door. He was sure it was sixteen. He remembered because of the joke she made in the letter that it was 'sweet sixteen'.

He couldn't wait for her approval, because there was a good chance she would reject the visit if she heard it was him who was there to see her. So he ran. He ran through the maze of doors that was inscribed in his memory from the times he came before. The doors weren't locked, but he wasn't supposed to go through them without consent or a visitor badge. He had to be quick, and would only get a small time to see her until he was found and removed. But there was time enough to tell her how he felt. Time itself seemed to slow down as he ran through the maze of doors. Every room looked the same. But then he saw a door with the number one above it, and followed it along to door number two, then three, four, five, six, all the way to sixteen. On the way he noticed the patients murmuring about the 'new guy'. Then a woman jumps out as if from nowhere and says to him: "Oh yes, you look awful! Just awful! And you came here? I was awful looking once, and I came here! And they wanted to replace my brain with that of a dog's! I said no. I want a normal brain! Don't you know what I mean?"

"Yeah. I guess I do. I don't want to be rude, but I'm actually not a patient."

"Well you will be if you hang around. That's how they got me." All that stress must have eaten away at her, she was paranoid with misted eyes leering in every direction. He heard a far off scream, just one of the many screams housed in the place, a place which he almost feared, as if it would swallow him up and he'd end up unable to leave.

"I just came here to see my... my... It's just I have to be going now. It was nice meeting you."

"Why are you here? Are you a narc?"

"No, I'm not a narc."

"Classic narc." Always says he ain't one." The woman carried on up the corridor.

Walking to number sixteen, he readied himself, took a big sigh, and knocked on the door. There wasn't any answer. He looked through the little window. He couldn't see her. He noticed he was being watched by a nurse, who was talking to a doctor.

As he walked in, she wasn't anywhere there. Not in the corner. Not in the bed. Not on the ceiling. He looked over at the table. Her diary was on top of it, spread open. He picked it up, and read from a random page.

The thing is, is that, even though I love Somnus, I still know that he killed someone dear to him. I can never forget it. I'm not sure if he can too. It was his brother. His own brother. Imagine me killing Beate! That's what it's like! He's always close to me. Literally. He lives in 17. I can hear him screaming about dreams through the wall. He's crazy, but I love him. I'm just worried that I am too becoming someone dear to him, someone he might end up killing. If he thought I was someone else... And who can I tell? Oh diary, if only you could tell me what to do instead of I you.

He threw the diary on the floor, opened the door and turned to the next room.

"Sir? Sir, where are you going?"

He ignored the nurse and walked in, seeing me on the bed with Somnus. He assumed the person in the diary. He thought I looked just a mess as the last time he'd seen me. Back in February. But I was still beautiful, he thought, even though a mess. When I noticed him there, I winced.

"Leo..."

"Get away from him, Maya."

"What? What are you doing here?"

"He's going to hurt you. He's a murderer."

"What? How do you?"

"Look, I know. I read your diary. Listen here, mate. You get out her room now. Now."

"Hold on. Who are you? Who is this, Maya?"

"I'm her boyfriend."

"Well she never mentioned you once. Maya, did you tell him I was a murderer?"

"No, Som."

"You think I'm a murderer, don't you? Say it. Go on. I know you want to. Say it!" Looking at the both of them, my head was about ready to fire off my body like a rocket.

"Fine. You know what I think. I think it's bad Som. I'm not saying you meant to do it. But. It's just bad. It made me scared."

"It makes me feel bad. Every day I've had to live with it."

"Live with it!" Leo shouts. "Every day! Imagine all the days your brother will never get, because you killed him! Maya. You need to make a choice. Me or him."

"Just back off buddy," says Somnus in a weary voice. There were hundreds of cockroaches on the walls, listening.

"And what if I don't. You'll kill me? Like you did your fucking brother?" Leo leapt at Somnus and threw him off the bed. I was staring from the corner of the room, horrified. He was hunched over Som and started punching him right in the head, over and over. The anger was so intense and his goddamn love for me was the same. The hate and the obsession mixed into a violent beating with both fists. Som's face was turning purple and gradually it became nothing but a puce pulp pile of mess. I was paralysed by fear and couldn't move. Blood ran all over Som's face and body. But Leo kept on punching him. He screamed at him as if he was the one who was crazy. As if he was the one who had killed before. I was crying, trying to hold him back, but I wasn't strong enough to do it.

"Stop Leo! You're going to hurt him!"

Leo pummelled his face one last time, his hands raw, his mind mangled, the man underneath him now unconscious.

"Get out! Get out! Why the fuck are you even here!"

"I came to get you back."

"Get me back? Get me back?! Are you out of your goddamn mind?! Look what you've done to him! Just get out. Don't ever come back, Leo."

I fell on top of Somnus. Everything became a blur.

37

After everybody came to straighten us all out, Wickman was taken away somewhere (hoping Hell), and Somnus was taken to a general hospital, but to me it really looked like he was dead after that last punch to the head.

I wanted to go to the hospital to see him, but I wasn't allowed to leave the ward. I thought about burning my tongue off or eating my hand so then I'd wind up in the general hospital. But like trying to die from not breathing or stabbing myself with plastic forks, it all came to nothing.

The next day I was lying on my bed, thinking about how many times I'd laid myself down on that same bed in the same goddamn position. How long had it really been? Was it really ten months as the calendars would have me believe? It felt like ten years. It really did. Time must slow down when you haven't slept for a year. I don't know.

I turned on my side. I began to hear something. Was it the Alphazites, returning? I braced myself and looked out to the room, seeing that familiar red LED light that blinked away in the top corner, as if watching me, as if waiting. But I waited and the Alphazites and anything else were nowhere to be seen. Then I noticed something shaking on the floor just by my feet. It was old Spencer Dustman. A drawn Spencer Dustman. Covered in dust. It animated like stop motion on the piece of paper.

"What the?"

"Please, don't go. Just listen to me." I stare agog. "They announced my death earlier today. I'm in a new world now. Don't worry about me." From the moving ink two of the Alphazites appeared alongside him.

"What are you guys doing there?"

"We are showing your friend here the next stage in evolution. Don't feel FOMO, as you humans say. For you, Maya, will also enter the next stage in evolution, when your own time comes."

"They're right, Maya. It feels like something is growing on my head. Is it happening, Axel? Is it happening now?"

"Stay calm, Som. It is happening." I looked at the animated ink, seeing the aliens each put one finger on his forehead, whereupon an eye came crawling out of his skin, blinking, darting around, and then finally looking right at me along with the other two.

"I miss you, Som. You and all your eyes."

"I miss you, too. It's been...wait. I'm seeing something. Oh right! How did I forget? There was a necklace on my old body, a necklace with a key. Did you manage to take it, out of curiosity?"

"No," I say to the drawing. "Why?"

"I want you to have it. So you can open my box."

"Your box? You mean that wooden box on your desk? So I finally get to see what's in there. But you've gone. Oh my god, what if they emptied your room already! I have to check!"

I ran out of my room and into the next room. When I walked in, someone different was there. I then realised I was in the wrong room, I had turned the wrong way. When I finally got to the right room, there was no-one there and the box was still there. But no key. So I put the box on the floor and stomped on it.

I looked at the ruins. Then I looked at my foot. It was bleeding. I noticed some glass or something sticking out of my foot. I winced and pulled it out. It was a purple gem.

*

I rolled my eyes but then stared intently at it. I had forgotten my foot was cut. But no, I had not forgotten. The pain had simply gone. I looked at my foot and the cut was gone. I put the gem in my pocket and started walking to my room. The broken box moved a little in aftershock and I heard a sound, it was the sound of that strange instrument Somnus had shown me. The mbira. I turned around, bent down and picked it up. Then I sat cross-legged on the floor and steadied the wooden block with the gap in my legs, and hit my fingers against the metal as if I was typing on a keyboard and it trilled in that beautiful way it did before. How could such a rudimentary object, looking so tattered as it was, produce such feelings of infinity? There was no sound more charming or beautiful. Nothing compared. I wondered with an air of mania if it had a certain power, something like the sleeping ring. Maybe the music did something to you. Or maybe that was the magic. Just hearing it.

I dusted it off, put it in my pocket along with the gem and made my way back to my room. While I strode through the corridor, I saw Old Bull and waved to him, but he didn't respond. I saw Rudie from her window, but she didn't respond either.

I got the gem out again in my hand and stared at it. I felt a strange rush, like a powerful drug. A drug I had never experienced. I tried walking to reception and got through the doors without anyone calling me out. I could see myself but I must have been invisible to others, I concluded. And so you know what I did, after everything that had happened? I left. Without a goodbye, without a bag of supplies. Just music and an amethyst.

I walked out of the front entrance. It was strange to finally be free, and to still not quite understand how it had happened. I began to walk to the train station and on the way I caught a glimpse of myself. Well, not myself. But the tail. Just the tail. It was moving right alongside me in the reflection of a shop window. I stood there still trying to understand. So it was invisible before, and now that I was invisible, it became visible? It looked like a fox's tail. I didn't question why no one else seemed to notice a random fox's tail floating in the air, and hurried to the station where I caught a train to the nearest airport. Usually airports are hectic and draining, but when you have an enchanted gem that makes you invisible it's not so bad. I didn't even need a ticket, I just followed people through the barriers. I got to duty free and a shop window reflected the tail again. I then looked across from me and someone else must have seen it in the reflection too, because they gasped and said to someone next to them: "You didn't drug my tea earlier did you? Look over there." He pointed at the window. "But it's not here. It's not here. But it's there!" He was pointing back and forth like a maniac.

I ended up on a plane to Seattle. Took ten hours. I sat down in one of the empty seats and tried not to cough. But I got the mbira out and played with it in my hand for a while, hitting the notes gently and staring out the window and seeing no reflection bar the tail. Passengers turned in their seats frantically, wondering where the ancient music came from. This amused me. The bad thing was I couldn't ask for food or anything.

After what seemed so long, we finally landed. I quickly exited before anyone else, and got out of the airport into the city. I had no idea where to go. I walked to a phone shop and stole a phone, again unnoticed. I turned it on and created an account so I could use the map. It asked me for my name. I typed: 'Maya Castro'.

When I got to the Map app I searched for Beate's house. It was the only place I could think of. It was about twenty miles north. I borrowed a taxi ride by getting in the spare seat with another punter. I was finding it strangely funny how no-one could see me. It was as if my dream had come true. To never be seen. I was always the girl hiding in the forest. To paraphrase that old saying I found in one of James Joyce's books: 'I am the girl that can enjoy invisible.' Even my clothes were not seen, and the phone was not seen floating out of the shop either. There must have been a cloak or something on all things I touched. But then how did the taxi stay visible? There was no-one to tell me.

The cab drove north, luckily, and I was only two miles away from the house. I decided to walk the rest. Now, unbeknownst to me at the time, my sister was not in fact kidnapped by anyone but had rather come to a strange and indeterminable end. I was unaware that the aliens weren't actually anywhere else but my mind; unaware that Sal Goodman wasn't anything but a figment; unaware that the Trump bombing was just a strange delusion; unaware that there weren't really bugs in the walls of Thorn Ward and no-one was actually out to get me at all and they really were just trying to help me. Yet the one thing I was aware of and that couldn't be denied was that I was out of Spector Park and free. I was free. On the run, technically. But free.

I journeyed far to find the house. But when I got there, it seemed she wasn't home. I went inside using the key she gave me and as I closed the door I smelt a really bad scent in the house. It was up the stairs, across the landing, in the bathroom. The door wasn't locked, and so nervously I opened the bathroom door and saw her spread-eagled in the tub and I knew she was dead because of the horrible smell and the way she looked. Her skin was blue and rotting away, her head was smashed in and there was bloody water everywhere. I panicked thinking it was an assassination or something and that it was by that far right militia, and that what that American guy Sal Goodman said to me and what the aliens said to me was true after all. I didn't know what to do. I'd never find the culprit. There was nothing I could do about it. I felt powerless. And it didn't even matter that I was powerless, because unknown to me there weren't any perpetrators to track down. It was a slip in the tub! That's all it was. As if she died for nothing. But she didn't die for nothing. Paranoid, I wept and fell to my knees slowly with the scent of death in my nose. Life, meanwhile, was telling me to get a proper burial sorted for her. I had to drag her rotting body out of the bathroom, and rolled her corpse down the stairs carefully to save my energy. When the body was finally in the garden, I searched for over an hour for a spade to dig a hole, and found one seconds before I was set to blow up in hysteria. I dug like I was looking for her, but I was simply putting her there. When the hole was deemed big enough, I pulled her into it, covered her lightly with a layer of dirt, chucked in all the flowers that were in the garden and orated a eulogy for her, all alone. I closed her eyes finally and shovelled the big pile of dirt to the side of me back over her until she was completely submerged and no one would know she was there except me. I maybe should have left after that but I couldn't bring myself to.

There is one thing I didn't mention before. I Robin Hood'd a bunch of meds from the dispensary room that day I left Spector Park. I took a pill every night at Beate's house, until I ran out and had to use the injections. When they ran out, I realised I could just enter a nearby pharmacy with the gem and take what I needed. Every time I ran out I got more meds using this simple technique. It never failed.

Years went by and it seemed as though my brain was starting to surrender to something. As if it were a slave. Though this had been going on for years, it was only now that I realised it. I was dependent on these pills. I became dependent on the gem, too. My mind turned to a vegetable. I saw my dream of being a writer smashed about me. I needed to write about what happened in order to cope with what happened. And so I cut myself off from the pills. Cut myself off from using the gem. At first it was hard, because I was full blown addicted to both to them. Of sedating my madness and being invisible to others. I craved those states to the point of madness, and when I finally cut myself off after years and years, I became so anxious that my whole body shook all the time and I couldn't stop it. And yet, in some weird way, I felt like myself again. See, the meds make you forget who you are. That's why you don't notice you've forgotten who you are, because the meds make you forget. I am me. I know that now. Although I fear this is only temporary, that I will lose myself again, take the pills again, and tear asunder any connection between me and the cosmos, as if I was exiled from the very fabric of the universe. But I am merely unnoticed. Unappreciated. Unknown. I am here as if I was a ghost of my own life. Here but not. And to add insult to injury, there's a good chance if you go crazy once, you'll go crazy again. Well I'm preparing for it. War is hell.

It's much harder to sleep and all nowadays without the meds. And when I can't sleep, that's when the psychosis slowly creeps back. At first, only slightly. But as the days go by and less and less sleep each night become zombie who shake and don't think smart fragile brain dead mind gone zombie who thought become reality when fear and contact lost with world. Eventually me sleep again and it seems to get better, but it always go back again, and then better, like never ending see-saw of sense. Sometimes I don't sleep for four days straight and start thinking I'm back in Spector Park. But I never tell anyone because I don't want to be thrown into another psych ward.

I guess there is no moral to this story. I can't find one, anyway. Staying away from drugs, perhaps that is the lesson. And yet madness just like I have seen, has happened to people who have never touched drugs. So I'm not sure what the moral is. What moral to pass on? What meaning? The meaning seems meaningless. Love came and went just as sanity came and went, just as the stars of the galaxy came and went, just as life came and went. I don't know what any of it meant. And I had a front row seat. Yet now there are only questions, not answers. Is the psychotic a hero in any sense, or just someone in the wrong place at the wrong time? I can't be a hero anyway, because I have not acted heroic. I have not acted badly, at least within my sense. But I am certainly not heroic and have done no heroic things. I have put up with things, bad things, but only for my own benefit. I fought it all for me, right? In the end, I'd save my own skin every time. I'm not recommending it or anything.

What moral there is in madness, I have not yet found. But there is moral in the maddened, if not in the madness. I think about all the people I met and wonder who was real. And if so, that they are still there, whilst I am not. It's still going on.

This is also something I ponder as deeply as I can: Are these types of institutions like Spector Park good? Is it treatment or confinement? Is society better off with us hidden? All using our own gems? Is taking their pills even good? Are hallucinations bad? Are voices to be met with axes to the head? What moral can I find, when everything is chaos.

To this day, I have never been able to figure out what really happened. Perhaps Som was simply Morpheus in disguise. And perhaps Morpheus was me in disguise. All I know is that I escaped, and have been living in Seattle ever since I got off the plane all those years ago, staying at Beate's place while she sits there supine in the dirt like an underground angel, and going to Hozomeen Mountain every now and then, as tribute, pretending Beate's with me hiking up the glorious thing. And the thing is, I'm not afraid any more. And I'm at the top. And I'm looking down. I chuck the gem over the edge of the mountain. Then I get out the mbira one last time and play it to the mountain and play it to Beate and play it to Som and play it to Dunley and Rudie and June and everyone with ears, still looking down, still wondering if falling off would stop the pain of existence, or if it would just be a mistake. Feet half off the precipice now, still looking down, mbira trills abound. There goes infinity again. Mountain monster wails a dream. Well I could end it all now. I feel as though it has been done, what needed to be done. The fat lady's sung. Everything was taken from me. Who cares? Meds or no meds, either way is doomed. Life's a trip. The tail wags once more. I could go right now. I could end it all right here for good. Feet still hanging off, still looking down, still thinking. Could have used that gem to get anything I wanted. Too late now. And the only thing I really want is dead in the ground. God, just one step. Just one more step. Number ten. Don't look back. Head up. Won't be so bad. It's just a ride. Can't be worse than mental pain. It's just physical. That's temporary. Nothing will ever rise to insanity. Just go, I tell myself. Follow the flower to the ground. It'll only hurt for a little while, I say against the high winds of the mountaintop. Hell, what happens next could be forever. In fact, must be forever. Either way, forever. Death is forever and so is life, it seems to me. It goes Life, Death - then what? It must be Life and Death again. And after that again. It must be the chicken and egg situation. Tortoises all the way down. If I should chuck myself off this mountain, will I not just become another soul born into this world who will end up despising their life to the point of suicide? And every life the same thing? Oh you'd say paranoia to me if you could, would you not?

Even if I didn't consider jumping, I know that I would still die eventually from old age, and there is no escaping death, and therefore life. It will happen no matter what. And I want to be relieved but I am disgusted. No, incensed. Minds eternally manic, and for what? And eternal pains, for what? I cannot endure the madness when it comes any longer, and I know it should come again. I stand still on the mountain peak. As if it was just a dream.

And it was, right? I am yet to wake up into death, I say to myself as the clouds foregather and a mysterious spaceship rockets through the air. And it was then that despite my certain fate – to be condemned to be free and free forever, either way I turned – that I gulped a huge breeze of air, shoved the mbira into my pocket, looked one last time at the view of scimitar shaped clouds curling round a dim and holy Sun, their currents sweeping the dust from the land into the sonorous sky and pollinating the world and therefore me, for I have not yet died, I have not yet died I tell myself and what a cursed talisman of life yet I have not yet died I scream into the air as a gust of wind jumps into my lungs and gives me a shock and I'm choking on air and adrenaline is pumping in my head... and as if turning the final pages, I turn myself and begin to hike down the mountain, all the way back to lonely Beate's, to write it all down and let my soul pass through the pages like a phantom through the wall; the scars of my words; the insanity of the structure and form. And then, having trapped it there, I will close the book tight, put it back on the shelf, and leave it there. Leave it there to age and rot, as I undoubtedly will. I shall become as wrinkly as Old Bull a thousand times over and never once figure out the damn plot. But while I'm here I might as well stick around. If the Earth's going down I'm going down with it. Might as well get it out now. Cough it up. All this my soul and the kitchen sink, I'll trap it all in ink. For if these words are ever seen, then I have not yet died.

PART III

Ducking Hell

38

Not being dead basically means having to live every day knowing you could die. It's nothing short of a very peculiar gimmick. A gimmick of life. It's mostly empty. Like space. Space is empty. Atoms are empty too. Life is empty like the atoms. Maybe death, then, is full. I do not claim to know shit about death but still I have a deep fear of it, because the plain truth is I haven't even lived yet. Empty years have passed like pages. I will tell you as much because I know you won't reply. The Reaper I'm not afraid of. I have seen things with unknown explanations a hundred times more fearful than an image of a Reaper. But dying before I've even lived, before I've seen my time, I am afraid of. And it is entirely possible. Entirely. It could happen at any point. It's possible as hell. How did it even come to this? This is where I will be slain? Here? Not ready for it. Curse a few others before getting to me, so I have some time. I just want more time. I desire no accolades or awards, just more time, perhaps a little money for my trouble. And in this flat there's time, albeit a strange, warped sense of time. But no money for the trouble. Time goes slower in the flat and yet quicker too. The clock on the wall goes up to thirteen. And why is it so hard to just leave the place? Because of the hotbox. It has almost become its own presence. A sentient, living thing. I've become trapped in it. I've become trapped in a twenty four hour hotbox. That's not even a metaphor. Ali decided to make a hotbox two months ago and it's still going on. Can't escape. It's goddamn tyrannical. It's distracting me from my work. No good ideas since he showed up. Not one. I'm uninspired.

    It's not all his fault, though, if I'm to be fair. Back in

the day when I could get words down uninhibited, I used to wake up not assuming I knew who I was, so that I might rise reinvented and not just string a few words together but string tomes of great meaning together. Yet now I know exactly who I am and I can't use that trick anymore. It might be every teenager's dream to be this messed up. They think that dream is a good dream. But really it's just depressing. Utterly uninteresting. And so too have I become. I am technically a man now, a man who may die having done not one noble or great thing. Not self-pity but merely self-examination. I'd do something about the situation but we're too stoned to sort it out. I don't even want to get stoned. Yet it seems I don't have a choice. I'd attack Ali with a butter-knife but as I said before, we're too stoned to do anything. Why the fuck am I writing this...

"Duell. What's this piece of paper with coffee stains all over it? Is this for the new book you're writing? You know, the book that's going to turn you into a Great? The book that will finally make people respect you? I haven't seen you write anything for weeks but you've sure been talking about it a lot."

"I think you're the one who keeps on talking about it but whatever."

"Are you even writing when you say you are? How can I believe you?"

"I wrote two books."

"That was over a year ago. What are you doing now?"

"I'm answering your questions. I don't have to prove myself to you. To others, sure. But not you, Ali."

"And yet I still feel like you're going to talk about it."

"This book is likely to change things."

"How exactly?"

"Well. I didn't write what I really wanted to with those

books. What I imagined in my head. I don't know. I didn't get it right. It just seems with this one, I can redeem myself. I can stop myself from being a joke. But this is the one. Not the fourth. This one. I can't write three bad books in a row. This one has to be good. Or else I'm a joke. And the only way to do that is making a great manuscript. A book that connects with its readers."

"The general public wouldn't know a good book if it hit them in the dick. Didn't *Purple Anchor* get zero sales the first three months? And *The Man With a Watch For a Head*? That got four I believe, and that was only because of the cover, which you didn't even do. Why do you think it will be any different this time?"

"How do you know so much about my career all of a sudden?"

"I'd hardly call it a career."

"I'd fight you on that point. But I've grown tired of doing so. I've lost money. When you add up all the profit and loss. There's nothing worse than devoting all your energy to something, and no-one even cares. I'd rather endorse someone else's book. But I need money."

"Obviously. The problem is you have no wit."

"If I make something good enough, it will get a deal eventually. If it doesn't, it's not worth writing in the first place. Right?"

"So you're relying on some fantasy of getting a book deal?"

"It's not a fantasy. Book deals are real things and I'm a real writer."

"Just because you wrote a couple books does not make you a writer."

"Of course it does. It's axiomatic."

"No," he says all too confidently. "Being a writer is a

state of mind, an attitude, which you do not have. You might like to pretend you're this sophisticated guy who writes in notebooks by candlelight with a giant quill in your hand but I know you. I've lived with you for nearly a year. You lie in bed with your laptop, type two pages and you're done for weeks. A real writer writes every day, not because it will get them a book deal but because they have no choice but to write. You aren't this person. You may have periods where you're writing, for weeks straight even, but let's be honest. Most of it is average at best and yet you are too precious about it. Granted I read *Purple Anchor* and thought it was okay. Good, even. But that character wasn't you. It wasn't you. I mean, you're not a fisherman. I've never seen you fish. You should write a book about how you can't ride a bicycle or that you're secretly jealous of all the successful authors. But you won't. I'm not saying you're a bad writer, Duell. But you are never going to be this thing you want to be."

"Your faith is touching, Ali. I'll quote Blake, then, seeing as you won't listen to me: 'The man who never in his mind and thoughts travelled to heaven is no artist.'"

"Icarus had that way of thinking, too. He melted, Duell. He melted."

"The sun isn't heaven. Heaven is heaven. You don't melt in heaven."

"And your version of heaven is, what? Being famous?"

"I'm talking about passion. The passion to be better."

"Why do you even want to be this Great writer? Why do you want to be better than you are? You can play that game your whole life. I'd say there's still time to cut your losses. Duck out."

"I'm not ducking out. I'm going to get better if it kills me. If it kills me, Ali."

"The reason you want to be a Great is the reason why you aren't."

I looked at the note on the coffee table, ignoring him. "This reminds me. It's burning day today."

"What?"

"Yearly book burning."

"Like those nutcases at church? You delightful man. Which books then? Don't be throwing in Proust and making out like it was too rudimentary for you. I know your tricks."

"I just tend to have a lot of notebooks around, random pages falling about the place. I don't like the thought of dying and having them found. See, you're my Max Brod, Ali. You think I'm going to trust you with these notebooks? These papers?" I picked up the note from the coffee table and placed it in one of the notebooks.

"What's the point of writing in those things if you're just going to burn them?"

"You know, Ali. I ask myself that question every day."

"No you don't, though. I told you. I know your tricks."

"Why do you keep saying that? What tricks?"

"See, you know I'm too stoned to explain myself. You're using that against me."

"If you're too stoned then stop the hotbox. It's been seven months, Ali. I can't take it anymore. I feel like I'm not even Forrest. I'm just a hotbox floating in space. Jesus, I have to get out of here. I can't believe it's taken me this long to realise. I'm done. I'm done, Ali. Help me lift my body."

"You are your body."

"That doesn't help the problem?"

"Here, take a hit on the wizard pipe. This shit gets you fired up."

"So you're recommending I smoke more? Just so I

have the strength to leave? Because I'm sick of the weed? And your constantly lit pipe that seems to never end? There's stupid, and there's stupid. I'm going."

"But this is your place."

"I can't believe you put *me* off weed. It was okay when I had a goddamn door for my bedroom, so the smoke didn't drift into my room... How do you get so stoned you end up losing my door?"

"I didn't actually lose it. I threw a hand axe at your door and it made a hole, so I got rid of the door."

"What? Where did you put it?"

"The door? In the river."

"Why were you throwing a hand axe at my door?"

"It was supposed to just stick out of the door so it looked cool. Trust me, if it hadn't made a hole but was just stuck there, you'd wake up, open the door and see a dope hand-axe sticking out."

"Did you not consider I might have opened the door just after you threw the axe?"

"It was a risk I was willing to take. Think about it anyway. Hand axe sticking out of a door? Cool. Hand axe sticking out of Forrest Duell's head? Even cooler. Not that I'd want to kill you. But you'd have to admit it would look pretty cool."

"Goddamn. I can't do this anymore."

"Wow. Mr. Drama over here."

"I'm not going going, I'm just getting out of the flat for a while."

"Wait, wait. If you are going yeah, Mr. Writer, Mr. Larry Angelo himself, keep the doors as closed as possible? Hotbox isn't smokey enough."

"Whatever. Bye hotbox. You sick motherfucker. You have enslaved me no longer. You have consumed me and ridden me with your bitter curses no more. I'm going out there, into the real world, to leave this cesspit and cleanse my lungs from your wretched ways. I -"

"Dude, come on."

"Sorry, got carried away. Alright. Bye."

"Wait, can you get milk?"

"What? There's milk right in front of you. I've had enough of your bullshit, Ali."

"Bullshit? I give you bullshit? Do you not remember I'm the one who saved your ass and gave you a job at the head shop? Do you not remember you would have been evicted if I didn't end up moving in and paying for half the rent?"

"I'm leaving because this place has made us into complete idiots. Stoned twenty four seven. What's the point now? I can't even remember my past. Any of it. Thanks for that, by the way."

"You are responsible for yourself, Duell."

I slammed the door, ventured up the front path and opened the rusted gate. I was glad to be out of the flat yet in actuality I didn't know where to go. As I stood there on the pavement, I begged for some idea to hit me on the head. For a book to hit me on the head. To fall from the sky spine first and land right on my head.

In the wintry chill, perturbed and frozen, I heard an engine crackling in the distance but no cars were around. I looked up the road straining my eyes and saw Ira Powell coming right at me sixty mph or so on his modded deathtrap. It was a skateboard with a delightful engine attached to the underside of the board that made it go way too fast. It was Ira's piece de resistance. His magnum opus. His crowning achievement. And he looked happy, too. Chuffed, even. No-one else in Krelboyne looked like that. But Ira the lovable fool he was, was happy skating around, getting dole, and not taking life seriously (as the wisest tend to do). He lived partly at his Nan's and partly at the head shop, round the back in a kind of tarpaulin (which he did because he said his Nan was always napping and he got bored being there). Me and Ali didn't mind him being there curled up in the tarpaulin, because we were bored too and we were bored because no-one ever came into the shop, except a few strange folk, and that was once in a blue moon. Yet sometimes, those blue moons came a dime a dozen.

In a failed attempt to be kind, Ira would try and drum up business for us by shouting incriminating things to any passersby that came down the street. Ira was always saying stupid things. On this particular day in December he says: "Wanna watch me bomb this hill? I'll do it coffin style." He pointed down the hill. It was a long way down.

"Does that mean dying, Ira?"

"Nah. Coffin style means you lie down back to the board. But yeah, I guess it could mean dying, too. You know. Maybe."

"I'm bored as hell. You wont hurt yourself though, right?"

"Trust me, you'll want to try it too."

"There's no way. I'm not crazy."

"Alright. See you on the other side!"

In order to maintain the illusion I was a busy person, I began to leave, but not before watching Ira bomb the steep icy hill just like he said he would. After a few yards he lies down on the board with his arms crossed over his chest and bombs all the way down coffin style yelping expletives.

I hung around, not hoping he would fall, but just checking he didn't. I would have relished the thought of someone I hated falling and breaking their spine, because I was no perfect person, and that was perhaps the one thing I did know about myself. But I didn't want Ira to get hurt. In fact, he was one of the few people I could rely on. I didn't want Ira to die. Because then I'd just be left with myself.

The biggest mystery of all: How Ira could seem to be so free. So happy and calm. What was his secret? Was it simply the skateboard? I was jealous of his seeming freedom and happiness in that freedom, as if his eyes were not merely rose-tinted, but actual roses, growing out his forehead.

After Ira was out of sight, I was left with my self and the cold bright day. I couldn't help but think about Ali's comments. Was I perhaps being too, precious? Should I have resigned myself to not bothering? Was Ali actually being unreasonable? Should you trust someone who throws hand axes about like ninja stars? Ira didn't need to write a masterpiece to feel a sense of happiness. All he had to do was be Ira. And neither did Ali need to write anything in order to be happy. I was starting to wonder whether I would ever be happy.

I stood there on the street, still waiting for that book to fall from the sky. Fall from the sky like that angel Juliane Koepcke. Landing with a thud, still in the seat, lost in the rainforest, all the other passengers of the plane dead. I wanted my big idea to fall from the sky like Juliane Koepcke and land right on my stupid head.

Feeling not just a tinge of embarrassment, I came back to the flat when I realised I still didn't know where to go and that I was still in wait for the angel book to fall.

"I thought you were going to be gone longer," Ali says

as I sit down on the sofa.

"Things change, my dear friend." I grabbed the pipe and hit it.

"Dear friend? What's happened? Are you okay? This isn't like you."

"You know, I realised something in the past seven minutes. I'm already doomed. I'm never going to write a good book. But that's where the relief is. It's not this giant monument anymore. I know I'm shit. Nobody gives a fuck. That's a good thing. I don't either. Nobody cares and nobody bothers me. I just need to stop kidding myself. I'm doomed. And I always will be. I'm gonna go hang myself on VR. See you later, Ali."

"If you're going to do that, at least jump off the cliff instead? You know I don't like you doing that shit but it's classier off a cliff."

"Like you know classy."

"Man I can rock a poncho and you know it."

"You can rock a straightjacket too, Ali." I got up from the sofa and walked through the
doorless threshold of my room, hearing Ali shouting at me as if there were still a door there: "Good to have you back, Duell!"

39

Later that night, after I came grovelling back to the flat for warmth, I went to the garden. I was thinking about Hope's assassination. Two weeks he had held the title of PM before someone blew up a train he was on, killing many others along with him. Those two weeks where Hope was PM were unreal. After his death, an election was swiftly cast and the Tories reclaimed their old long-standing position. Hope was dead. But Boris was still alive. And that was perhaps proof no just God existed. I reminisced to those long-gone two weeks, almost mystical they felt, where life seemed hopeful and no-one was pissing on me.

There was a surreal, almost purple fog that had foregathered in the garden. I grabbed a rusted bucket and threw one of my notebooks in. I lit a match I got from this hotel in Edinburgh and threw it into the bucket, watching flames rise as the terrible writing disappeared forever. Now I just had to delete all the digital work. To my own estimation none of it was good so it wasn't hard to say goodbye. After that I retired to my doorless room and passed out from drinking red wine, listening to Kurt Vonnegut read *Slaughterhouse 5* on my phone. I somehow woke up at Get Head (the head shop Ali owned), amid the sounds of the Dresden bombing in the background of my brain. It was as if the travel was wiped from my mind. The empty bottle still in my hand with the lid missing, queer scents coming out, as if I had mixed it with a spirit while intoxicated. I wasn't even meant to be in. I leaned forward on the stool behind the counter and looked around.

Like my drinking the night before, I was working solo, since Ali had a day off, thereby cancelling my own pre-agreed day off. All things considered, it was pretty easy to do the job. No-one came in or bought anything really but the store made money from illegally selling weed on the side. If we didn't sell any official products, say in one week, then I still got a wage because of the weed deals. But Ali handled all that and I hoped no-one would come in asking for the stuff.

I spent an abundance of my youth sedated (and gladly) yet while I was working at the shop I never got stoned.

There were constant reminders of weed everywhere in the shop but I resisted somehow. I was constantly reminded of weed while I was there and yet worked sober because I didn't want to mix business with pleasure. I waited until business was over. Incidentally, there was a good chance if I was stoned at work I would forget something or give the wrong change or somehow end up asleep in a crate in the Pacific Ocean.

The bell of the shop rang. "Do you sell crow here, lad?"

"No. Who told you that?"

"That skater round back."

"Well technically we do but officially we don't."

"What does that mean, fella?"

"I can't do it, sorry. My colleague sorts that stuff out. He's not here today."

"Fine, I'll just grab a pack of Sterling and I'll be out of your hair."

"We don't sell cigarettes here."

"God, you don't sell anything do you? Well, I'm off to get drunk. Bloody drug legislation. Crow's still illegal? But pints and spirits at every shop in the land! They've been promising to legalise it for years. Bloody useless government, am I right lad?"

"You're right."

I waited for the guy to leave, then walked out of the shop. I went round the back of the building. On the way a newspaper flew into my face. The headline:

'QUEEN BLAMES VR GAMING FOR VIOLENCE AT EIGHTH ANNUAL BREXIT CELEBRATION'.

I grabbed it and tossed it in a nearby bin. I was surprised the Queen was still alive. Not surprised by her delightful comment. To listen to anyone who sat on a golden throne would be truly absurd. In fact, to listen to a newspaper headline would be perhaps even more absurd. In my anger, I walked moodily up to Ira. He was doing tricks off the curb, landing hard-flips like nothing, showing the underside of the board as it spun around.

"Ira, mate. Stop telling people we sell weed here."

"Oh shit. Sorry, Forrest."

"It's fine..."

"I just keep getting confused. Because of all the posters of weed you have at the shop. I keep thinking it's legal and that."

"England is backwards right now. Bat-shit backwards. And Krelboyne is Backwards Capital. Happily nestled in the status quo. We however, in this goddamn shop, are the ones going against the grain."

"I miss living in Amsterdam."

"You weren't exactly living there. You were homeless. It was more like dying, no?"

"Yeah but it was okay. I crashed in some nice alleyways with people, talking all night, drinking, stargazing."

"You're really a glass half-full guy, aren't you Ira? How I envy you."

Walking back to my station, Ira followed me like a dog. He was telling me about the homeless people he met in Amsterdam. He said some homeless guy there was planting apple trees on one of the streets where lots of other homeless people resided, so that they could all take the apples and eat them for free. Eventually, when the trees grew and bore fruit, the guy, Ira says to me, was juggling the apples and someone was filming it and he became known online as the 'homeless apple juggler'. Ira said the guy basically became famous.

"I can juggle. But am I going to be famous from it? No. What a jip." The shop bell rang, abruptly rousing us from conversation. A wild-haired man walked in, then proceeded to take out a pistol and point it at us. I wasn't even meant to be in, goddammit.

"Give me the money in the till."

"Umm. There isn't actually any money in here."

"Fucking give me the money!"

"Look." I picked it up and turned it around so he could see it. I opened it and showed him the empty till, bar a lone blue fiver.

"What is this fucking place? Why's there nae money?" He was still pointing the gun.

"Business is bad."

"Aye? You're not making the most of it?"

"No weren't not," says Ira.

"It's a tough gig, aye. Tough economy."

"It sure is," Ira continues. The guy lowered the pistol. "To be honest boys, I was planning on robbing you blind, but this is just a toy gun, lads. I was just hoping to get some cash cause wee chance of finding a job in this economy. I won't be robbing you nae more."

"Thanks strange gunman." I rolled my eyes at the ground. Only Ira could say something like that.

"You better get some profit so I can rob you proper! Hahaha, no. I kid. I'm a changed man, now, boys. I won't be robbing you nae more. Good luck with your business, lads." The bell rang as he left.

"Well that was bizarre."

"Just another day at the office I guess," says Ira, cracking his fingers.

"Ira. You don't work here."

"Go round back?"

"Go round back."

"I lost my tarpaulin."

"How?"

"Wind. Can you get me another one at the tarpaulin shop?"

"There's no such thing as a tarpaulin shop, Ira."

"Maybe that should be our business then! If there aren't any about? Woah, did we just come up with a million dollar idea?"

"No?"

"Alright. I'm gonna go to the bowl and skate a bit before I head back to Nan's."

"Alright mate. Good to see you. Don't run into that gunman."

"Oh yeah, good shout. Peace!"

I loved Ira's stupidity. It was a silver lining in my terrible cloud of a life. He always made me laugh with his stupidity. His stupidity was genius. It was a light. It was enlightening. Illuminating. Sometimes stupidity is poisoned by evil, yet I was not in the presence of such a person. He gave me the parka I was wearing that day in December. The one I always wore every winter. It was nice as hell. Dark green with a simple hood, big pockets and warm fleece all inside. Ira just offered it to me one day and took it off his back, saying I could keep it because I was chapping cold with it being one of the coldest winters. It was a nice gesture since at the time Ira had very little money and the parka was so warm. So you can bet your life savings that Ira was a good guy.

After I locked up the shop, I beheld a tulip joint sitting idly on the icy tarmac. I figured it must have been Ira's because of that time he told me he always carried a rolled tulip in his pocket just in case he died, so he would have something to smoke as he kicked the bucket.

"Well...he's not dead yet."

I walked home smoking Ira's death tulip and got a hit of motivation to write something down. I figured it was unwise to just give up completely. Not halfway through it, I put the tulip out carefully and placed it in my jacket pocket.

When I got to my bedroom, and loaded up the computer, I lost the motivation instantly. Despite this, I sat there for hours looking at the blank screen, trying to not let it defeat me. I got the tulip out again and smoked it to the bone in hope of kick-starting my brain. At one point Ali mime-knocked on the 'door'.

"Knock knock. How's the writing going?" I stared at the blankness.

"Yeah, good. Salinger's gonna shit when he sees this."

"Are you lying?"

"What? No."

"So it is going well?"

"That's what I said didn't I?"

"Yes but you're a compulsive liar. And Salinger's dead."

"Ali, I'm n-"

"I just don't get why you won't admit it's not going well."

"Fine. It's not going well. I haven't written anything. I haven't had a single good idea for months. I'm a hack. I'm deluded. Are you happy now?"

"I'm not unhappy."

"You know why I can't write? Because I don't have a door for my fucking bedroom."

"I don't think that's really an excuse."

"I can't concentrate. You need to pay for a new door."

"Is this really about the door? Or is it about your

inability to write something not worth burning?"

"It's about the door."

"Are you sure?"

"Yes, I'm sure."

"I will get you a new door once you have a good idea. Agreed?"

A month went by. Ali didn't get me a door.

"I give up," I say to him. He had been standing once again in the threshold, watching me try and fail to write something down. It was as if he was watching me like a zoo animal. Typing with my monkey paws.

"Finally."

"You're supposed to tell me not to give up."

"I stand by what I said."

"Jesus. Is it really so hard to give me some encouragement?"

"You think you want encouragement. But you don't. If I encouraged you, you wouldn't write anything good. You'd feel good about yourself. So you wouldn't write well. I'm doing you a favour."

"A favour? To undermine me at every opportunity?"

"Yes. You don't want someone giving you false praises do you? Or perhaps you do?"

"Well, no."

"And you want to write something good, right?"

"Yes..."

"Then grow a pair, Duell. The point is, it shouldn't matter if I'm encouraging or not. It shouldn't matter if there's a door there or not. Nothing should matter. Write. Or don't write."

40

"I heard they concocted a fake university just so they could arrest the students and extort money from them. A fake university. Farmington, it was called."

"You know, the whole problem with ICE and the US borders, is that not enough people know what's still going on there."

"That's not the problem. People do know. The problem is people don't care. Same thing with global warming. The human race is doomed. But no-one cares. Bangkok's already underwater. And no-one cares. ICE? Forget about it."

"Do you care?"

"Sometimes I do, Duell. Sometimes I forget about it."

"Well that's it. People forget."

"Can you imagine if we didn't forget? If every day we kept on thinking about those innocent prisoners, those kids in cages covered in their own shit, and the ever conscious guilt of having our own rooms and our own freedom while they don't? To never forget that? We'd be tormented with nightmares."

A grey-haired woman with a red beret who really looked like she came in by accident opened the shop door, rousing the bell from silence, and hobbled slowly up to us. She had chunky spectacles.

"Hello there, I was wondering if I could use your toilet?"

"Sorry. We don't have a toilet."

"No toilet? Oh. I see. Well, I'm going to need some Imodium then, dear."

"We don't sell Imodium here."

"No toilet. No Imodium. What do you sell, then?"

"We sell paraphernalia."

"Oh. Drug paraphernalia? That's not good, dear."

"Why are corner shops okay, where they sell cigarettes and spirit, but this place isn't?"

"This shop is offensive to the people who live here."

"Offensive? Nothing that is human should be offensive to you."

"Terentius. Noice."

"Drugs are not good."

Ali chimes in once more:

"I guess you didn't get good enough shit."

"Oh," she says. "I assure you, dear. I got good enough shit." Bell.

"What were we talking about anyway?"

"Wait. I forgot."

"Ah well. I'm sure it wasn't anything important."

"What's Ira doing out there?"

"He's talking with his psychic."

"Piss off."

"I'm serious. That's his psychic."

"He doesn't look like a psychic. He's wearing a goddamn tracksuit. How long have you known about this, Ali?"

"Too long."

"Then why didn't you tell him psychics are frauds?"

"Hold up, Duell. He might just be the one."

"The one what?"

"The one who's really a psychic."

"Okay, hell with this. I'm going out there."

"Your shift isn't over."

"Taking my break then." I walked out of the shop bell — and saw the mysterious tracksuit-clad guy already walking off. I went up to Ira.

"Ira. He's your psychic? What the hell, man?"

"Yeah yeah. Trust, since I've been seeing this guy my

chakras have opened way up. According to him, anyway."

"Do you even know what a chakra is?"

"It's some sort of, thing."

"Well that clears that up. What do you do with this guy?"

"Well he starts by reading my mind, then gives me advice on how to handle the future and stuff."

"Right. How does he read your mind?"

"He just looks at my forehead for ages."

"Wow. Just wow, Ira. What else can he do? Levitate? Raise the dead? Turn Xbox One's into Xbox Two's? What's this guys name, anyway?"

"Casio."

"Wait. Jake Casio? That guy who used to sell us weed when we were teenagers? That Jake Casio?"

"Yeah."

"Ira, you idiot. He's not a psychic. Don't you remember Casio back in the day? He was a dickhead. He was always pranking and robbing people. I can't believe you sometimes, Ira. I hope you don't pay him."

"Of course I pay him. You have to pay for a reading."

"How much do you pay Casio, Ira?"

"Not much."

"How much?"

"It's complicated. Basically there's three easy installments every month. Since I got a full year subscription I go to him every week. A hundred quid each installment. He said it was only for his exclusive customers. Pretty sick, right?"

"So you pay this guy three hundred quid every month?"

"It sounds like a lot but it's not really."

"How did this even become a thing? In what complete

nonsensical train of thought would lead you to believe that Jake Casio was a legitimate psychic? Doesn't it hit you that he just made all this up to goof you? To trick you, Ira. You have to stop paying him. How'd you even have that much to burn?"

"I haven't told you this yet. But my Nan died a while ago. I sold her flat. I've been living on the streets again. Well, not streets. The woods. Dunno why I thought to sell it but I've got so much money now. And I kind of like sleeping in the woods anyway so it's really not an issue."

"Oh. I'm sorry about your Nan, Ira."

"Thanks."

"Listen, do what you want. I just think it's a bad idea but what do I know about good ideas? I just don't trust Casio."

"I dunno man. He seems pretty legit. You should come by his place sometime, you know. Check it out."

"Yeah, right. I'm guessing it's at a haunted house, too."

"Don't doubt the haunted houses, man. But no. It's at his mum's yard."

"Of course it is."

"Just come by with me sometime. I'll use one of my vouchers for a free reading. Once you see him you'll know he's legit."

"Jesus. Fine. I'll come along. But you're not changing my mind about psychics. I'm serious, Ira. If you want to waste your nest egg you might as well give it to me. But you know I'm not that kind of person. Let's go see your dopey psychic. Life's already meaningless."

"There's the spirit?"

41

While me and Ira were at Casio's, Ali Anand was leaning his elbow on the shop counter with his hand in a fist, supporting firmly his languorous drooping head. His eyes red. His mood nonchalant. He inhaled a bag of vapour and called his girl and basically did everything he could to not work. He knew it was all messed up anyway. If he got caught selling weed, the whole shop would be closed.

Bell.

"Alright mate. What's this little operation then?"

"We're a head shop."

"Oh, right. That's why it's called Get Head. Looked like some sleaze shop. You should consider changing the name."

"Sure. How can I help you?"

"Got any pocket knives?"

"We don't sell pocket knives here."

"I really need a pocket knife."

"Can I ask why?"

"There's this plastic shit caught on my pet bird's fur. I need a knife."

"Oh, what bird do you have?"

"It's one of them, flying ones. Can't remember the specific name."

"You can't remember the type of bird you have?" He looked blankly at Ali. Ali continued: "There's a hardware shop up Grenflower. They might have something."

"Cheers. You know, you Muslim lot are alright."

Bell.

"Sartre was right. Hell is other people."

...Bell.

"Oh. It's you two. Get this, that guy who just left. He just assumed I was a Muslim. Fucking people in this town. Hold on. Why you two look so weird? How was the psychic?"

"He goddamn mugged me. Well, he was trying to. We got away on Ira's board."

"Why did he try and mug you?"

"I kept telling him how psychics are bullshit, and that he was basically conning Ira and that he had to refund him. But he refused and just got violent. Then he tried to do his psychic shit on me as we rode off. Said I'd never get a book deal. What a joke, right?" They looked blankly at me.

"You shouldn't have pissed him off like that," says Ira.

"We got away didn't we? And we didn't even have any money on us to be mugged in the first place."

"Yeah. It's like that saying. If you spend all your money you'll never get mugged."

"That's not a saying."

"Well it was said, right?"

"Stop confusing me. Your dumb is infecting my dumb."

"Anyway, Duell," says Ali. "Wanna tell me why you ditched work for all this?"

"Ira practically bent my arm about it."

"Ira. Here's a reading for you. Everyone is a piece of shit. You can't trust people."

"But I can trust you guys. Right?"

"Ira, you can trust me. Don't know if you can trust Ali, though."

"I'm trustworthy."

"Would a trustworthy person break their housemate's door and chuck it in the Thames?"

"Would a trustworthy person get all whiney about a

fucking door?"

"You've got a door. You don't know what it's like to not have one."

"Do you want me to give you my door, Duell? I'll do it. Just so you shut up about it."

*

One day, I was feeling particularly reckless. I wanted to know if skateboarding and bombing down the hills was what made Ira the happy, carefree person he was. I needed data and I was now willing to do anything to find out. So on this day, bored and despondent at the till of Get Head, I left my post and ventured to Ira round back, who had somehow managed to no-comply over a disused fridge that had been left there.

"Yo."

"What's up, Forrest."

"Ira, I wanna bomb a hill. Can I use your skateboard?"

"I've been waiting for this," he says. "Okay. Why not this hill we're at now?"

"This one? This is a bit steep."

"Doesn't look steep to me."

"I walked up that hill to get to work. It's definitely steep."

"Do what you want, man."

"Fuck it. Gimme the board." I took the board and carefully placed it at the top of the hill. I inhaled the cold air, took a step onto the board, almost lost balance but soon regained it, rolling downwards faster and faster and already I knew why Ira was so damn happy all the time. Because he was doing this. It was going faster and faster and faster and faster. Joy and excitement pumped through me like holy adrenaline. And then I bailed.

It was about halfway down. The board continued down the hill and crossed paths with a car at the bottom, breaking the wood in two upon impact. Ira heard me calling him. I was still on the floor. I was clutching my leg.

"It's broken."

"What is?"

"My leg. Owwwww. Goddammit. Why did I think this would make me happy?" I lay there on the street in agony.

"You definitely think it's broken?"

"Yeah. I broke my wrist once. But this is something else."

"You know why you broke your leg? You were leaning too far back."

"That's little comfort now, Ira."

"At least the bone isn't poking out?"

"Yeah. That's something to cling to. God." I looked up to the sky and it started to snow. "C'mon. Now? Well I guess white is the colour of death. Fitting."

"Stay with me, Forrest. I'll call help. I'll ring 911."

"That's America. Ring 999."

Half an hour went agonizingly by on the snowy street.

"It was me who smoked your death tulip," I say as we wait.

"What?"

"You dropped your tulip outside the shop the other day. I smoked it."

"That's okay, man."

"Is this karma? Because I didn't tell you?"

"I think you're just bad at skateboarding."

"Do you want it back? There's none left but I can give you some of mine."

"Keep it in case you die."

When the ambulance finally came, I was taken swiftly to the hospital. Once they drugged me that was it. My last question to the nurse was: "What's going on?" and she replied: "Purple haze." I couldn't even remember if Ira was still there or not. They promptly realigned the bone, put it in a soft cast and sent me to bed until the morning where they would be drilling an eighteen inch rod into the middle of my tibia bone. They said they would be cutting open the kneecap and that it may go south. When they told me that I wished I was still messed up on the ketamine. Eventually after a semi-horrible night in the hospital I had my surgery. One more night of sleep there and I was allowed to go, walking out with crutches and a big boot. They told me I had to set up a repayment, an absurd amount, which, in all fairness, was not the nurses fault for simply delivering the message. It was because of Donald and Boris. And all the people who subscribed to their bullshit. I simply ignored the bill, just like I had with my student loan repayments, knowing I would never be able to pay any of it.

If I even moved my right leg in the slightest way the pain was excruciating. I got home after a very hard walk. When I got to the threshold of my room, I saw that I couldn't see my room. A door was there. In the frame. There was a note on the door.

'I hope you like this door. It's my door. I don't need it anymore. I'm fleeing the country. The shop was getting heat. Don't go into work. They're going to flatten the shop. Get out while you can. I'm sorry about your wages. But it's either this or jail. Luckily there was no official paperwork of you working at the shop, so right now you're invisible. Stay

invisible. You never worked there, you never met me. I'm going to miss you, Duell. I hope you can be happy somehow. I've left a oner under your pillow. Burn this after reading. Peace brother. Break a leg.'

"Goddammit."

42

Two weeks drifted solemnly by and I still hadn't found a job. Heaven knew how miserable I was. The leg ache was getting frustrating and I had just used my last codeine tablet to help with the pain. Failing all else, I tried to write something down, knowing that Ali and his smoke was gone, and that the door was back. Yet none of that helped. Ali was right. It didn't matter if I had a door or not.

I didn't want to do it, but I ended up asking Ira for a few hundred quid just so I'd have more time to find work. At the time I let him crash at the flat since Ira had sold his Nan's flat like an idiot. But that meant he had a lot of cash. I took this borrowed money and set a plan to find a job. The problem with finding a job was that no-one wanted to hire a guy who had just broken his leg. I couldn't even hang myself on the game since I had to sell the VR headset. Existential crises aside, Ira managed to be a better housemate than Ali was, because he didn't criticise me. He really thought I was a great writer. The idiot. In Ira's mind me and J.K. Rowling were cut from the same cloth. He even read my first novella. He said his favourite part was when the manta rays approached Tim and began talking to him.

"Oh man. Those manta rays!" he shouts at me while he's stoned-to-shit on the carpeted floor. "Those guys were funny! One's like 'I'm manta gay, guys. I'm coming out the coral.' You're such a good writer, man."

"You really think that, Ira? You think I'm good?"

"Well to be fair your book was the only one I ever read. But I thought it was good."

"You should read more books. Feel free to take from the bookshelf. There's good stuff there."

"What would you recommend?"

"*1984.*"

"Okay." He got a pen from his jacket pocket and wrote '*1984*' on his hand. "I'm guessing it's about the eighties?"

"Not really the eighties you're thinking of."

"If you think it's good then I'll read it."

"That book got me addicted to reading. I read it when I was fifteen."

"Oh, so back in the eighties then?"

"I'm not that old, Ira."

"You're getting on a bit, though."

"So are you."

"We're getting on a bit but we still look young."

"Yeah. We're at the physical peak of our lives. I mean, apart from this leg. It's all downhill from here."

"Downhill? So we can just bomb it then, can't we?"

"Not this hill, Ira. Not this hill."

Once the winter was itself dying just as the autumn had before, the days were a bit brighter and more colourful, albeit rainy. Yet feeling we were spending too much time indoors and seldom time out, we took a visit to Krelboyne's favourite watering hole to get shit-faced, thinking that, if we got drunk enough, then we'd come up with some great idea. We'd write it down while we were drunk, so when we were sober again we'd still have a note of the great idea. But as it turned out, we just lost the note when we were drunk. That great idea is somewhere out there. Maybe not even in Krelboyne. Maybe Belgium.

After that night of drinking with Powell, I woke up in a skip with a bad hangover. Then I woke up again. But the hangover was still there. At least the skip was just a dream. Yet did its manifestation mean something? Was the skip a metaphor for something? I was rubbish? There was nothing in me but stench and decay? That's what it was telling me. I grabbed a tall glass of water from the kitchen, thinking about Ali and where he was. At least in all this time I hadn't had any trouble with the law. Like Ali said in the letter it was easy to stay invisible. I could hardly walk. And I had nowhere to go anyway except Krelboyne's favourite watering hole, luckily seconds from the flat (and that's why it was the favourite). I was glad he was gone in a way. But for some imponderable reason, I missed Ali criticizing me. It was weird.

I drank the water until my head hurt less. Then I made coffee and put a pop tart in the toaster. As it toasted, I thought about Vincent Vega being in the bathroom, reading his copy of *Modesty Blaise*, staking the flat in case I happened to be there so Vega could whack me. But my life just wasn't that interesting. The pop tart still tasted good. That made it worse somehow. My whole life, was somehow uncomparable to a pop tart. I saw on my phone that it was 1st April. Didn't even matter. It's always April Fools' Day when you're perpetually confused about the world. Then Ira comes out the bathroom holding a wet magazine.

"Morning, Forrest."

"It's four in the afternoon."

"Oh. Well, good afternoon."

"Don't feel too bad. I only woke up twenty minutes ago."

"You know," he says. "In a way, time is meaningless. Take those people who only eat cereal at breakfast time. It's like, you can eat Frosties anytime you want."

"Yeah. You know, you were making a great point before that tangent. Time's meaningless. The door is meaningless. We live, regardless. We write anyway. We write anyway, Ira!"

"Ah, I don't know if I want to be a writer, man."

"Sorry, I was just getting carried away. I'll see you later, Ira. I've got a brain baby I need to deliver."

"Okay. What shall I make for dinner?"

"Cereal. As your suggestion?"

"Nice. Good luck with the writing."

"Thank you. You know, sometimes the muse just hits you, Ira. We make the meaning when we do. When we live. There is the meaning and there alone. Yeah. Yeah. Okay. I'll meet you at dinner. I'm about to chow down on the biggest goddamn manuscript write-up since *The Epic of Gilgamesh*."

"Sweet."

When I got to my room, with this new found realisation that I had to be the change I wanted to see in my life, I loaded up the computer again, and when I beheld that blank screen, something just snapped and I was once again dumbfounded. I thought drearily that I couldn't make that meaning. That the meaning was pointless to find anyway. That nothing mattered and everyone was a piece of shit like Ali said. But something told me that wasn't true. That there had to be more to it than this. With self esteem all but extinguished, I turned off the computer and left the room, unsure if I would ever find my muse. And if I did find it, what would it even say to me?

"I gave up again," I say, sitting down on the sofa, resting my one crutch next to me.

"Oh. Sorry to hear that."

"How do people do it, Ira? Maybe I should just hire a ghostwriter. God, new depths of depravity."

"A ghost writer? Do those exist?"

"Not an actual ghost. Just some tool to write my ideas for me. But I haven't even got any ideas. I'm done beating my head against a pole. I'm a hasbeen."

"No you're not."

"You know, Ali would have probably said something like: 'you need to have been first before you can be a hasbeen, Duell.' God. I miss him."

"Did he tell you where he was going?"

"No."

"Well. Maybe it was meant to be this way."

"If my life was meant to be this way, then whoever's responsible needs a ball kicking."

"God?"

"God doesn't have balls, Ira."

"Maybe you just need inspiration. Something to jolt you out of routine."

"I have always had this fantasy of making a book group. Like, just getting some random people to come over and discuss books. But Ali never wanted me to do it."

"Well, he's not here now, right?"

"I just think it might be a bad idea."

"You'll never know until you try it. Maybe it's a good idea. Maybe it's that great idea we wrote and then lost."

"Huh. I guess it couldn't hurt to try. You wouldn't

mind if some people came over once a week or something, would you?"

"Sounds fine by me. Can I join the group?"

"Sure. Yeah. You know what. I think this is going to be good. I'm excited."

"That's it, man. We got this. We're golden."

"Golden. Yeah."

43

I woke up screaming. On this occasion, I was actually in a skip. Yet I believed it was a dream. I was so confident it was a dream that when I got out of the skip I yelled at some random person on the street.

"I created you, bitch!"

"You what?"

"Yeah and that! I created that too! Clay in my hand!"

"Shut up right now or you're playing a mug's game, hear me?"

"Wait, why aren't I waking up?" He was walking closer. "Hey. Hey! Wake time. Wakey wakey! Oh shit. Did I really wake up in a skip?"

"You're crazy, mate! Go to bed."

"Just to be clear, I don't sleep in a skip. This is an anomaly. A one time thing."

"You like rubbish. I don't judge, mate."

"Rubbish? I definitely don't think I'm rubbish. Right? I'm not rubbish, am I?"

"At what?"

"Nevermind." I walked away in shame. As if calling out madly to a heavenly plane, I waited yet again for that remedy, that mysterious book, to fall from the sky. I imagined it as by some alien writer, written with strange unfathomable hieroglyphs, the ink serenely glowing. But what was the alien writer saying? It was fun to imagine things like that. Almost wanting it to happen for real. Would I die broke and forgotten? Who cares, as long as I can board a mothership and speak to aliens about their amazing book that fell on my head when I came out of the skip. Would I die alone and unloved? Who cares, when you can just fall into someone else's story.

When I got to the flat I took a shower with my leg hanging out the door, in order to get the skip smell off me. I couldn't even be bothered to piece together why I ended up there. It just didn't interest me. When I was shit-faced drunk, I tended to do embarrassing things. It was better that they stayed unknown to me.

In the shower I was thinking about Franz Kafka's Metamorphosis. I was thinking about it because I was considering it for the topic of the first book group meet-up. I wanted the text to be fresh in my mind. A haunting book, but I liked that about it. I wanted to be haunted.

After I got dressed I walked into the living room and saw Ira wearing his new VR headset, and grabbing at imaginary things with two strangely glowing gloves on his hands. It was the newest VR machine out.

"What are you doing, Ira?"

"I'm fighting a grizzly bear."

"Wow. That sounds like fun."

"Yeah. It's pretty intense. Who'd have thought having loads of money meant you can buy well nice things? Ahh! Don't eat me! Shit. I died."

"Can I have a go?"

"Yeah. Here." He took the gloves and the headset off and passed them to me. "Have fun."

I put it all on and looked around. I beheld an alluring, verdant woodland. I was holding onto a wooden staff.

There was no bear in sight. Yet there was a woman. Up the way. She waved at me. I was curious so I walked up to see her. But as I got closer, she turned away and ran into the darkness.

"Am I supposed to follow her?"

"Who?"

"There's this girl in the woods with me."

"What? That's not supposed to happen? Are you sure?"

"I'm sure. There's a woman."

"I'd say follow her, but that's a bit creepy."

"It would be creepy if she was real, though. Right? She's not real."

"I guess. Follow her? You might get laid. Virtually anyway."

"She's so fast. Wait, I think I see her stopping."

"Ooh, tension!"

"Shut up, man." I got within ten feet of her. Yet it was something I didn't want to see. It was this girl I knew. A girl from my past. She was right there. Waving and smiling. And it enraged me because that wasn't her doing it. It was this virtual thing. And yet it looked as real as life. Her smile began to irritate me, and yet still I missed it.

"Forrest. It's you."

"You're not her."

"I miss you, Forrest."

"No you don't. You're not her. Why are you here?"

"I don't know. Why am I here?"

"This is not how I want to see you. This is fake. You're not her... however much I might want to trick myself that you are. I have to get out of here." I took the headset and gloves off, threw them at Ira, and went to my room, vowing never to use VR again.

"How can she infect my thinking like that?" I say to myself. "It's been years since I've even seen her... I don't even think about her, but then some night once in a blue moon I'll have a dream of her standing there in my mind. What is that? I don't want her there. I don't want to be reminded. It's not an obsession, because I go months without even thinking of her. Yet something in my head won't let it go completely. She was, out of everyone encountered, the only tolerable one. And yet to her I was just some guy, a blip, a mistake. So why is she still in my mind? I should have greater pride than that but I know I have no pride at all. I may lie to others about that but not myself. I've been on my own. I've become a hermit. Writing my stupid books. I've let love pass me by. Why can't the book fall and knock some sense into me? She probably doesn't even remember you exist. You know why? Because you're Forrest Duell. No-one remembers you exist. She doesn't remember either. It's not her fault. Nobody remembers. But isn't there good in that? I don't get hassled by people. I don't get anybody calling me up. I don't get tricked by women. It's good. You don't want to be known. You don't want to be loved. But the thing is, I do want to be known. And I do want to be loved. Because that would mean I wasn't a screw-up. God, talking to yourself. Get a grip, Duell. Get a grip."

44

When me and Ira were at the top of Hummer Hill, holding the newly printed flyers for the book group, I looked down placing my crutch-end carefully on the ground so I didn't fall down the hill. I beheld the town, my mouth and nose beset by strong thick winds. Everyone looked like beetles.

"So. Which direction should we chuck them?"

"We want to get as many people to see the flyers as possible. Not many people are into books unfortunately. We live in a sad world, Ira. We need a big hit count. Chuck them this way. Ready?"

"Ready."

"And chuck!"

A gust of wind made the flyers dance around in the sky, before falling down onto the unwitting town of Krelboyne.

"What did you write on the flyers anyway?"

"What do you mean, Ira? Didn't you look these over before you got them printed?" Ira picked one up that had fallen nearby, straining to read.

Like books? Want to join a book group where you can talk about books with other like-minded people? Come by to 8 Speare Street on Tuesday 21st @ 7pm to discuss Metamorphosis!

"Is it a good idea to write your address?"

"How else will people know where to go?"

"I guess. It's just. Who knows who the hell will show up."

"Ira. Goddamn. Why are you saying this now? We just chucked all these flyers. Who would come, except people who were into books?"

"Serial killers. Or robots."

"Just stop it. You're the one who said it would be a good idea. The great idea we lost."

"I just thought it would be fun to throw them off a hill."

"And you thought, me having a broken leg, would enjoy climbing this hill?"

"I thought your leg was better."

"It's clearly not better. I just don't whine about it. It really hurts still."

"I'm sorry."

"Let's just get the hell out of here."

"I'll call a taxi so when we get down there you won't have to hobble."

"Cheers, Ira."

When we got to the flat, I asked the driver if he could take me to Cafe Kaiser so I could have a coffee and get out of the flat for a bit.

I arrived, waiting in line, looking at the pastries. I ordered a jumbo latte and sat down with my laptop set on the table for writing. I looked across the cafe and saw someone point at me.

"Wow. It's you. The writer!"

"Who, me? Well, I wouldn't call myself the writer. But thank you. Would you like an au-"

"Lucius Bosch! Big fan!" I realised she was pointing to the person behind me. I didn't even stay to drink the coffee, and I loved coffee. I just hobbled out with sixty-five percent less self-esteem than when I came in.

How stupid, to think someone would actually recognise me. How ineffably stupid. I mean, I had sold books. Nothing like Lucius but I had sold some. Not enough, though. Yet didn't it feel nice in a way, to be hidden? Sure, it didn't feel nice to be broke. It didn't feel nice doubting myself at every opportunity. But it felt nice to be hidden.

"What the hell is Lucius Bosch even doing in this town? Hey. Taxi!"

"Where you going, lad?"

"Speare Street."

"Okay. Hop in." I hopped. "I saw your flyer."

"You did?"

"Yes."

"What do you think?"

"Nobody reads books anymore, kid. Especially not Kafka. People would rather watch TV."

"You know Kafka?"

"Great writer. Are you a writer?"

"I guess so. But I'm not a good one."

"Want my advice? Write movies. Not books. You like eating, don't you?"

"I do. Isn't it a strange world?" I looked out the car window and saw, to my surprise, a man on a pennyfarthing, clad in lycra. It was a weird and not unamusing sight.

"I've never seen that in all my life," says the driver.

After a swift journey, the car was suddenly brought to a stand-still and I readied to get out. I wondered how the driver knew it was my flyer.

"Here you are sir. We're here. That's £10."

"That was quick. Here you go."

"Thank you. Have a nice day."

"Cheers. Hey mate. How did you know it was my flyer?"

"It's you, isn't it? On the back?"

I took the flyer from him and the driver sped away. I didn't realise until now that on the back of the flyer Ira had put an embarrassing picture of me dazed in the skip that night we ventured drinking. It was my mistake for letting him be responsible for it. I didn't even know if

Ira made a mistake or if it was a prank. But Ira didn't make pranks. I looked morbid in the picture. And it was black and white too, which for some reason made it worse. How many had we chucked over that hill? About a thousand. Dazed, in a thousand skips all over Krelboyne. I took a moment to laugh at myself. And then I couldn't stop laughing. I grabbed my side and choked on the laughing. I was such a joke even I couldn't help but laugh at myself. It felt kind of invigorating. Cathartic. I shrugged thinking of the flyers. As they say, a picture paints a thousand words. And I didn't care for any of them. The photo would sure sieve out the regulars. Maybe some real freaks would show up. People also ensconced in garbage.

45

The evening before the big night, at 7pm, the buzzer went off unexpectedly in the flat. I put down my bowl of bolognese and walked over to the machine.

"Who is it?"

"It's Alan."

"Alan? I don't know an Alan?"

"No. You don't know me yet."

"What's up?"

"I came for the book group. I saw your flyer?"

"Oh, right. It's actually scheduled for tomorrow, Alan."

"Oh, damn. I got the date wrong? Shit. It's just. Now's a real bad time for me to be outside, if you get me. Could I come inside for a bit?"

"I guess. Come on up." I held the button. Shortly after there was an oddly orchestrated knock on the door and I opened it. A stumpy white guy wearing a grey cossack hat and a black & red striped jumper, who was presumably the Alan in question, was looking at me with doleful eyes.

"Hi."

"Hi. So, Alan. What's so bad about being outside now? Too cold?"

"Well. That's not actually it. You might not believe me, but I was abducted by aliens the other night."

"Oh, really?"

"Yeah. One of them was called Kevin. Or I think he thought my name was Kevin. Either way, there's a Kevin involved. I don't want it to happen again but I feel they're close. They're out there. I can feel it. I can feel it, man. They're watching me. Waiting to pounce."

"Okay. Have you considered it was just a dream?"

"Hold on, Forrest," says Ira. "I think he's onto something. I had a similar experience the other night."

"You were just fucked up on k, Ira. I'd see aliens too if I snorted a bunch of horse tranquiliser. So, you were saying you were abducted, Alan? What does that even mean?"

"They grab you, then they observe you. They do experiments."

"Look. I don't doubt the existence of aliens. But chances are they're not near us, and they don't abduct us. I think you're safe. People have weird mental earthquakes at times. They think they've seen aliens."

"I saw them clear as I see you."

"Anyway, Alan. The meet-up is tomorrow. Maybe you should come back tomorrow and we can talk about it then. I'm sure the aliens won't grab you while you're out. They already got you, right? You're good. You're golden."

"Okay. I will come back tomorrow then. I've been reading the story. I've nearly finished it.

"That's great, Alan. My name's Forrest, by the way. This is Ira. He's also part of the book group."

"Nice to meet you, fellas."

"Well, let me get the door for you. We'll see you tomorrow."

"Bye, guys."

"Will he be alright, Forrest?"

"Of course he will."

As Alan James walked nervously down the street, he was checking the sky to see if they were coming again. He started to hear the unusual sound he had heard the first time. It was too late. The spaceship was already directly above him. A neon beam encased him and lifted him up whereupon a mechanical door opened for his entry. He cried out, hoping someone would hear. But no-one heard anything. A businessman happened to be walking down the street yet any trace of Alan's voice was muted from the mysterious beam. Still, he managed to witness the sighting, walking down the street and fortuitously looking up a mere second before Alan and the ship evanesced into the skyline. He quit his job in the stock market shortly after that.

*

In the morning, I was doing some stretching exercises to make sure the muscles in my leg didn't atrophy. The pain had been reduced but the bone wasn't fixed yet, and wouldn't be for a few more months. Yet I could walk around with no crutches. The rod in my leg allowed me to walk around much sooner than if I hadn't

had the rod put in. I had to pay for a permanently numb knee and muscle damage, though, from the surgery. I ventured to the kitchen and found some frozen chips. I placed them on my kneecap which although was numb ached at the same time, and then made another coffee and put another pop tart in the toaster, as was my tradition, and I again imagined Vincent Vega being in the bog and how I would kill him. Maybe with my bad nutrition. Wasn't the axe still in the flat somewhere? Did Ali take it with him? Was he planning on using the axe, like some Dostoevsky character? While the chocolate pop-tart toasted I went looking for it.
After an hour I stopped looking. It wasn't there. Ira came into the kitchen.

"This is a bit early for you, Ira."

"I like skating about when there's no cars."

"You realise it's noon? I just meant even noon is early for you."

"Oh."

"Want some coffee?"

"Sure."

"So. What did you think of *Metamorphosis*?"

"Metawhatphasis?"

"Kafka? The book we're meant to read for the book group? Remember?"

"Oh, shit. I didn't think we were meant to actually read it. I thought we'd read it at the book group."

"No, we're supposed to read it before the meet-up so we can talk about it together. God, I should have realised you'd get confused."

As the day went on, I was getting nervous about who would come over. Or if no-one came over at all. I decided to prepare a dinner for my guests, yet it was really a selfish reason because I wanted something to distract me from the wait. I looked in one of the cupboards and set to making some spaghetti and a carbonara sauce to go along with it. By the time it was nearly ready, someone beeped the buzzer.

"Can you get that, Ira?"
"Sure. Hello. Who's this?"
"Harper."
"Are you here for the book group?"
"Yes I am. I do have the right place don't I?"
"Yeah. I'll buzz you in."
"Thank you."

After what seemed like a very long time there was a knock on the door. I opened it and beheld a smiling woman, about seventy years old, cane in hand, with deep indigo hair.

"Hi. Harper, is it?"
"Yes. Nice to meet you. And your name is?"
"Forrest."
"Well hello, Forrest. Am I the first one here?"
"You are. Well, Ira's here. But he lives here. Ira! Come say hi to Harper." He came out of his bedroom, doorless now since Ali had taken it out.

"Hi, Harper. Ira Powell." He proceeded to shake her hand.

"Pleasure. Harper Dennison." There was an awkward silence.

"Would you like some food? I made dinner for whoever's coming tonight."

"Maybe in a bit, dear. Thank you, though."
"So did you read the book then?"
"I did. Well, I have read it before. But I re-read it for tonight."

"Great. See, Ira. She read it. She re-read it."
"How was I supposed to know I was meant to read it?"

"Ignore him, Harper." I then whispered to her so Ira couldn't hear. "Between you and me, I only let him come because he's my friend. He knows nothing about books." She smiled at me with her bluey-green eyes. They were quite noticeable because of her blue hair. It made her eyes very prominent. It made them glow.

"So what do you do, Harper?"

"I'm a librarian at the Krelboyne Zoology Museum. But really I'm a scientist. I've been one for fifty odd years."

"How did you get involved in all that?"

"I realised when I was seven that I wanted to be one. My father was a scientist. He told me when I was a kid there was a creature in the ocean that was nearly as old as Shakespeare. Of course it was the Greenland Shark, but at the time I thought it was The Lochness Monster. As I got older I started focusing on regenerative biology, since my father died of a severe case of muscular dystrophy. I wanted to find a way to stop it for others. He's kind of the reason I became a scientist, I guess."

"Wow. How interesting. And now you just chill in the library?"

"Pretty much. I still read all the new papers but I do take more time to relax these days. I like it at the library. No one comes in. It's easy. Quiet too. I have all the time I want to read my books, and play with Vincent."

"Who's Vincent? Your kid?"

"No. He's a pet. He's an axolotl."

"What's that?"

"They are the most extraordinary creatures. Salamander that lives in the sea. They have these goofy big faces. I adore them!"

"So it's in the library with you?"

"Yes. I take him nearly everywhere with me. In a tank.

We've become quite a pair. Always finishing each other's sentences. Joking."

"Hah. I can't believe I haven't heard of this animal before. It makes it seem, I don't know. Magical."

"It's funny you should say that. They are a bit magic."

"How do you mean?"

"Well, they-" BUZZ BUZZ BUZZ.

"Sorry, I just have to get that." I got up from the chair and went over to the machine. "Hello?"

"Is this the book group?"

"Sure is. Is it just you?"

"I brought someone with me."

"Okay. C'mon up."

"Thank you!"

When the door knocked again, this knock sounding like a loud scattering of pent-up force, I reached for the doorknob and opened the door. Meanwhile, Ira was doing his best to entertain Harper.

"Zoot?" He asks with a misty air, gesturing the spliff to her.

"No, thank you." She then, unable to hold it back, starts coughing.

"Oh shit," he says. "I'm sorry. I should lean out the window. Hold on." He moved about three inches still sitting in the same place, but now blowing the smoke straight out the window instead of Harper's poor lungs. "Woah, is that a fox out there?" The fox stood there by the window, still, staring at him.

"Ira. What are you doing?"

"What, Forrest? I always smoke when I read books."

"Oh my god... We're not reading books. We're talking about reading books. And what do you even mean when you 'read books'? You read one book in all your life. And it was shit!"

"It was your book, man..."

"Shut up. Guests are here and you're not ruining this night for me."

"Okay. Fine. I'll shut up."

"I'm just stressed. I didn't mean that."

"Whatever, Forrest. Enjoy your night. I'm not going to ruin it for you."

"Wait. Ira. Come back. I'm sorry. Don't, uhh. Umm. Excuse me, guys. Harper, this is Paddy. He's a priest. And this is his, umm, this is his acquaintance, Klara? Paddy and Klara, this is Harper. She's a scientist."

"Wow," Paddy says to her. "I love your hair. What a fascinating look. Blue as the day is long!"

"Thank you. You have nice silver hair. Silver as a spoon." They shared a laugh. At that moment I couldn't help but notice a white powder dripping from Paddy O'Driscoll's nose. I then looked over at the girl he was with. She was holding onto his waist. She couldn't have been older than twenty, yet he must have been fifty. It was weird. Was she coked up too? God, I thought to myself. This is imploding.

Paddy was wearing the typical Catholic Priest outfit. All black except that little white collar, yet perhaps that was just more cocaine. I slyly watched him. I could tell, easily, that he was charged on uppers. I could deduce from his frantic conversation with Klara, the mysterious young blonde European who held onto his waist, that this wasn't a one time thing. That this was his regular shtick. His jaws were clenching a lot which made his Irish accent even more hoarse. I looked at him and foresaw my own aging. Hell. Maybe if I was an old man like him, I'd snort some coke. I mean, people in that situation, being that old, are going to die anyway. If you lived a full life, then why not? I still wasn't happy about it. Yet I asked for this. Anyone was welcome. That was the point. The buzzer went off again. The flat was running out of places to sit. I hadn't really thought this through. I flocked to the machine.

"Hello?"

"Yo, is this the guy who lives in a skip?"

"What? I don't live in a skip. I obviously live here."

"But are you the guy?"

"The guy who what?"

"The guy in the picture. On the flyer."

"Guilty as charged."

"Can we come in?"

"Well, did you read the book?"

"Book? What book?"

"*Metamorphosis*?"

"Doesn't ring a bell."

"This is a book group for people who have read it. I'm sorry b-"

"C'mon, mate. Let us in."

"Us? How many of you are there?"

"There's four of us. Oh, and some straggler's here too."

"There's five of you? Have they not read the book either?"

"Hold on. Straggler! You read this book by Frank Something?"

"Franz. Not Frank."

"She says she has."

"A miracle. Okay. I guess you guys can come up. We're about to start."

When they came, I could hear them all hiking up the stairs like Vikings. There was a simple three beat knock and murmurings. I opened the door, and it was just like seeing the worst possible thing. There were these two tall women, one wearing a fur coat and incredibly long eyelashes, and the other with so much make-up on it should have been a federal crime. To be blunt and also a bit shallow, they didn't look like the people who read Kafka. Nevermind them, there were these two guys who were with them who looked even worse fitting. As it turned out they were an MC and DJ duo. I thought to myself, these are the people who respond to a flyer about books? These people? I had expected intellectuals with corn cob pipes to turn up. What a fool I was. And then I noticed the obvious 'straggler'. She was a young woman, dressed in a dark green cardigan and pink blouse. It was obvious she wasn't with the garage boys or the two outlandish birds. She was a reader. You could tell it from her demeanour.

I introduced myself to everyone and we all sat in the living room. I had to stand.

"So. Hi everyone. I thought we could go round and say our names and a bit about who we are. I'll go first. I'm Forrest. I'm twenty four. I write books. But no-one buys them." I let out a nervous laugh. The room was silent. My attempt at self-deprecating humour wasn't working. Everyone just looked sad for me.

"Harper?"

"I'm Harper. I'm a librarian. Lived in Krelboyne all my life. I won't go on. It's nice to meet you all."

"Thank you Harper. Who's next?"

"I'm Matt but you can call me MC Emme Cat. This is my partner in crime, DJ Moose. We're into bass music and that. Bad basslines."

"Yeah. Basslines."

"Bad basslines."

"Yeah. The baddest basslines."

"Okay. Who's next?"

"I'll go. My name's Faye. I'm a nurse. I love reading. But I'm so busy I don't usually have time. I like using audiobooks because it seems to be easier to get through stuff."

"Yeah, audiobooks are a good way to read. Well. Not read, exactly. But it does the job."

"You don't even have to move! It's great."

"Well, thank you Faye. I'm glad we have a nurse with us. Nurses are the angels of the world. Anyone else want to jump in?"

"I'm Klara. I am from Sweden. I came to England to be a director. But so far that is just a silly dreams I guess. I also like reading. I would like to write a story and make film about it."

"I gotta title for you," says Matt. "Stock-Cum-Syndrome."

"I am not making porno? That is not funny."

"Well round here love, cum is a funny word."

"Maybe to a bonehead like you," she says, smiling in self-assurance. "Babe. Go."

"I'm Paddy. I'm a priest, obviously. I paint recreations of William Blake's famous depictions of Hell in me spare time. And snooker. Love me some snooker! Why's there no snooker table?"

His jaws were clenching, his eyes were popping out, his mouth was agape. Agape over the word snooker. Man he was fucked. Why did no-one else seem to notice? Right then Ira walked in.

"Sorry to interrupt. Do you remember my password, Forrest?"

"For what?"

"My computer."

"I don't know? 'I'm an idiot'?"

"Nah, I already tried that."

"I don't know, man."

"Ah, it's cool. Anyway I think I left a zoot here I forgot to smoke. Can I just grab it?"

"...Sure."

Then Ira proceeded to navigate the packed room, climbing over people to get to the corner. It was so stupid.

"You smoke, mate?"

"Yeah."

"MC Emme Cat. This DJ Moose. Moose! Wake up! We're gonna bun a zoot with this matey."

"We are?" Ira says.

"Well you got a zoot, don't you?"

"I don't even know you man. You haven't even asked me what my name is and you're asking me to bun you up?"

"Listen Matt," I say. "I could smell the weed on you when you came in. You've got enough for yourself. Don't be a dick to my friend. Because you're on thin ice. One more stupid comment and you're banned from the book group."

"Whatever."

"Okay. Has everyone been? What about you two?" The two as yet unintroduced ladies were both transfixed to their phones. It was as if they weren't even conscious of being in the room. "Okay. Why don't we just start talking about the book, then? Anyone have any first thoughts?"

"Yeah, why were you in a skip?"

"Thoughts about the book?"

"Were you looking for your shitty novels?"

"Shut the hell up, Matt. I told you. You had one more chance to be civil. You need to go."

"Or what?"

"God. Why are you even here? You and your pitiful brain couldn't comprehend a paragraph of Kafka."

"Rah. You wanna go? You wanna start something?"

"Fuck. Off."

"We'll go. But we're taking this." He turned to the wall and grabbed the painting of the four-headed Hydra off the wall.

"Oi! That's mine! Oi!" I tried to take it off him but he pushed me to the ground.

"C'mon Moose. We can sell this for some cans."

"Give me my fucking painting back!"

"Sorry skipboy. It's been a pleasure." He started for the door, but then out of nowhere Ira just rugby tackled him to the ground. It was insane. O'Driscoll cheered. Ira picked up the fallen painting and handed it back to me. The garage boys quickly scuttled out.

"Thank you, Ira. That guy was getting on my nerves. Sorry about all that, Klara."

"It's fine. Some boys will always be boys."

"I guess so. Right. Enough of that horrible interlude. We haven't even discussed the book. Oh, wait. I made dinner. And I forgot about it. Anyone hungry? I can heat it back up."

"I could eat."

"Me too."

"Yep."

"I'll have a little bit."

"Give me five minutes, guys."

"Well. At least we won't starve like Gregor," says Klara.

"Shit. Is someone dead? Who's Gregor?"

"The guy in the book, Ira."

46

With some of us on the sofa and some in the kitchen, the group all ate the pasta in a weird silence. I offered Ira an apology and asked him to stay. After all, he saved me from that imbecile. And he helped me put this thing together, slipshod as it was. Feeling happy that Matt had gone, I readied everyone, gesturing the copy of *Metamorphosis* in my hand. We all congregated back in the living room to finally talk about the book.

"I don't think it's a metaphor. I think he actually was a giant insect."

"Who? Kafka?"

"Samsa."

"Who's that?"

"The protagonist."

"What's a protagonist?"

"It means he's the main character."

"Oh. Okay." Ira tried to write protagonist on his forearm with a pen he obtained from his jacket pocket. He gave up.

"Does anyone think it's a metaphor?"

"It must be," says Faye, who up to now had been all but quiet. "I think there are multiple metaphors. His insect like nature means he is different than the rest. As at work he feels different to his co-workers, and his boss looking down on him, like an insect. But also it shows how shallow people are. They reject his appearance. He knows he is not a monster, and yet everyone treats him as if he were. But he sees it all. He sees them looking at him. He sees the crawling legs with human eyes."

"That's a good point. There isn't just one metaphor." At that moment something felt wrong. I felt I had to throw up. It was not expected. I slapped my hand across my mouth and ran to the toilet, thereupon yakking into the bowl. When I raised my head, I felt strange. My eyesight was blurring. I looked in the mirror and felt even stranger. I felt like I was on something. I realised something then. Those mushrooms I had cooked into the food. They were not mine. I didn't buy any mushrooms. It must have been Ali's stash. I beheld again my bizarrely outlined reflection in the mirror on the medicine cabinet.

I walked back out. People seemed concerned. "What's going on? Are you okay?"

"I threw up."

"Oh. Was it the food? Did you not cook it properly?"

"No, I cooked it fine. It's. Okay. Don't panic. But I kind of slipped up. Those mushrooms, in the sauce. They're actually magic mushrooms. My old-housemate left them here. I just didn't think. I'm so sorry, guys."

"Christ."

"Woah. I am starting to feel it," says Klara. "Paddy? Can we go? I need to go."

"Calm down, gal."

"But I want to be with you. You understand?"

"Listen, Boris. It was great to meet you but we have to shoot off."

"It's Forrest."

"Oh sure. Come on, lassie!" He slapped her bum as they began to leave.

"Bye, Klara. Come back next week, will ya?"

"Oh yeah! I just have to go now. I feel weird."

"Listen," I say to her at the front doorway. "I have some medication that can stop a trip. I can give you a pill if you want."

"You know, I think I'll ride it out. I quite like magic mushrooms."

"You're being very gracious. Well, good luck with the priest."

I was left feeling a tinge jealous of O'Driscoll. Klara had a great aura. And he was such an oaf. Coked up at a random person's book group. Anyway, I was no better. Wait. Was I saying that in my head or out loud? God.

I didn't even realise half the people were panicking. The two tall models were screaming and the nurse was quiet but looked in horror. Harper was taken aback, quite rightly.

"Harper. I'm so sorry. Are you doing okay?"

"Yes. Thank you."

"I've got pills. They can stop a trip. It just takes a couple hours. Do you want one?"

"You know, I think I'll be okay."

"Are you worried?"

"No."

"Are you mad at me?"

"No, Forrest. It was a mistake. It was a mistake, right?"

"Of course. I would never do that to even my worst enemy. Really."

"Well. I'm going to go home and try and compartmentalise all this. Good night, Forrest. I had fun tonight." She stood up slowly and made for the door.

"Will you be back next week?"

"I will."

"Then you get to choose the next book."

"Oh great. *Frankenstein*!"

"*Frankenstein* it is. Let me walk you out, Harper."

"Oh no. I can manage."

"Are you sure? It was great to meet you."

"You too. Bye Forrest! Muah!"

She left, her blue eyes still seared into my mind. I was really messed up on mushrooms. I was at the part, about an hour and a half in, where it really starts to get going. I was unsure whether to take my antipsychotic pill and stop the trip or not. I wasn't scared, but I was perhaps not mentally ready to deal with it. I asked the two tall models if they wanted the exit pill but they insisted they weren't going to take any more drugs, and carried on screaming and eventually just left the flat without even saying bye and me still not knowing their names or why they showed up in the first place. Ira was still giggling weirdly, babbling about the 'fox of truth', whatever the hell that was. Meanwhile, Faye was looking bad. I went up to her. She thought she was turning into a bug like Gregor Samsa.

"Faye. Can I give you a pill that will stop the trip? Do you feel bad?"

"I feel horrible. Please help me."

"Okay. I'm going to give you what the doctors gave me when I was seeing too much stuff. Hold on." I searched my pockets, and found a sheet. I gave Faye a pill.

"Listen, it's going to take a while to take effect."

"God. Why did you do this?"

"I'm sorry. I didn't want to do it. It was an accident. I don't even do that stuff anymore."

"God..."

She sat there on the kitchen floor, closing her eyes fiercely, as if trying to get away from visions. Her appearance began to frighten me. Her fear was getting me nervous. I reached back into my pocket and produced another pill.

"Down the hatch, I guess..."

I left her to be alone and sat next to Ira while we

tripped. He was still laughing at nothing and unable to explain himself. He thought the fox was still there by the window.

Now that nearly everyone had left, I relaxed a bit, feeling glad the night was cut short. I just hoped that everyone was okay. And that they didn't go on any drug-induced killing sprees. Eventually after an hour of watching a 'show' on the blank wall (hallucinations), Faye came into the living room from the kitchen floor and said she felt normal again.

"Good. That's great. I'm so sorry, Faye. I really messed up."

"You were there to help. Even though you did cause the problem in the first place. But. I can tell it was a mistake. Still, this has been a crazy night. Thank you."

"Thank you for making a crazy night?"

"No. That would be silly. Well, I'm going to go."

"Take care, Faye. You coming next week?"

"I'll have to let you know."

I sat down and looked up at the painting of the hydra. It undulated and sparkled. Maybe if I erased one of its heads, two more would grow back in its place.

It was soon after Faye had left, that the medication began to work on me too, and I felt my trip disappearing. Ira was still laughing to himself and deep into the most intense part of his own trip. He was chanting every now and then, gibberish, lying on the floor in the stupidest position. I went to my room, but not before draping him with a nearby blanket.
"Good night, Ira."

47

"I don't need therapy. Had it before. Didn't help."

"This isn't therapy, Forrest."

"What is it, then?"

"This is a dream of you being in therapy."

"What?"

"So tell me, Forrest. Why do you feel you have to attend therapy in your dreams? How does it make you feel, knowing this is how you're spending your dream time?"

"I have to go."

"We have thirty three minutes yet, Forrest."

"I'm in charge of my own dreams."

"Then why do you dream of being in a skip? Of being here in therapy? Of seeing some girl you don't want to see? Why dream these things?"

"You didn't even mention the dreams where I'm killed. Those are constant."

"Well," the therapist says, raising a hypodermic needle to my face. "Some things you can't change, Forrest."

I woke up trying to pull the needle out of my neck and slumped in embarrassment when I realised that it wasn't really happening. The therapist was right. Why did I dream those things? I couldn't remember the last time I had a good dream. Either the sun disappears or there's a huge tidal wave or a monkey grabs a gun and shoots me. What a jip.

As I pulled myself out of the bed, untying myself like a thread, I started to remember that last night happened. Oh, it happened. That was no dream. What exactly had happened? I remembered throwing up. But where? Did I puke on someone's head? I went to find Ira to ask him.

Yet when I got to his room, I saw his skateboard wasn't there. He must have been out skating.

How did he do it? How was he so nonchalant about skating? Knowing that you could fall off at any minute was what made it exciting for him. And the engine making it go even more stupidly fast... I couldn't believe how one little mistake on that deathtrap could result in two broken bones in the leg and need of surgery and months of recovery and exercise. It was so stupid. People are so susceptible. We have bones that break. We have skin that bruises and cuts. We have heads that snap off. We have all these imperfections. Eyes that can be stabbed. Cells that can be infected. Thinking that can be brainwashed. What God would make a creature such as this? And to top it off, it gives you nightmares in your only time of respite. There cannot be a God, then. I mean to say, there cannot be a good God. For if it was good and it could really do anything, it would answer. It would turn darkness into light. But as it stands God is on permanent vacation. It's not dead. It simply faked its own death. It's on the run. It's fleeing the country. It's not taking responsibility anymore. It shat out the universe and flushed us down the toilet and it's not going to answer anyone. That's not even what depressed me. I didn't want God to help. I wanted help from people. If God showed up right before I died, after a long and arduous life, I was sure I was going to give it Hell. I'm old and decrepit and about to die and then it shows up? I'd tell it to get out of my face. The nerve of some deities. Phoney as humans.

Of course, I didn't believe such a cruel creator really existed. But I was sure it was more accurate than declaring it all-loving. To me, it seemed only love was all-loving. I kneeled not before a god but to life itself.

All its charms. All its beauty. It was to me the only thing worthy of devotion. I recalled what Wilde had bluntly stated in *De Profundis:* "The faith that others give to what is unseen, I give to what one can touch, and look at. My gods dwell in temples made with hands; and within the circle of actual experience is my creed made perfect and complete."

*

While Get Head was being torn down like a temple of its own, and the status quo was being maintained, Ira happened to be skating by the wreckage and told me about the bulldozer after he got in.

"Man. Lucky you didn't go there. One of the guys knows you."

"Wait? One of the guys knows me? What one of the guys?"

"One of the construction people. Or are they deconstruction people? I'm gonna go with deconstruction people. One of the deconstruction people."

"What did the guy say about me?"

"He said he knew one of the guys who worked at the shop. Knew his face or something."

"Ali?"

"Yeah, could have been. But it could be you."

"I'm not very memorable, Ira. My life has shown me that bleak truth."

"Bleak truth schmeak truth. You're memorable. You have a memorable face."

"Are you trying to help, or just trying to make me paranoid? They know nothing. I never gave out my name at work."

"Yeah but don't you think Ali said 'Hey, Duell!' or 'Duell, shut up' or things like that at work? So someone might know you're Duell."

"No-one knows Duell. That's the point. Only Ali did, now he's gone. It's over Ira. I'm the uncatchable man. Because no-one knows who the hell I am, not even me."

During this, the bulldozer was flattening the only shop of its kind in pitiful backward Krelboyne. Probably to be replaced by some common thing, a pub most likely, where the drug is drinkable and therefore not deemed a drug. A little boy on a trike was looking over at the destruction, clapping his hands and cheering.

"You know," I say to him. "I'm wondering why that Alan guy didn't show up to the book group. Remember him? He said he was abducted by aliens."

"Maybe they got him again?"

"That's ridiculous. There has to be another reason."

"You said yourself aliens probably exist. How come psychics are bullshit but aliens aren't?"

"Oh, psychics exist. They're just frauds."

"Still, they could be out there. Aliens."

"Well yes, it's one thing realising that, another to assume they give a shit about us. He probably just got the date wrong again."

"I liked him."

"Yeah. You two would have got on like a house on fire. Dumb likes company."

"Hey. I'm not dumb."

"Don't worry, Ira. I like your dumb. It's one of your good qualities."

"It is?"

"Sure. Ali wouldn't get it. But that's because he's a cynical man. He's not like us. We're dreamers, Ira."

"Dreamers? What do you dream about then?"

"Not being in a skip, Ira. Not being in a skip."

48

It was my twenty fifth birthday, which I couldn't care less about, other than that it was now not unbecoming to eat some cake for breakfast. So I was eating some cake for breakfast. Ira was still asleep. I heard the letterbox flap and went to investigate. A flyer for some pizza place and a postcard. I picked up the postcard. There was a photo of an old storefront in sepia. The sign said 'CHEMIST SWENY. DRUGGIST'. I turned it around and read the note.

Thought I'd send you a postcard. I'm enjoying my new life. Time without you has been most productive. I learnt how to fix cars. I also learnt how to fish. I'm not saying you were weighing me down, Duell, but still I am impressed with my progress. I hope you too have had progress. Anyway I bought this postcard as a small gift for your birthday. It's from a historic shop in Dublin. James Joyce wrote about it in Ulysses, chapter 5. I know the only thing you know about Dublin is James Joyce. Come to Dublin. There are more things in Heaven and Earth, Duell, than are dreamt of in your philosophy. Come to McDaid's Bar. I'm always there (when I'm not fixing cars or fishing). Make sure you burn this postcard. Sorry if it was somehow sentimental to you.
Ali

"Come to Dublin?"

"Come to what?" says Ira, just now appearing from his room.

"I just got this postcard. It's from Ali. He's in Dublin."
"Where's that?"
"Ireland, Ira."

"Ireland? Woah."

"He wants me to come to Dublin. Like I'm doing that!"

"Why not?"

"Dublin's probably cool but his note... it seemed. Suspicious. I doubt it's going well there. He's just trying to rub me up the wrong way again. Like he always did. He'll do whatever he can to prove that I'm more worthless than him. And now I'm far away he has to send a postcard just to push the knife in."

"What if he's genuinely happy with how things are going?"

"But why does he get to be genuinely happy and I don't?"

"I think he just decides to be happy."

"Surely that's not how it works?"

"I don't know, man. The only thing I know how to do is skate."

"I wish I could be as care-free as you, Ira. But I'm just not that person."

"I like who you are."

"You do?"

"Yeah."

"Even though I poisoned you with magic mushrooms?"

"Simple mistake."

"You're too good for this Earth, Ira. I don't deserve you. I don't deserve anything. Not only do I ruin my own life, I have to ruin everyone else's. I hate myself so much I end up hating everyone else. I'm some sort of, disease. I just need to do the honourable thing."

"Honourable thing? What's that?"

"Killing myself, Ira."

"What? That's not an honorable thing? Please don't do

that."

"I won't. I'm not going to. I'm just saying, I need to. There's the conflict. That's my conflict. I spend every day wanting to kill myself and yet every day I don't."

"It wouldn't be the same without you around."

"It would be the same. If I wasn't around no-one would even notice."

"Look, man. You can do this all day, beating yourself up. You can kill yourself. Or we can both go to Dublin and see Ali. What's it gonna be?"

I decided to go to Dublin with Ira. I didn't want to get on a plane because of the metal rod still inside my leg, so selfishly I made us take a train instead. I didn't have any paperwork to prove I broke the leg. It was nearly fixed now and I didn't want to be searched by anyone. The flight would only take an hour but on the train we could probably stash weed, though that would take ten hours and it wasn't even cheaper than a plane ticket. Yet I had this weird fear of airplanes, thinking it would crash. I would never be spared like Juliane Koepcke, I thought. I would be like everyone else. Going down imagining that Bright Eyes song and struggling to get my last thoughts out, seeing my life slip away in total panic and horror, wondering why I didn't just take the train. So we took the train.

It was on the train that I realised even trains crash. But we were already aboard, so I swallowed my paranoia. I settled down in a window seat next to Ira. He got out a book. It was *The Man with a Watch for a Head*.

"Ira. You're reading my book?"

"Yeah."

"You realise you could be reading George Orwell? Or Lucius Bosch? You know, a real writer?"

"You are a real writer, Forrest. Just because no-one buys your books doesn't mean you're not a writer."

"Can you not say that so loud? God. Why am I such a loser? At least I haven't resorted to writing self-help. Those guys are the worst. Actually, those people that do TED talks are probably the worst. Remind me, Ira. If I ever do a TED talk, kill me."

"What's a Fred talk?"

"Nevermind. How come you chose this one to read?" He turned the book over in his hands.

"I just thought it would be a long time, and the cover looks really cool. So I just took it."

"But that's my thing."

"What is?"

"Reading on the train."

"Where's your book then?"

"I didn't bring one, Ira. Huh. I guess the tables have really turned. I'm just going to stare out the window and contemplate my own futility." I looked out the window. We hadn't even left the station yet. There was a guy with a very long beard on the platform with what looked like an eagle on his left shoulder. It must have been Eagle Man. I'd heard about him, that he was a wood-pigeon exterminator. Because the wood-pigeons were sometimes deemed annoying with their repetitive hooting, and also pests to vegetation, people hired him to hunt the pigeons using his eagle. I knew about him without even meeting him, but that day through the train window I saw him up close for the first time. The way I found out about Eagle Man was that I used to have this friend Billy who hired him, because the hooting near him was so constant and loud he couldn't get it out of his head, and actually went crazy thinking he could hear it in the night. Even though he took up Eagle

Man's services, new pigeons showed up in all the trees near his house. It was an unwinnable battle. He couldn't stop hearing the hooting, until it was all too much, and he jumped off Krelboyne Bridge.

I wrote in a notebook with a yellow pencil: 'Why is death always on my mind?'

At one point we had to get off and make a change. When we arrived at the new platform, it was packed, so me and Ira sat down against this wall, and I could have sworn the girl on my left who had sat down next to me was the girl from the VR headset. It looked just like her. Yet I was scared to turn my head and look at her properly, in case she noticed me, so I never found out if it was her. The train came and once I saw her walking off to get to the train, we hurried the opposite way to be sure I didn't end up sitting next to her. I didn't want to deal with that. I didn't want to see her. And yet I did. A paradox. How would I even react if we were to bump into each other? I would most likely have pretended I didn't see her, like I had before. That she was nothing but an invisible ghost, out of not resentment or spite but simply fear, afraid of confronting her and forcing us to engage in small talk of some kind, which would not only not be satisfying would also feel fake. But then would I regret not doing anything? To tell her the truth would open me up to her tearing me apart, perhaps with only one simple phrase. Or maybe she would have just said nothing at all. I remembered how, a long while after the original 'tornado', she asked me for help writing poems for her coursework, because she hadn't planned accordingly, or she just didn't care, and I agreed to help her. I stayed up through the night distilling my thoughts into the poems. Hoping she might cotton on through reading them, so I wouldn't have to say it out loud.

Three hours went by on the train. Ira was still on the first couple pages of the book.

"Ira. Trouble reading?"

"I keep forgetting what I've just read, so I have to keep going back. Reading's long."

"You know, an audiobook would probably be better for you. You could listen to a book while you skated, with headphones."

"Does this book have an audiobook version?"

"No. Who the hell would want to do that? I wish there was someone who would."

"I can do it."

"Your voice is a bit goofy, Ira. Plus you know you'd still have to read the book if you were going to do the voice-over?"

"Yeah I'll pass then. Maybe someone in Dublin will do it."

"You know, I do like the Irish accent. There's something about it that just shits on ours. It's eloquent."

"Yeah. It's nice in the ear." Then someone from behind interjects, in a deep Irish accent: "Did you hear that, all? This fella likes it in the ear!" A few people laughed.

"See, Ira? Eloquent."

As we waited for the train to get to Dublin, still about three hours to go at this point, I watched Ira sleep against the back-end of the seat in front of him, using *The Man with a Watch for a Head* as a pillow. I took out my phone to take a picture of him and saw an email. Someone had left a review. So it finally happened, I thought to himself. It finally happened. A review. I clicked through, and saw it. How many stars? One. And the comments? - 'Derivative prose. He's not fooling anyone. The one good bit? WHEN IT ENDED.'

I should probably skip all this nonsense about what happened before we got off the train. Basically Ira did his usual gimmick and realised belatedly that he had left his luggage on one of the platforms. I should have realised he'd do it but I didn't think Ira could keep on being stupid. I thought there was a limit. That eventually he wouldn't do something stupid. Yet that never happened. There were new depths to his idiocy. He said it was empty anyway so I say: "Why did you bring it then?"

"Everyone else brings bags to stuff."

"With things in!"

I didn't bring up the review to him, but I was still thinking about it. Well, one star is better than no stars. One star out of at least one hundred billion. And that's just our galaxy. How small and pointless my life seemed, when I thought about those stars and how many there were. Countless clusters of beauty. Their light still visible even after death. Ghosts of illuminated presence. In Krelboyne you can see them, because it's such a small town and there are a lot of open fields which encourage a good night for the stars to come out. I always thought I was apart from those stars, and I was, but I mean, not even of the same material. I knew we are of the same material in a literal way, for the stars material is the founding, embryonic material for our own creation, yet I still felt I wasn't fully part of that process. That I somehow showed up ten minutes late or something. Why did I feel so alone, on this train? Why, in all the billions of people accounted for, did I feel I could not talk to hardly any of them? I spent too much time worrying I was terrible at the craft of writing that I seldom sustained any friendships or relationships. I would never live up to what I wanted to be. There is a reason I'm not a star, I thought. For they have purpose. They know what they're doing. Twinkling diamonds bigger than Jupiter, made in crucibles that would put Dante's Hell to shame, nascent in the black night, emerging, coming out to say hi like mischief on Halloween, bright dilated pupils orbiting their own mad heads. Stars. The holiest things. Unsullied by humans. Untouchable. They are born like us and they die like us, yet they will never meet us. We are one and the same and yet in a different world. That's why I like them so much. And what mind-bending photography I had seen. One enchanted picture encompassing the entire known universe. Like some magical art. Science is not far from magic, in the things it can produce. Virtual Reality so advanced you can see things that are kind of like hallucinations. Which explains why I saw that girl in Ira's Grizzly Woodland game. This does not occur in everyone, but a small percentage of people. It is because the visuals and immersion, being practically indistinguishable from reality, confuse the brain (in a small percentage of people). And that's when I realised what this girl was. A hallucination. That's all she was to me now. Her name and an image of her. That was not knowing someone. That was knowing a hallucination. A dead star.

49

We wandered around the port after we departed the train, Ira trying to skate the cobbled streets. I tried to talk to him about the insanity of how long the crusade of Brexit had been, just so I could use this line I thought up on the train ride: "You know, the money wasted on Brexit would have been enough to build a time-machine. Funny, right?" Ira simply nodded and picked up his board with a swift kick on the tail which bounced it up into the air.

We wandered up Samuel Beckett Bridge and went to a few museums, Ira seeming happy to do so. We visited Kilmainham Gaol, a jail turned museum, which used to house Irish revolutionaries, imprisoned by British forces. Ira just thought we were at some police station, wondering why no-one was locked in the cells. We also ventured to the Irish Museum of Modern Art. There was this piece by Mary Swanzy which immediately piqued my interest and I must have stared at it for a long time trying to figure out what the painting was, ignoring all the other ones by mere happenstance. Ira said it didn't make sense but that he liked it too. In true Ira-esque fashion, he proceeded to hassle the staff member about the painting.

"Hello. I'd like to buy this one."

"These aren't for sale, sir."

"Oh, I see. Playing hard-ball so I'll cough up more? I know your game museum man. And I will play. Is two grand enough?" Ira got two grand in notes out and waved them to the guy.

"Sir, like I have said, it's not for sale. None of these are."

"What kind of auction is this?"

"This is an exhibition, sir."

After we couldn't resist the poison any longer, we went to McDaid's to find Ali and have a drink with him. We obtained a table and put our stuff down. I noticed the ceiling was unusually high. I told Ira to wait with the stuff while I got drinks (with his money). As we were in Dublin I got whiskey for us, neat. It was good to have food in your stomach if you were going to drink straight whiskey, yet it made you drunker if you were starved. So I got very drunk. We ended up going out for a smoke with someone I didn't even remember talking to. That level of drunk. I felt vulnerable, as if in my stupor I would be too dim to have my usual wits about me. I then felt compelled to drag Ira out with me and find something to eat before I got conned by someone.

"What about Ali?"

"We'll come back after I've eaten."

"God you're being paranoid."

"It's not paranoia, Ira. People target drunkards. And I am drunkard." Then Ali appears as we get outside. He goes to hug Ira and fist bumps me after.

"So you bloody mentalists. You actually came."

"Yeah, well I was going to kill myself, but I thought I'd do this instead."

"Glad to see you didn't. So, how's life in Krelboyne? I almost forgot what it's like being here so long."

"How long have you been here?"

"Nearly two months."

"That's not that long. I thought you said you learnt how to fix cars? And fish? You can't do all that in less than two months, can you?"

"Yeah that was a lie. Just for the record, though, that and more can be done in a single week."

"What?"

"What I wrote on the postcard? Yeah that was bullshit. No. Are you kidding? No. I'm trying to become a PI. There's a lot of crime here."

"A private investigator? Are you serious?"

"I haven't been able to buy the license yet. But it's coming."

"I should have known that fishing thing was bullshit. You haven't changed at all."

"I thought you'd be happy for me. I used to do crimes. Now I prevent crimes. That is classic change."

"What crimes have you prevented?"

"Well, nothing yet. But something's gonna pop off soon. I've been staking out this guy's flat. His girlfriend thinks he's cheating so she asked me to find out. I'm going there tonight. You want to come with me, guys?"

"That sounds so cool," says Ira. "A stake-out!"

"No, that sounds so dumb."

"Well, I help people."

"This is just some stupid dream, Ali... you're never going to help anyone. You're probably just going to get killed."

"That's why I want your help. Please?"

"I thought the point of a private investigator was that you work alone?"

"I could easily do it without you. But it's going to be more fun this way."

"Okay. I get it. You don't do this to stop crime. You do it because it's fun. Jesus, Ali."

"You can have more than one reason for doing something, Duell."

It was nearing nightfall in Dublin. We were sitting in Ali's car staking out the area, looking for the guy who fit the description made by the client. She provided a picture for a reference. In the picture he was wearing suspenders, green ones, under a tan coat. He was white with a brown crew cut, about 5 ft 10. His name was

Frank. He looked like a real sonofabitch.

To pass the time, apropos of nothing, Ali asked us what was the most 'embarrassing thing' that had happened to us.

"I'm not answering that."

"Come on, Duell. There's gotta be something."

"That's the point. There's many somethings. I guess if I had to choose one... God, I wasn't going to tell anyone this. Back in the day, I had councillors because I was so messed up. Well, I had a crush on one of them. A mad crush. But I never said anything to her about it. Whenever she came over to talk, I would imagine all this stuff in my head. I wanted to fuck my councillor. That embarrassing enough?"

"Damn. That's the one to beat. Pahahahahaha. Ira?"

"I shat myself on a school trip once."

"That's disgusting. I think Duell's is more embarrassing, though."

"What's yours?"

"I don't have one. I just wanted to hear yours, you fools."

"Of course. What's the plan, Ali? Is the guy ever going to show up?"

"It's not Ali. It's Aziz. Aziz Fontaine."

"Aziz Fontaine? What, you're not Ali any more?"

"No, Ira. I am Aziz. And you're... you're Dean. Dean Cooper."

"Ah, sick."

"And you Forrest... you're Melvin. Melvin Munch."

"Why does Ira get a dope name and I get Melvin Munch?"

"I don't know, Melvin Munch. What do you think Cooper? What should we do if we catch this guy cheating?"

"Dunno... just, like. Tell him not to do it again?"

"Oh, Dean. We're too far into the rabbit hole to let him slide like that."

"We're literally not. Again you're making your life a movie."

"Silence, Munch. Our time is now. I see him."

"Huh, yeah. Green suspenders under a tan coat. He's with a girl."

"It's not Jessica. Oh, this dirtbag is going to pay."

"What do we do?"

"We wait, then walk in and catch them in the act. I put something on the latch earlier so we won't get locked out."

"No-one's gonna get hurt right, Ali? I mean, Aziz?"

"Hell yeah he's gonna get hurt, Cooper. This is the heart of darkness. There's no sympathy in the heart of darkness."

"Please tell me this is a dream. Please tell me this is a goddamn dream."

"It's a dream," says Ira.

"I didn't mean literally tell me."

"Sorry, Melvin."

While we waited in the car, Aziz revealed some cocaine.

"Fuck no."

"Ira?"

"Yeah go on."

"Why are you doing this, Ali?"

"Aziz is a coke-head. It helps him solve crimes better."

"I see. You're really crazy now, aren't you? Being a PI just so you can snort coke with a clear conscience. I'm leaving."

"You can't leave now. This is where the story gets good."

"Fine. Whatever. So are we all three going inside to confront them?"

"I'll take the lead. But you two are gonna be behind me."

"God..."

"Are we scared, Munch?"

"No, just reevaluating my life choices."

We got to the door of the flat. Aziz looked at us, nodded, and opened the door, removing the post-it-note from the latch. When he stepped in, we followed slowly, and heard a woman screaming. Yet it wasn't because we opened the door. Something else was happening.

"Help me! Help!"

I followed Ali and Ira followed me. We walked into the open bedroom. The man was forcing himself on the woman, holding a knife in the air.

"He's a rapist! Help!"

Ali socked him, repeatedly, but the guy didn't even flinch. He put the knife in his mouth like a maniac and donkey punched Ali so damn hard he fell to the carpet floor. When I stood there in shock, not doing anything, Ali turned to Ira.

"Dean! Do something!"

"Uhh...uhhh..." Ira, seeming distraught with indecision, then proceeded to lift his skateboard up behind his head and swing down smacking the guy's face with the metal trucks of the board whereupon the knife flew out and his jaws caved in and blood and teeth splattered onto the walls. He stumbled about, then ran out of the building a hot mess.

"Goddamn, Dean."

"You saved me. Thank you. He forced me to come inside with him," she says. "He said if I made a scene he would stab me! Thank you. Thank you so much."

"No worries. If you get a problem again. Come back to me. Me and my colleagues will sort it out."

"Thank you..."

"Fontaine. Aziz Fontaine."

"Mr. Fontaine. Thank you all. Well, we should all get out of here shouldn't we?"

"Of course. Have a safe night." Ali picked up the knife that had fallen and we walked outside. "See boys. That was real justice! Felt pretty good right? And you, Ira. You stepped up."

"I just panicked and the board was in my hands." We walked out into the street and left the woman.

"So, Duell. What have you got to say now? We just beat up a rapist. We stopped that woman from being raped. Maybe killed. That's got to feel good, right?"

"I guess. It's just. Won't he still be out walking around and snatching up women? It's not like we arrested him."

"But he'll think twice before doing anything again. Now he has the fear of us."

"Fear of you. I'm out. This shit is too intense for me, Ali."

"C'mon Duell. Where's your sense of curiosity? Shouldn't a writer have that?"

"I have enough curiosity. Your level of curiosity is psychopathic."

50

When I decided it was time to leave Dublin, Ira didn't want to come with me. He wanted to stay with Aziz Fontaine.

"C'mon man. Ali said we'd be helping people. He even

thinks he's close on the trail of a white supremacist ring... I finally have a purpose here."

"But that's what's so good about you, Ira. You didn't need a purpose. You're not really going to stay are you? I need you to help pay the rent."

"Maybe it's time you found a job. I can help you out one more month's rent but that's it, man. I'm staying."

I left them and took a flight to Heathrow, staring out the window of the aeroplane the entire flight. Now I am truly alone, I thought. Without Ali's burns or Ira's idiocy, I was truly with myself. No friends but the mountains, as the Kurds do say. I could write in total peace now. Maybe I should have listened to Ira, about getting a job. Yet in all honesty I didn't want to do that. To take a desk jockey position for some bullshit marketing company? That which seemed to be the only job going, since I couldn't wait tables or serve at a bar having had no experience with such things. I was poor but I had prose. I had a goal. Not money. A masterpiece. Money makes people mad but I was mad the day I was born.

I knew it was all a fantasy, though. I had to get a job now. I'd gone so long without working, apart from Get Head, because of the incident.

I was sectioned some years ago, for taking too much of this psychedelic, and I was completely insane, so they gave me this money to help, and I had lived off those benefits for years. Every two weeks I was wired enough money to be glad about it. I was convinced I was a fraud, because sometimes I would lie to people asking me what I did for a living, and say the money came from book sales. Yet sometimes it's hard to tell the truth about that kind of stuff. I never wanted to tell people I went crazy but invariably had to because everyone always asks you when you meet: 'so what do you do for money?' I mean. Don't they?

For years and years, I took this money pot and blew it to shit. Without working at all. Only writing. I had inordinate time, yet it didn't stay that way. A short while before I met Ali and he moved in, I got a letter saying those benefits had been stopped, since I could no longer 'prove' I was ill (I had stopped picking up my meds). In all fairness I didn't feel like I did in the ward any longer. Yet I might still have needed the pills in the future. I knew it could come back at any point and was frustrated they didn't seem to care. When they took the benefits away, Ali semi-serendipitously offered me the job at Get Head and to move in and pay for half the rent, for the place I had lived for the past three years, all previously paid for by the government. Yet now they didn't want to help, and not even Ali or Ira was there to help. I didn't have friends to leech off any more. The pressure to get a deal, whatever it was, in this new climate, was immense. I would have done anything I could to avoid taking a full time job that I wouldn't be able to handle. Perhaps I would have lost all self esteem and wandered pathetically back to my parent's house to live there. The very thought made me sigh. It's not that they were bad people, it was simply that I was itching to be freed from them, being together so long. I was daydreaming about Stephen Fry getting expelled from a Latter Day Saints tour when the tour leader said to everyone: "In the afterlife, you are reunited with your family and will be with them forever," and Fry replied: "And what happens if you've been good?"

As long as the book I wrote was good enough then everything would be okay. But I was lying to myself. I knew I wouldn't be able to do it. I wasn't Stephen Fry. I couldn't do it. I didn't have the capabilities. And yet I had to. Within a month.

I even thought about making a story about Aziz Fontaine but I didn't want to give Ali the satisfaction. It would have been fun to write-in his untimely death, though.

Instead of trying to get a job, or landing a deal, I found other ways to get money. I sold the VR headset Ira left at the flat and got £600, and I also signed on for dole. Those two things bought me an extra month's rent. I bought myself some time.

At the moment I finally thought I had a good idea, I hurried to find a notebook, and the buzzer went off which made me jump, making me forget my idea. I let them into the building without even asking who it was. I was that angry.

I waited for the knock and sternly opened the door. A young woman was staring at me.

"Can I help you?"

"Hi. My, grandmother. Harper? She told me about the book group. I wanted to come and check it out. If that's okay."

"Oh, right. That explains why you look so much like her. That blue hair doesn't fall far from the tree, I guess?"

"I got the idea from her."

"And who gave Harper the idea?"

"Marge Simpson. My name's Mel."

"Nice to meet you. I'm Forrest."

"Can I come in? Am I the first one here?"

"Actually, the book group has been abandoned. No-one wanted to come back since this, umm, incident. So how come you came but your grandmother didn't?"

"Actually. She died the other night."

"Oh. I'm so sorry."

"Before she went she told me about your book group. She told me to read *Frankenstein* by Mary Shelley so I did."

"I guess we could still do the book group? Just a one-on-one session or something? If you're free, that is."

"That sounds fine."

As we sat down on the sofa, I couldn't help but notice how attractive she was. I started to feel nervous. I grabbed *Frankenstein* with both hands.

"I can't believe Mary Shelley penned *Frankenstein* before she was twenty. What a bitch, right?" I was real nervous. She laughed, I could only assume, in pity. But still, I was glad she did. "Any first thoughts?"

Yet strangely, there were no first thoughts. You know those times, seldom they may happen, when two people are just staring at each other, and something comes over both of you, compelling you to kiss and not bother with first thoughts? Well that happened. I kissed her again, and could feel that she was smiling as our lips pressed together. I pulled my head back and opened my eyes. She not only looked like Harper, and had the same blue hair, but she also had the same bluey-green eyes. It was as if I had gone back in time and seen Harper as she would have been.

She took my shirt off and so I took her blouse off. She smelt nice. And I smelt of weed. We kissed again, our bodies pressed together. I probably don't need to go on. You get the idea. We fucked. No big deal. But it was unbelievable. I wasn't sure if that was because I hadn't had sex for two years, or that it was because I found her so attractive.

And even though we didn't get to discuss the book, she stayed over and we talked about it in the morning. It was a good buffer for potential awkwardness, to escape into Shelley's vision for a while. We discussed the possibility of imbued life, with her explaining that they'd need to understand how life even began before they were to uncover the secret of how to resurrect it. We ended up pretending to be monsters of our own, after having imbued each other with the 'spark of life'. Lightning trembled in my hand. She began to eat my forearm, moaning incoherently.

"Hey. Cut it out. I'll eat you too."

"Maybe I want you to do that."

"Wow. You're funny."

"Sarcasm?"

"No really. I think you're really funny. And smart."

"I just bit your forearm. That's not really smart. But, if you were an axolotl, and I bit off your arm, it would grow back exactly as it was."

"Axolotl? Hey, isn't that the salamander thing Harper had?"

"Yeah! Since she died, I moved into her flat and have been taking care of it in her absence. I'm kind of a scientist like her. Well I like to read about it, anyway. She told me a lot about them. How they can regenerate almost any part of their body, even their brains."

"Wow. I wish I was an axolotl when I broke my leg. Might have healed quicker."

"How did you break your leg?"

"It was about six months ago. I was skateboarding and fell off and my right leg snapped."

"Is it better now?"

"Kind of. There's ripped muscles still, but the bone is

fine. There's a rod in my tibia."

"I think I can fix those muscles for you."

"You can?"

"Harper had been working on something, she'd written it down in her notebooks that I've since looked at. Instant regeneration. She had equations written down which although at first seemed uninspiring led me to a fascinating application of these equations to experiment. It seems to work. If you will let me, I can give you the serum."

"You're yanking my chain, aren't you?"

"I used it on myself to fix a sprain I had, but I think it should work just the same. Can I give it to you?"

"Okay..." She produced from her handbag a little vial and syringe, inserted the syringe's head into the strange topaz liquid of the serum, and pulled up on the plunger. It glowed in her hand. She then looked at me, waiting on a final nod of agreement. I nodded. She began to feel for where the muscles had been damaged. It was behind my right knee.

"The gastrocnemius," she says. "Okay. Are you ready?"

"Let's do it."

She injected the leg. There was a feeling of intense strangeness, as if liquid was bubbling inside my leg. As if the atoms were being realigned.

"How long will it take?"

"Almost instantly."

After only a few seconds, already I could feel the weak muscles imbued with a new energy, a kind of fire, a Promethean flame, strengthening the adjoining bonds and growing in power. They were not ripped now but pretty much fully joined. There was no pain. No pain at all. I tested this new strength by lifting the knee high up in the air and straining, which usually caused a deep pain, yet which now seemed as easy and pain-free as it was on the left leg.

"It works. The muscles are strong again..."

"Told you." She put the equipment back in her bag.

"Thank you so much, Mel."

"Don't thank me. Thank Harper. It was all her idea. So, maybe now you're better you'd want to come by the flat sometime and see Vincent. He's also part responsible for your leg getting better, in his own little way."

"I would love to see it. I need to see this guy in action."

"We don't hurt him, though. Not that I'm saying you would. It's just, Harper said never to hurt Vincent, even if you could make a huge discovery from it. She used to experiment on other ones, but never Vincent. Vincent's special."

*

When she opened the door of her grandmother's flat, Mel gestured to let me in. The tank was in view. There was movement.

"Here he is."

I looked up close to his curved head, with an appearance of a big wide smile, and beheld several beautiful orange-red gills that surrounded its head like some mane of an underwater lion. It turned away and swam a bit, looking around, its tail undulating.

"He's beautiful. Is it Vincent because he's orange? You know, because Vincent Van Gogh had ginger hair?"

"No. It's because he likes to paint. Like Vincent Van

Gogh. Well. I introduced a waterproof miniature art set to his environment. I put the brush in his mouth and he painted stuff like Jackson Pollock. I don't make him do it or anything, he gestures towards the brush all the time. When I move the brush somewhere else in the flat, he gestures to that place. That's when I know he wants to paint."

"Can all axolotls do stuff like that?"

"It's not a common thing, no."

"Can I see some of Vincent's art?"

"Sure. I think it's somewhere around here. Here." She passed some small pages of Vincent's art. It was real bad.

"Looks cool. Vincent, you're pretty smart aren't you? Better than anything I could do. Gee, it's amazing what your grandmother told me about them." I loomed over the tank, seeing his curious goofball expression. "Cut my head off, I die. But cut your head off and you regrow it. Brilliant!"

"Well, not exactly. You can technically remove a third of the brain and it will regrow to full health, but no more than a third."

"Still cool."

"Yeah."

It floated around in the tank with that goofy face and flower-like gills. It looked like a mythical being. But this one avoided metamorphosis, Mel said to me. Its main power was regeneration. It could regrow considerable parts of its heart and even spinal cord within a matter of weeks. One question arising: Why did God make humans bereft of these abilities? Why did it take a scientist to see this injustice and hack the system? If God could do it for the axolotls then why not us? No answer came, save Vincent floating in the tank of water.

"How old is he?"

"Five. He's a teenager."

"And how old are you?"

"I'm. I'm twenty five. The age deterioration starts, I guess."

"Me too. Dying and all."

"You look only eighteen, Forrest."

"Time has been kind to me. I should imagine when I reach thirty I'll age real terribly."

"Men tend to look better the older they get."

"Yeah, wrinkled foreheads and big ears and bony faces. Looks good, right?"

"Are you worried about getting older?"

"Well, I'm already twenty five. I haven't done anything worth all that time. Michelangelo sculpted The Pieta at twenty four. And Carrington was only twenty one when she made her famous self-portrait."

"You are a baby, Forrest. You can't compare yourself to others."

"I imagine being older and regretting stuff I didn't try harder at. That I would look back on my life and see that I had done nothing. That's terrifying."

"You're not an old man. You still have time. Like you said, time has been kind to you. It's still being kind. It's giving you time. You have time, Forrest. You have me."

"I do?"

"Why do you think we've been inseparable since I came to the flat?"

"I'm scared, Mel."

"Why?"

"Nothing ever works out for me."

"Maybe because you don't give it a chance to?"

"Should I ignore my brain and listen to my heart? Because my heart is telling me I feel something but my brain's paranoia is telling me that's going to cost me somehow."

"Okay. Don't listen to your heart, or your brain. What does your gut say?"

*

I decided to not embrace the thought of us, that I was somehow betraying Harper by sleeping with her granddaughter within five minutes of meeting her. Harper was dead, but I still felt I was betraying her. Even more so. I was betraying her ghost. I left Mel that day feeling something given to me and yet taken from me, too. I felt sure and yet uncertain.

I resolved to write something and not delete it this time. This time, I would write as if carving with a chisel. Permanently.

... Melvin was frozen in shock. It was then that Fontaine, having been pushed to the ground by Greta Linberg's kidnapper, signalled to Dean Cooper, slyly sliding a metal pole across the floor. Dean picked it up and smacked the kidnapper with the rusty pole, his jaw smashed apart by the metal. The man fell to the floor, unconscious.

"And that's how you take down a real sonofabitch! Cooper, get that duct tape off her. Untie her."

"Sure Fontaine. Is this guy dead, or?"

"Who cares. Anyone willing to take Greta hostage deserves to be dead. Greta. Are you alright?"

"Yes. Thank you Fontaine. How did you find me?"

"A little sleuthing around. It's kind of my specialty."

"It's nice to know not everyone is a total bastard. Or an idiot."

"People want to kill you just because you won't stop

talking about climate change."

"I'm used to it."

"The world is fucked. It's been a pleasure to save you, but unfortunately me and Cooper have more tasks to account for."

"Thank you Aziz Fontaine. You're my hero!"

"Ah," says Dean. "I got this dickhead's blood on my pole."

"Take it as a reminder of today, Cooper. We just made the world a little less shitty."

How the hell did Aziz Fontaine turn out to be such a hero? I was the one who wrote it and not even I could understand that. I sought to make his character an anti-hero, someone who makes rash decisions and creates problems by dreaming too big, but he damn saved Greta Linberg from a kidnapper and even I knew I couldn't delete that.

After a few days of writing for my new book 'Fontaine and Cooper', I felt I had worked too much. My head felt off-the-wall and I wasn't sleeping regularly. I decided to scrap writing any more, since I had already managed fifteen thousand words, and go see Mel. The flat was only a few minutes away.

As I got to the front door, I thought about Harper. And how Mel said Harper never had a proper funeral. I thought about getting in contact with all the book group people to see if they would come to a funeral for her as guests, since Mel said no-one else would come. I wanted to surprise her, yet that felt kind of morbid considering it was a funeral, so I asked her first before arranging anything.

"A funeral? For Harper? Oh, I don't know, Forrest."

"Don't you think it would be good? To say goodbye?"

"I guess."

"I really liked her. She was nice. Didn't know her for very long. But still. I liked her."

"Forrest. I can't do this. We can't throw a funeral."

"Why not?"

"Because she's not dead. She's me. I'm Harper."

51

"Huh? You're her granddaughter."

"No. I just made that up so you wouldn't call me crazy. I'm her."

"What?"

"While I was hallucinating on those mushrooms you cooked for me, at home, I found myself as if in another dimension. I don't remember how I did it, but I did something to that serum, I changed it somehow. And then. I injected it."

"You injected it?"

"Into Vincent. I injected it into Vincent, for some unknown reason. He was never an object of experimentation, yet something compelled me to. I don't know what. And so I injected it into him thinking it would make him 'magic' or something just as bizarre. Then he started appearing younger, though I assumed at first this was merely a hallucination. Yet it didn't go away. After the effects of the drug subsided I still noticed him as being much younger than usual. He was fourteen originally. Then he was about, to my estimates, only five. I decided to inject myself with the serum too in a kind of madness. Accounting for the genome difference. All while on the mushrooms. And now I'm sober I can't remember how I did it. But it works. It works, Forrest."

"Please don't mess with me. This is really strange what you're saying, Mel."

"I'm not Mel. I'm Harper. Mel doesn't exist."

"I'm sorry. I have to go."

"Please don't."

"I don't find it funny."

"It's not meant to be funny."

I got outside and flagged a taxi on my phone. No- one would pick me up. I stood there on the street waiting in the rain. I couldn't help but notice a handbag snatch. I didn't even try to help. Aziz Fontaine would have done something about that. Got the handbag back and beat the guy up, too. Yet I wasn't Fontaine. In the black night, and out of the blue, Ira Powell happened to appear, on his skateboard. He saw me and waved yelling my name, not noticing the car coming down the street. He was so transfixed on seeing me there, as if he were in a desperate situation, that he failed to see the car as he crossed the road. Incidentally, Ira hit the windshield, cracking it apart. He and his skateboard fell to the ground with a loud thud. Why was he here? I went to look. Blood was everywhere.

"Ira... Ira..."

"What, where am I?"

"Settle down."

"Are you a? Are you a penguin? What's going on? Am I dreaming?"

"You're right. I am a penguin. No dream. My name is Verso. You have come to the Asphodel. It's your time."

"My time?"

"You died after you got hit by the car. I've been watching, because I'm your Watcher."

"My Watcher?"

"On my 100th birthday, I was assigned to watch over one human the day of its birth, and throughout its whole life. That I should choose such a person as you, was even beyond my knowing. You see, you came here after the accident because I requested it from the High Penguins. I told them your death was unjust. That it fit the mandate for premature death. I brought you here so you could return to Earth alive, Ira."

"What if I don't want to go back? Things are bad there."

"You don't want to live?" It flapped its great black flippers and paced around the ice. Ira looked around. They were standing on top of a giant iceberg. Glowing butterflies and curious trails were flying around his peripheries. Such a strange dream, he thought. But the penguin kept on talking, raising and lowering its flippers in unison with its speech.

"So how would I get back, if I wanted to do that?"

"It should be relatively easy. You just have to make an account to the Elders. The thing is, right now we are in the middle of The Congregation of Watchers."

"Right."

"You see, each human ends up in their own Asphodel after death, with their own universe and own Watcher. But the Congregation is implemented to bring a select group of Watchers from each universe together, so that they may discuss with the One how to deal with their humans better. Right now, Penguin Palace is filled with the Congregation, and will be as such for the next week. We have a few days to wait here until the Palace is clear and we can speak to the Elders. They are the mavens. They will help us."

Ontop the icy peak, Ira could see other icebergs in the

distance, carved into intricate architecture. There were other penguins standing on top of them. They were about as tall as humans. Not unsettlingly giant but weirdly big. They had white bellies and orange beaks, with a streak of gold across the side of the beak. It was enthralling for Ira to see this world. He had an angel looking down on him. And it was a goddamn penguin.

"What would you like to do?"

"Can we look around?"

52

Once he got to the hospital, Ira was already declared dead. His spine had been destroyed in the crash, his heart had ruptured against broken ribs. Ira was dead. She was with me at the hospital. Too much had hit me all at once and I couldn't make sense of it. Too great and sudden.

"I'm so sorry, Forrest."

"You have to tell me the truth now. Now he's gone. You have to. Or we're done. Who are you?"

"I'm Harper. Harper Dennison. I'm the old lady you met at the book group. I know it sounds ridiculous, you may think I'm deluded, but it is true and I must be honest."

"If you are her, what did you say to Paddy when you met?"

"That his hair was silver like a spoon."

"...Harper?"

"That's what I'm telling you."

"So, that's why you said you 'moved in' to your grandma's flat. It was your flat all along."

"Yes."

"This is insane." I really began to doubt her at this point. Nothing sounded so nutty as this. "Could this really be true? You've made a discovery? You're... younger?"

"It appears so." We stood there in silence at the hospital entrance, our shadows strange silhouettes on the concrete.

"Harper..."

"Yes, Forrest?"

"There's no way you could figure out how to bring someone back to life, is there? You know. Using science? Or is that just fantasy?" I turned around and stared back into the doorway, hoping Ira would come back out and it all would have just been a simple misunderstanding, or a joke.

"I don't think so, Forrest." She held my arm and rested her head on my shoulder. "I guess I could try, though."

*

High beyond the mortal world, the Asphodel revealed itself to Ira. In manifestations of a holy nature, otherworldly to his half-comprehending gaze. He beheld the queer creatures that were housed in the icebergs all across the vista. Big penguins with loud human voices echoing against the winds. Ontop the black water below, a mesmerising effect: lights reflected off the water's surface, the source of the lights being the work of the penguins. It created a busy yet relaxing night time feel, not unlike an old Parisian alfresco cafe, or a neon Tiki bar just by the shore of an island in Croatia.

Verso gestured with his flippers to Ira, wanting him to get on his shoulders.

"You look all slippery."

"Get on, Ira. Don't you want to look around?" Ira succumbed, climbing on top of the great animal. "Hope you don't get queasy."

"Wait, are we flying somewhere? I thought penguins can't fly."

"We are not mere penguins. Ready?"

"Let's go, Verse. What else is there to see? Maybe a big dragon in the sky? Or a monkey's paw and we get wishes or something?"

"That is W.W. Jacobs."

"Oh, is he another penguin?"

"He's a you. A human."

"Never heard of him. So, what is there to see?"

"This is pretty much it. Is this not enough? I can fly faster."

"I'm just a bit bored."

"Well, this might pique your interest. There is, I shudder to say the name. Molocth. An underworld in the black water's depths. They say there is a fallen penguin down there. A Lucifer, you might say. It can kill a human simply using its mind. But since it is so deep down in the water, it cannot harm you."

"Right. So what you're saying is no swimming?"

"Don't worry. I have a spell cast that will keep you holding onto me."

They flew above the wind-swept water, its oily blackness dotted with the city lights and their own reflection. Ira's gaze was hung on the surroundings. The icebergs reached out of the ocean as fantastically tall igloos, made into the strangest and detailed of forms, with small square windows displaying the quintessential penguins, the denizens of this world, flapping their flippers and pacing around inside. Some were aloft in the black sky. They, and the stars, bejeweled the nightscape.

It seemed upon inspection that the only things the penguins really did were eating fish from the ocean and talking to each other, about politics, about the Asphodel, about their humans back on Earth, about the fish. A lot about the fish. As they flew there afloat, swiftly dodging the icey buildings, Ira beheld a penguin below disappearing as if into a portal.

"Where did that one go?" he says, pointing.

"Intervening."

"Huh?"

"It has left to intervene on Earth. There is probably something wrong with its human and it is deciding to intervene. A Watcher may intervene for its human, but it must be worthy of intervention. You may only intervene when it is absolutely necessary. Watchers must choose wisely."

"You seem wise to me, Verse. How many times have you intervened for me?"

"I haven't. You've been fairly self sufficient. Wise? I am only learning, like you. You are wise, are you not, Ira?"

"I don't know anything."

"Said Socrates."

"I've heard of that guy. Didn't he part the waters?"

"I don't think it was him."

"I'm stupid, aren't I, Verso?"

"You are not stupid, Ira. If you had said you knew everything instead of nothing, then I would have doubted your intelligence. But you admitted you know nothing, and that is everything. You may struggle to pick Greek philosophers out of a line-up, but you have a secret power."

"What is that?"
"You are yourself."
"Well yeah. Who else am I meant to be?"

Days drifted by, not without their charm, yet back on Earth only mere hours had been accounted for. The dimension change was enough to distort time itself. Akin to seeing Harper from once an elderly woman into a twenty something. That also distorted the time. When I realised we couldn't throw her a funeral, because she was not in fact dead, we decided to get one together for Ira thinking he'd need it more than the 'Old Harper' (this was a term Harper coined about her old self, her old body. Old Harper. As if some purer person than who she was now). When it became apparent that we didn't know who to invite, since Ira never went around with any other people save me and Ali, I fell back to my old plan to invite the illustrious book group people, whom I was able to contact when we all exchanged phone numbers before eating the weird spaghetti.

At the funeral, me and Harper waited for the other guests. Paddy had agreed to oversee the ceremony, though I made it clear to him that Ira wasn't a Catholic and that he didn't want a Catholic funeral. Paddy was fine with it for some reason.

I breathed in the summer air. It was like shards of glass in my lungs. Faye, the nurse, had brought her infant daughter, Fern. She was wailing.

"How long did you know him?"
"So long. We were maybe ten when we met. He's always been around."
"This must be tough."
"It is. I never knew anyone that died. Why couldn't it

have been me? I would rather it have been me."

"It is sad," she says.

"I wonder what happens after death. Is some veil lifted? Do we carry on, in some way?"

"You're asking like you expect me to answer you, Forrest."

"Well, I'd ask God but he's on the run and won't get back to me."

"I'm sure Ira's at peace. Rest."

"Yeah. His last rest."

"At least it's a rest. Rest is good."

Meanwhile, in the Asphodel, where he had been soundly sleeping at Verso's house, Ira was loudly awakened by the big penguin.

"Ira, wake up. Now is no time for rest! We have been summoned by the One. We've been summoned by the One! We have to leave now!"

"Good. Being here with nothing to do was getting on my tits. I'm ready for the One! Who's the One?"

"The One? Well, you know how I'm your Watcher? Well, the One is my Watcher. The Watcher who Watches All Watchers. It has chosen us to be present at the Congregation, with two other Watchers. This is a very big deal. Meeting the One is a true gift."

"When do we go?"

"We go now. The One does not wait."

"Can I take a dump first?"

"You'll have to hold it in. There's no time." Ira held it in while riding on top Verso's back. He was squirming all over the place. They flew fast, straight up. The black water below was haunting. To look down was scary for him, but he enjoyed it the same way he enjoyed bombing steep hills in nutty positions. It was dangerous, but it was fun.

"Where are we going, exactly?"

"We're going high up, so high that we'll be able to see the One."

After hours of flying upward, Ira was nearly dying to go to the bathroom. There wouldn't even be time for a bowel movement any time soon since the One was waiting. He'd have to talk to the One, while simultaneously thinking about how he really needed a shit.

At the moment they entered the ethereal Heights, where the One was patiently waiting, the funeral for Ira was in motion and the guests had arrived. Paddy was at the altar, holding a lit cigar. He coughed up a loogie behind him and began. The baby Fern continued to cry and you could see it was getting in the way of Paddy's thoughts. But then she started to laugh instead, high pitched giggles, after spotting a robin fly down to her hand and look up at her, before darting off again. She kept on laughing. Then, after a good long laugh, more crying. That was some bi-polar baby.

"God," Paddy mumbles silently to himself. He then raised his voice so all could hear. "Death. We cannot escape it. It comes for us when we least expect it. What are we to do when confronted with this abysm? We must realise life is futile. God won't answer. Its silence is our sentence. And Hell is nowhere else but here on Earth. This is Hell. We're in Hell, watching our friends picked apart by the void. There is no hope in anything. No hope in God. The world is a cruel mistress. I mean, what's the point?" He stopped to puff his cut cigar. The crowd looked beyond concerned. Unphased, he continued: "I mean. All this life of torment, just to end up like old Ira here, pushing up the daisies. I guess what I'm trying to say is, everything is pointless. Rest in Peace Ira, old boy."

"Well that was a disaster. Was hoping for the Serenity Prayer. Nice to know we got the Nihilist's."

"C'mon. I think 'everything is pointless' would look very nice on a needle point pillow."

"I know you're trying to make me laugh, but I am incapable."

"Boris. Get up here. Let's get this over with."

"Wish me luck, Harper."

"Good luck, darling." I walked up to the altar. I hadn't prepared anything to say. I still hadn't fully come to terms with it. Ira lay there in the open casket, with his skateboard next to his legs. That skateboard would never be ridden again. I turned to face everyone. I cleared my throat. I felt my heart pounding against my chest. Sweat was dripping from my ears. Would it have been rude to just run away? To not deal with it? I asked myself this rhetoric pointlessly. I wanted to run away from this nightmare. But I didn't. I stood there, not saying anything. A minute went by and I did not say anything. Two minutes went by and I said nothing still. Three minutes nothing. Five minutes nothing. I stood there saying nothing, just as Ira was saying nothing. I couldn't speak. I couldn't get out any words. No words. In an air of guilt, I signalled to Paddy to lower the casket.

*

"Is that the Sun?"
"No. That is the One."
"It's blinding, Verse."

"Its light is very powerful. Be careful not to stare too much at the light, Ira."

"I can't help it."

"We're reaching the top. Get ready."

And it was as if a doctor had just pumped him with an anaesthetic. The world vanished from his eyes. He came to, in the presence of his watcher Verso. They were sitting at a big round table. There was also an elephant-headed man, and a gigantic squirrel. In the middle of this round table, the One sat, hovering. Ira was getting nervous.

"Can we bun up here?" he says as he reaches for a spliff in his pocket.

"Ira. Not now."

"But that elephant guy is smoking a blunt."

"It is his religion. That is why he is allowed."

"Maybe it's my religion too, then."

The elephant headed man then spoke, again with a human voice, but very deep. His big ears waved about. "If boy gwarn end up in the Asphodel let him toke. Ain't nuttin wrong with the ganja."

The One's voice resounded through the misty heights. "Enough of this. Where is your human, Quentin?"

"He'll come."

"Can you put out the fire? You'll need to remember what I tell you. Your human is out of control, Quentin. You intervened to save him. Yet only betrayal has he accomplished thereafter."

"Somtimes it good to intervene. I was naht to know he would do such a terrible thing."

"The voice of his brother's blood cries to me from the ground. And you intervene again? You try to help him. But now I must intervene." Its rays of iridescent lightning shone forth. It turned to the squirrel. "Navi.

Your human, Dunley, has been in the anteroom for thirteen Earth years. That is about a hundred in the Asphodel. A hundred years has your human been in this room. I do not think this is fair. I think it may be better if Quentin's human were sent to the anteroom instead of Dunley. Dunley has done his time. Too much, I should think."

"If the One gwarn tell me, I'll abide. It true, Leo lost his way."

"Then it is settled. Dunley will return to Earth, under your supervision, Navi."

"Of course, the One! Of course. Thank you!" The squirrel's bushy red face showed excitement. "I'm sure he'll be eternally grateful to you for this kind gift."

"And now you, Verso. You are one of my most respected Watchers. You have always done what is right. You have guided and helped create a good human. Without intervening once. Yes, Ira may not be the smartest of men, but his heart is bigger than any other human's. He is fearless too. A desirable mix of traits. He will, under your hand Verso, be returned to Earth to live his life. Now my command has been made, I shall go."

"So I'm going back to Earth?"

"Yes, Ira." He beheld the One, directly. It made him blind.

"Sick."

At the funeral back in Krelboyne, the casket was lowered nearly all the way down. Harper was placing flowers on the casket. For a second she thought she heard something. Someone talking. She shook her nerves off but in unforgettable madness did the casket door swing open and Ira came bursting out. Half of them were screaming. Half just gobsmacked. I ran up to him. He woke at his own wake.

"Ira... you're alive. You're alive! What's going on? I'm so confused."

"Yeah, I dunno either. I had this weird dream."

"So you were never really dead?"

"Oh yeah, I was dead. But now I'm here. Woah, is this my funeral? Hey, everyone."

"This is unbelievable. I can't believe it. This is great! You're still here. My buddy's still here!"

"Glad to be back."

"Ira, we need to celebrate. But wait. Hold on a second. Why were you even in Krelboyne last night? Why did you come back?"

"Oh yeah. Ali. It's Ali. He's in trouble."

"What kind of trouble?"

"They took him."

"Took him? Who took him?"

"Neon Nazis."

"You mean neo Nazis?"

"Yeah. I feel bad, I left instead of trying to help... They nearly had me too but I escaped before they really figured I was there. They're some scary people man. Skinheads, with swastika tattoos. They're called the Dublin Deimos Club. They go to this underground pub in Dublin to meet up. That's where Ali is. After we started investigating them, well they clocked Ali and weren't happy that an Indian was investigating them. Turns out white supremacists hate people from other countries. Anyway, I came to Krelboyne to find you because I didn't know what to do. I thought you might know."

"I don't know, though."

"We should go help him, right?"

"Help Ali? Doesn't sound great."

"Come on, man. Yeah he puts us down, but that's because we're friends. Friends chat shit. But friends have each other's back. They might be torturing him right now. Groin stuff. Groin stuff, man."

"How are we going to save him? How? Break him out of the Nazi stronghold? I'm not going. I'm not gonna goddamn die before I've even lived. Not for him." I walked off, ignoring it all. Would Ali have even done the same for me? No chance. Yet after a few solemn minutes, while the funeral folk had all but wandered off, I realised that Ali may indeed have done it for me. Just because he tortured me with abuse didn't mean he didn't care for me deep down. I couldn't keep on letting down my friends. I walked back.

"Okay. Let's do this Ira. Let's go back to Dublin."

"Yes!" I turned to Harper.

"I have to go. I'm sorry. Our friend Ali is in trouble. We have to go get him."

"Don't do this, Forrest."

"My whole life I've done nothing for anybody. Ali is my friend. So I'm sorry if you don't want me to, but I'm going whether you approve or not."

"Can't you just call the police instead? This sounds a bit crazy."

"If we call the police they'll kill him. We can't risk it. It'll spook them. And Ira knows exactly where he is, don't you, Ira?"

"Yeah."

"Okay. I won't stop you. Just please. Be smart. You can't just burst into this pub and grab him. How are you going to get inside? You need a plan. A good one. Because this is the only funeral I'm going to."

It was while me and Ira walked back to Speare Street

that I had an idea for how to get inside the pub.

"We dress up as Nazis?"

"Yes."

"Will that work?"

"Well. We'll have to look the part if we're going to this pub. Plus they must have seen your face. Shaving all that long hair off will hide you a bit, but it won't be enough. You'll have to be silent when we're there. I'll talk. You just nod in agreement with me. I'm Jay and you're Silent Bob. Got it? We need to shave our heads, and get tattoos."

"Tattoos?"

"Yeah. We need to get swastika tattoos."

"I don't want to get that, man."

"Okay, Ira. Your plan is to do it with a biro? Fine, that's fine. They'll just rub it off, see it's fake, and shoot you in the face. That's a good plan, Ira. Great plan. We need real tattoos. That way, our cover is believable. I mean, who would be crazy enough to get real swastika tattoos if they weren't really Nazis? It's foolproof."

"Don't you think they'll find out we're faking?"

"Who knows. But we need to act."

"Okay. Let's do it. For Ali."

"For Ali."

53

Using the tattoo gun Ali's old friend Dusty had left at the flat, I began to draw a line on Ira's upper arm.

"Well, when in Rome."

"There's the spirit, Ira. Don't move. I'm gonna do it."

"Wait, let me chug this beer real quick..." He emptied a nearby Stella. "Okay. Go."

I pushed the needle into Ira's pale skin. He says: "Man, I don't think I'm going to get laid after this."

"Maybe there's a nice Nazi out there for you. Anyway. Girls are an odd creature, Ira. They're like mushrooms. Some are nice. Some trip you the fuck out. The rest, are poison." I began another line.

"What about that girl you were with? With the blue hair? What's she?"

"She's two of them."

"Poison?"

"No."

Ira reacted fairly well to the pain. After I was halfway through, it got kind of weird to draw it, because the reality was setting in. I was tattooing my good friend with one of the worst possible symbols (granted it was usurped by Hitler when originally it was a symbol of peace, yet for a lot of people it was impossible to go back to that peace for some reason and only a demon or a madman would walk around publicly with the pattern on their sleeve knowing full well about the Nazi's use of it). I consoled myself with the thought that we could simply get them covered up with a bigger unrelated tattoo after the mission.

"This is so messed up."

"Agreed."

Once I had drawn it on him, I gave Ira the gun and meekly presented my arm. Ira got to drawing the despicable lines on me. Would the gods forgive us?

"This is not how I imagined my life would be. Well, it's a certain spontaneity, I guess."

"Yeah, man. Life is unpredictable."

"Like, you were dead. Still don't understand. They said your spine was destroyed."

"I know. It's a mad one."

"I guess I've heard of people coming back to life but you were declared dead for time. I really hope it's not just a dream. Some mad-ass dream." Then Ira slapped me in the face.

"What the hell, Ira?"

"Sorry. Isn't that what you do when you try wake someone from a dream?"

"That really hurt you donut."

"So this needle in your arm is fine? But the slap hurts?"

"Yes."

"And…we're done."

As the needle finished painting my skin with its sharp inky tip, I knew it was done and (thanks to Ira's slap) that it was no dream. There was no going back now. I had nearly completed my transformation into true Nazi white trash. Obviously, this was something not to tell anybody. Because no-one with any intellect would understand.

Maybe it was because I was so bored with my life that I agreed to do this. So I'd have something to write about. So I wouldn't feel deprived of purpose. Or maybe I just wanted to help my friend. In any case, I wanted to die having done something good. Then, and only then, I thought, could I die unafraid.

"Welcome to Hell, Ira."

"Hah. Are we crazy?"

"Perhaps. But with good intentions. We're going to need aliases. Nazi names. I'll be… Drake. Drake Hugo. What's yours going to be?"

"Charlie Hitler."

"Think again."

"Harley Chittler?"

"Really? That's the name you want to pick? Okay. Harley Chittler. Sounds Nazi-esque, I guess. I'll just call you Harley."

"Sweet. What's the plan now, man?"

"We shave our heads."

"Can't we just wear bald wigs?"

"That won't work. I know you've been accustomed to your long hair, Ira. But this is nothing compared to the tattoo. Your hair will grow back."

"Okay. If it has to be done. Clipper me, Hugo."

*

We took a flight to Dublin, wearing wigs covering our newly bald heads and jackets that covered our newly inked tatts. When I went through the detector at the airport, it rang because of the rod. I hoped to God they didn't ask me to remove the jacket.

"Can you please take your jacket off, sir? We have to ask since the machine went off."

"I broke my leg and they put a metal rod in. I haven't got anything I haven't already shown you."

"Okay. I still need you to take the coat off."

"I am very cold."

"It's August, sir. Please. Take the jacket off."

"Fine." I took the jacket off and quickly hung it across my right arm, which hid the tattoo from the security guard's view.

"Can you put it down over there? I need to give you a quick pat-down, sir. Is that okay?"

"Go for it." I put the jacket in the corner, the tattoo now in clear view despite my attempts at hiding it. Luckily it wasn't too big. The security guard pat me down from behind, not finding anything. I didn't know what to do after the guy stopped the frisk and turned to my front. All I could think of was furtively crossing my arms, with my left hand over the tattoo.

"Okay. You can go through, sir."

After the flight, which was spent in anxious sleep, we landed at Dublin Airport. We went through customs and the woman asked if there was anything we had to declare.

"We have nothing to declare but our genius."
"Smort."
"And those bags, sir?"
"Oh, yeah. Our bags, too."

We arrived in the open city with trepidation and a peculiar animal drive. The sun was starting to set and casting the first shadows of boundless night. I asked Ira where we were going.

"Room 102," he says.
"Oh, so next to Room 101?"
"Huh? Yeah I guess."
"You never read *1984* did you, Ira?"
"I was going to but I left it at yours and then I went to Dublin and all this shit popped off. What's Room 101? This place is called Room 102."
"Room 101 is where humanity's worst fears live."
"Okay." Ira scratched his nose. "So if Room 101 is where scary shit happens, and Room 102 is next to 101, then, what does that mean?"
"It's. It's fear's neighbour. Or fear's brother. That's what it means. The greek God of fear was called Phobos. Phobos had a brother that was also a God. He was called Deimos. The God of terror. Or, terrorism? That must be

why they're called the Dublin Deimos Club. Man that is crafty. Room 102. Okay. Let me type it in my phone."

"It's off the grid."

"It's a private bar? We can't just walk in?"

"No, man. I think there's a password you gotta give the matey at the door or something."

"Goddammit."

"What do we do?"

"I guess we'll just scope out the place, see if we can get a clue. Can you read lips?"

"Yeah I can, actually."

"Okay. Tester. I'm going to silently speak out a phrase. I want you to read my lips and tell me what I said. Got it?"

"Okay." I mimed 'haberdashery' just to mess with him.

"Haberdashery?"

"What? You got it! I'm surprised you know such a big word."

"I don't know what it means. I just know it's a word."

"Right. So you can read lips. We should stake out the pub from afar. I have binoculars."

"I concur."

"You concur do you? That isn't another word you secretly don't know the meaning of, is it?"

"You see right through me, Hugo."

"Don't call me Hugo. Not yet. That's the name of a sick Nazi fuck. I'm Forrest right now. My time to be Hugo will come."

*

We could not have foreseen what happened that moment me and Ira got to this secluded alleyway next to the pub. Up above. A man was falling from the sky. Like

Juliane Koepcke had all those years ago.

The man was yelling. Yet it almost seemed he was elated. He managed to fall on a nearby pile of old mattresses, which roused some pigeons to flight and also the bouncer, who had just let in a small group of regulars. The bouncer walked over to the mysterious man, leaving the basement door open.

"Who are you? What are you doing here, screaming?"

"I'm back. Dunley Novak's back, bitches! Damn, where am I? Is this... Dublin?"

"To be sure. Gear got you down?"

"Not down. Ah, the air. The space. Sorry. This must look real strange to you." He got up from the pile of mattresses. "I was trapped in this room. For a very long time. They let me out I guess."

"Jail?"

"A kind of jail. Yeah. Do you know the year, by any chance?"

"The year? It's 2029, lad."

While the bouncer was distracted with the imponderable man, I nodded to Ira. We took off our wigs and jackets and put them away in separate bags.

"Okay, Harley. Looks like we got lucky. We go now. Sneak in, pretend we're just one of the crowd. You ready for this? It's do or die."

"Ready, Hugo."

We walked up as quietly as possible, the guard still talking to the strange man who had inexplicably fallen from the sky, and went through the open basement door and down the steps, emboldened by our plan to save Ali. At our entrance, with bated breath, we were greeted by a thick, tempestuous cloud of smoke, and a raucous, dark laughter. It was like a dungeon. Grey brick walls with inordinate graffiti and flags of the swastika adorned proudly at all sides, and the bar topped up with enough drink to knock out a blue whale. The booze had evidently been making the crowd of thugs more thuggish still. I was getting nervous seeing some of the figures filing past. People that looked much stronger than either of us. We seemed like a couple of lanky kids in comparison. We weren't physically at a match with the rest, but it didn't matter, because we had a dark secret (we being Harley and Hugo). Harley and Hugo were some sick motherfuckers. We didn't have big muscles, but we were twisted. We didn't need to be fit and strong to gain the crowd's respect. We just had to be some sick white motherfuckers. And so the plan was to act as such. To spout the most racist of things in front of them, the most depraved and denigrating of things, in hope they might agree and carry us on their Nazi shoulders.

We acquired stools by the bar, the bartender clad with a swastika on his forehead. Before either of us could order a drink, two men from behind came out of the darkness and were leaning over us, hanging onto us, as if totally blitzed.

"Finnley! What's the craic? I was all on me tod thinking of you then speak of the devil!"

"What's the story, Sean? Spouting your gibberish again I see."

"You ready for later? Seamus says the bombs are nearly ready."

"I'm always ready. Why do you look so happy?"

"I'm just looking forward to it. Plus, we got a new one. We got a new one, Finnley. Right in the supply closet with the other."

"What is he?"

"He's a Muslim to be sure."

"Like the one we've nearly beaten to a pulp? I can only wonder what it's like in that supply closet." He bust a gut laughing, his pale white face turning pink. "Good thing we can be out here, eh lads? Guinness, Murphy! Here's some nicker."

"Chasing the bar stool tonight eh, Finnley?"

"To be sure, I'm going to lose your outlines by the hour I promise you that Murphy. Ah. Tastes fantastic." He decanted the Guinness into his gob. Then, he finally sees the person he'd been leaning on. Me.

"Who are you? I don't recall your face. Who are you boy?"

"Me? I'm Hugo. Drake Hugo."

"Hahaha! This boy thinks he's 007! Is that your name, then? What are you doing in Dublin, lad? Shouldn't you be in Windsor Castle choking on caviar with the Queen?"

"We hate England. It's a pile of shit, so we left."

"Oh you do, d'you? Talking smack about your own land. Shame. Be proud of where you hail, lad." He took a swig of his drink. "But as it happens, we're not keen on England either. But you're white. That's all that really matters." Everyone in earshot clapped in agreement with Finnley.

"Who's this with you, Hugo?"

"Harley. Harley Chittler."

"Harley Chittler? Your face is familiar to me. Why?"

"I just have one of those faces."

"Ah, this lad is funny. You know. I don't understand something." His face turned severe. "How you two got in. Because to be sure you've never been here before. What's the story there? Eh?" He grabbed me in a headlock.

"Well," I say, stricken by fear. "We got kicked out of our regular club and... we're... we're a... we're a friend of... John's. John's brother. So we came here."

"I see, you're mates with Leeroy? John's brother?"

"Yeah." He let go of me. I was so goddamn glad that worked.

"That explains it. So what did you happen to do to get booted out of your old club?"

"For being too, I don't know, I guess the word is, depraved? We're kind of sick. We've done stuff to people. Well, not people. They're more sub-human."

"Blacks and such?"

"Yeah. Not just blacks. Browns too. Me and Harley are especially interested in Muslims. We love killing them, torturing them. Don't we Harley?"

"Sure do, Hugo."

"Well today might be your lucky day, lads. A little bird tells me there's a sub-human or two among us." He let out a maniacal noise.

"Oh?"

"But before that business. Let's quell our thirst a while. Before dessert."

"Sure. Me and Harley love getting wrecked, don't we Harley?"

"Sure do, Hugo."

In the dirty, windowless supply closet, Ali noticed the stranger begin to cry.

"We're going to get out of here."

"Right. We're dead, man. We're dead."

"Brothers stand together. Are you going to sit, or stand with me?"

"Is it... just because of our skin?"

"To them we aren't even the same species."

"What did they do to you?"

"They cut me all over with a machete and beat me. Next they're going for the eyes. They were laughing about it as they left. I will get us out. What's your name?"

"Yusuf."

"We're getting out of here, Yusuf."

"I pray to God you're right. I don't think I could handle losing my eyes." He looked down to the floor, seemingly embarrassed. "Sorry."

"There are worse things in Heaven and Hell, Yusuf. Such as, what I'm planning on doing to them."

"What can you do? What can we do? We're chained to the ground, man."

Feeling Yusuf's breath on his face — they were that close to each other — Ali looked around the small room and discerned a set of keys hanging off the back of the closed door in front of him. "There's a key. I bet it opens these cuffs."

"Where?"

"On the back of the door. Behind you."

"But we can't stand up. How do we get to them?"

Back in the bonhomie of the bar, with the red flag waving proudly, the Nazis were singing a song.

> *"The great replacement will never come. We're going to white wash the land in one. The great of us, the masters, come, and chain the soulless to the sun!"*

"Why weren't you boys singing?"

"Sorry, Finnley. Too drunk, I guess."

"If there's ever a reason it should be that one. I'm seeing doubles boys. Need to sober up. We're going to show these scum the proper way. We're going to let you and your friend in on the pool."

"The pool?"

"We all take turns. Now is yours."

"Well, let's do it then. Come on, Harley."

"Coming, Hugo." We reluctantly followed Finnley to a side room. Inside there was a giant en-suite full of weapons and lavish furniture, and the supply closet, which when Finnley opened, displayed Ali and another gentlemen chained to the ground with metal cuffs. Ali saw it was us yet did not show any surprise. He knew as soon as he saw us that we were there to get him out. He played along, as if he didn't know.

"Who are these guys? Haven't you done enough?"

"Shut up. You know the rule, number seven. Talk down to us one more time and your lips are coming off. And that's no metaphor."

"So. What's his name?"

"He doesn't have a name, Hugo. It's number seven."

"Okay. Number seven." I punched him in the face, knowing that we had to play along if we had any chance of saving him. Maybe I just finally wanted to punch the guy. Couldn't be sure.

"You're evil!" he shouts, dramatically. "I am human, just like you. We're not numbers! We have names!" Finnley went over to the torture wall. He picked up a metal muzzle.

"We made our own scold's bridle. This one pierces not only the tongue, but the eyes. I think we should give it to number eight first. Don't you, number eight?"

"Please. Don't do this. What have I done to you?"

"Soul-less ape!"

"Stop. Don't put it on me. Stop! Stop!" He fixed the muzzle onto Yusuf's face. There was nothing we could do. He turned some screws on the device and Yusuf began to scream. Then someone knocked on the door.

"Finnley. We need you. The fruity. We're doing the quiz on the fruity and we need you."

"I'm busy."

"We got five hundred nicker riding on it."

"I'll be out in a moment, Seamus." Seamus went.

"So I have to attend to something. You boys, feel free to fuck them up. Just don't kill them. Not yet."

"Got it, Finnley. These two are in for a world of pain." Finnley left for the bar. The timing was auspicious. I took a heavy breath of stale air. In that moment hope seemed real. Ali whispered:

"Guys. Get the mask off him. Hold on, Yusuf." I looked for the screws that Finnley had turned on the device, and turned them again in the other direction. Yusuf screamed again. I then felt for the back straps, and loosened them. I pulled the muzzle off and chucked it on the floor, seeing the gentlemen's face. I beheld holes in his eyes. Blood was raining out of them. He looked in agony.

"We need to get you guys out so we can take you to the hospital. What's your name?"

"Yusuf."

"Don't worry, Yusuf. We're getting out of here. All of us."

"I must hope you are right."

"Duell. There's keys for the cuffs. On the back of the door."

"I see them." I went over to the keys and grabbed them. I leant down to their locks, grabbed Yusuf's cuffs and put the key in. But it wouldn't turn.

"These aren't for the handcuffs..."

"What? They must be."

"Nope. They won't turn."

"No. No no no..."

"It's fine. We just need to break this lock."

"With what?"

"There's loads of weapons over there. Hold on. Is that my novella on the table? What the hell? Is this one of yours, guys?"

"Nope."

"No."

"So a Nazi is reading my book? A Nazi is reading my book?"

"Focus."

"Sorry. It's just. Nevermind. What about that hacksaw?"

"That's going to be too tough to cut. It's too thick."

"There's a power saw here."

"Great. Let's use that. Hand it over here, Ira."

"Here you go."

"Won't they hear it going off?"

"Yes, but we have the perfect get-out. We're literally meant to be torturing you. Just scream when we're cutting the chain."

"Okay. Hurry up, Duell. Cut this quick."

I turned on the power saw, and bent down to their chains. I sliced one with the saw, and Ali and Yusuf screamed in turn, yet Yusuf was perhaps wailing for real due to the scold's bridle's cruel effect.

I kept a steady hand, slowly lowering the blade against the metal. When I was done with the first chain, I moved onto the second. Eventually, after a couple minutes or so, all the adjoining chains became separated from the cuffs. They were free. Ali stood up. Then Yusuf. They walked out into the open room. There was a gigantic persian rug on the floor and a plethora of weapons on the walls. Knives, guns, grenades and axes shone a menacing light. On one of the desks, there was a picture of a mosque with red arrows drawn on it and notes that were too illegible to discern. No-one noticed it.

"I have an idea of how to get out," I say. "But we need to act. We need to get these two out of here without anyone knowing we're saving them."

"It's impossible."

"No. See how we tricked them before? We lied. So. We lie again. We say we've got your sisters locked up somewhere else. That you told us where they were and used our links to get them kidnapped. And that we need to bring you two, just so we can 'rape your sisters' in front of you. It's so depraved. So sick, that they'd have to let us go and do it."

"But we're not really doing it?"

"Exactly. That way, we're allowed to leave. Then we just split."

"Will that really work?"

"Anyone got a better plan?"

"Yeah, Duell. We take these weapons and kill every one of them."

"That's a stupid plan."

"Fine. I'm taking some grenades, anyway." He filled his pockets with the grenades.

"You're not using that. You'll kill us all, Ali." At that moment steps were heard from the door.

"Quick! Sit back down there in the closet! I hear someone."

Finnley appeared, just as Ali and Yusuf had returned to their original place.

"Heard you using the power saw?"

"Yeah. Cut their fingers off. Fed them their own

fingers. No big deal. Say, Finnley. I was just wondering. Could we take these two out of here for a bit? See, we got their sisters locked up somewhere nearby. We want to take these two and bring them to their sisters. We're planning on raping the girls in front of them. I know it might seem maybe even a bit, I don't know, *too* fucked, but would you oppose the idea?" Finnley leered at the tattoo on Forrest's arm.

"It's not too fucked, lad. Not at all. I see why you were kicked out of your old club. Just bring them back alive, Hugo."

"Of course. We just want to have a little fun."

"You remind me of me when I was younger," he says. "Here are the keys to the locks. But if they get free, it's your head, Hugo. Understand me? I'll kill you and them and I'll be whistling as I do it."

"Of course, Finnley."

"Alright. You've got an hour." He left for the door. I steeled myself.

"Okay guys. We're walking out. It's happening."

"Thank you, Hugo."

"I'm not Hugo, Yusuf. I'm Forrest."

"Thank you, Forrest. I can't believe we're getting out!"

"Shh. Let's go."

We walked out to the bar, 'Hugo' stiffly holding Ali by the shoulders and 'Harley' holding Yusuf. Everyone in the pub was cheering, no doubt because Finnley told them all about our depraved 'plan'. We continued through the thick smoke, up to the stairs, and when we reached the basement door and opened it, Ali turned back, holding the grenades he had picked up in the torture room. He pulled a pin out, then another, and yet another, dropping the three grenades down the stairway slamming the door yelling: "RUN!" and then, not four seconds later, three huge explosions which rattled the Earth.

54

It was 2025. The day Hope was assassinated. Headed for darkness at the speed of light, I was twenty one and undergoing my first disquieting meetings with madness. A Duell family barbeque. It was summer. Dead people were singing on the radio. While we all sat there in the garden drinking, I began to think my brother Mike was cooking human meat on the grill. Everybody was eating it without any qualms. The dead people on the radio continued to sing. My family urged me to eat something. Reluctantly, I bit into a hotdog. It tasted horrid. My head felt like a warped vinyl, a melted frisbee. A boomerang that didn't come back. Eating human flesh. The song of the dead undulated in the air. My father was talking to me in an unknown language. It seemed some intelligent creature from space had used my father as a tannoy and was trying to talk to me. There was apparently a war going on, a psychic war. They needed my help. The only price to pay, a pain that felt like the brain itself was crumbling like ruins. It was the price of 'knowing'. In return, I would live for hundreds of years on the peaceful planet where the guardian, now speaking through my father, had been sent from. At the same time, I heard medical equipment being turned on and people talking who were not present. It was as if my actual body was somewhere else. In a hospital far away. But I saw myself in the garden. Didn't hear any birds. Only the voices and the medical equipment. I denied what was happening, for it was too hideous, and went inside to the kitchen to see a vision of everything setting alight with flames and so panicking came running out to explain but no-one understood what I was saying. They were still eating the meat.

It's the brain that's supposed to be in charge. It's what helps us understand reality. But something in my brain wasn't operating right any longer. Stuck in a dream. Alas the dream might change and warp, but it is forever a dream. A dark, unending corridor where the exit has vanished.

55

The bouncer came running after us. And Ira did something magnificent. He deftly turned around and struck him down on the temple with his skateboard in a swift, powerful swing. The guy was out cold.

"Shit. I got this dickhead's blood on my board," he says. "Still, sick weapon."

"What were you thinking, Ali?"

"They were asking for it, Duell."

"What do we do?"

"We need to get out of here. Ira, can we all get on your skateboard? Will we fit?"

"I've done it with three people before. Not four, though."

"We've got no choice. We have to leave here. Everyone, get on the board. And don't fall off. We're going fast."

They stood in file on the wood but there wasn't enough space. They had to split up. Someone had to exit the board.

"I'll do it," says Yusuf. "I'll stay."

"But we need to take you to the hospital, man. Your eyes and tongue are bad. Someone needs to take Ali and you. I'll stay. You guys go ahead."

"Are you sure, Forrest?"

"I'm sure. You guys go. Quickly. I'll find my way. Get them to a hospital, Ira. Then get the fuck out of here. I hope you boys make it."

Ira stood in front on the board, Yusuf and Ali hugging onto him as they flew wildly across the horizon, and I realised I should get the hell out of there before any Nazis came out of the now smouldering basement. Police and firefighters were already arriving at the scene from the sound of the blast. I had to vamoose. I reached into my bag and produced the long blonde wig I had worn before, in the darkness so as not to be spotted, and got on a random bus which had parked up portentously across the street.

When I sat down, I was paranoid. The place we bombed (well, Ali bombed) was only a short distance from the bus. They could get on. And then we'd all be stuck with a vengeful Nazi on the bus. No. I had to get off. I hurried back to the front door to leave, but it had already started its journey and I couldn't leave. People looked at me like I was another drunkard. God, if only they knew the truth.

Ali had most likely killed at least two thirds of them, possibly all of them, since no-one came out after us. It was crazy. I told Ali not to mess around with those grenades. Still, I couldn't help but behold it as an amazing move. Something Aziz Fontaine would have done. Not Melvin Munch.

In the misted twilight air outside, trickles of rain on

the bus-window glistened with the lights of the firetruck that was departing from view as the rattling bus drove on, the destination still unknown. At one point, the bus had a kind of turbulence, and the wig fell off my head. The old woman across from me laughed, says:

"Oh, that's happened to me before." Then she noticed the swastika on my arm, which I had almost forgotten about. "Oh me god. Nazi! Get off the bus!"

"No. You misunderstand. I am an actor. I am shooting today! That is all."

"My apologies. Sometimes it's hard to know what's reality round here."

"Yes. Sorry to scare you. I abhor the symbol myself. I had no choice but to wear it. For the shoot."

"I understand."

*

"Oh my god. He did what?"

"He just chucked them, and told us to run. It was insane. Like something in a movie. He bombed them to Hell. He didn't even need to do it. We were already out of there."

"I can't believe it. Did Ira get them to the hospital in the end?"

"I don't know. He won't pick up his phone. I'm sure they're fine. Are you glad I came back okay? I told you I would."

"I am. You're not going on any more crazy adventures, right? I still need to give you your home-coming gift."

"You really don't need to. All I want is you."

"Well, good. Because that's the gift. Me."

"I love it. Why didn't you wrap it, though?"

"Too excited to give it to you."

"Can I open it now?"

"Yeah. Unbox me. Unbox the fuck out of me."

"You really know how to talk like a modern girl, don't you?"

"I may have been born in the sixties but I assure you, we talked like that back then."

"I thought it was all. Oh swell! The maid has made my member blush upon her countenance! Not 'unbox the fuck out of me.'"

"You might be a century or two off. How old do you think I am?"

"I don't know. You were old. Now you're young. How do you even add that age up?"

After, she says:

"Forrest. Can I ask you something?"

"Sure."

"Those pills you take. Are they, safe?"

"I don't take them."

"Oh. What were they for, then?"

"It's nothing. I used to need them but now I don't."

"Right. So you used to take them? For how long?"

"Years, on and off."

"And you just stopped taking them cold turkey?"

"Yeah."

"I'm no expert but that doesn't sound too good. Maybe you're supposed to be taking them?"

"Just drop it, okay?"

"But I'm only saying because I ca-"

"I said drop it!"

"Fine. You think because you're the only one who knows my secret I'll put up with this? I want you to get out."

"Whatever. See ya, Vincent." I slammed the door

behind me. Already I was taking her for granted. Already the regret was seeping into a headache of guilt. But she kept prying. Why would I want to talk about the thing that most feared me? Why on earth would I want to do that?

When I made it to Speare Street, I walked up to number eight and saw an eviction notice on the door and all my stuff sitting outside.

"Goddamn. I'm locked out." The four headed hydra painting was there next to a bag. Except, it wasn't four headed anymore. It was eight headed.

I went to the woods that night to sleep instead of going back to Harper's. Just like Ira used to do. I ensconced myself between a couple bushes and saw what looked like a huge load of strawberry donuts on the ground, but which were in fact a colony of fly agaric mushrooms. They had red bulbous heads dotted with little white spots. They were magic, like the liberty caps Ali had. I thought about eating them, thinking it might help with the writing of the story I was still trying to craft. But I didn't. I had already bitten off more than I could chew with those things. I merely looked at them intently, deciding not to partake. That was maturity. I might have been sleeping in the woods after being evicted but at least in some respect I had matured. Psychedelic drugs were all fine and good at one point in life, but that point for me was over. Way over.

Still, it seemed the gods decided I would still be fated to feeling ill of some sort. I felt an abnormal, unpleasant wave throughout my body. My brain lit up like coals. I was feeling mentally vulnerable. Hadn't been sleeping well the past few weeks, and unbeknownst to myself I was sliding into delusions. Feeling an episode coming back to me, like it had before when I'd been off the pills for a while, I began to contemplate my lover, and her reality. Was she just a delusion? Caused by not taking the meds? It got to the point I needed to run out of the woods and back to Harper's because I left the meds there and I needed to take one, to quell the horrid feelings of paranoia.

"Forrest. You're sweating. Calm down."

"Are you just a delusion in my mind? It would all make sense, would it not? Because I still don't believe you made that discovery, I don't believe that you are who you say you are, and I need you to tell me right now because I'm losing it. I'm slipping away again. I know I am. So. Please. Just tell me who the hell you really are?"

"Listen, just calm down. Your medication has been taken. All this madness is going to go away, okay?"

The very word made me horrified.

"Don't say that. I'm fine."

"You're clearly not. Just go lie down in the bedroom. I'll leave you be."

"You know, I do care about you. Whoever you are."

56

It's strange seeing the moon in the morning. It seems like it shouldn't really be there at that time of the day. I seldom woke up in the morning to see any such things, but I would often stay up so late as to fall slap-bang into the next day, thereby seeing the morning moon at dawn, surreally peering over at me from out my window, quietly, morosely, as if it had been up all night from some bender with a bunch of comets and now began to finally fall asleep, in plain view, like some hungover angel in a diner at daylight, and crumbling to dust like a vampire in the sun.

Sometimes people say being crazy makes you a real good creative. Well, I don't know if that's true. I was for all intents and purposes going crazy that night in the woods, yet I didn't know how to turn that into great prose or anything. The feeling was perhaps unexplainable. Ineffable. All I could think of was what Hunter Thompson said: "If you're going to be crazy, you have to get paid for it or else you're going to be locked up." Well, Larry Angelo wasn't getting shit.

Luckily the meds did their thing and I woke up that morning, from a long sleep, as if it were all a freakish dream. I felt sedated and dizzy. Harper handed a cup of coffee.

"Drink this."
"Thank you."
"You know. You were really scaring me last night."
"Yeah. I should probably explain."
"Okay. You know, don't feel like I'm forcing you to talk about it. If you'd rather not, that's okay."
"No. It's silly to hide from it. I'll tell you. I have a genetic component for psychosis. I inherited it from someone in my family. It was brought out of me when I took this drug. And so they put me on these pills. But I didn't like being on the pills. So I stopped. But when I stopped, I went hypomanic, which was great for writing the books. But it got worse and I went crazy again. So I took the pills again. But then I hated being on the pills. Stopped. Went crazy again. And so on. I don't know what to do. I guess last night, well it'd been a real while since I last took them, and it must have got to me. I'm sorry I scared you. I'm sorry I didn't tell you that I'm a

screw-up."

"No. Don't be sorry. That's not screwing up."

"There's things I cannot even share with myself. Yet with you, it's easier."

"Please. It's my pleasure. It's nice having you over. So, what are your plans for today?"

"I'm going to try and write something. I might need six more coffees."

"Only six?"

After the first coffee, I took to recreating Burroughs' and Gison's cut-up technique on some old Daily Mail (from the 2010's) left in the flat. Maybe I just wanted to destroy it. I cut out and meshed together random phrases from the paper and glued it into my notebook after. It said...

£1000 bonuses for staff who
were once worshipped by the Aztecs for being food of the gods.
Seven in 10 English want Scots to watch
a snakepit of insurgents
and business leaders
stabbed and drowned in a butt of malmsey wine.
The two leaders of the Scottish National Party want to break up.
Alex Salmond replied: 'speaking as a homosexual, I suppose
the Queen is thought to be alarmed and saddened by the prospect.'

After the second coffee, I made some real weird ones, using only words found in the newspaper, none of my own creation. It said...

Carpets can be found in the Sistine Chapel
but jumping around in time and hopping between
Warsaw and London.
At just £1.49 it's an excellent investment, because
there's no getting away from God or
Jeremy Clarkson.
She seeks the help of a two year old
gynaecologist who has grown rich performing illegal
operations.
Into every aspect of her life - even controlling her own
body,
fishnet tights studded with pearls generate confusion.
A black and white photo
of tsar Ivan the Terrible
laid on the spot where she died beside a zebra, only to
re-emerge as a video version of himself, underwater.
Many banks have said
the Taliban
grabs his crotch,
up and down like hammers inside the piano. Where are
the robots?
Presumed dead.

I needed another coffee after seeing that shit. After my third helping of caffeine, I wrote...

My Circadian rhythm has killed itself.

After the fourth coffee, I wrote...

Idea for a book. A cup of coffee is the protagonist for some reason. We see inside the cup, so to speak. No. That's terrible. Start again. Goddamn. It's like these people trimming their hedges don't even care that I'm insane. If that guy died today, all he'd have to remember of his life was that he trimmed some hedges. What a joke.

After the fifth...

If you're going to use a loud machine to do a pointless task, then make it a musical instrument or make it nothing. All for the benefit of having your Adonis hedges trimmed. 'Oh behold, my hedges are not perpendicular, I must fix this!' No you mustn't. You're the one that's not perpendicular. The hedges aren't the problem. It's you. You're the goddamn problem. Coffee's made my anger blossom. Maybe five is too much.

After the sixth...

There's a mountain in Germany called The Wank. See, this is why I burn my notes. Great. Now I've spilled coffee everywhere. I'm going to bed.

57

Autumn stumbled into delightful view. The air was serenely cooler and I was glad of that fact. While I stayed at Harper's, I heard back from my old gang, old Fontaine and Cooper. Immortal Ira called out of the blue one night to say everything went down fine, that Yusuf got medical attention, and that after he decided to leave for the US to be a skater there and enter the competitions and such. I was proud of Ira. I was only semi-proud of what Ali said, though, when he called. He said he was also planning on going to America, but to fight ICE. Vigilante style. I told him it was a stupid notion, that his over-confidence almost led to him being killed, and yet he still wanted to risk it all just to kill some fuckers for, I don't know, revenge I guess. And then, that morning in September, I turned on the news to find that a law had just passed, making cannabis legal to purchase and own in the UK. Well, that took some time indeed. So after I got that stupid call from Ali, and I saw the news, I called Ali back letting him know weed was legal in Blighty now and that he should stay in Blighty and hurry to get a bud-tending job instead, since that really was his only specialty. And that the vigilante business was something for someone else, a character in a book, in a film. Not a real person.

They both asked me what was going on with my own life. I lied and said I had a great book I was writing. I even lied to Harper about it. That I had the greatest idea for a story. I don't know why I lied to them. I couldn't lie to myself, so I guess I needed to lie to them.

I even lied to Vincent, Harper's axolotl. Vincent could paint, but he couldn't write. I had that over him. He might have been able to make art and regenerate like a superhero, yet surely the animal couldn't be conscious of any of it. I was conscious of it.

I became quite obsessed with watching him while I tried to think of what to write. I imagined it could talk. And it would say: "Don't you dare touch my brain, human." On an otherwise unremarkable day, I was looking at him again as I drank my morning coffee.

"Harper. Does Vincent look, I don't know. Smaller?"

"Vincent?"

"He looks real small." She got up from her chair. "Oh, God."

"What? What, Harper?"

"He's dead."

"He's dead?"

"He... reverted to a fetus-like state. Almost, as if. As if he carried on getting younger. Past the point I had intended."

"What does that mean?"

"I guess his nervous system couldn't take it. It seems I didn't know what I was doing when I used that serum." She wrung her hands. "I thought I simply reversed the age to a certain point, but it's carrying on. Why didn't I notice before? No... I was busy looking at research. I've made a wretched mistake."

There was a curious painting of Vincent's that was left in the tank floating next to his dead body. His last one. It was a simple arrow. Going backwards.

When it became apparent to Harper that she herself may have still been getting younger all this time like Vincent had, we resolved to note any physical changes. Every day she looked younger to me, but perhaps that was just love blinding me. But a few weeks went by, and then into months, (still nothing good written during this time) until it was nearly the new year. And the horrible truth? She was getting younger still. There was no denying it. She looked younger. Maybe only twenty now instead of twenty five. She was perhaps going to take seriously ill unless she figured out how to stop it. But as the weeks went by, her aging continued down the strange backward path it had taken, accelerating, while mine maintained its regular wave. By New Years Eve, she was reduced to a haggard sixteen year old. It seemed she found it hard to remember things that had happened, and even questioned who I was claiming she didn't know me. I told her about her experiment that went wrong. But soon, she began to completely forget about it. She became unknowledgeable. She unlearnt all the majestic things she had once known. She was now, in this state, unable to fix her own mistake. She never foresaw this turn of events. It was her fait accompli, already decided before she became aware of its ramifications. She had unwittingly chained herself to the Caucasus Mountains. There was no changing her wave of direction. At least by her hand. She was a different person now. If she had known what it would have done at the time, she never would have delved into the thinking any further.

When it came to New Years Eve, I suggested that we go out drinking but she didn't want to. She accused me of wanting to get her drunk just so I could sleep with her. I told her I only wanted to get drunk somewhere. I said I didn't feel that way about her anymore, that I wasn't going to do that, that I didn't want to do that, to her or anyone her age. She nonetheless flipped out when I asked her again if she wanted to go out drinking, storming out of her own flat saying she wasn't coming back.

"Forget you. You're just a weird creep, Forrest. Why do you want to hang out with a teenage girl?"

"Because you used to be older. You're not remembering that you used to be older. It's not my fault this happened to you." But it was.

"You're the one who's old."

That night I went out and drank alone at some bar. I couldn't even enjoy the new laws. I didn't feel like getting stoned. I wanted to drown my sorrows. I wanted to be submerged like Bangkok.

The clock was getting to midnight. Everyone else in the bar was cheering as the clock counted down. I wondered why the hell they were doing that. The clock of time was ticking. For Harper, it was ticking the wrong way. What would happen when she became only a fifteen year old? How would she survive out there? I felt my very presence was only tormenting her, so I didn't try and track her down, which may or may not have been the best decision. I left her to do whatever she was doing, still staying at the flat incase she came back. But she never did.

2030 was hardly the greatest beginning of a decade. I had stupidly expected that by now the world would be different. But newspapers still flew into your face. Money still made people mad. Plastic mountains still foretold doom. Nothing seemed different.

A few more weeks went by. I was getting cabin fever. I tried looking through her notebooks in case there was a clue to fix her condition, but gave up after I couldn't understand the simplest things. In anger I threw the notebooks onto the floor. Then I heard a knock on the door, so I went to open it, and there this little quivering girl was, perhaps only six years old. With indigo hair.

"Can I come in?" Her clothes were all baggy and her shoes didn't fit.

"Of course." She came running at me, crying. "It's okay. It's safe here."

"My head feels funny."

When little Harper was back, I felt both happy and terrified. It seemed she was getting younger by the minute. I was afraid of what she couldn't see. The backwards arrow. But I also felt determined, in making sure she was okay. I felt I had a purpose for once in my life. And my purpose was to help her. Even if she would die in the end, just as Vincent did. If her future was foretold, I would make her last moments on Earth as comfortable as I could. It was my duty. That was my purpose now. The deranged urge to come up with some great book meant little now in comparison. I saw how phoney it all was. Even if an idea eventually came, even if the Midas touch had finally found me, I knew that I couldn't turn away from her to write it. She was the only thing I cared about now. It's odd when that feeling hits you, that all you previously strived for is made meaningless. That you're somehow responsible for something beyond yourself. She was, herself, the manuscript I had failed to write. She was the gold of the Midas touch. A gifted curse. The light of night and the dark of day. The everything. And like a beautiful flower, she would wither away and I would only be left with a memory. The woman who traversed time, who transcended time. She had tried to duck Hell. To suspend her judgement day. Yet there was no ducking Hell.

58

"Hey, little girl. I've got a present for you."
"What? What?"
"It's under this blanket. Let me remove it." I took the blanket off the water tank. She saw the axolotl.

It was a pink one. I had bought it for her to cheer her up. When she beheld the creature, she stared at it, and then me, and then it, and then me, and then, while gazing up at the water tank with her head pressed against the glass, she let out an adorable giggle.

"I love it! I love it. It's my little pet."

"What are you going to name her?"

"Pink! Pink. You and me are going to see the world," she says, grabbing both hands onto the water tank with eyes lit up and a smile pinned onto her that invoked a peculiar idea within me, an idea that maybe the world wasn't a stolid dumping yard.

I tried to figure out her mistake. Exerting all my intellectual strength and will, so that I could save her from the pain she was in, and her head feeling 'funny' (which I understood as much more dark than a simple short lived anxiety). I read nearly everything she wrote as an adult, even going on to further research online, but it repeatedly dawned on me that Harper had done something which was unprecedented. When I ended up contacting various scientists online for assistance, they all thought I was a troll when I repeatedly said in the emails: 'My friend has reversed her age and it's gone wrong. Please help.'

I tried, and tried, to understand how. But this wasn't some make believe film where the hero cracks down and saves the day, and I knew it. I was just a guy. An average guy who seldom took care of himself, let alone another. It was hopeless. Even 'Old Harper' couldn't figure it out. She may have cracked it in time had it not been for the exponential degrees her mad path took. Soon what had once taken weeks was now happening in a matter of hours. And I, with hardly any scientific training, was supposed to outwit the smartest person I'd ever met.

Within a few days, she had grown even smaller and weaker. Perhaps three, now. She was unable to play much with her new pet Pink. She eventually became so ill she refused to eat and wouldn't talk or look at me or even Pink, so I knew it was bad. And then, one cold night, she called out:

"Floris... Floris..." I got up from the sofa and went to the bedroom. She was coughing up blood. "Am I sick?"

"Yes, angel. I'm sorry. I tried to fix it. But I couldn't understand how. It's not because I don't love you, angel. Don't be scared."

"Am I going to go to Heaven?"

"Yes. You are. And it will be a magical place. With birds singing, and the sun, shining."

"It sounds nice."

I held her in my arms while we sat on the bed. I was making the duvet wet with the tears that I couldn't hold back. I was trying to be strong for her. But I couldn't help but tear up. She said: "Why are you sad?"

"It's nothing, angel."

"Is it because I'm sick?"

A compulsion hit. To fix this before it was too late. I couldn't just let her die. I walked over to the notebooks that had fallen, picking them up and laying them out on the bed next to Harper. I scanned them, looking for something, desperately, madly, turning pages, turning my mind, forcing an epiphany where none would come. I went to the living room with the books and read there for hours. By nightfall, I was almost demented with insanity. As the seconds counted menacingly on, more maddening was the situation, more hopeless was the outlook. I eventually decided to abandon the notebooks and spend time with her instead. If she had needed me and took ill while I was off looking at the books, that would surely have driven me to the apex of mania. So I went into the bedroom and brought peach ice tea with me, her favourite drink. She said she didn't want any. It was while I sat there with her, just looking at her and nothing more, that I saw her shrinking. Almost imperceptibly. Yet still so. In a strange rewind of life and atoms. She couldn't talk now. Didn't know how. She must have been only a few months old at this point. She wailed like that baby did at the funeral, yet even more tired and lethargic were the wails. She continued to shrink, now unable to lift her head, becoming ever more weak and malleable, and within a matter of seconds — and it was seconds — it was then that the inevitable happened. She crumbled into the bed. Her head tilted off to the side. Her last breath was taken. Or perhaps it was her first.

I closed her eyelids. I kissed her on the forehead, covered her with the duvet, and left the room. Then I left the flat. Pink was left floating.

Outside, it was snowing. I fell to the ground and lowered my head. Then I looked up. I saw my cruel creator, staring back at me.

"Why did you do this to me? Answer... Why? Why? If you're there... you're evil... silent and evil! You hear me! I know you do! You made us and you spat on us! Figures out of clay... For your amusement! Fuck you! Fuck you to hell!"

They heard this.

"Are we perhaps taking it too far?"

"Xenon. Aren't you curious to see how far we can take this?"

"I can't hide from the fact they seem to have a sentience, Gluplap."

"Sentience? They are soulless. Merely characters in a video game. The game you created, Xenon. We are the ones with sentience. Remember that."

"Gluplap, sir. I really think you need to hear me out

on this one." Xenon wrung his three hands and looked at Gluplap. "Some of the characters are starting to figure out that they're in a simulation. I started one a few years ago, called Maya. She was sent to a mental ward because of her visions. She was seeing through the simulation. I sought to create a game so advanced there would be infinite possibilities. But what I hadn't anticipated, was that the characters seem to have developed their own thoughts. That we can't detect. We can create the entire planet Earth for them, we can give them love and hate and wonder and oblivion. But the one thing we can't do is hear their thoughts. Sentience must be residing there. That is what I fear. Perhaps we should destroy the game."

"Your legacy? Do you know how many Zeefdorians play this game?"

"It is a curse I have cast and nothing more."

*

A lonesome year passed. Guided by a malevolent spirit of self-harm, I refused to pick up my medication, seeking instead the uncontrollable hypomania. I stayed at Harper's flat in lieu of somewhere else to go and was taking care of Pink, the only one who seemed to stick around. I fed her earthworms every day. It always looked like she was smiling, even when asleep. Perhaps she had merely accepted life's absurdity, something which I had not yet been able to accept.

Four more years passed. Full of bad writing, loneliness, and earthworms. Nothing the least bit edifying. I had half expected Pink to be dead by now. I expected myself to be dead by now. I had fallen into another hole of drug-taking, numbing my days and nights for years with seldom any good words written. Only three pitiful words in five years. Thirty year old me had resolved to suicide. I went to where Billy jumped. Krelboyne Bridge.

No-one was around. I climbed the railing and looked over the edge, and took one minute to think before doing it. *Am I seriously going to do this? Hell. I'm curious enough.*

I took out a joint and lit it while I looked at the drop below. The smoke was harsh in my lungs. I said my final 'prayers', threw the half finished zoot over the edge, and when I leapt from the bridge, I had already decided this was not what I wanted. I reached out desperately for escape. But it was too late. I hit the water. And landed on my old door which happened to be floating at the bottom of the river.

Failing suicide, which I did not take as a sign so much as an intervention I didn't ask for, I began to write a story about a young woman who finds a book of magic in a wastebin and inadvertendly casts a curse upon herself, which makes her immortal. She learns this when she jumps off a bridge but survives. She is severely depressed and just wants to end it. But she can't because of the curse. Eventually, 'killing' herself over and over again becomes a mere game to play. She does five finger fillet every breakfast and the wobbly stool & rope dance every evening. She becomes addicted to killing herself. Her favourite thing to do is to put on a bulletproof vest and shoot herself in the head.

The problem was how to end the story.

It was while gazing in the mirror one hungover day that

I realised how much older I looked. The drugs had done a real number on me. Time had too. My skin was stained and my forehead was wrinkled. There were brutal bags under my eyes which foretold my entropy. But there was a way out. Harper's spare vial. The one left in her handbag. Going out like this would ensure I would die. And there would be time to be young again as an added bonus. Not much time. But time nonetheless. How ugly I thought myself in that mirror. I had taken to drinking a lot more, and sometimes snorting heroin. I was getting ill. It was time to feel the force of the backwards arrow.

I emptied the handbag, readied the syringe, injected the serum into my forearm and took a seat next to the mirror. I watched the creases in my skin slowly fade away. I observed the few grey hairs I had acquired on the sides of my head turn back to the familiar dark brown. I began to look youthful once more. But death was still waiting and I knew it.

In this new mind-state, things felt different. Surreal. Writing was impossible unless it was written backwards. Lines of heroin did not go into my nose but instead out. Food wasn't eaten, it was thrown up and stored in the fridge. The bombs of Dresden flew up from the ground.

In this inestimable paradox of time, life soon made little sense to me. It was not that the world was going backwards. It was that my mind was. I was out of sync.

I left the flat to pick up some more brown off my link, which seemed to numb this feeling of going in reverse. My thoughts ran in impatient wait. *Is this a good idea? Of course it is. Gonna die anyway, right? Might as well enjoy it. I wonder if they have smokes in Heaven. I wonder if I'll come back as a cigarette. And someone will light me up. And I'll burn like Joan of Arc.*

Outside, in a nearby alleyway, I waited still for the guy to show up. It was while craning my neck and looking up to the snow dappled sky, that I noticed a comet dance through the night air. *I'll burn like that thing.*

Hours later I woke up in a hazy drug-stupor. I would have had a big old beard by now had it not been for the fact I was getting too young to be able to grow one. Yet the swastika tattoo had still not vanished from my skin.

It was going much faster this time. It must have hit my metabolism in a different way. Or maybe I just used too much of it. My shoulders were unbroadening by the second, like an unfurling flower in swift rewind. By the time I got to the mirror to see this, already I could see myself growing shorter and smaller in the reflection. Unbidden, my clothes in kind grew bigger on me. I shrunk. And shrunk. And shrunk.

When things got too confusing to really understand, I walked out the door, down the stairs, out the front entrance and into the street outside. Then when I couldn't walk, I crawled to a gutter, weak and frail. So quick was this transformation. It almost seemed like the end. The aliens above were observing this.

They turned on the neon magnet and lifted me up into the ship. Just in time, they took me to the incubator and realigned my biological clock using their sacred machines.

After the surgery, and after they told me about the game, I decided to stay with them instead of going back to the simulation. I grew up with the aliens, as if I was their pet. Indeed, I was their pet. And they spoiled me. They showed me untold wonder. That my sorrow, which I had been dealt with for nearly all my life, the loneliness, the failures, the insanity; all these sorrows had made me what I was. They recited a song to me and from these enchanted tongues, I knew for the very first time that nothing in my life was meaningless, that nothing in the world was meaningless either, that to endure suffering was a magical state and therefore I was magical, as they were magical. They nurtured me, until I was nearly a man. Until the darkness of my confusion had been illuminated into truth by a holy beam found within my suffering. They sang...

> *"Who never ate their meal in sorrow*
> *Who never spent the midnight hour*
> *Weeping and waiting for tomorrow*
> *They know you not, ye heavenly power."*

How much sense there seemed within those words, to realise my life did have meaning. A heavenly power. That even in the depths of despair, which I had all but lived, there was an oasis in the nadir reflecting the moon and stars before me. I saw that the door which rudely saved me was not rude but in fact the opposite. It became an angel to me, that old door. It was as if I had ascended to Heaven. Where holy voices resounded. They sang it everyday, and everyday I was in awe and everyday it made more sense.

> *"Who never ate their meal in sorrow*
> *Who never spent the midnight hour*
> *Weeping and waiting for tomorrow*
> *They know you not, ye heavenly power."*

To them, this was merely something learnt as a child, such was their intelligence. Yet still everyday they sang to me, and I grew and I grew, and my heart grew alongside me. To hold resentment would only destroy me. And so I grew. And so I grew. And then I was a man once more. Yet now, the pet, it seemed, had gotten too big. Too big for the house. So they put me in a cage. Krelboyne Park Mental Hospital.

More by the Author:

A Nocturne for End Times
(Published 2020)

Lightning Source UK Ltd.
Milton Keynes UK
UKHW011823090223
416682UK00001B/192